"Author D. Barkley Briggs braids ancient strands of Arthurian myth together with his own homespun thread into a complex tapestry of magic and meaning, bravery, and brotherhood. When the roll call of ambitious fantasy writers is called, you'll find that Briggs has earned a place in that book of names."

—JEFFREY OVERSTREET, author of
Auralia's Colors and *Cyndere's Midnight*

"D. Barkley Briggs has penned a rousing fantasy packed full of Norse and Celtic mythology with a hearty dose of Arthurian legend. With a wide range of emotions, he moved me from the sadness of loss to the giddiness of comic relief, all the way to the excitement of heart-pounding tension. Strap on your armor, pull out your sword, and get ready for an adventure!"

—M. C. PEARSON, director, Fiction in Rather
Short Takes (FIRST) Blog Alliances

"Doors shall open, doors shall close. And shadows follow. Something waits for young Ewan and Hadyn Barlow in the seemingly endless broken tangles of the briar patch behind their new home. Fleeing grief and broken dreams, the Barlow brothers discover strange secrets and new worlds right outside their door that will change their lives forever. *The Book of Names* weaves a tale that is both thrilling and wrought with hope. D. Barkley Briggs is a new and welcome voice in fantasy fiction."

—WAYNE THOMAS BATSON, author of THE DARK SEA
ANNALS (Living Ink Books) and THE DOOR WITHIN TRILOGY

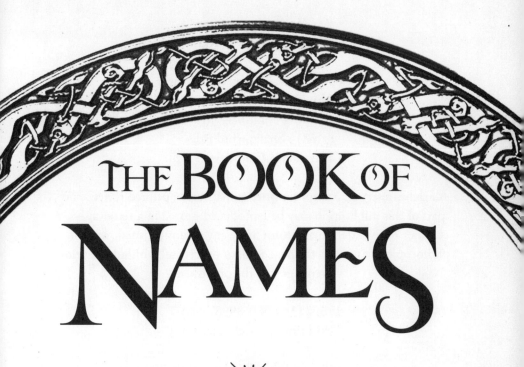

THE BOOK OF
NAMES

LEGENDS OF KARAC TOR

LIVING
INK
BOOKS
Writing Worth Reading

D. BARKLEY BRIGGS

The Book of Names
Volume 1 in the **Legends of Karac Tor** series

Copyright © 2011 by Dean Briggs
Published by Living Ink Books, an imprint of
AMG Publishers, Inc.
6815 Shallowford Rd.
Chattanooga, Tennessee 37421

ISBN 13: 978-0-89957-863-7
First Printing—February 2011

Originally published by NavPress in 2008

LEGENDS OF KARAC TOR is a trademark of
AMG Publishers.

Cover illustration by Kirk DouPonce, DogEaredDesign.com

Cover photo by IstockPhoto, Shutterstock, and Dreamstime

Cover layout by Daryle Beam at BrightBoy Design, Inc.,
Chattanooga, TN

Interior design and typesetting by Kristin Goble at
PerfecType, Nashville, TN

Creative Team: Rebecca Guzman, Michael Van Schooneveld, Reagen Reed,
Darla Hightower, Arvid Wallen, Sharon Neal, and Rick Steele

Look for *Corus the Champion*—the next book in the
Legends of Karac Tor series, releasing spring 2011

Printed in Canada
16 15 14 13 12 11 –T– 7 6 5 4 3 2 1

For Hanson, Evan, Gatlin, and Gage.
My heroes.

What if sorrow was a doorway,
And memory, a gate?
What if we never passed through?
What worlds would go unfound?

In final days / Come final woes
Doors shall open / Doors shall close
Forgotten curse / Blight the land
Four names, one blood / Fall or stand

Great one falls / Fallen low
Rising new / Ancient foe
Darkest path / One turns back
Blade which breaks / Anoint, attack

Once and future / Lord and land
Hidden tomb / Burning brand
Bone and earth / Warriors rise
Haste the day / Of bloody skies

Aion's breath / Aion's curse
Making song / Made perverse
Cold beginnings / Wild cry
Truth revealed / Fates divide

Secrets lost / Secrets found
Eight plus one / Hel unbound
Beast shall come / Some must go
Doors shall open / Doors shall close

Hanging prince / Vision seen
Ancient gate / 'Neath crimson green
Nine shall bow / Nine shall rise
Nine shall blow / Nine shall shine

Falling fire / Burning pure
A thousand cries / For mercy heard
Plagues on water / Horns of dread
End of days / Land be red

When final days / Bring final woes
Doors shall open / Doors shall close
Fate for one / For all unleashed
War of swords / Slay the beast

—The Ravna's Last Riddle

CHAPTER 1

Black Birds

I n short order, the afternoon sky cooled from blue to marbled gray. Strange clouds teased the senses with a fragrance of storm wind and the faint, clean smell of ozone. Invisible energy sparkled like moonlit dew, mostly unseen, but felt. It was damp. A perfect day for magic.

Hadyn Barlow would have none of it. Standing alone in an empty field on the back of their new acreage, Hadyn saw nothing but the colorless smear of his life in the brooding, late November landscape. Everything around him was distasteful: rural Missouri, leafless trees, dead grass, winter coming on strong. Most of all the hatchet in his grip, and the humongous, despicable briar patch sprawling in all directions right in front of him. Each and every blister, every callous earned hacking its branches, screamed from

1

his hands. As for magic? He rolled his gray-green eyes. There was no magic in the world.

He was in a mood. Something gnawed at him. Really, the last thing he needed was more irritation, but something other than cold prickled his skin and he couldn't shake it. The feeling was frustratingly abstract, like sitting in a theater, anxious for the curtain to rise, wondering why you've come since you don't even know the name of the play.

Whatever. He rolled his eyes again for the umpteenth time. *Dumbest thing I've ever heard.*

As the oldest of four brothers, his was the cheerless task of preparing the land for a purchase of cattle next spring. A ridiculous thought, since his dad had never owned a cow in his life. He was a history teacher for crying out loud! A college professor. Hadyn's shoulders slumped. Didn't matter, everything was different now. Though Mr. Barlow didn't let his boys curse, Hadyn did, low and mild, just to prove the point. Life stunk. That was the brutal truth.

While standing in the field and bundled in flannel, his stomach fluttered—almost the same feeling that occurred every morning right before school. Three months into an anxious, friendless sophomore year, Hadyn knew the sickening feelings of exile.

But not this. This was different. This was feathery and floating, not churning. And it wasn't morning anymore.

He sniffed the wind, studied the field, saw a fox scamper in the distance. Heard the soft whistle of bobwhites. For weeks, this had been his routine. Go to school, come home, do chores. In that respect, today was no different, except for the clouds—big slabs, strange hues. Not normal Midwestern storm clouds.

"Get a grip, Hadyn," he said aloud, his breath hanging in the cold air.

It had begun before school, as he stood by the mailbox with his brothers, waiting for the bus. Nearly imperceptibly, as mild winds stirred from the south, something had shifted. Hadyn listened to the wind in the leafless oaks and elms of his yard, hissing with a high, dry laughter. He noticed the breezes scampering like playful ghosts through the brittle cornstalks in the neighbor's field across the road. Even then, something had felt odd. Later at school, outside the cafeteria, eating lunch alone again, the wind had shifted north. No big deal. Missouri weather was always temperamental, pinched between warm gulf winds and Canada's bitter cold. Shouldn't have mattered ten cents.

But then he saw it, actually saw it, after the last bell on the ride home. Sitting with his face pressed against the window, lost in daydreams about driver's licenses, cars and no more stupid buses, Hadyn watched the skies open and spill. Low banks of clouds came tumbling from the horizon like old woolen blankets, gray and purple. Weird. Like that scene from *Independence Day* when the alien ships first appeared. He didn't know what to think. Only that it looked . . . otherworldly. Like God had put Van Gogh in charge of the weather.

And there it was again. The dry-mouthed, queasy feeling.

He glanced around at other kids on the bus. They were all oblivious: earbuds, iPods, and such. Hadyn became transfixed. It always went like this when a puzzle formed in his brain. How many times had the whole family heard Dad's affectionate retellings of little Hadyn comprehending the alphabet at a precocious twelve months? Not merely reciting the ABC song, mind you. Hadyn could actually select the correct letter from a jumbled woodblock puzzle and insert the letter into the proper slot when asked.

"Hadyn, can you give me the D? Okay, now get the R."

And Hadyn, such a serious little boy, determinedly sucking his pacifier, would put his chubby little fingers on the correct letters. He didn't speak before age three; refused to, his dad always said. But when he finally decided to talk, sentences gushed out. Big vocabulary. He had always been bent toward structure, patterns, logic. So for the sky to grow strange and moody in the middle of an otherwise typical, dreary day bothered him. He was moody enough. Didn't need any help. Worse, now there was an itch, and he felt compelled to scratch. Identify the moment. Name it!

Wet fish guts? Not quite. *A full wet diaper?* He remembered those well enough from when the twins were little, but no. *A three-day-old slice of cheese?*

Yes, that was it! Cold and damp, just like the day. Another lousy day, not a gouda.

Oh that's bad, he thought, disappointed in his own...cheesiness. It was getting worse. *Velveeta, actually.*

There, finally!

Another lousy Velveeta day in the life of Hadyn Barlow, he decided, feeling a small measure of relief. He fumbled for the zipper of his coat as another icy breeze cut through his clothes. Perfect.

He should have been hopeful. Only two days until Friday, then came Thanksgiving break. Two days. He could make it. When chores were finished, a roaring woodstove waited for him back home. Hot cocoa. But none of it brought any consolation. Until dusk, he was still stuck outside in a field with hatchet and hedge shears. Stuck in a foul mood, stuck with a knot in his throat. Just plain stuck.

"A little bit every day, however much you can manage after school," his father would remind him. "And don't look so grumpy. The days are getting shorter and shorter."

But not any warmer.

"*Grr!*" he growled. Hadyn had chosen to clear the massive briar patch by reducing it to tunnels. Probably not exactly what Dad had in mind, but, well, to be honest, he didn't really care. He was the one out in the cold. With several tunnels mostly complete, he reentered the biggest one now, clicking his shears at the endless mess of thorns and branches, alternated with halfhearted swings of his hatchet. The briar patch sprawled a couple hundred feet in every direction, comprised of overgrown nettles, blackberry bushes and dense cottonweed. Untended for generations, the underbrush was so thick and tall a person could easily get lost in it, especially toward the center, where the land formed a shallow ravine that channeled wet weather rains toward the pond on the lower field. Hadyn guessed the height at the center point would be a good twelve feet or more. The thing was enormous.

It was a ridiculous task. Dad had to know that.

"Why not just burn it?" Hadyn had asked him. Burn it, then brush hog it. Throw a hand grenade in and run.

Mr. Barlow never really answered, just rambled on about a good work ethic and clearing it by hand. After the first day of mindless hacking, Hadyn started carving tunnels. His plan was to craft a maze out of it, maybe create a place to escape . . . at least have some fun before his dad made him level the whole thing.

Fun? He caught the word on his tongue like a spoonful of medicine. *Fun is soccer with the guys back home.*

He paused a moment. Home was a city, not a cow pasture. Home *had* been Independence, the suburb of Kansas City whose chief claim to fame (other than being the birthplace of Harry S. Truman) was that Jesus would return *there*, at least according to one of numerous Mormon splinter groups. Skateboards, traffic.

Rows of houses. Noise. Friends. Now, everything familiar and good was exactly three hours and twenty-nine minutes straight across I-70 on the opposite end of the state. Might as well have been the opposite side of the planet. For the last four months, the new definition of home was three hundred acres in the middle of nowhere, away from all he had ever known.

Newland, the nearest town. The name felt like a smack in the face.

New school. New faces. New troubles and disappointments. His dad had tried to make a big deal of the "new" thing. This would be a *new* start for their family, a *new* chapter, blah, blah, blah. A change from sadness to hope, he told the boys. Hadyn hated change.

He didn't want new. He wanted it how it used to be.

How it used to be was the last time his world had seemed normal and right. How it used to be was when they were a family of six, not five. A familiar pang sliced across his chest. He would have traded all the unknown magic in the world for five more minutes with . . .

Mom.

A full year had passed since she died, but his mental images of her remained vivid. A beautiful woman with porcelain smooth skin, naturally blonde, witty, vivacious. All four boys shared her spunky attitude, and an even mix of their parents' coloring, somewhere between Mom's fairness and Dad's darker hair and complexion. As he took full possession of his adult body, Hadyn was tall for his age, muscular and lean. Some days his eyes were smoky jade, others, iron gray. He had Anna's cleverness.

His parents had been saving money for several years, studying the region around Newland with a devotion Hadyn could not fathom.

What was so special about Podunk, America? Yet he could not deny how happy his mom had been to think about life in the country. And that was enough, once upon a time. But now? Without her, what was the point? Why couldn't they have just stayed in Independence? Moving wasn't going to bring her back. Didn't Dad know that?

For the second time that afternoon, a tidal wave of loneliness crashed around him, leaving him gooey with a sticky self-pity he didn't want anyone to spoil. He took one more angry swing that achieved nothing. Done or not, he was finished for the day. Dad would just have to deal with it. He had six unconnected tunnels so far.

Like I give a rip about these stupid tunnels, he thought, crawling from the center toward the mouth of the largest, longest shaft. *Or this stupid land, or town, or patch of*—his knee jammed against a thorn protruding from the soil—*thorny! ridiculous!*

A dozen choice words sprang to mind. He bit his tongue, honoring his dad. Tears streamed down his cheek. It wasn't just the thorn in his knee. After about forty more feet, he emerged to the westering sun melting in the sky. The otherworldly colors were gone. Only the cold remained. And now, a bleeding, sore knee.

Behind him, he heard rustling grass and the high-pitched notes of his brother's tin whistle. He wiped his eyes on his sleeve so Ewan wouldn't notice. Like his mother, Ewan was quite musical. Even more like her, he was sentimental. She had brought him the whistle as a gift from Ireland and he carried it everywhere. The sight of him wandering the field playing a spritely little tune might have seemed humorous to some. It annoyed Hadyn. As his brother drew closer, the song trailed away.

"Hey, Hadyn."

Hadyn grunted.

Ewan tucked the flute into his back pocket. He wore blue jeans and a blue embroidered ball cap, initialed ECB.

"Wondered how things were going."

"Did Dad send you to help?"

"Yep. Got done with my chores. Sooner than planned."

"Bummer."

"Major bummer," Ewan peered past him, toward the briar patch. "You to the center yet? With the main tunnel?"

Hadyn didn't bother to reply. With only two years between them, the two brothers had always been the closest of friends and fiercest of competitors. They understood each other even more than the twins sometimes. But they were opposites. Hadyn was studied and cautious. Ewan was quick and generally fearless, comfortable with long odds. No one could make Ewan laugh—gasping-for-air, fall-on-the-ground cackling—like Hadyn. And no one could frustrate Hadyn, or, with the sheer power of silliness, cheer him up when a sullen moment was about to strike, like Ewan. At the moment, Hadyn did not care to be rescued from his mood. He let his silent response wrap around him like a barrier against further penetration. But Ewan's gaze had drifted from the briar patch to the low sky, paused there.

"What do you make of that?" he dimly heard his brother say. Hadyn followed Ewan's pointing finger straight into the sunset. At first he saw nothing. Then it was obvious. Several large, black birds were hovering low on the horizon. Even from this distance, it appeared they were headed straight for the two boys. Only a hundred yards or so away, they drew swiftly nearer. They had a raucous cry like ravens, only larger, throatier, and if possible, blacker.

"Cawl-cawl," they cried.

Hadyn counted four total, wings outstretched like stealth bombers in formation. There was something organized and determined about their flight. It lacked animal randomness.

"Do they look strange to you?" Ewan asked, cocking his head.

Hadyn pretended to be uninterested, found himself saying, "What's that in their claws? Are they carrying something?"

"Yeah, I see it. Sticks?"

"Too thick. And too heavy. Wouldn't it be?"

Ewan held up his hand to shield his eyes. "Man, they're fast. Flying right at us. What are they?"

"Dunno. But—"

"Look out!" Ewan dove to the side, knocking Hadyn over with him. They hit the ground on a roll, turning just in time to see the birds swoop suddenly upward, arcing high into the sky, turn, then turn again. The lead bird, larger than the others, croaked loudly; the other three responded. Over and over, the same phrase, like a demand: "Cawl!"

They were pitch black, with none of a crow's deep blue sheen. In the failing light, they were black slashes, all wing and beak. Not elegant in the air, but fast. Disappearing against the lightless eastern expanse, they reappeared as skimming shapes on the horizon, before gliding up and out in a wide arc. Soon, the curve of their path came full circle, attempting another pass. Both boys nervously scooted further outside the angle of the birds' approach.

"What the—?" Hadyn said, hatchet raised and ready. The birds *were* carrying something. Clearly visible in silhouette, each held a long, thick tube in their talons.

The brothers hunched together, tensing their bodies. Hadyn held his breath. The birds didn't veer, nor seem to aim for them. Instead, they formed a precise, single-file line, a black arrow shooting toward the main tunnel of the thicket. With a final loud croak—"Cawl!"—and not a single flap of wing, all four swooped straight into the hole, one after the other. As they did, each released the object clutched in its talons. The tubes clattered together with a light, tinny sound at the mouth of the tunnel, literally at the boys' feet. The birds' throaty noise echoed for a moment before evaporating into the faint breeze passing over the dry, broken grass.

Hadyn and Ewan stared at the tunnel, then at the objects. Then at each other. Back at the tunnel. In the same instant, each of them leaped toward what the birds had left behind: four thin, black metallic tubes, trimmed with milky white bands top and bottom.

Hadyn picked up a tube, rolled it between his fingers. It was about the length of Ewan's Irish whistle, but thicker, maybe the circumference of a quarter. Not heavy at all. In the middle of each tube, finely wrought in scripted gold filigree, the letter *A* appeared.

Ewan lightly shook another tube, listening for clues. It sounded hollow.

"Don't we have to sign for delivery?" he deadpanned. "These look important. What are we supposed to do?"

"How should I know?" Hadyn said, flicking his eyes cautiously toward the tunnel. "Where'd they even go? I mean, really. Are they just hiding back there until we leave?"

"You're kidding, right?" Ewan said. "Some birds dive-bomb us and drop these really cool tubes. You have one in your hand. And you're concerned about the birds' exit strategy?"

Hadyn mulled it over. "Maybe they're some sort of carrier pigeon, but . . . do carrier pigeons even fly anymore?"

"On *Gilligan's Island*, maybe. TV Land. Listen to me, why are you talking about this?"

"Because it makes no sense!" Hadyn shot back.

Ewan considered. "Okay, maybe you're right. Maybe those birds really are carriers of some sort. Obviously they are." He held up a tube. "Maybe they're trained to do this when they need to rest? Drop their packages, find a hole, rest, then grab their stuff and carry on."

"So . . . what should we do? Flush them out? No way I'm crawling back there in the dark."

Ewan didn't reply. Instead he dug into his pocket, pulled out a small flashlight, and scuttled into the tunnel. "Wait here," he said.

"Watch it back there," Hadyn cautioned. Secretly, he wanted Ewan to go and knew just how to punch his brother's buttons to make it happen. But those claws looked sharp.

While he waited, Hadyn examined the tubes further. He shook one tube, flicked it, smelled another, picked up and twirled the third and fourth tubes. Every effort yielded the same muffled sensation of something barely shifting inside. Maybe a rolled-up piece of paper? If the ravens (or crows, or whatever they were) were carriers of some sort, a written message did make the most sense. But who in the world still sent paper messages . . . by bird? By raven, no less. Hello, email anyone? Facebook?

Presently, Ewan reappeared, breathing hard.

"No big deal," he explained. "Must have flown out the other tunnels."

Hadyn frowned. "Are you telling me they're gone? The tunnels don't connect yet."

"Really?" Ewan's eyes widened. "No, I guess I didn't see any others, now that you mention it."

The two boys stared at one another as evening enfolded them. "Must have crawled through the branches," Hadyn said, though he hardly sounded convinced. The briar patch was thick. "Are you sure you didn't see them?"

Ewan rolled his eyes. "Hello? Big, black flappy things. Yes, I'm sure." He grabbed one of the tubes, shook it again. "This band looks like ivory, but it's hard to tell in this light."

"Reminds me of one of Mom's necklaces."

Ewan grabbed the end and twisted. "Only one way to find out."

Hadyn didn't try to stop him. Curiosity had gotten the best of both boys. The lid twisted off with surprising ease, followed by a thin hiss of sealed air. Ewan wrinkled his face. "Smells old. Yuck. Here, take my flashlight. Shine it over here."

He tapped the open end against the palm of his left hand. The coiled edge of a piece of thick, cream-colored parchment slipped out. Hadyn leaned in closer. Ewan gingerly teased the scroll out. The grain was heavy like woven cotton, with rough edges trimmed in gold foil. Both boys let out long slow breaths. Neither the silver moon hanging off the treeline, nor the winking stars provided light enough to clearly see. Hadyn shook the flashlight, trying to squeeze a few more lumens out of the batteries, as Ewan slowly unrolled the parchment. Pinning both ends to the ground, both boys read at once the simple message beautifully scripted on the inside in golden ink:

You have been chosen for a life of great purpose.
Adventure awaits you in the Hidden Lands.

—A

"Dude!" Ewan whistled softly. "Looks like something Gandalf wrote. Or King Arthur. What's the Hidden Lands?"

Hadyn, being the son of a history professor, and who actually knew the legends of King Arthur—which, of course, Ewan knew, too—was already reaching for another tube. Within twenty seconds, all four tubes were opened. Four identical parchments lay spread on the ground, illuminated by flashlight. Golden ink glimmered, each with the exact same message.

You have been chosen for a life of great purpose. Adventure awaits you in the Hidden Lands.

Hadyn grabbed the four sheets, rerolled them, inserting each back into its thin metal sleeve. "We need to head home before Dad gets worried," he said. "You take two, I'll take two. Stick them under your shirt and act cool. I have no idea what these are. But they're our little secret."

He puffed up for a moment, the older brother. Still out of sorts with the world.

"And none of your games, either, Ewan. I mean it. I'm not in the mood."

CHAPTER 2

Ancient Stone

Somehow, the search for clues made chores more tolerable. When Friday afternoon finally rolled around—school bell, Thanksgiving break—it was a gift. Ewan asked his dad if he could start helping Hadyn clear the brush, and Mr. Barlow, impressed with his initiative, allowed it.

First thing Saturday morning at the briar patch, as in the previous two days, the boys took turns scanning the sky, scrambling through the tunnels, searching for clues, then backtracking and searching again. For anything: bird droppings, loose feathers, tracks, anything. No luck. The arrival of the black tubes and the curious messages held inside had piqued their interest, though they weren't really sure why, except for the wild flights of fancy a boy's mind was prone to take. They joked as if they were hacking through the Amazon or discovering a lost Mayan city. This was as

15

close as either had ever been to a quest, Indiana Jones–style. The plain fact was, birds didn't carry messages like that, not anymore. They certainly didn't just disappear. For whatever reason, it fell to the Barlows to solve the puzzle of where and how the birds had passed through, or out of, the maze.

About mid-morning, just for fun, Ewan began referring to the whole briar patch as the Hidden Lands, just like the scroll said. Hadyn thought Avalon or Camelot sounded more intelligent and sophisticated. He could be snooty about stuff like that. Everyone and their dog read Harry Potter, but Hadyn had always preferred Arthurian legend, though not much of late. A fifteen-year-old (almost sixteen) found other things to be interested in. He mentioned it anyway. Camelot?

"Not bad," Ewan agreed. "Or even Narnia. But I still like Hidden Lands best."

They took turns hacking deeper into the main tunnel. It was slow going. The nettles and branches were so tangled, so thick and so tall that even a little progress took a long time. Various layers of dead, matted foliage in the upper branches formed a canopy through which very little light passed. Underneath their fingers, the damp earth smelled of worms and rotten leaves, forcing them every now and again to return to the entrance for fresh air, casting their eyes searchingly toward the sky.

As Saturday turned from breakfast to lunch, the boys were cold, stumped, and disheartened. They had amassed zero evidence of any birds ever flying into the tunnel (except for the parchments and tubes, of course). Come lunch, trailing home, they floated the idea of abandoning the secret and telling their father what had happened. The idea was distasteful for a variety of reasons. First, Dad would probably be disgruntled to learn that they were wasting time instead of working. He might move them on to other chores. Nothing could ruin a good adventure quicker than actual chores. Second, above all else, telling Dad meant admitting they couldn't solve the puzzle themselves—an awful thought.

Upon arriving at the house, they peeled off their winter coats, gloves and hats, aiming straight for the woodstove to thaw. Mr. Barlow was busily at work on five plates of the family favorite: PBJs with banana.

"Hi boys," he said in a raspy voice, wiping crumbs from the countertop. He looked wrung out.

"Your cold getting worse, Dad?"

Strolling to the fire, Mr. Barlow laid a strong hand on each boy's shoulder. Standing about six foot, fairly fit, with an angular face, coffee-colored hair, and deep-set eyes, their dad was neither a true farmer, nor the bookish, retiring academic one might expect of history professors. He had a scruffy, short-cropped beard, ready for winter. Happened every year about this time. Hugging their necks, he only lightly kissed their cheeks, careful not to spread germs. When he pulled away to cough, it sounded rattly.

"The echinacea hasn't really kicked in," he said wearily. "And I don't want to pass anything on. Gabe's already coming down with it, I think." He called to the twins upstairs. "Barlows . . . lunch!"

Tearing down the stairs came the twins, all hands and arms and sandwiches, chewing and gulping milk before their rearends had even hit the seat. Garret noticed Ewan. "You been working out in the field? On a Saturday?"

Glancing at Hadyn, Ewan played it cool. "We're making progress."

Gabe wasn't impressed. "You're nuts. It's freezing out there. And

I have a cold." He certainly didn't act sick, but Dad's concerns had apparently convinced him.

Garret rolled his eyes at Gabe. They were fraternal, not identical, but similar enough in appearance. In temperament and personality, though, it was night and day. "I want to see what you're doing, but Dad won't let me. Why's that again, Dad?"

"It's big kid work," Mr. Barlow answered casually. "No distractions. Right guys? You are remembering to work, aren't you?"

Hadyn, mouth full, said, "Umm, sure. But you said I could make it fun, remember?"

"Yeah, Hadyn is the king of fun," Ewan said drily. "A regular barrel of monkeys."

The snarky comment landed him a punch on the shoulder. Ewan clutched his arm, laughing. The twins laughed, too.

"Well maybe I'll just come out there with you sometime to check on your progress. How's that sound? After I'm feeling a little better."

"Sure," Hadyn answered evenly. "Just tank up on vitamins."

After lunch and back at the briar patch, the afternoon sky was clean and bright above them, the air crisp and pale and blue. Hadyn contemplated the main tunnel. Light penetrated into the shaft twenty feet or so. Beyond, the center of the briar patch was probably another forty feet farther on.

Ewan said, "Maybe they have a nest in there somewhere."

The oldest Barlow shook his head. "If they do, we've scared 'em away from it. I just can't believe we haven't seen a single scratch on the ground."

"Couldn't they have just crawled through the branches?"

"I suppose, but those were pretty big birds. Not little sparrows or even quail. Besides, we're back to tracks. That's all soft mud back in there. No grass. And yet no tracks. If they just crawled out, we'd know it."

After a moment of silence, Ewan said what both were thinking. "It's like they just disappeared."

Hadyn grabbed the hedge trimmers. "It'll all disappear if Dad thinks we're moving too slow. If he shows up with a brush hog, we'll never know the truth."

They began again, each with a flashlight this time. More crawling, more musty-smelling earth, more thorns, more cold. More clipping, snipping, hacking. Hadyn, as lead engineer, wanted to aim for the center rather than mess with connecting tunnels. They took turns chopping and dragging branches to the brush heap outside. Hadyn knew his dad wouldn't approve of so much wasted, duplicate effort; definitely not the easiest or most efficient way to clean the place.

"This is going nowhere," he groaned after another hour of toil. "We're well into the center. If there's anything to see, we should have seen it by now." He sighed, "I just don't get it. Are we crazy? We saw four birds, right?"

"And have four metal thingies to prove it. They flew right into this tunnel. Then—"

"Poof. Gone."

Ewan wiped a thin bead of sweat from his forehead. "Okay, what if we try to connect to that first shaft back there," he pointed. "You know, the small one coming in from the left side. You thought it was pretty close to this tunnel, didn't you?"

Hadyn sighed. "I had that much tunneled before the birds came. Starting over means all of this"—he waved his hands futilely—"has been a waste."

"Maybe not. If the other shaft is that close, maybe the branches thin out. Enough for the birds to have slipped through. Think about it—we've never even bothered looking down the other tunnels."

For lack of a better option, Hadyn agreed. They backtracked. Hadyn stayed in the main shaft with the trimmers, while Ewan crawled outside the briar patch with the hatchet and reentered through a smaller, narrower side shaft cut to intersect the main shaft at about a forty-five-degree angle. In the darkness, Ewan sounded surprisingly close. Perhaps only a few feet.

"I see your flashlight!" Ewan called. "Can you see mine?"

"I see it. But we've got some big stuff between us. Is that a tree stump?"

"Nah, looks too tall. Hang on."

Ewan's flashlight laced through the branches. Next came dry cracking noises and the dull chomp of his hatchet. A few minutes later Hadyn heard: "Nope, not a tree stump, don't think. Hold on, I'm to it now. One more swing . . ."

Another sound, brighter, like metal on rock. Hadyn winced at the vibration it must have caused.

"That's gonna leave a mark!" Ewan groaned.

"You okay? Sounds too big. Better just work around the—"

"Stone," Ewan cut him off, voice trailing away. "It's not wood. But . . . what in the world?" Hadyn pulled at the branches between them until he glimpsed the outline of Ewan's head and the silhouette of the object. He heard Ewan's soft, low whistle.

"Hadyn, you ought to come around here."

Hadyn scurried out of one tunnel and into the other, following the line of his brother's flashlight to the object itself, at least the part they could see. The edges revealed cut stone, not like a random formation of rock. Dried vines plaited the surface, curving out of reach, out of sight. Something stirred inside Hadyn to look at it—something wild, like the feeling you get on a moonlit path through the woods, or on finding hidden doors in an old house, leading to secret rooms. Or words on a scroll trimmed in gold. A bubble of words rose through the dark waters of memory.

Great purpose.

Something caught in his throat. A feeling. He tried to identify it, couldn't.

"C'mon," he said. "Let's see what this thing is."

They began clearing a wider swath, discovered that the full stone reached over the thicket like an arch. Before long the relative positions of arch and tunnels made sense. An arch has two base pillars. With Ewan having discovered one, the arch curved up and over from that point, planting its other base in an uncut portion of the briar patch on the other side of the main tunnel. Hadyn had inadvertently channeled the main shaft through the space underneath the arch.

"We dug right through it," Ewan breathed.

The boys worked until their lungs ached and their flashlight batteries grew weak. Hours passed. They connected the two shafts and built a mini-cavern around the arch, all hidden in the belly of the briar patch. Finally, they plopped down, exhausted, to gaze upon their labor.

In front of them, approximately five feet wide by five feet tall, stood a smooth curve of ancient stone. The stone itself was three-sided, like a wedge pointing in and down, meaning the footprint of each base was triangular. Its weathered surface was quilted with lichen and fungi, so that neither boy could tell if the color was indeed black, or if the surface was darkened with age and decay. Brittle vines clung to the surface. The boys scraped the vines loose, then rubbed the lichen and spores with their gloved fists until the growths broke off in clumps.

Suddenly, Ewan said, "Hey, run your hands up here. Along the top curve. Do you see those?"

Hadyn shined his light. "Are those letters?" He traced the surface with his fingers, felt a series of crude, oddly angled slashes and dots. "Ewan, what is this thing? That's not English."

"Maybe Indian?" Ewan replied, glancing at the back side. "Same marks back here." He rolled his forefinger left to right over each carved shape. Age and vegetation made it difficult to distinguish one from another. "I think I count nine."

"Me, too. We should get—"

Never finished. Three short air horn blasts cut him short. Their sound echoed across the fields. Dad called it the Von Trapp, his signal for "Come home *now!*" Ewan began gathering their things. Stumbled from the tunnel, together. Overhead, stars.

"Oh, not good."

"How long have we been in there?" Ewan wondered aloud.

"I'd say long enough for Dad to get worried. He's probably gonna kill you."

"Fat chance! I'm just the hired hand. You're the boss."

Hadyn lingered a moment longer, staring toward the unseen arch. Then broke into a sprint over the dark fields for home.

CHAPTER 3

Curious Codes

Fortunately, Dad didn't kill them.

He didn't say much of anything, actually. After dinner came free time, then bed, leaving the brothers to plot and scheme late into the night. When morning finally came, they begged their dad to let the whole family stay home.

"Take a day off," Hadyn said. "Even from church."

Surprisingly, Dad agreed. Or perhaps not so surprising. Though they had been in Newland four months, Dad had only recently found a church everyone liked. Plus, his cold had gotten worse and Gabe was starting to drag. Probably a relief to stay home, especially from church. Good excuse. At the one-year mark, Mr. Barlow was a notably quieter man than before. More tentative. Anna's death had left him weary of the world. Hadyn saw the difference, even hurt for him, but, if he was honest, also resented how much his Dad had changed. Their home was different now. Spiritually. Emotionally. Even socially. It was complicated.

Hadyn knew more than the rest of his brothers, if only because he was older. A couple of weeks after moving to Newland, when the house was still a mess of unpacked boxes and luggage, Hadyn had found his father's laptop open. On-screen, Dad's most recent journal entry practically dared him to snoop. The words were confessional:

Well we're here, sort of. So much to do. I'm so proud of my boys. They're handling the move better than expected. But how can this place ever feel like home without Anna? Now that we're finally here, I feel more stuck than ever. My unending grief is a hellish No Man's Land, trapping me between the longings of a past I can no longer possess and a future I can no longer enjoy. From the moment Anna passed beyond my reach, all of life has become at best, second best. Every day I have to make myself be strong, smile, breathe . . . for the boys. But oh, how I loved a girl named Anna! I am rooted to the ground of her soul. How do I uproot? How do I move on?

Hadyn, having read it a dozen times, still remembered the words, the guilt of reading, stealing his father's private thoughts. But really, it wasn't much of a secret. Fairly often at the beginning, even now, Dad would randomly and tenderly grasp one of his sons and say, "I miss your mother so much," or "It shouldn't be this way." He was always apologizing, always trying to comfort, to make space for their grief and yet say hopeful things. Hadyn got it. Dad wanted them to have hope for the future. But always, faraway in his eyes, was the ache to see beyond this world into another.

That look . . . *that* was what Hadyn resented. The burden of it. It was not something a son was meant to carry. Haunting and vacant, like a black hole. Hadyn dared not enter the pull of its gravity. His plate was full enough. Adding more pain was beyond his emotional range, beyond any fifteen-year-old boy's.

It was exhausting, all the continual processing, the churning. Mercifully, his reverie was interrupted by two eager voices. The twins, eyes pleading. No church meant playtime.

"Hide-and-seek? Either of you? C'mon! Betcha can't find us."

The older boys were together on the couch, whispering. They eyed each other warily. All they really wanted to do was get out the door, but not with two nine-year-olds trailing curiously behind.

"I'm not really up for games right now," Ewan said diplomatically. "Besides, I thought you guys were about to beat Mario?"

"Been there, done that. Yesterday." Gabe smiled. Sure, he was sniffling and his eyes looked puffy, but it took quite a bit to knock Gabe down. "How about basketball?"

"Too cold."

"We could wrestle."

"Too much noise," Mr. Barlow answered, passing through the living room on the way to his office. "Roughhouse outside if you must." Which, of course, they were not going to do, and Dad knew it. It was the kind of impossible, inarguable logic adults were known for.

"C'mon, let's play *something*," Garret begged. "We'll let you guys pick."

Hadyn said, "Chess it is. You up for a thrashing, Garret?"

Garret's eyes widened. He loved chess. Ewan blinked, started to counter. Hadyn cooly intervened, "Ewan, why don't you and Gabe play something for a little while. Then maybe you and I can do something together, later, while the twins do their own thing."

A coy expression crept over Ewan's face. "C'mon Gabe," he said, scrambling upstairs.

Hadyn felt clever and wise. He faced Garret gravely. "One condition," he whispered solemnly, glancing over his shoulder as if he were telling a secret. "You can't beat me like you did last time."

Garret grinned, dashed off to find the chessboard. The games began.

A couple of hours later, it all ended in a pillow fight upstairs, with Mr. Barlow mercifully allowing more noise than he preferred. When their dad finally called out, "Alright, enough boys! Cool it down. It sounds like a herd of elephants up there!" the twins, breathless, decided to watch TV, and Hadyn and Ewan realized their golden moment had arrived. With new batteries in their flash-lights, an old toothbrush, a ball of steel wool, paper, crayons, and pencils in hand, they bundled up and dashed out the back door. After a couple hundred feet of fairly clean woods, the fields opened wide in front of them.

In spite of his distaste for it, this really was a beautiful part of the country, with low-ranging hills, blue streams, and many fields of corn, wheat, and soybean. Hadyn saw the beauty through tears, hearing his mom's voice as he ran. Full of laughter. Countless times, she had tried to win his heart for the move to Newland, saying, "*Out of the city, into the woods. What could be better for a bunch of boys?*" or "*Hadyn, think about it! The home of Mark Twain. Huckleberry Finn. It has adventure written all over it!*" Now as he ran through those very woods, he was not sure whether he ran toward the memory or from it. He saw her face, her smile, burning like the sun in his brain. He remembered how beautiful she was, platinum hair catching light like an angel's wings. It wasn't long after those very memories that the chemotherapy started, and her beautiful hair began falling out.

Fueled with fresh anger, he ran harder, leaving Ewan behind. It took him roughly ten minutes to reach the briar patch, a couple minutes faster than usual. His chest heaved in the chill air. Ewan came up behind.

"What's gotten into you?" he choked, bending over.

"Nothing. Let's just do this."

They dove into the main tunnel and scurried to their newly formed cavern. Other than the hard sprint, Ewan did not seem to notice or care about Hadyn's agitation. Immediately he began fingering every notch and crevice of the stone arch, as if rubbing the surface might cause the stone to change to gold.

"It's like finding treasure," he whispered. "Only better. Makes me think about Mom. She did this kind of stuff in Ireland, you know. All those old ruins. She would have loved this."

Bad timing. Still hearing her echo in his head, Hadyn tried to ignore Ewan. He managed to choke out a few incoherent words by way of reply.

But Ewan, still full of wonderment, pressed the point. "She would have. I'm just saying."

The older Barlow whipped around, shoved his brother hard in the chest. "She's gone, Ewan! When are you gonna get that through your head? G-O-N-E. Gone!"

Ewan's face reddened with anger, embarrassment. Tears leaped to his eyes.

"You think I don't know that?" he shot back, kicking at Hadyn, forcing him back, then lunging at his stomach. The two tumbled to the ground. In the cramped space, Ewan flailed his arms and fists wildly. "She's not gone to me! She's not! Hate life if you want, but I want to remember her!"

Hadyn, caught off guard, was late in blocking. One of Ewan's blows landed hard on his shoulders, another in his gut. Enraged, he smacked Ewan upside the head, shoving him away. This time,

Ewan didn't try to rise or retaliate. He turned off his flashlight and lay in the dark, breathing hard.

Hadyn felt the anger drain away, felt ashamed. He put his hands to his face.

"Ewan . . . I'm so sorry."

"Just shut up," Ewan whispered. Slowly, he rolled to a sitting position. "You think I don't know she's dead? I know it every day." He turned his flashlight on. His eyes were bloodshot and swollen. "But she'll never be gone. Not to me." He wiped his eyes. "Jerk."

They sat together, alone, on the cold ground. Time passed.

"Let's get this over with," Hadyn sighed, breathing into his cupped hands. "Today's too cold to stay out for long. If we get back and have a more normal day at the house, it might keep Dad from getting suspicious." He crawled to his knees, made a lame attempt to switch gears. "Have you noticed? He's been watching us funny."

Didn't work. Ewan didn't respond.

They took turns with the steel wool and toothbrush, gently scrubbing the top of the arch, smoothing the surface, careful not to chip the stone. Hadyn held a piece of lined notebook paper against the stone and Ewan colored. The tension didn't disappear, but eased. Although the first attempt to etch with pencils didn't work so well, trial two, with crayons, did. Two sheets per side were needed to capture everything. Ewan used a different color crayon for each face, then they compared the etched paper copy to the original.

"Perfect," Hadyn declared with satisfaction. The marks were bold and easy to read. He felt certain they could figure out the meaning. Probably some sort of language. Clues all over the Internet about stuff like this.

"Let's g-g-go," Ewan said, teeth chattering. "I need warmth."

Back at home, the woodstove was joyously ablaze. Ewan cradled a warm mug of cocoa in his hands, staring soberly into the flames, silent. The fire behind the glass wildly took wing, like a caged bird thrashing about, struggling to rise in flight, be free. As Hadyn watched his brother, he knew the feeling. Ewan had been sitting there, reading, drinking, occasionally writing in his journal. For over an hour, like Dad. Hadyn tried to conjure words to make it right, but knew it would only make things worse. Most times, as now, he just held it inside.

Besides, he was on a mission with Google. Laptop, far couch, away from foot traffic. Gabe, listless on the other couch, stared out the window through bloodshot, watery eyes. The virus had finally caught up to him. It soon became apparent that Hadyn had no idea how to Google for *this*. How do you describe the shape of random marks on a strange stone? Search results were both nonsensical and entirely unrelated.

Unexpectedly, Garret plopped down beside him. Hadyn angled the screen away.

"Not now, Garret. I'm busy."

Garret shrugged. He was nearly always agreeable. He ambled over to sit by Ewan instead, folding his legs, propping his chin on his fist. This time, he seemed heavy. Ewan sipped his steaming drink.

"I miss Mom," Garret sighed.

It was softly spoken, but loud enough for everyone in the room to hear. Hadyn felt like kicking himself all over again. Really, how many times can a person screw up in one day? He watched the words take their toll on Ewan, watched him close his eyes, thrown headlong into the pockmarked minefield of his own emotions. The twins were still trying to find their own grief, to give it a voice. They were only eight when she died.

Ewan looked into Garret's face, groping for words. The fire crackled and hissed.

For the second time that day, Hadyn felt drawn into a slow boil. Mad at himself. At the world. At God. It was all so unfair. Ewan was right. *Jerk.*

Watching Ewan hold his mug, Garret said simply, "She fixed really good hot chocolate."

Ewan nudged his little brother with a tight, slight smile on his face.

"The best, right? But don't tell Dad."

Garret's nose wrinkled. "He doesn't put enough chocolate in. Mom always put extra chocolate in. Plus, Dad always fixes it too hot."

Ewan put his arm around his little brother's shoulder. He had been so proud when they were born because he *finally* got to be a big brother.

From the couch, fighting fever, Gabe moaned pitifully, "I miss her, too."

"We all miss her, guys," Ewan replied gently, glancing at Hadyn. "In our own ways."

The open space of the great room fell silent. Hadyn coughed.

"Ewan, when you get a chance. I need to show you something. Please."

"Not now."

"It's the *code.* For our . . . spy game."

"Spy game!" Garret whirled his head. Such was life at nine years old—short attention spans. Hadyn should have known better.

"Sorry, Garret. Sorry, Gabe. It's a secret."

Gabe hadn't moved since the pillow fight and wasn't about to move now. His only protest was another soft moan. Garret, on the other hand, deflated. "Can't I just look? You never let me do the fun stuff!"

Ewan climbed to his feet, took his mug to the kitchen.

"Better let me check this out, Garret," he said self-righteously. "You know Hadyn. He blabs a lot and doesn't always think of others."

Touché. Whatever it took. Hadyn dashed up the stairs, taking them two at a time. When Ewan finally joined him, his brother closed the door, took on a chastising tone.

"You know we're going to have to play spy with the twins now, don't you?"

"Hey, you're the genius that put me on the spot. You knew I was working on the inscription."

Ewan smirked. "So it's an inscription now? How official. I hadn't been informed."

"Here's another news flash. I've got nothing. Zip."

"You've been searching for what, half an hour?"

"First, drop the superiority thing. I said I was sorry. And try *three* hours. But it wouldn't matter if it were days. I'm not getting anywhere."

Ewan's tone shifted. "No hits, for real?"

"I've Googled everything I can think of. The only logical thing is that it's Indian something-or-other. But most Indian tribes didn't even have an alphabet, and the Cherokees' looked totally different. I'm stumped."

Hadyn sat cross-legged on his bed. Four sheets of etchings were spread in front of him, taped together to form one side in brown crayon, the other in blue. Ewan stared at the rubbings for a minute, blank-faced.

"Well, any ideas?"

Ewan shrugged. "You're the puzzle guy, not me. I have no idea."

"Humor me. At least pretend."

"Fine, try working on the message in the tubes instead of the arch. How's that?"

"Like?"

"Like . . . what could *A* stand for? Or something else."

Hadyn groaned. "*A* could stand for *anything*. That's not really helpful."

"See! What do you want me to say? It's gibberish! It's not an alphabet."

"Not one that we know. But it doesn't have to be an alphabet to have a pattern to it. Look, this mark and this mark are the same. And this one is the same as this mark on the other side. I just can't figure it out."

"Hadyn, face it. We need Dad's help."

Not the answer Hadyn was searching for. Ewan's response might be virtue, might be vice. He was the more flexible and adaptable of the two, but also generally quicker to throw in the towel . . . on some things. Hadyn, on the other hand, walked a fine line between tenacity and sheer stubbornness.

Ewan reached under Hadyn's bed and pulled out one of the slender metal tubes. He ran his finger along the scrollwork *A*.

"I wonder if the birds could be connected to all this?" he mused.

"You mean to the arch?"

"I know, it doesn't really make sense."

Even so, it was a new thought. Both silently pondered.

Hadyn pulled one of the scrolls from the tube, read it silently, vague intuitions gnawing his brain. Ewan idly fiddled with his tin whistle, waiting.

"What about this? What if we make a *drawing* of the marks by hand, then tell Dad it was something we were working on at school. Or something like that. I don't want to lie. But that way he might not suspect anything. And we might still get help." His face brightened. "After all, we're afraid Dad's going to figure us out, but why exactly? What do we expect? Why would he automatically think we've found some ancient monument on our land, just by showing him these marks? I mean, this is *Missouri* for crying out loud. We don't have cool stuff here."

Ewan chewed the thought like a piece of caramel. "Because if the marks are written in our own handwriting, Dad wouldn't have a reason to connect it to anything else . . ."

"He wouldn't have a reason to suspect anything, really. A rubbing obviously looks like it came from something. But a drawing—"

"Is just a drawing. Maybe from a book."

Hadyn nodded. "Or a game. Or a school project. Not a strange, arched rock doohickey on the back of our land. I don't want to spend my entire Thanksgiving break stuck on translation." He stuck out his right hand. "Deal?"

They shook hands.

"Deal."

"Okay, I've done my part. You draw. Let's hope it works."

Ewan smiled confidently. "Dad'll know what it means. He's studied stuff like this for years."

CHAPTER 4

Secrets

Mr. Barlow frowned. "I have no idea what it means," he answered flatly.

The two older boys stood in their father's office downstairs, located just off the den. They had just presented him with a single sheet of paper, bearing Ewan's best renditions of the markings and a totally flimsy cover story.

"For extra credit over the break," Ewan explained, trying to capture the right mix of innocence and conviction. "Hadyn couldn't figure it out. We're studying . . . Egypt . . . in class. If I get it right, it'll be cool. The whole class is clueless."

Technically, Ewan and Hadyn had reasoned, the arch *was* like an extra credit project. Just not a *school* project. An after-school project. And Ewan had, in fact, studied Egypt at school earlier in the semester, so that part was accurate. Sort of. Lastly, his class was, in fact, clueless about everything they were doing. Creatively worded truth. Hardly foolproof, they knew, but the secret was part of the fun.

As his dad studied the drawing further, Hadyn's eyes began to drift. This office, though different from the one in their previous home, was also very much the same, being a repository of various centuries-old artifacts. Hadyn had grown up imagining his dad's office to be some secret chamber in a faraway castle. The air always smelled old and musty from dust and oiled calfskin, and shelves lined with leather-bound books, fastened with blackened brass clasps. Faded old maps hung on the walls, the daring conquests of other eras. Hadyn didn't have a clue what half of them described, nor what the thick parchments were, laying in uneven bundles here and there, tied with twine. Even the desk was old, with a broad, waxy top all but lost under a chaos of papers and books. The only modern item visible in the entire room was the large, flat-screen monitor sitting on the left side of the desk, toward which Mr. Barlow seemed ever affixed—pecking incessantly on the keys, writing his latest book. Searching, always *searching*. It consumed him.

Really, what was there to find? Like nearly any adult enterprise, his occupation was B-O-R-I-N-G to the kids. History for seventeen years at UMKC. A frequently published academic. He was even considered an expert on northern European history, though his interests and pursuits had increasingly shifted from classroom to fieldwork over the last decade—less textbook, more applied archaeology. After volunteering as an amateur assistant on digs during his college days, he had progressed to something of a "professional hobbyist," but was not an archaeologist by training. Pretty straightforward stuff. But Hadyn had no idea how controversial his dad had become. His views on "theoretical early European civilizations" were radical to say the least. Some called him a quack, one more crazy pseudoarchaeologist.

Didn't matter, because it was on one of those early digs at the Hill of Tara, "on the green hills of Ireland," that a young Reggie Barlow first laid eyes upon the young and lovely Anna Leigh. She had spent two weeks at a place called Newgrange before he arrived, then another three at the Hill of Tara. Anna was no radical. As a young anthropologist, she had the perfectly respectable mission of exploring the local customs of primitive Celts. But then, for better and worse, she met and fell in love with Reggie, busily searching for evidence to support his budding ideas. After marrying, they published an underground rag together on "speculative archaeology" that quickly developed a fierce and critical following.

Mr. Barlow leaned back in his chair. The leather sounded like secrets about to be revealed. Suddenly, their plan seemed rather thin.

"Where did you say you found this inscription?" he asked, pleasant enough—especially factoring in the aches and fever—but his eyes were fixed on Ewan.

"I copied it from another sheet," Ewan said, technically true, "but don't know what it means." He tried to sound like he was answering the question, while really avoiding it. "It seems like a pattern of some sort. Are they hieroglyphs?"

"No. Which of course your teacher would know."

A half shade of color drained from Ewan's face. "Maybe she's trying to trick us. Maybe *that's* why there's extra credit in us figuring it out."

Mr. Barlow's red-rimmed eyes shifted between his sons. He released the paper, letting it float to his desk, grabbed a tissue, and blew his nose. "They look runic to me, but unlike any I've seen before."

Hadyn attempted to sound casual. "Runic?"

"Think Viking. Runes were the alphabet of ancient Europe before Roman alphabets took over. There are stones with similar runes all over northern Europe, left by tribes of the British Isles, by Scandinavians, by the ancient ancestors of Germany. Some of those stones predate the pyramids. The people didn't have paper and pens, so they carved on small rocks and gigantic boulders. Usually these were burial stones or ceremonial stones. Called dolmens, runestones, monoliths, menhirs. I've studied many of them. I've seen marks very similar to these, in fact."

Hadyn wondered if Ewan's heart was jackhammering like his own. They had to play it cool. Failed.

Ewan fumbled for words. "So . . . not Egyptian."

An unreadable smile played at the corners of Mr. Barlow's mouth. "I commend you for being so committed to your school assignments. Over Thanksgiving, no less."

"Yeah, you know . . . no big deal. We were bored."

"You know, it's interesting," Mr. Barlow continued, leaning forward to study the paper again. "There's dozens and dozens of famous sites with runic inscriptions all over Europe. But even with decades of study by many brilliant minds, the purpose of these stone monuments is still, largely, a mystery. Even the meaning of certain runes are unknown. A runic inscription can state one thing, but also form a riddle that means something else. For example, a runestone may tell a story, but hidden in the letters, it may also reveal a date. And that's just the tip of the iceberg, really. We know some stones performed certain basic, highly precise calendar functions. The angle of their shadows or a keyhole that allows a beam of sunlight through at a certain time of year may mark the winter or summer solstice. Some of the markings record historic events. Even more puzzling, many of the monoliths seem meaningless. A bit of magic and uncertainty surrounds most of the stones. Especially," he paused for effect, slowly raising his eyes, "the runestones that have been discovered in North America."

Both boys swallowed. Neither moved or even breathed.

Mr. Barlow pulled out three recent volumes from the shelves behind him. "The Fletcher Stone, in Nova Scotia. The Spirit Pond Stones in Phippsburg, Maine. The Heavenor in Oklahoma, which may be as old as AD 600. And the most compelling and enigmatic of all, the Kensington Runestone, discovered in 1898 in Kensington, Minnesota. Right at the headwaters of the Mississippi. All of these, in varying degrees, suggest that Scandinavian explorers traveled to North America, probably predating Columbus by at least a hundred years, possibly several hundred. Their presence may have even been more permanent than conventional wisdom allows. Settlers, not just explorers. Even if not, they left clear evidence of Viking culture behind."

"In runestones?" Ewan breathed.

"Well, in one sense, there's not a lot of proof. But what we do know is hard to explain away. Triangular, Scandinavian mooring holes for anchoring ships are drilled in rocks in Maine, Minnesota, Iowa, South Dakota. Viking implements—halberds, battle-axes, spears, and boat hooks—have all been identified. Several American Indian words are highly suggestive of Norse origin. And there were blue-eyed Mandan Indians who knew about Christianity before the first settlers arrived. These same Indians lived in square, medieval-Norwegian-style buildings. Way too coincidental to be coincidence, I think."

Ewan's eyes danced. "So, these runes. Are they letters? Does it spell something?"

"Could be letters. Could be symbols for colors. Or sounds. Or shapes. Could be anything. Actually, I'm quite intrigued. I've never seen some of these markings before. And yet . . ."

"What? Yet what?"

Mr. Barlow smiled. "I'm sure you drew the runes well, Ewan, but it would be helpful if I could study the original letters more closely. Maybe you could show me the photo your teacher used? Is it in a book?"

Ewan cleared his throat. "I'd have to look for it."

"Actually, I'll probably just talk to your teacher after the break. While commendable, and pleasantly surprising, this may be too difficult for seventh grade."

Mr. Barlow studied Ewan's sheet once more, gathering his eyebrows like storm clouds above the bridge of his nose. A puzzle and memory darted across his eyes. He grabbed another book off the shelf. A thick stack of papers from his drawer. Put on reading glasses. Thumbed through the book to a foldout full of strange runes. He scanned the markings, darting back and forth between a photo of a particular stone and Ewan's meticulous, hand-drawn recreations of the runes. Then he turned to what looked like a manuscript for a new book. Back and forth, twice more.

"I recognize these," he murmured. "I couldn't place it at first. Here, take a look at this."

He waved his sons forward excitedly, showed them the title of his manuscript: *Ancient Civilization Portals: Dimensional Travel in the Formation of Early Civilizations.*

Both boys leaned over his desk for a closer view. The caption above the photo he had turned to read: "Kensington Runestone." Hadyn wiped his sweaty palms on his jeans, trying to appear calm. Mr. Barlow pointed to three different runes in the book, all of which were circled.

Then he pointed to three different runes on Ewan's sheet. They matched.

"There are so many of these things, in America and all over the world, I created a new category for them: Ancient Civilization Portals. ACPs. I've been pressing my colleagues for answers, stirring a hornet's nest. A lot of people don't like my theories. My hunch is that they were meant for more than just calendars and markers, but the conclusions I draw are too radical for most." He pointed to the photo again. "You boys don't know it, but I've studied the Kensington Stone firsthand. I worked on one of the modern translation teams in 1998, deciphering the inscription. I assisted Dr. Nielsen in 2002, when we proved the stone's linguistics were plausible for a fourteenth-century expedition. History tells us King Magnus Erikson of Sweden authorized a voyage as far as Greenland in 1354. From there, down the Hudson Bay—it's not hard to imagine the rest, which matches the year mentioned on the stone. Geochemical analysis helps further, suggesting pretty conclusively that the stone was buried long before the arrival of Europeans in the region. Some, however, claim the Kensington is a much more recent forgery. Part of their argument is that it contains runic forms never verified on any other runestone. These," he tapped the three circled runes, "have never been seen anywhere else. In Europe. Anywhere. Until now."

Silently, all three absorbed the weight of the moment. Hadyn compared the runes over and over. They were, indeed, the same. Identical, in fact.

When Mr. Barlow spoke again, his tone was soft and intimate. He looked at each boy as if telling them his own precious secret. "I've often wondered if those Scandinavians, or perhaps Viking sailors from centuries before—if they found the Hudson Bay, if they found the Mississippi—what would keep them from sailing farther south? All the way down? Why stop at Kensington? After all, these men were relentless explorers, nautical geniuses. And if they did sail south, might they have left other runestones? If so, somewhere along the banks of the Mississippi is a likely choice."

He rose stiffly, moved to the east window, gazed longingly toward the slow, unseen current of the Mississippi a mile or so away, comfortably hidden by three more farms and many, many trees. "Boys, I will tell you a great secret. It's time you knew."

He kept staring out the window. Hadyn's skin began to tingle. His mouth, suddenly, was dry as cotton.

"This," Mr. Barlow said, pointing to Ewan's drawing, "is why I bought this land. Your mother and I worked for years. We searched old maps, old writings around the world. We read everything we could find. Years! We were about to give up. Then one day at an old library in Norway, we found a major clue that there might be another runestone, perhaps even greater than the Kensington, somewhere in this area, specifically even on this land. Or at least a nearby farm. A thousand years ago, the Mississippi was even wider than it is now. Did you know that? We stand on its ancient shores. So when this old farm was put up for sale, we jumped at the chance."

He kept talking, but the words became detached in Hadyn's brain. Something nameless and familiar was stirring deep inside. It was bothersome. Like a question you know the answer to, but can't recall. Later, Ewan would tell him he had felt it, too, like whispers of a song he thought he should know, but couldn't sing. For Hadyn, it was a longing, almost a sadness, rising in his throat. He pushed it aside. The words on the scroll blazed in his heart.

Chosen.

Dreamlike, the room almost seemed to fade away. In a rush of revelation, Hadyn heard a raucous cry and the flapping of dark wings, saw in his mind's eye a replay of the flight of the birds from that first night, when the scrolls were given, as the sun collapsed; realized how they had formed a black arrow, pointing straight into the tunnel. To the arch. He knew in a flash, then, that Ewan was right. Everything was connected. The scrolls were not the only gift left behind. The flight of the birds was part of the message.

They passed through the arch. And were gone.

In that moment, Mr. Barlow turned from the window to face them. Hadyn saw something almost like anguish in his eyes, deep memory. And tears. In a voice drenched with reverence, like spring fields are drenched with rain, he said,

"Enough of the games, boys. It was clever. But first thing tomorrow, I want to see the runestone you have found."

CHAPTER 5

Dreamsong

That night Ewan dreamed a strange, beautiful dream. It was dark in the dream, so dark he couldn't see the black birds, but he heard their loud wings flapping all around him. In fact, he realized, the darkness was their wings, and it shimmered. He heard their dissonant cry. It made sense to his ears, like a voice speaking.

"Call! Call!" they cried. In the color of the blackness he felt the soft touch of mystery, like petals on a flower.

The flapping wings disappeared, and Ewan found himself standing on a green mound overlooking three white towers and a broad valley with a ribbon of blue winding toward the sea. He listened. The sound of the water tinkling over the rocks was clean and bright, as though crystal pipes were being struck. The water played like a melody in his head. It was haunting. Sweet and simple, only a few notes, but seemed *so* familiar. In the dream he realized his skin had become like stone, that now he was lying in the bed of the stream, and the water on the pebbles was making music as it flowed over him. He saw magical winged creatures all around him, lying down, as if weary. Weeping, turning to stone. Again and again the music played, ceaselessly, burning itself from deep memory into conscious thought. Soon, his skin, his teeth, his bones started vibrating. He had become the song.

Within the dream, the song called him. Urged to movement, he stirred, humming the tune. He dressed quickly, heavy coat and boots, favorite ballcap. Stuffed a few things in his pockets. He floated, through the river, through his room. The water was trapped. A music riddle. The song must be released. Down the hall, down the stairs. On the wall, the clock read 5:13 a.m. He saw, he could read, but he moved in a dream.

Outside, the night was still heavy and dark. Bitter cold. He glided along, ambivalent to the snapping of twigs underfoot. Soon he was across the field, the urgency of the tune lofting around him. It was a needful thing, this dream, whispering nine notes.

A song that *must* be sung, a tune that must be played.

Even so, when he reached the briar patch, looming large in the darkness, he hesitated. What was happening? Was he awake? Or dreaming? Why these wild compulsions? He felt foolish. Still the melody rose and fell within—a watery, lilting tide, transfixing him. He found himself staring, unable to purge the memory of silver notes strung like pearls in the air before him, straining within, to be made known.

Called, the birds said.

Some things could not wait for sense to be made of them. In the dream, Ewan stood on the shores of the crystal stream again, coaxed downward into the water by melody. He resisted one last time, then fell, plunged into the depths, swimming the channel, crawling, toward some unknown, dark heart.

His eyes glazed over with sleep, somewhere between the waking world and the world of dreams. Somehow he knew this—knew it, but not in a way that mattered or could be resisted. Pulling his tin whistle from his pocket, he played. Having never played the tune before, his fingers effortlessly knew the notes. He played the melody: nine sweet, beautiful notes.

Nine notes, nine times.

As he played, the runes began to glow pale blue, shining like timid December light on morning frost. Nine strange symbols pulsed, arcing up and over his eyes, carved in stone. Underneath, in the open space, the air trembled. The song felt released. In the darkness of his reverie, Ewan studied the glowing runes, curious to see what the other side looked like, if they glowed on both sides. Time slowed. He tucked his whistle in his pocket.

And crawled through.

Lights flared, briefly, blinding his eyes. The darkness of the dream faded, replaced with a very real absence of light. He was awake, alert, confused. And dizzy.

Reaching out with both hands, he grasped for something firm until his senses cleared. Fumbling through his pockets, he found his flashlight, flicked it on. Beneath him was soft, moldering earth. Above him were what looked like thick, twisting roots, thrusting down into the soil, some gnarled and strong, others rotting apart. By some strange occurrence, he was in a cramped space, a cavity of earth and rock and moss. He was on all fours in a crawling posture. How did he get here? In his winter coat, no less. Since when did he wear his coat to bed?

Panic rose. *Where's my room? Where am I?*

He clamped his hand over his mouth, twisting left, right. Nothing familiar, no landmarks in sight. He was under a tree.

Softly came the remnant of a melody. Of a river, singing to him. His dream came flooding back. He had been swimming—where? crawling through the tunnel?—had played the tune, seen the runes glow. Had passed through.

That's why they disappeared! he thought, remembering birds, swift in flight. *They must have flown through the runestone.* The epiphany was both wonderful and terrifying.

As Ewan's eyes adjusted, he noticed a narrow hole above him, and beyond, a brighter shade of twilight. The hole he was in was warm and smothering. He wiggled free of his coat, turned off his flashlight. Listened carefully for any sounds he could recognize. The loudest in his ears was his own ragged breath.

Then, a new thought. *I'm still dreaming. Too crazy. Waking up, playing the tune, coming here. All part of the dream.*

He reached out, put his hand on a rock. It was firm and cool, quite solid to the touch. He dug his fingers into it as if it might turn into some ephemeral dream powder. It did not.

Definitely not dreaming.

He adjusted to a crouched position, carefully pulling himself up to the opening to peek out. The opening was draped with vines, obscured by a large rock to the right and underbrush to the left. With what few cracks of space he could peer between, Ewan saw that he was in a forest of some sort; quite literally in, or at least under, a tree. He saw no signs of life, man or animal.

Something dropped on his neck from above, scampered quickly down his shirt. Furry and wiggly. Once sleepy, Ewan came utterly *alive*. He screamed nonsensically.

"*Ahhooooo-ahh-aii!* What was—? . . . No, get . . . *off* me! *Mmph . . . aiigh!*"

He had no judges, no audience, which was a shame, because if he had been an Olympic gymnast he would have surely won the gold. Or if a yodeler, the entire nation of Switzerland would have been proud. Whatever it was, bug or mouse, the moment it slipped down his shirt, Ewan began shrieking, flailing his arms, cavorting wildly about. In two seconds he was out of the hole, over the rock, shirt stripped, and jiggling every part he could jiggle. On the ground by his cast-off clothing, a fat, furry caterpillar crawled away as fast as it could, probably as terrified as its unfortunate victim.

Ewan slumped against a rock, breathing hard. Very slowly, he became aware of the silence surrounding him. There was a light rustle of leaves in the buttery breeze, a skittering of squirrel feet somewhere behind. Blue-jeaned and shirtless, he surveyed his new environment. It was a forest. The tree he had crawled from stood to his left, a large, sprawling oak with meaty roots that tangled on the surface before plunging into the earth. Funny thing, though, looking at it from ground level . . .

I can't see the hole.

Panicking for the second time, he dove toward the underbrush, poked his head into the hole, felt around, shined his light, looking for anything familiar: another hole, a tunnel, runes, the arch. Just as he feared, nothing. Back on his feet, he turned a slow circle. The woods were old and stately, well-spaced, minimal underbrush. He stood on a footpath. As best he could guess, it was early evening, though it could have just as easily been early morning.

"Think, Ewan," he told himself. He was surprised at his momentary calm. "Think."

It seemed pointless to call for help. The woods were empty. He tried to retrace what had happened in his mind, feeling a vague sense of body memory, dressing in his coat, wandering to the briar patch, carrying his flute. How could he have sleepwalked that whole thing? Played music, crawled through? Yet he knew it wasn't a normal kind of sleepwalking. But then . . . what? He had obviously been transported somewhere. That would explain why it was so warm here—*here* being someplace altogether foreign. Was stuff like that even possible? Teleportation was science fiction and magic. Crazy stuff. He donned his shirt and ball cap, grabbed his coat.

Though the melody from his dream lingered, it had begun to fade.

Okay, fine. I'm just going to assume I'm still dreaming. And if I know I'm dreaming, I should just do whatever I want.

It made as much sense as any other plan. But which way, left or right? What did it matter?

He turned left. When he did, she was there. He gasped.

CHAPTER 6

Fairies and Gnomes

Beautiful was too kind, too tame a word, to describe the slender woman before him.

Ewan had heard of such creatures. Bedtime stories. Stuff like that. Not like her though. She was unlike anything he had ever seen except in picture books as a child. Fanciful drawings and legends. Now, here, with his own eyes, he saw her. Luminous, silvery. Standing behind one of the trees off the path. Or floating, perhaps. She was about his height, willowy, with thin filamental wings that glittered almost beyond visibility and hair that swam in the air as if in water. The air around her appeared soft, almost liquid. She looked young, utterly captivating, staring back at him with a puzzled expression that nearly stopped his heart. He wanted to go to her, catch her like a firefly at night, just stare at her. He was thirteen. The surge of desire he felt was not a thing of lust, but wonder.

"How?" she said. Her voice, like a plucked harp string, hummed with surprised awareness. "How is it that you can see me?" She wasn't talking to Ewan. Her question, spoken aloud, seemed like a private musing.

"How is that you have wings?" Ewan said, marveling. "And glow?"

The fairy's eyes darted up to the sky, then left and right. "The moon is not full. There are no pools of water. No reflections. You have no silver talisman. How is it that you see?"

She seemed annoyed, intrigued. Ewan took a step toward her. She skittered back, from one tree to the next. Her dress, green and sheer, revealed nothing, floating with her. Her wings vibrated like a hummingbird. She seemed both nervous and fascinated, no less by him than he of her.

"I'm sorry. I didn't mean to frighten you," he apologized.

"I saw you come. Through one of our—what is your wordspeech?—doorgates." She blinked. "How did you find it?"

"I don't know. I played. Music."

The girl twitched and twittered her feet, like a cat with wet paws. She studied Ewan unreadably, came to a decision. "My Lady will require this news. There will be a reward."

She turned, wings blurring into motion.

"Wait!" Ewan said. His heart stirred and he did not know why. Surely, to see her go.

The fairy paused in mid-flight, tossed her head, found Ewan's eyes. "If you were of age, you would already be lost to me. It is good you are yet young. I will take it into account that you bear no mischief. No salt or iron. My Lady the Queen awaits."

And then she was gone. Ewan realized he had been holding his breath. He let it go, looked around. Now he felt doubly lost. And nearly heartbroken, though that made no sense at all.

He sat a moment, breathing slowly. Was she real? What was this place? He resumed his walk, heading north, or so he guessed. One thing became clear: it was evening, not morning. Light was failing. Getting stuck in an unknown forest at night was a tad creepy. Unless, of course, it meant *she* might flutter back.

He twitched his head, blinking free of her spell. The urgency of being transplanted to this land, the looming fear of night, pressed upon him. The woodland path rolled among sloping land not altogether different from their farmland, yet nothing around him was identifiable as home. A pang of longing struck his heart. Hadyn was probably still sleeping. Night fading there, approaching here. Weird.

He had to get back.

He kept up a brisk, wary pace, ranging over hills that were higher and more broad than the gentle, treeless slopes of Newland, winding up and down, left and right, rarely straight ahead. After traveling probably two or more miles, he heard a sound that stopped him in his tracks. Over the next rise, a voice.

It sounded gruff, maybe even angry. Ewan instinctively dropped to the ground. Crawling on his elbows toward the point where the path curved over the hill, he peered into the weakening light. Saw nothing, yet heard movement. Finally noticed a figure cloaked in green, blending almost magically with the underbrush. The fabric shifted colors to match both shadows and thinning light as needed. The creature stood with its back to Ewan. It was a short, stumpy man. Short as in midget short.

Vertically defeated, Ewan thought with a smirk.

The little man had a brown knapsack slung over its shoulder and scavenged the ground with a stick. Ewan couldn't see the creature's face at all. He had to strain to hear his words.

"Bah!" the creature snorted, stomping the ground, shuffling sideways another pace or two. He pried back fallen leaves with his stick, stooping to pluck something from the ground. His movements were neither stunted nor awkward.

"Morels, schmorels," the little man sniffed disdainfully, holding the object aloft. "Paltry puffballs. Bah!"

Can't wait to strike up a conversation with this guy, Ewan thought.

As if reading his thoughts, the creature swiveled toward him, sniffing the air. Ewan ducked, waiting several moments before slowly edging up again. The creature was back to poking the ground, but Ewan now had a full glimpse of his face. It definitely *wasn't* a man. It had a snout nose, set between high bulging cheekbones, a jutting forehead and a thick, trimmed beard of bright red hair. It was every bit the little trollish monster of fairy tales, only better groomed.

Occasionally it would sample the harvested goods; more rarely, it would drop one in its knapsack. Ewan surmised them to be wild mushrooms. Perhaps berries from nearby bushes.

Inspecting one final mushroom, it made a noise like a sneeze, "Shame for Flogg! Fit for pigs, not priests."

With that, it gave up, trudging along the footpath away from Ewan. Ewan waited for the creature to get a safe lead before following. The sun was setting quickly. Shadows draped the trees, forming a dark canopy of leaves that whispered in the breeze. Moon and stars appeared as distant, barely glimpsed promises, mostly hidden. When Ewan finally crossed a stream of clear water, he realized he was mad with thirst. Fearing time to drink might cost him his guide, he pressed on. After rounding two more tree-thickened hills, the woods thinned abruptly. He came to stand in the clean wash of ivory moonlight, a sky blazing with stars. To his left (west?) the hills flattened, hinting at a wide expanse of open fields stretching into a far, unseeable darkness. Immediately below, along the base of his hill, was a little village of uniform architecture—simple, stucco, square box dwellings. Candles flickered in the open windows and a thick outer wall glowed with torch fire. Rising from the village came the faint sound of many voices. Singing? Chanting?

The path down the hill to the village was bereft of the cover of trees or shadows. Ewan crept along slowly. Not too slow or he would lose his guide. As he passed along the outer wall, the chanting again drew his attention. It came from somewhere farther inside one of the inner buildings. It was a doleful, warlike hymn. Minor key, serene and austere.

> *"Everking, Lord of Wind,*
> *Speed arrows to the mark.*
> *Pluck Thy bow and loose the shaft*
> *Ere Light succumb to Dark.*
> *Aion's breath, from north to west*
> *Aion's fire, from sacred pyre,*
> *Aion's wall, defend us all,*
> *Let banned and damned depart . . ."*

For a brief moment, Ewan was torn between locating the singers—they sounded like monks or something (maybe they could help)—and continuing to follow the creature. Maybe it would be better to just stay where he was. Typical for a boy of thirteen, curiosity trumped caution. Just ahead, the little creature opened a heavy wooden door, ducking into a narrow atrium between buildings. When he disappeared behind another building, Ewan quickened his pace. A warm blaze of light spilled into the shadows from another door ahead and to his left. Hugging the stone wall, he caught the door just before it closed and tiptoed inside.

Instantly, he felt a metal blade pressed against his throat.

"Manling be following Flogg, now, eh?" rasped the creature. He was so short, he had to stretch his arm to reach Ewan's neck. "Thinks Flogg has no ears? Might as well three elephants a'follow me."

He grabbed Ewan by the sleeve, shoving him forward. He was surprisingly strong for his size, had an iron-fisted grip. They were in a storehouse or pantry of sorts. The walls were shelved with earthenware, wood-slat boxes, and sacks of dried grains. The rafters, clogged with hanging stalks, roots, and leafy things, filled the air with yeasty smells and pungent spices. Even stronger was the smell of cheese. Ewan was shoved forward again, through another door, into a broad, rustic kitchen with a hearth fire, two large black kettles suspended over it, a heavily scarred chopping table in the center, and every size and shape of cutting instrument one could imagine hanging above.

"Flogg hunting morels to break the fast. On the morrow. Felt yer eyes." He scraped the tip of the blade against Ewan's skin. A warning against brave ideas. "Look atcha . . . what kinda manling wears such strange rags ya'? Did carnivale down Portaferry snag an orphan? Bah!"

"Please don't hurt me," Ewan said, trembling. "I'm lost. I don't know where I am. I came here for help—"

"Shuttin' the mouth! Whines like a lass with new dressings and no offers to dance!"

"Please . . . ," Ewan whispered.

"Please, wheeze, fleas, sneeze! Sneezing and freezing. No pleases! Go you to the Father, I will. Spy on Flogg no more."

In one swift motion, Flogg transferred his knife from Ewan's throat to the small of his back. "Step it, manling. To the Circles."

CHAPTER 7

Mirroring

The melodic humming, the song Ewan had heard, increased, pulsing along the hallways like a bass line at a rock concert. Earlier, it had sounded reverent. Now it sounded like war.

He didn't have time to notice, really. The sharp tip of metal against his lower spine kept prodding him forward. The building he found himself in was spacious, but plain. The walls were made of fitted rock and mortar, well lit with ensconced torches. The roof was thatched and high. Flogg pushed and shoved Ewan down one hall and then another, then a third, before the last hallway opened into a large, round chamber with a peaked roof sweeping upward. A massive cedar pole supported the center. Here, the chanting crescendoed.

Electricity tingled in the room. Ewan forgot for a moment the knife stinging his back. Power radiated from the front, where a clean circle of polished bronze hung from a thin wire, and where, under that bronze circle, a fierce ritual now unfolded. Nearly a dozen men wearing robes of gray stood in a circle facing inward, both arms raised, palms out as if pressing against a barrier . . . or forming one. Their wordless chant thickened into a droning, sonic wall. In their midst, a vaporous creature twisted and writhed. The creature seemed the color and substance of roiling smoke, bird-like—all claws and wings and gaping, knifed maw. Something like a spine of jagged teeth ran along its massive beak, and its face was spotted with dozens of frenzied eyes darting in every direction. It was horrific, and altogether otherworldly. Ewan flinched to look at it, nicking the skin of his back on Flogg's knife. The collective energy of the robed men seemed barely able to restrain the creature. Its tortured, raging cries came from some nightmarish realm Ewan did not ever want to visit.

Now Ewan saw a girl standing in the midst of the circle, facing the beast. Her garb was more dress-like than a robe, not gray, but purple, the color of squeezed, summer blackberries. Unlike the men, she was young, with light brown skin and dark eyes. Her hair, black and straight, whipped about in a torrent of unseen winds, stirred as the creature writhed about. Rather than backing away, she leaned her trembling body into the wind. She held something like a square of mirrored glass. Only not glass. Ewan couldn't be certain, but the mirror seemed watery, translucent. The girl's lips were moving. Ewan couldn't hear a single word, but saw her edge closer to the beast, which thrashed, making sounds like tearing metal, like a wild boar, cornered, run through with a spear. Still, the girl edged forward. Her face tightened with strain.

The creature retaliated, swiping a claw at the girl. Ewan heard fabric tear. She nearly dropped the square, watery device. Black wings thrashed. Again, she edged closer. Gathering her strength, she raised the mirror high above her head and cried aloud.

"*Aione yl oSova!*"

At once, the encircling men grew silent, lowering their palms.

For just a moment, the entire chamber seemed to inhale its breath. The girl, the creature, paused. In that moment, the beast turned, looked right at Ewan. Something like surprise, then rage, then desperation registered simultaneously in its many, hollow eyes. Straining against its unseen bonds, it seemed to gather its energy for a final leap. *Toward* him. Instinctively, Ewan shrunk back. There was no need. The girl swept her mirror downward so that it passed through the vaporous form. The creature screamed a final time, a sound so raw it might melt stone or cause a man's heart to fail. Then it vanished into the glass, absorbed in an instant.

Silence.

The men bowed low, as one, shoulders sagging. Each raised their hands, cupped their fingers, making a sign over their hearts. The shape of an open circle. They wordlessly dispersed after that, except four. One old man whispered intently with the girl in purple for several moments before wearily taking a seat in a wooden chair near the front of the circular chamber. He was clothed in a gray so dark as to nearly be black. Two other men, robed in lighter shades of gray, attended him. The girl with the mirror was plainly exhausted. Her chest heaved. After a few more words with the elderly man, she bowed deferentially and turned to go, bearing the mirror carefully in both hands. As she did, Ewan saw the creature, flattened, transfixed, whirling deep in the glass. Though it made no sound, it still seemed to be watching him. Ewan let slip a little, panicked heave of air.

The older man lifted his eyes at the sound, noticing Ewan and Flogg now for the first time. He registered surprise. He had a salt-and-pepper beard (mostly salt), a studied, careful face, and eyes that struck Ewan as both patient and curious.

"Master Flogg," the man said in a warm, gravelly voice. "You should have waited outside."

"Was outside," said Flogg, bluntly. "Hunt'ring sun meal. Caught other somethings."

The old man hid his mouth behind a casually placed hand. Ewan thought he seemed amused. He had a fleshy, circle-shaped scar on his forehead that had whitened with age. "Master Flogg, I thought you told me morel bread and fresh berries would be the morning meal. Did you return from the forest with a different recipe in mind?"

Flogg shook his head irritably. "Too old, this manling. Already tough, the meat." He prodded Ewan in the back. "Flogg caught him sneaking. Food thief . . . spy. One of the lost ones. Father will know."

The other men, whose faces were barely discernible under their deep hoods, lifted their gaze ever so slightly toward Ewan and his captor. The older man stepped forward from his chair, leaning lightly on a long staff made of willow with a thick, knotty top.

"How many times have I told you, Flogg?" he said in a mild, scolding tone. "Cutlery is meant for the kitchen. Instruments of violence have no place in the Room of Circles."

Ewan searched the room. Not only was it circular in shape, but the walls were painted with endless patterns of interlocking circles. Bronze discs hung in a manner that appeared to mark the cardinal points of the compass. Flogg glanced sheepishly at Ewan, then his knife. He frowned.

"Too tall the manling without blade."

"Yes, I'm sure. Of course, you do your clan proud, Master Flogg. I will see to this boy now. Thank you."

Flogg scowled once more at Ewan. At close range, he was even more ugly than seemed possible, with skin that cracked like old leather. His eyes roamed from Ewan to the old man, back to Ewan again.

"Any ideas, and the pounding I'll givya! Ya' be singin' with your behind, it be knocked so far up ya' brain. Brg!"

He turned and stumped away. Though he stepped hard, his footsteps made almost no sound on the flagstone. When he had departed, Ewan nearly collapsed. He had been tensing every muscle for so long.

The old man in front of him shaped a circle with both hands, fingers and thumbs. "Peace, little brother! Goodness! Peace to your road. I am Eldoran, Father of the Gray Abbey. Come . . . you look spent."

He gave Ewan a cup of water. Ewan gratefully gulped it down.

"Where am I?" he whispered. "Please tell me. And also, what was that . . . that thing?"

"Poor lad. I can see Master Flogg has frightened you. You will have to forgive his manners. He is a master chef and a loyal friend. But we all know how grumpy gnomes can get." Eldoran studied Ewan for a moment, his clothes, his face. The ball cap. He seemed to consider his own words. "It is normal to be afraid after seeing what you've seen. Watchers are evil. Spirit and air, slaves of great darkness. Do you not know of these, my boy?"

Ewan shook his head. He could not stop his hands from trembling.

"How'd she do that? With the mirror?"

Eldoran leaned close, close enough for Ewan to see the circular scar on his brow, wrinkled with age. "You are not from any city or part of this kingdom, are you? Your clothing is . . . strange. Sit and speak now. Tell me your story. Brother Melanor, bring bread and fruit for our guest. He looks hungry."

The man wearing the lightest shade of gray bowed his head, made the sign of the circle, and departed. He returned shortly with a wooden platter of simple fare, a half loaf of dried bread, grapes, and some other kind of small green fruit that was delicious. Ewan ate hungrily, mind racing. It seemed ridiculous to even attempt to tell his story. Who would believe it? But with few options and nothing but time, he told the whole tale from start to finish. Newland, Missouri. The briar patch, the tunnels, Hadyn. The birds, the scrolls. The arch. The tune and the glowing runes. When he finished, his belly was filled and his heart calmed, but a fresh ache for home nearly overwhelmed him. For the first time yet, it occurred to him that he should be very afraid.

Eldoran didn't utter a single word while he spoke. No questions, no comments. He merely listened and watched with a serious, attentive expression.

"By the Nines, I have heard such things," he mused after a long silence, stroking his beard. "From long ago. Legends of old. But Call Birds haven't flown since the time of the great mirling, Tal Yssen. If even then. This is sober news, indeed."

"They have a name?" Ewan asked. "So you don't think I'm crazy?"

"Oh no, no!" Eldoran said, shaking his head. "Of all the things you have said, the Call Birds and the gifts they bore are the most strikingly true to my ears, the most impossible to deny. The arch and markings and such I am less certain of. But the Call Birds"—he shook his head, seeming to size Ewan up with new appreciation—"that part suggests you are of royal blood, to be so Called."

Ewan snorted. "Hardly."

"Call Birds are the ancient descendants of Runnin himself. He who was present at the Mercy of Aion. It is a proverb in our land: *When you are Called, you dream. When you dream, a new world opens.*'"

Ewan wiped his mouth. "Yep, that's pretty much how it happened. Frankly, I expect to wake up at any moment, safe in my own bed." He tried to play it off, finding no hint of humor in Eldoran's eyes, nor the other men, whose faces remained hidden under their cowls. It was all just too weird. Ewan whispered, "So this is all for real? Father Eldoran of the Gray Abbey, Flogg the gnome . . . and a really *ugly* spirit bird?"

"Watcher," Eldoran said gravely. "Oh, my boy, yes. For good or ill, you are wide awake." He slapped his thigh. "Gracious, look at me! I'm ashamed of myself." He glanced at Ewan's ball cap and pointed at the letters. "Modesty has prevented you from saying your name. Young Lord Ecbee, I presume? Is that your family crest?"

Ewan pulled his cap off, saw the letters ECB. Embarrassed, he answered, "No, no. I'm just Ewan. Ewan Carter Barlow. ECB."

"Well, Ewan Carter Barlow, you have presented me a great mystery. And none too soon, for we live in troubled times. I must ponder further. For now, it appears to have fallen to me to serve as first ambassador of my world to yours. Therefore welcome, Ewan Barlow of New Land Misery. Welcome to Karac Tor!"

As he spoke these words, the door toward the kitchen burst noisily open.

"Let him go!" demanded an angry voice. A familiar, wonderful, angry voice.

Ewan leaped to his feet. "Hadyn?"

There, wildly brandishing his Swiss Army knife like it was a sword of great doom, stood Hadyn. He wore a winter coat tied around his waist and a dangerous, wild expression.

"Let my brother go!"

He broke into a run toward Ewan.

CHAPTER 8

High Callings

H adyn didn't get far.

Slipping from the shadows behind the door, a gray-robed figure thrust the tip of his staff toward Hadyn's feet, sending him thudding to the floor. The impact jarred the knife from his grip as it clattered across the flagstones. He rolled over, found the same staff now pressed hard against his chest. He struggled to rise, but the monk bore down even more. He groaned.

"Relent," said the monk. "You have entered a place of peace."

Ewan shouted, "Stop it! That's my brother! That's Hadyn!"

Eldoran's deep voice boomed. "Sorge, release him. I am in no danger from this boy, I think."

Sorge relaxed his pressure, but did not lift the staff. "If you are truly kin, you will recognize the health of your brother. We have caused him no harm. You would be wise to treat us the same." He removed his hood, extended a hand. A thin smile played at the corners of his mouth.

"It was an ill-considered plan," he said softly. "But large of heart."

"Courageous indeed," Eldoran agreed, striding forward with Ewan at his side.

Hadyn rubbed his sore chest and looked into the face of the monk called Sorge, roughly fortysomething, with a jaw like an ox and a melting gaze. He was black, his head completely shaven, except for a long, braided ponytail in the back. He too had a circular scar on his forehead, about an inch wide. Branded. Hadyn reached for the offered hand, pulled himself up.

Was nearly knocked to the ground again by Ewan's fierce, grateful embrace.

"How did you get here? How in the world did you find me?" Ewan exclaimed incredulously.

"I'd like to know the same thing," Hadyn said wryly. "First, what world are we talking about?"

"The Royal Kingdom of Karac Tor," Eldoran replied with a flourish. "Peace upon you."

Hadyn blinked. "I don't suppose that's anywhere near St. Louis?"

"Totally different world," Ewan whispered urgently. "I don't know how or why, or even what that means, really. All I know is that I dreamed a tune and played it at the arch. The runes glowed and I crawled through to look at the other side. Next thing I remember, I'm here."

"Okay," Hadyn breathed. "That's a start. Because when I heard the back door open last night, I couldn't figure out what in the world you were up to. I woke up to go to the bathroom and saw a light out the window. It was you, with your flashlight, heading toward the arch. I couldn't believe it. It must have been four or five in the morning. What were you thinking?"

"I don't remember thinking," Ewan admitted. "It was weird."

Hadyn's green eyes narrowed, a gesture of practiced, brotherly disapproval. "Anyway, I got dressed and tried to catch up to you. I heard your flute ahead of me, but when I got to the tunnel, you were gone. The runes were glowing. I was afraid. I thought I should get Dad, but then the glow started to fade, and I didn't know if I could make it back before the glow was gone. So I crawled through, too."

Ewan smiled. "Did you see her?"

Hadyn cocked his head. "Her who?"

"I saw a woman. A fairy, I think—all glowy and stuff. She was slender, with large eyes and wings and silver hair that swam in the air. She acted very surprised that I could see her. She said she had to tell her queen."

"A Fey Folk?" Eldoran said. "You *saw* one of them?"

"I think so." Ewan grinned at Hadyn. "Hey, did that hole under the tree freak you out? I had bugs dropping all over me."

Hadyn scrunched his face. "*What* are you talking about?"

"When you came through the arch. The nasty hole under the roots of that old tree. That's where I landed before I saw the fairy . . . Fey Folk thingy . . . whatever she was."

"Not me. I was on a path on a hill. And I found this on the ground." He held up Ewan's tin whistle, adding, "Your tennis shoes leave pretty good tracks, by the way."

Ewan grabbed his flute with relief. "I had to crawl so Flogg wouldn't see me. It must have slipped out of my pocket."

"Flogg?"

"A gnome. Mean little bugger."

"But a good cook," Eldoran replied, amused and troubled by the whole exchange. He regarded Hadyn quite seriously. "Welcome, Hadyn, brother of Ewan. The tale of your coming is equally curious to me, but it seems you too have been Called."

Ewan elbowed Hadyn. "The birds. He's talking about the birds."

It took a moment for all the pieces to connect. "*Call*," Hadyn exclaimed. "*That's* what they were saying."

"It is said they have the power to fly between worlds, and it seems the legends are true." Eldoran shook his head wonderingly. "I dare say a true Call has not been released in many long generations."

Hadyn pulled from his coat pocket two black metal tubes, banded with ivory, scripted on the side with a fancy capital *A*.

"If you know about the birds, I bet you'll know about these."

He handed the tubes to Eldoran, who took them delicately, almost reverently. Melanor pressed in to see. Sorge seemed perplexed. Father Eldoran gently removed the tube's cap and tapped the casing until a thin corner of the scroll emerged. He tugged it free, unrolling it gently, studying the grain of the parchment, the weight of the script. Then he read aloud:

"*Chosen . . . for a life of great purpose. Adventure awaits you . . .*"

Eldoran spoke slowly. His faded blue eyes caught the oily light of a dozen torches like sparks in a mirror.

"An auspicious omen," he said, stern and joyful.

"So this is the Hidden Lands?" Haydn asked. "This, right now?"

"That is an old name," Eldoran replied. "But yes, little brother. You have come to the Hidden Lands, more commonly called Karac Tor."

"And where exactly *is* that?"

"Not where, perhaps, so much as what. We are a kingdom without a king. But first, come, both of you. I will tell you more. We shall take refreshment in my study. Elder Sorge, join us."

They moved from the large, open chamber to a smaller room lit with candles—Eldoran, Sorge, Hadyn, and Ewan. Melanor and the third monk were dismissed to their chambers for meditation and rest, but not before Hadyn noticed that they too had the same round, white scars on their foreheads. Sorge brought more bread and slices of sharp cheese, like cheddar, a small cup of wine for the Father, and a tangy concoction of apple and lemon juice spiced with fresh mint leaf, sweetened with a touch of honey. He called it Alm Tea. The boys found it delicious.

"What is this stuff?" Ewan said, holding up a piece of yellow cheese. "It's amazing."

"Ah, well, how polite of you," Eldoran said with obvious pride. "We are simple men, but we work hard. Doolin, Braghe, Chadar. We trade our cheeses around the kingdom, to help fund our work." He smiled. "*Better bread with cheese than a feast without.* Or so we like to think."

"He's being modest," Sorge interjected. "In the south, they call that cheese you are eating *eldoran.*"

Father Eldoran grinned broadly. But this was not the time for bragging. When both boys were suitably refreshed, he opened his hands to them, "Allow me to share with you the history of our land."

So he began.

"As I've already said, Karac Tor is, regrettably, a kingdom without a King. Yhü Hoder, the first man, ruled for five hundred years before passing the scepter to his son, who passed it to his son, and so on. A long-enduring dynasty was forged on a throne of wisdom and quiet strength. This was the Age of Crowns. It was followed by the even more glorious Blessed Thousand. Ten centuries of unsurpassed beauty, prosperity, and advancement—the golden age of Karac Tor.

"But that was many hundred years ago. The King's line was cut short and the royal scepter passed into legend. To maintain order, the King's Governors assumed power, dividing the land into their own fiefdoms. The Five Dominions formed. We gained a few years' peace and order, but ultimately, it was a selfish, disastrous plan."

"All we did was exchange one great war for dozens of smaller wars," said Sorge.

"Wars and warlords," Eldoran added. "Then, thirteen generations ago, a noble Governor named Archibald rose to influence. He united the land and brought peace, much as a King would do. He was a good man, but it was not an easy peace."

"Nor holy, much of the time," Sorge added.

"Ahh, now, be charitable, Elder. The Archibalds did much for the kingdom. We are indebted to them." He turned to Hadyn and Ewan apologetically. "Sorge is clear-eyed as a hawk and twice as fierce. He speaks the truth. The problem is"—he groped at the air for words—"the virility, the goodness of the kingdom has languished under the Archibalds. We have a sense of our history again, and decency—"

"But we have no courage," Sorge murmured. "No heart. No will to fight the rising tide."

"What tide?" Ewan asked.

The two monks exchanged worried glances. Eldoran let his gaze drift past the walls to the green hills beyond, like a man in a cave trying to see farther into the darkness than his lamp allowed. He stirred his wine with his finger, shook his head. Shuddered.

"We dare not speak it. Not yet. It is an ancient evil. But like the tide, it *is* rising."

Sorge folded his arms. "You see, little brothers, life is a delicate balance, wavering between order and chaos, virtue and corruption—"

"Between the Mercy of Aion and the Wrath of the Devourer," Eldoran said gravely.

"It is a perpetual struggle. The Abbeys were ordained to achieve fullness of revelation and thus preserve righteousness. We are a brotherhood of three distinctions: White, Gray, Black. Preeminent among us are the Whites, for they are the chief custodians of the two great tasks, to study the Book of Law and keep the Book of Names."

Ewan motioned in the air with his hands. "I'm really sorry, but I'm not getting this."

"Yeah, me neither," Hadyn said. "What's the big deal with a Book of Names?"

Eldoran looked genuinely surprised. "The big deal? Why, names are our greatest treasure! Surely you have such a book in your world. A magical, sacred book?"

Hadyn opened his mouth to answer, but Sorge cut him off. "The Book of Names reveals the great plan of Aion," he explained, as if this were a fact everyone should know.

"Go back further, Sorge. Tell them of Yhü."

Sorge nodded. "Yhü Hoder was once the friend of Aion, but then he drank the forbidden waters of Mount Bourne. Part of Aion's judgment against him was that he labor without rest until he had recorded the history of Karac Tor to come. He was given a powerful gift of foresight, to name every man, woman, and child who would ever be born unto the end of the age. So it was. And so it is."

"Every person who has ever lived, in one book? C'mon."

"Ever lived or *will* live in this world," Eldoran's eyes twinkled. "Yes, it boggles the mind. We call all of it, collectively, the Book of Names. There are millions of pages."

Ewan was catching on. "Let me get this straight. You mean some kid's name who will be born tomorrow is already listed somewhere on a scroll or something . . . before he's even born?"

"Exactly. It has never failed. Thrice a day—dawn, noon, and eventide—the Chief Curator reads aloud the names given to that day."

"So when that kid grows up, he could go and read about himself? He could find out what he's going to be doing in five years? Who he's going to marry? Stuff like that?"

"Not quite," Sorge said. "First, though every new name is readable to all, they only appear as each person is born. It is part of Yhü's magic, the magic of creation. Second, a person's deeds are visible only to that person, not another. Third, only major deeds are recorded. Perhaps five or six. Or ten."

"It is the greatest treasure of the kingdom," Eldoran declared in a voice that left no room for dispute, "entrusted to the care of the White Abbey, for they sit in the shadow of the library Yhü constructed to house his great Book. The Whites take the honor very seriously. Rightly so, I might add. It is a stern and reverent task."

Sorge fingered a grape. "All for the sake of righteousness. So extreme fidelity is how the Whites contribute to the balance of wisdom. They are unbending, legalistic."

"And most unpleasant. Merciless on nearly all matters." Eldoran cleared his throat, as if to clear his thoughts. "They are Stewards of Truth for a reason. On the other hand, the Black Abbey to the north is another matter. Theirs is the way of mystery, the unknowable secrets of Aion. Their rituals bring power to the service of peace. Thus, their part of righteousness relies more on awe than creeds. The woman you saw in the Banishing Ring with us, Asandra, is a mirling of the Black Abbey. Her rank and gift allow her to capture Watchers with blessed water. Mirlings exercise the mirrorling arts to cleanse the land of evil." He paused, suddenly tired. "But only a few remain these days, and none so skilled as Asandra. Cassock halted their training for nearly two decades. During this time many *mismyri* slipped through."

"Watchers," Sorge clarified.

The word made Ewan shiver. Sorge continued.

"It is dangerous work. Some Blacks have lost their way, drifting into blasphemy."

Eldoran sighed. "Thus you see the need for balance. Power is necessary, but only the Books are true. Thus, Whites and Blacks."

"Book of Names, Book of Law," Ewan said, holding up two fingers, trying to keep it all straight.

Eldoran leaned forward. For a moment he hesitated, briefly glancing toward Sorge with a kind of tenderness. "Nemesia was one of Cassock's brightest pupils. Some twenty years after she became a mirling, she strayed from her vows and refused to repent. She veered from mystery to darkness, from ritual to sorcery. We saw it too late. Our discernment failed. Now she ascends. For months now, all over the kingdom, reports have arrived of children drifting about like wraiths. Parents claim the very souls of their sons and daughters are being stolen. Many, many hundreds have asked for prayer."

Hadyn said, "What do you mean, stolen?"

"Stolen. Taken captive. Young people, disappearing."

"Not disappearing," Sorge spat. "They go to the Tower of Ravens. To *her*. I would swear it."

The image was striking. Ewan pictured zombies wandering the empty fields.

Sorge clenched his fists. "If I had been wiser, it would be different now. But I was a fool."

"It is no longer your guilt to bear, Elder Sorge. Have peace, sit down. Governor Archibald is not blind. The City of Kings overlooks the Isle of Apaté."

"Precisely. He *over* looks."

Eldoran unrolled one of the invitation scrolls. "So we thought, but what of these, my brother? Have faith! The Governor has released the birds of legend, with invitations bearing his name: *A* for Archibald, the twelfth in the line of Archibalds. He must have a plan." Eldoran glanced admiringly at the Barlow brothers. "And I must send a courier to convey the glad tidings, that his answer has arrived. Here they are, within the walls of our very own Abbey!"

Ewan was dumbfounded. "Here what is? Who is?"

Hadyn dropped his head. "He thinks we're the answer, Ewan. He's talking about us."

Eldoran beamed, motioning like the presenter of gifts at a ceremony. "Obviously, you! He called for Champions and you've come. You boys are the answer to our many prayers."

CHAPTER 9

Homesick

A lump formed in Ewan's throat. Champions?

"I'm sorry, what did you say?"

"Haven't you been listening, little brother? You have been chosen. Karac Tor's Champions are gone, too busy with their own affairs, with wine and dance and song. Many have grown old and died. Mac'Kalok is blind. Corus of Lotsley is lost among the Fey Folk."

"Or worse," Sorge said quietly.

"The Abbeys have prayed and Archibald has repeatedly summoned the kingdom's former Champions. None answered, to stop Nemesia. It seems Olfadr Everking has reached to your world for hope. Yet I must say, you are so young . . ."

His voice trailed away.

"Mr. Eldoran, I don't know how to put this," Hadyn said firmly, trying his best to be reasonable. "But we're not your Champions."

"Oh, no need to be modest. I don't understand it either, little brother. But to you falls the privilege of righting the wrongs. You hold the scrolls."

"No, we *found* them by accident. And they aren't our wrongs to right! We're here by mistake."

"Nothing in the will of Aion is a mistake."

Pretense and politeness were not working. "Fine, then *you* fix the balance thing. You save the lost. Why do we have to?"

Eldoran leaned back in his chair. "Our Order is not like that. The first Grays were weary warriors who traded their weapons for vows of peace. They gave up battle for gardens and cheese making. Men grow tired of blood." He began pacing the room. "Ours is a task of prayer. We serve wisdom and righteousness by finding the balance between reason and faith. Do the Grays really think wraiths wander about? Of course not. It's childish superstition. But the part about losing the soul . . . ahh, now that part rings truer to my ears. And it shakes me to my core. If the soul of a generation is lost, the entire kingdom goes with it, slipping quietly into darkness. The Dukes and land barons are too distracted right now, sharpening their swords to raid each other's lands. Nemesia's shadow will engulf us all and no one will notice until it is too late." He lowered himself to the table, noisily sipped his wine. "The dark is rising. But for you to be here"—he shook his head—"the situation must be far more grave than I was willing to admit."

Ewan bit his tongue. Sarcasm came so easily.

I'll take "Sorry to Disappoint You" for $200, Alex.

Hadyn, touching his arm, mumbled, "Ewan, I think they think we're someone we don't think we are."

"I think that's a double negative," Ewan replied. "But it sounds right."

Eldoran quietly stroked his gray beard. He held up the scrolls. "Who do these belong to?"

Hadyn began prowling the room. It was obvious how Eldoran was trying to pin them down. "I honestly don't have a clue! The stupid birds dropped them, that's all."

"At whose feet were they dropped?"

"It could have been anybody's!"

"Even so, someone was there, at that exact spot, at that exact time. Or forgive me. Were others nearby? Was there a crowd? Could the placement have been mistaken?"

Hadyn didn't answer. He looked trapped.

"And who picked up the scrolls? Who read the invitations? Who claimed them?"

"This is messed up," Hadyn whispered. Ewan felt sorry for him. The briar patch had become a rare bright spot for his brother. It wasn't supposed to become a life mission.

"We don't belong here and you know it," Hadyn continued. "We didn't know what the Hidden Lands were, or the birds. We didn't know we'd end up in another world. Is that the way this Ever King works? Trick you and make you do his bidding? Besides, I can't do this to my dad. Our family has been through too much already."

"You *answered* the Call, little brother," Sorge said solemnly.

"I'm not your brother!" Hadyn cried, loud enough to make Ewan flinch. Hearing his voice echo off the walls, he slumped forward in defeat. "Listen, I'm not trying to be rude. It's just that I'm not your Champion and neither is Ewan. We're from America. I don't even have my driver's license. Honestly, I don't know what you think we're supposed to do."

"Yes, that is difficult. What do you think you *should* do?"

Hadyn sighed. "We should go home. Show us the yellow brick road. Let us go."

Eldoran stroked his beard. "I understand that you do not feel connected to us. But the Grays have a proverb: *Eventually, all are brothers.* Perhaps even from one world to the next."

Ewan attempted to be diplomatic. After all, the monks couldn't hold them prisoners, could they? "Sir, we're sorry for all the trouble your planet is in, or wherever we are. But you can see that we really shouldn't be here, can't you? It's a mistake."

Eldoran wagged his finger. "Providence is never mistaken. Only misunderstood."

Hadyn said, "Listen, we've asked as politely as we know how. If you'll just show us the portal, we'll be heading home now."

"The what?"

"The runestone. Where is it?"

Sorge stubbornly crossed his arms, brushing back his sleeves. But when Ewan caught sight of a plain bronze band on his forearm near the elbow, the monk quickly pushed his sleeves back into place.

"We do not have this power," he said simply. "It is of the Fey."

"Show us the runestone!" Hadyn demanded.

Implacable as stone, Sorge stood to his feet, squared his body to Hadyn. Even under his loose robe, his stance and the grip of his hands on his rosewood staff suggested a muscular frame. Ewan stepped between them, feeling haggard. Technically his day had been pretty short so far. But with all the weirdness, and the stress of capture at knifepoint, it felt quite long already. Behind him, edgy and protective, Hadyn said, "You can't keep us here against our will. You *can't*."

"Stand down, little brother. You are in a place of peace, remember? It is no more our task to return you than it is your task to help us."

"Sorge, Sorge," Eldoran chided. "Oft have the Hidden Lands been ruled by coercion, yet none have ever prospered to take what the heart is unwilling to give. 'Tis not the way of Aion." Ewan felt the old man's comforting hand rest on his shoulder. Trembling, he buried his face in his hands to hide his fear. As cool as all this probably was and should be, he simply wasn't prepared. It was overload.

The Father's eyebrows wrinkled with tender concern. "You are obviously distraught, my boy. I'm sorry for that. But please believe me when I say—now that you are here—I truly don't know how to send you back."

"Under the tree," Ewan raised his head hopefully. His eyes were streaked and red. "It must be there."

"Doubtful," said Sorge. "Fey magic isn't like that."

"How do you know? We could try."

"You yourself went back and looked. You said so. Think, little brother. You both crawled through the same portal on your world, yet one came out under a tree and the other came out on a path in the woods."

The effort of hope so briefly risen, fallen, consumed the last of Ewan's strength. He turned to Hadyn, asking questions without words.

"It'll be alright, Ewan. We'll figure this out."

Eldoran strummed the tabletop, thinking. "The only option I can see is to send you to Stratamore. If Archibald called you, he must know how to return you. Rest here tonight. Tomorrow we will make plans for your journey south."

Hadyn took a slow, calming breath. "Okay, sounds like a start. Thank you."

He added, "I'm sorry. Truly sorry we can't help. We just don't belong here. And my dad needs us."

Eldoran shuffled to the wall, rang a little service bell hanging there. Brother Melanor hurried in, hands dutifully clasped in front of him.

"Show these fine young men our guest quarters," the old man instructed. He sounded neither bitter nor angry.

"Please don't be mad at us," Ewan said, to Sorge for some reason. "We're just kids."

Together, following Melanor, they passed through the halls in silence. They might as well have carried rocks in their bellies. Ewan wanted to throw up.

Behind them, unheard, Sorge leaned near to Eldoran's ear, whispering. "It's a mistake, Father. Let it go from your heart. Those boys could not possibly be the Champions we need. Someone else was meant to find those scrolls." Watching them disappear into the shadows, he mumbled, "Yet I must say . . . for a moment, it seemed like hope had entered our world."

Eldoran straightened his back, determined and prophetic. "Hope never stands alone," he said in a dry, husky voice. "It is born of valor and perseverance. It rides the back of courage."

One by one, Sorge pinched the burning wicks of the lit candles. The room progressively darkened. The darkness was great and heavy as all the world in that moment, smothering his last words.

"Then we are doomed."

CHAPTER 10

Escape by Night

A voice. Hissing and harsh. Exasperated.

"... must I beat on a pot with a spoon? Merciful Aion! Awake, Lord Ewan ... awake!"

Ewan sat upright, eyes wide. Two faces slowly formed from the stain of night. He tried to focus. A lone candle fingered the walls with light and mercurial globs of shadow. Two murky figures loomed above him: Hadyn to the side, and Sorge, leaning over his bed, shaking his head in amazement. In the darkness, Ewan could only see the man's eyes and teeth.

"Woe should the War of Swords begin while you slumber, Ewan Barlow. You sleep greatly! Rise now, make haste."

"I'll take Cheerios," Ewan mumbled sleepily, falling back onto his bed. "Some banana slices, too, thanks."

Fingers jabbed his ribs. Hadyn said, "Ewan, knock it off. Wake up. This is for real."

"What?" Ewan whined. He sat up again, rubbed his eyes. "War of what?"

"There's no time," Hadyn snapped. "Just do it."

"Gather your things. Dress quickly."

But wakefulness was a gradual process for Ewan, like crawling out from under a warm, heavy blanket. Eventually, a few things became clear. First, that Hadyn was *already* fully dressed; furthermore, that he wore native clothes, not his own—simple, loose-fitting shirt, brown trousers, sandals, cloak pinned at the neck; and third, that he appeared quite awake, even alarmed. Ewan strained his face to assemble this new information. Thankfully, Hadyn read his thoughts.

"Yes, away. To home hopefully. But there are . . . problems."

"Dangers," Sorge said plainly.

"Dangers getting us home?"

"No, to get you to Stratamore, where we will find out if it is even possible to get you home. First things first, Lord Ewan. Quickly, dress!"

Ewan rose, finding Hadyn would no longer meet his gaze. He was clearly worried and trying to hide it. The younger Barlow accepted the shirt and pants Sorge gave him without question, feeling rapidly more alert. Nervousness, like claustrophobia, seeped into his skin.

"Leave your lettered head piece," Sorge said.

"The hat." Hadyn whispered, replacing it in his hands with the small, thin shape of his tin whistle. "How many times do I have to find this for you?"

Ewan snatched his hat back, stuffing it into a loose back pocket. The feel of the whistle in his hands became a kind of portal to home—unpassable, except for the wanting. A great, lonely distance opened inside him as they hastened along night-wrapped corridors, arriving at last in a torchlit antechamber which reeked of manure and old, wet straw. Beyond were the stables. Father Eldoran was there, looking tired. He greeted them grimly.

"One of our Brothers had a dark dream this night. In the dream, a rift opened in a gray sky, followed by thunder, as two arrows were shot from a great bow. Just then, sunlight broke through the clouds. But the sound of thunder had roused Watchers from their slumber. They pursued the arrows across the sky, intending to capture them before they found their mark."

Ewan glanced at Hadyn, uncomprehending. Eldoran continued.

"The Brother who dreamed woke in a cold sweat and came to me in the middle of the night to interpret his vision. It was about the two of you, I'm certain. It troubled me enough to wake others. While you slept, we took counsel together, the Gray Elders and myself. After much deliberation and prayer, we came to one mind. Our judgment is that the dream is a clear message from Aion—a warning. Your coming to this world is not an accident, nor has it gone unnoticed by forces of evil. Last night I was too taken aback to realize the obvious: moving from one world to another does not occur without a great release of power."

Sorge spoke next. "Somehow, that power has marked you, according to the dream. We don't know how. Perhaps in many ways."

"Marked doesn't sound so good."

Father Eldoran's answer was rough and unequivocal. "Like it or not, young men, you were Called. By accepting, you each chose that Calling, whether by will or by accident. I know this means little to you, and that you have no interest in the workings of Karac

Tor, or the weaving of law and magic by which our world is bound. Your aim is simply to go home. In good faith, we are utilizing every resource to aid your return. Nevertheless, when you accepted the Call, you came with power. You saw Fey Folk, with no moon. How can this be? It is because you are marked. And evil, which never sleeps, has taken notice. In short, you are now in danger."

Ewan felt a surge of fear, knew he must confess. "Yesterday, when that mirling did her thing with the Watcher—there was a point in the ceremony when the Watcher looked straight at me. I was at the back of the room, with Flogg. It clawed at the glass as if it was trying to get at me."

Eldoran thumped his staff on the stone floor angrily. His bushy eyebrows twitched. "Eldoran, you fool! Of *course* they are known. A Watcher saw them with its own eyes!" He glanced at Sorge. "Now, indeed, you must make haste. We will have even less time than I hoped."

He placed his hands on the brothers' heads as an act of benediction. "Speed and secrecy are urgent to your task, and miles matter more than sleep. You journey south, under cover of night. If you are going to get home—and I make no guarantees—you must first get to the City of Kings. Archibald must know you are here."

"But we don't know the way."

"I do," Sorge countered. "I am taking you myself."

The door from the antechamber to the Abbey swung open, slamming Ewan's shoulder. In stomped Flogg, mad as a hornet.

"Ready," he groused. "But no manling whines or Flogg be crackin' heads."

Eldoran glanced toward the Barlow brothers. "Flogg shall accompany you, as well. Gnomes have an excellent sense of the land and . . . other skills."

Ewan didn't much care for the gnome. Knife to the back and all. He started to protest.

Flogg cut him short, waving a finger at Eldoran. "And no crying from Father when bowl grows cold soup."

"Of course," agreed the older man.

Flogg whirled to face both Barlows, wrinkling his snout. "And no complainin' for fast movings if manling feetsies start to hurt. Flogg helps get manlings home Flogg's way."

"You've got to be joking!" Ewan said. "The troll is going? Is someone going to take away all his knives first?"

"Hah!" Flogg stomped his foot. "Good! Flogg go back to kitchen. Morel stew need more salt. Manlings on their own."

Eldoran waved his hand peaceably, "My favorite stew can wait old friend. They need you on this journey more than I need my soup, though believe me, I will miss it. And don't worry, the boy will learn better manners in time." To Sorge, he said, "Go quickly. Dawn will break soon. You should have better cover along the Old Way through the hills to Threefork. Flogg, gather your things. And please, kindly check on Asandra, if she is still in the kitchen."

"No need. I'm here."

The mirling stepped out of the shadows at the far end of the hall, robed in purple. She wore a silver chain around her neck and silver rings on every finger of her right hand. Hadyn's eyes widened to see her. Her skin was smooth, her lips full. She was exotic and beautiful—almond-shaped eyes, thick; flowing hair as black as night. She was a mix of races, dark and light. Perhaps a Native American princess.

Except this wasn't America.

"Asandra, Lords Hadyn and Ewan. Little brothers, may I introduce you to Asandra the mirling? She is traveling to Seabraith on official business for the Bishop Cassock and will accompany you for the first leg of your journey."

Hadyn thrust out his hand rather awkwardly. Asandra regarded the gesture with disdain.

"This is how we greet on my world. We shake hands. I'm Hadyn."

"So I've been told."

"Right . . . Eldoran just said that, didn't he?" he laughed nervously. "That mirrorling stuff sounds pretty cool. Did that take you long? . . . to learn?" His voice trailed away.

Ewan snickered. "Nice. Smooth. Ask if she's on Facebook next."

"Shut up," Hadyn said.

Sorge seemed discomfited by the mirling's presence. His expression was both careful and blank. "Are you . . . sure, Father? We need speed."

Eldoran missed or overlooked the subtlety. "Yes, I agree. If only we had enough horses. But they would tire quickly in the hills, I'm afraid."

Asandra, not missing Sorge's point, smiled coldly. "If you are afraid I'll slow you, I won't."

Flogg, grumbling something gnomish—more like a sneeze than an actual language—dashed off, returning momentarily with a leather satchel half his size slung over his shoulder. A heavy, black cudgel dangled from his belt. In the firelight, his red beard and face looked like dried clay.

"Packings and smackings. Flogg ready."

Eldoran said, "Perhaps you should carry your bow, Elder? The Order would permit it."

Sorge unfolded his arms from his gray robe, his fingers curving easily around four grooves worn into his quarterstaff. Evidence of many miles travelled in service of the abbey. He held it easily, naturally. A ready threat, a trusted weapon. It seemed an extension of his own skin.

"I took a vow. My staff will do."

The old man gave a gesture of acceptance more than approval. He squeezed Sorge's arm, like a father to a son, then leaned close to his cheek. At first Ewan thought it was for a kiss, then he saw the old man's lips moving. He strained to hear. Words like leaves, falling to the ground.

"If trouble befalls you, have no doubt the Tower of Ravens is behind it."

Sorge nodded curtly, telling his companions, "Jackals have been wandering north of Redthorn as far as the southern Shimlings. It is a sign of things to come. We must be alert."

He set off. The boys followed. Flogg and Asandra brought up the rear.

Eldoran blessed them with a wave of his hand. "Aion smile on your road. We shall pray the court of Archibald finds you well, then safely home."

As his voice faded, Ewan realized he would probably never see Eldoran again.

CHAPTER 11

Gray Morning

The five travelers passed out of the Abbey, east, through the Gate of God. Almost immediately they reached a narrow, sturdy wooden bridge to cross Plumwater. Sorge informed them that it was the third watch, which Hadyn, after a few more questions, estimated to be roughly two o'clock. The sky was empty of stars and moon, covered with a thick layer of clouds. Hints of turbulence could be glimpsed overhead from time to time, felt in the thickening air. South and west, lightning flashed, briefly illuminating the dark southern plains, transforming them into a vast, waving sea of rolling grasslands.

"Lightning is an empty promise," Sorge said. "The Midlands beg for rain."

Ahead and to the east, like billowing sheets, the dark hills furled into utter blackness. The five climbed in silence, picking their way carefully along a goat trail up the hillside.

From the rear, Asandra spoke a low, ominous warning. "I sense a Watcher in the hills. He is far away. But he is searching."

Sorge flashed a look of displeasure and fell back to discuss the matter. Obviously, the mirling was being chastised, probably for speaking aloud, making the boys nervous. She took the correction with stony silence and defiance in her eyes. Sorge quickened their pace, traveling a lightless path with no torch or moon to guide their steps.

Ewan caught up to the monk. He wanted to get his mind off Watchers lurking in the dark. "So what's the circle mean? On your forehead?"

The monk huffed with the effort of his pack. "Aion . . . has no beginning. Our loyalty has no end. Thus, an endless circle."

Ewan almost had to jog to keep up with his long strides. "Okay. So why Gray? Why not White or Black?"

"Grays are called Waykeepers by some. We labor among the people, with the people, as healers, singers, farmers. Some, even, as warriors. We build and keep orphanages. We give aid to the hurting and stay connected to the earth, the stuff of life, in ways the other abbeys cannot sustain, for it would dilute their task. Our task *is* those things."

"So you were a warrior once, right?"

"Once, long ago. A Master Bowman."

The hesitation in his reply made Ewan curious. "Is that what that bracelet on your arm means? Some sort of warrior thing?"

Sorge flicked his eyes from the trail to Ewan. Back to the trail. Asandra, apparently, was also curious, having quickened her pace enough to join them.

"What happened?" she asked.

Her tone, relatively pleasant, seemed incongruous with her blankly rigid stare, leaving Ewan to think there must be more. Sorge did not seem bothered, only tired, casting his gaze ahead to the next rise of hill.

"I lost my way. Lost a friend." He wiped sweat from his brow. "I lost many things."

He pulled ahead after that, as the hills grew steadily higher, rougher underfoot. Took more effort, concentration. Two hours slowly passed, then three. With dawn, the world slowly changed clothes, exhanging the cool cloak of night for scarves of gray fog wrapped around the hills, suspended in twilight.

"Trampings and stampings. Brg! Should be cookin' and cleanin'. Flogg likes. But no!" It was a random complaint, and no one bothered to reply, but Ewan was irritated. Gnomes, it seemed, were cheerless little creatures.

The mirling, her face hidden beneath her cowl, continued her dark glances to the heavens. They trekked in single file for a long time, no one speaking, until far to the south rose a high, lonely wail. Sorge froze. The cry was faint, almost unhearable, but another echoed it. Then another. Then all three at once. Ewan shivered at the sound. They were haunting howls of lust and anguish.

Asandra began moving again. "We mustn't pause, even to rest."

They set off, dogged and wary now, moving from peak to valley, peak to valley, over the seemingly endless hills. Dawn drew near. The cover of night would soon be gone.

"Hadyn," Ewan whispered between panting breaths. "I'm scared."

Hadyn pursed his lips. "We don't have time to think that way. Just keep moving."

Which, of course, made Ewan feel even more the younger brother. Small and weak. But how was he supposed to act, fleeing for his life over hills he had never seen in a world totally disconnected from his own? With a gnome and a monk? And a whatever she was . . . a mirror woman. And what was this place? Another planet? Another dimension? He dropped his head, trudging along. The hills, looming large, all seemed to be crawling with prowling beasts, at least in his imagination. He had little choice but to keep moving.

Unexpectedly, a hand touched his shoulder. He almost jumped out of his skin.

"I'm scared, too, Ewan," Hadyn finally admitted. "Just don't think about it. Sorge will get us there."

It wasn't much, but it was enough. Hadyn's fingers were even trembling.

Morning broke with a mixture of relief and dread, the sun straining through low, brooding swathes of cloud. Though visibility came as a welcome companion to the five travelers—or at least to Ewan, Sorge still fretted. They had traveled hard for hours and paused now for breath on the crown of a tall hill, easily the highest yet, one which offered commanding views in all directions.

"The Watcher?" Sorge asked, bending over, hands on his knees.

Asandra caught her breath. "Not near at least, but I still feel him. Close, yet never within reach. He will try to avoid me, you know."

"Yes, but is he searching or tracking?"

From his tone, Ewan knew the latter must be the worse, though he didn't quite understand why. Neither sounded good. Asandra studied the skies.

"I don't know."

"Then figure it out."

Asandra eyed the monk coldly. She pulled her hood over her face, retreated from the group. Sorge saw Ewan's fear, pulled him near. He pointed. Ewan followed his finger. The hills rippled away below them, miles and miles of green undulations, looking much like a crumpled green skirt flung to the ground. Ribbons of thin fog still clung to the valley beds. Further west, the hills gradually flattened, abruptly ending. Plains began. And right there, on the hem of the hills, tiny in proportion, so far away . . .

"The Gray Abbey," Sorge declared. "See those small lights? And the thin gray wall of the watch tower on top of the hill? From here, like just a few pebbles. I stood once with Corus on this very hill, on our way to see Har Halas in Brimshane. We laughed and battled. By nightfall, we took shelter among those pebbles, at the Abbey. Even then, long before my vows, it felt like home to my soul. And Eldoran, like a father to me." He sighed. "We stand now on the highest hill of the Shimlings. These are the oldest mountains in all of Karac Tor, once high, frosty peaks. They are but little hills now—green, beautiful and forgotten. The trader's routes all follow newer roads. We take the Old Way."

"Hah! Older trackings Flogg thinks. Under rocklings, not over."

"Yes, Master Flogg, but we can't. You can't either. No rollwols. Our friends are frightened enough at the moment."

"*Rulvôl,*" Flogg sniffed.

"Rold gold?" Ewan repeated. "Those are pretzels in my world."

Whistle in the dark. Make a joke. Distract yourself. Whatever it takes.

"Say again?"

"Pretzels. They come in little bags. I don't much care for them."

Sorge frowned. Standing near the cracked bed of a dry little stream, he spat on his fingers, took a small chunk of hard clay from the ground and began spinning it between his thumb and forefinger. He walked as he spoke, toward a stand of trees.

"Rollwols are secret underground passageways," he explained. Faster than could be seen, he held a little clay bowl in his hand. "Humans are forbidden to enter rollwols. A gnome can be cast away from his people forever for betraying one of their locations. But they are very proud of their secrets. Flogg wanted to boast."

Though early still, the day was already hot. And dry. Sorge, glancing irritably toward the sky, mumbled, "Swords and blood . . . a little rain, please! We'll take cover under those trees and eat, but no lingering. Here," he handed the clay bowl to Hadyn, "use this if you like. Flogg has water."

Soon they were munching on plums and honeybread, sharing small sips of water. Everyone was thirsty.

Hadyn said, "Sorge, I really work better with a big picture. What's our plan?"

This line of thought seemed to please the monk. "Good, yes. We aim for the foot of Avl-Argosee, and the river town of Threefork. The lake is barely visible from here. Over there, on the horizon," he pointed east. The boys saw it. A thin, vast stretch of blue. Lake Argosee, it seemed, was enormous. Sorge took a stick, cleared a patch of dirt, and began scratching lines.

"We're here, moving southeast. In Threefork—here—is a captain friendly to the Abbey. A patron, really. He's done well for himself, is mostly retired, and works only when he wants. I will send Flogg ahead to secure safe passage for us on his ship, south across Champion Bay to Stratamore. Simple, really—as long as nothing follows us."

Nearby, Flogg motioned toward the monk. The gnome's voice sounded distant, strained. He sat with both hands pressed flat on the grass, palms down.

"Walkings and stalkings all around," he whispered. "Too late."

Catlike, Sorge sprang to a crouching posture. "Blackest gates of Helheim! I had a feeling." He took a breath. "What do you see?"

Flogg appeared to be sucking up the earth's vibrations through his fingers. "Other feet. Shadows. Near. Manlings being watched. And wings."

"I sense it, too," Asandra said, closing her eyes. "Something . . . not Watchers."

"Hush!" Sorge said, motioning with his hand. "Lay down. Be still."

Both boys dropped to their bellies. Flogg's white eyes, heavy-lidded in his trance, seemed oblivious. Sorge scoured the hills.

"I see nothing. Are you sure, Flogg?"

The gnome's milky gaze slowly gained color, focus. His breath evened. "Flogg may lie," he groaned. "Not stone."

"Swords and blood!" Sorge fumed quietly. "Which way?"

A shadow in the air, far away. Asandra saw first, cried out.

"There! Too many. It is a Flight of Crows!"

Sorge looked, saw the dark knot flinging across the sky. Moments before, it had been clear and blue. Now it thrashed with darkness. He leaped to his feet.

"Merciful Aion! This way!"

Whatever morsels of food they held or chewed were spit out, cast to the ground. Grabbed their packs. Began sprinting down the hillside following Sorge, his ponytail whipping in the breeze behind his shaven head. Ewan felt his blood pounding in his face. Behind them, a cacaphony of raucous cries grew terrifyingly close, loud. The beating wings of many birds, hungry and vicious. An eerie warm wind sprang up, which had not been before, bringing the birds near with frightening speed. Ewan glanced over his shoulder, stumbled on a rock, cried out. Hadyn caught him, hauled him forward.

"Watch your eyes!" Sorge cried. "They strike the eyes!"

The birds swarmed closer. Hadyn pushed Ewan ahead to shield him, and screamed as the birds clawed him, gouging with their beaks.

"Don't look back!" Hadyn hissed. "Run!"

His lungs were about to explode, but he somehow found the will to run even faster. Saw at the base of the hill a tiny hut built of blue river stone, mortared with clay. Sorge, running. Flogg, surprisingly swift on his short legs. The hut. Nearby, a small pond rimmed with cattail and pampas grass. So strange, so serene. People fleeing for their lives. Birds, like demons, swarming in a dark cloud behind. Surreal.

"Inside, inside!"

He dove headlong inside, collapsing in a heap. The birds shrieked, enraged. Hadyn broke through last of all, a raven still attached to his back, digging into his flesh. Flogg slammed the door shut. The back of Hadyn's shirt was red with his own blood. Sorge leaped forward, grabbed the bird, and wrenched it away. It thrashed, pecking madly. The monk roared, spun the weight of the bird's body in a circle around its own neck, instantly snapping the spine. The flapping wings stilled.

But that was only one bird, inside. Outside, a storm of wings continued.

CHAPTER 12

The Stone House

Everyone labored to catch their breath. Asandra reached gingerly toward the patches of blood on Hadyn's shirt.

"I'm alright," he panted. "Worry about me later."

Outside the birds clattered, beating their wings against the thatched roof. They squawked and cawed and pecked the stone. There were many dozens.

"This is the Stone House," Sorge managed between breaths. "A way station for pilgrims en route to the Abbey." He offered a wan smile. "It's supposed to be a simple shelter from the rain, a place to reflect. It is old."

The space was small, a single room, one door. High up two small, round—

"Windows!" Ewan said.

Sorge saw, tore off his cloak. Hadyn did the same. The windows were simply open holes, no glass, which they stuffed full before retreating to the corners. Flogg, fingering his cudgel, prowled the room. The small space darkened considerably, but cracks of light still shone through. For his part, Sorge seemed fixed on the west wall, the wall that faced the direction from which they had come. After a few moments, he laid his staff on the bare dirt floor, crept forward. First he put his ear to the stone, then his lips. Whispering, almost cajoling it seemed, he pressed his index finger into the rock. The effect was like sinking a hot iron into soft wax, as his digit slipped into the stone up to the third knuckle. Ewan let out a hushed cry of surprise. He had seen something similar at school, with a potter spinning a lump of wet clay on his wheel, then pinching it to suddenly draw forth the cavity of a cup. But that was soft clay, not hard, brittle stone. The gesture was so simple, so effortless, it almost seemed *normal*. Still whispering, the monk twirled his finger, molding a channel about two inches wide. When he withdrew, light and grass were visible on the other side.

"They've stopped," Ewan said, noticing the silence.

Sorge peered westward. The birds were hushed, the air was still. Sweat poured down Ewan's forehead. Hadyn, too, was flush with heat and strain. Ewan saw gouges on his back.

"Are you okay?" he whispered.

"Hush!" Sorge commanded. "Master Flogg, I don't see anyone. What does that mean?"

"Any*who?*!" Hadyn demanded. "And what did you just do with your fingers?" He surveyed the room with wild eyes. "Will somebody tell me what's going on? Why are crows attacking us!"

"Not crows," Asandra corrected. "Ravens."

Hadyn pressed into the wall as if, by chance, he might force himself into the cracks of the mortar and disappear. "Whatever! People don't just stick their fingers in solid rock where we're from. And birds don't hunt people. It's the other way around."

Sorge flicked a hand. "Shhh!"

He squinted once more into the hole. "Five figures," he whispered, "approaching from the west. The ravens are with them. I don't understand. How can a Flight of Crows last so long?"

"Dark magic. Blackest Hel," Asandra murmured, mostly to herself. It was answer enough.

Sorge presented the options. "We could flee. But I think it unwise. Or fight."

"Fightings, smitings!" Flogg said eagerly, patting his satchel. "Five they, five we."

"Not a full five, friend. These boys know nothing of battle and we have no power over the birds. It's too dangerous."

Flogg spat. "*Ügthilik ngolo ligk'na bôr.*"

Sorge translated, "Courage, he says, not numbers."

"No, no, this has nothing to do with how brave we are," Hadyn challenged. "Besides, what do you want us to fight with?"

In reply, Flogg merely licked the side of his cudgel with an ugly, purple tongue. Ewan felt repulsed, but the gnome was determined.

"Name enemy. Then fight."

"How do we fight birds?" Hadyn exploded, wiping his forehead to keep the blood out of his eyes. "And might I point out, we are *all* hiding—all five of us. Not just Ewan and me."

Sorge grew thoughtful. "We must think. First a Watcher, now ravens. Nemesia's will is bent on finding you. I am certain of it. We either fight, run, or hide. That's it. But we need to decide quickly if we are going to run."

"Fight," said Flogg.

"Hide," said Ewan, "here in the Stone House. At least we have protection."

"I agree. We close the door and lock it until they pass by," Hadyn said. "If you want to call that hiding, so be it. I call it playing it cool."

"My vote would have been to run, but," Sorge glanced out his peephole again, "I fear it is too late for that now. And to be true, the birds are too swift. A Flight of Crows is sorcery. The birds fly swifter, with focus and greater rage and always seem to multiply. Very well. Ewan, lock the door. Everyone else up against the east wall. Stay flat and still. If Aion smiles, the door will hold."

Ewan scooted on all fours, fumbled for the latch, and slid the bolt. They all pressed against the stone wall. Flogg was obviously irritated. Outside, amidst scattered, low voices, a sound drew near. Feet crunching on pebbles.

Ewan said, "Sorge, your hole!"

Sorge smeared the rock face with his fingers. The surface sealed under his touch as if made of paste. Taking staff in hand, he drew himself to his full height, alert, ready. Sounds of pacing feet now ringed the Stone House. Only the four walls stood between the hunters and the hunted.

Once, then twice, the five outside circled unseen. Their movement was slow, deliberate. Ewan heard the light sound of flapping wings return. Claws scratching on the roof. A few birds, squawking. On the third circuit, something like fingernails began scraping the rock wall. Inside, the air thickened. The air grew miserably hot and clammy, making it hard to breathe. Ewan realized a strange thickness had begun oozing under his threshold of conscious thought, like smoke under a door, making it difficult to think. He tried to focus on a spot on the far wall. Beside him, he felt Haydn slump against the stone. Matted blood was stuck in his brother's hair, dried and smeared on his face. His ragged breath sounded like Ewan's own.

What's going on . . . ?

Sorge had said there were five, but a single voice now rose, directionless, drifting like a leaf in the wind, leeching through the stone, shiftless and flat.

"Who travels . . . so far?" the voice said. Male, not old, it sounded neither curious nor fearful, stringing words together like pearls on an open loop, then letting them tumble thoughtlessly to the ground, unclaimed. The other four voices rose faintly in response, moaning like wind on a barren plain. "Who journeys . . . through skies . . . to the home of . . . despair?"

More soft strides on padded feet. More scraping. More bird noises. Strangely, no shadowed forms even attempted to peer through the high windows. They could have easily pulled the fabric loose. It was as if they truly didn't care. Perhaps a joke meant to scare.

But they did care. A fist suddenly slammed the door so hard the wood planks rattled. Ewan jumped. Hadyn clasped his brother by the wrist. Sorge placed a steady hand on the shoulders of both boys, left and right. He touched a finger to his lips to focus their thoughts. *Shhh . . .*

Another thump, this time harder, as if one of the people outside had taken a heavy stone from beside the pond and was trying to smash the door apart.

"Who crosses the hidden . . . barrier . . ."

The door rattled again, a bone-jarring sound. *Thunk!*

". . . to trouble holy men?"

Thunk! The birds went wild, dancing and squawking and pecking.

"Plans come to nothing. Yours. Ours. Nothing. The world will . . . come to nothing. Hide and prove us true. Or join us. Or fight and be consumed. It matters not to us. We are the—"

Thunk! Surely the door would shatter at the next blow. Ewan found himself straining to concentrate. He couldn't be sure if he had heard aright, but that last word, drowned amidst the clank and noise, echoed inward with vague and formless despair. *We are the . . . Nameless. Was that what he said?* His head spun. The voice was oily, speaking questions with no regard to their answer, leaving a murky residue that was altogether foreign, yet arrived in his brain with a sense of relief. Ewan tried to shake his head to clear it. Hadyn made a similar gesture. He wanted to scream, to force out the numbing cadence as it continued.

"Do not imagine great things, outlanders. You have come for no great purpose. Let me show you . . . the way of peace. Nothing matters."

Other voices joined in, creating a soft, uneven chant: "Nothing. Matters. Nothing. Matters."

It slowly grew, seemed ready to crescendo. Ewan braced for the door to splinter. Wings flapped wildly. Sorge's knuckles were white on his staff. Asandra's face glistened darkly.

"Nothing matters!"

Then, nothing. Except the sound of feet trailing away to the south, lost amongst the whispering grass and the generous curves of dimpled land; lost in the slow circles forming on the water where the silent gulp of silver perch topped the pond for mosquitoes. Birds and voices alike. Gone.

Hadyn sank to his knees. Even in the warmish light, his face was pale. "We shouldn't have come, Ewan. We should be home right now, not here. I'm so sorry."

Ewan thought he should be the one apologizing. After all, he came through the runestone first. But he didn't have any words. No feeling. No thought. Like a song in a minor key, he felt transposed, removed from one world to this, and from this to a place of numbness.

"That kid's voice," he mumbled. "What was happening? I feel so . . . numb."

"What do you mean?" Sorge asked, concerned.

"It wasn't just words. It was in my head. More than normal."

"I felt it, too," Hadyn gasped. "Totally freaked me out. Who was that?"

"No doubt, the wraiths of legend," Asandra said. "They sounded like young men, young women. My age. Your age. But their souls are empty. You can hear it in their voices."

Sorge moved. "Be thankful, little brothers. I do not know what just happened, but there is a dark magic at work."

"Must go," Flogg interrupted, stepping toward the door. "Words later."

He reached out his hand to the bolt, pulled. Pulled again. The latch didn't budge. He braced his stance and yanked. Soon he was pounding the wood with his fist.

Nothing.

"Rust?" Asandra said warily. But no, the latch was clean, black iron.

Sorge, Flogg, and Asandra all took turns inspecting the bolt, before consulting in low tones. Flogg reached into his bag. "None of your fire salts, Flogg. The room is too small and we have nothing to hide behind. The boys would likely be killed."

Ewan coughed. "We *are* in the room, you know. What's the problem?"

Sorge answered with a story. "Long ago, when Duke Tiernon sent his army to bring the sorcerer Zynwl to justice for his crimes, they found the keep of Zynwl fastened shut. Zynwl had built a tall tower and made it difficult to take, with no windows and only one gate at the bottom. So Tiernon called upon his great ally and dear friend, Soriah, the greatest Elder in the history of the Gray Abbey. Instead of contending with Zynwl's evil and dragging him out by force, Soriah bound the one door to the earth, as if the fortress were a tree taking root. Zynwl never escaped and eventually flung himself off the tower to his death."

Ewan was too tired to think. "Thanks. That'll be a fun one for the kids, someday."

Asandra folded her arms with familiar haughtiness, but took up the riddle's explanation. Her answer chilled Ewan to the bone.

"Sometimes the way you beat an enemy is not to conquer, but to *confine*. He's telling you we're trapped."

Sorge touched the iron latch once more. "The door is word-locked. We are sealed inside."

CHAPTER 13

Blood Visions

Thee small gray mouse twitched and writhed, but was miserably unable to escape the delicate iron grip of the woman who held its tail. Lowering her face closer to the creature, she looked into its eyes as they rolled back into its head with fear. Her hair was a black fire.

"Too, too easy," the sorceress laughed. Pale pictures lingered in the steam rising from the pot beneath her hand, engulfing her fingers. Images of five creatures: a monk, a gnome, a young woman with hair as dark as her own (and power she recognized), and two brothers, trapped in a small stone house of prayer. Sealed inside by the strength of her will. She watched, wrapped in a cloak of silver pinned at the neck. She stood alone, surrounded by black stone and fire. Her long, silky hair, banded in silver, blew in a slight, unseen breeze. Tall and slender, she wore a plunging gown that made her beauty plain.

"Tsk, tsk," she purred. "I had not even laid my full trap."

As the ghostly image began melting into curls of misty white, the gnome in the vision was still pounding on the door with his fist. Fading from view, the circular chamber also drained of power, though plumes of steam continued to boil up from the small pot of polished brass. The little mouse continued to squeal at the heat. Nemesia did not. For all the fire and moisture, the air remained unusually cool—the kind of cold that makes you feel you are being watched, that runs up your spine and clings to your skin. On the woman's shoulder sat a large black raven with glossy, tar-colored feathers. Unblinking, the bird stared at the small, delicious creature dangling helplessly in the vapors. It flicked its black gaze to the table beside the pot where a dozen more little mice nervously skittered about in cages, watching the boiling pot with wide, white eyes.

Ravens were the faraway descendants of mighty Auginn's illustrious line. Lesser birds, by far, but Nemesia took pleasure in the symbolism of defiance, perverting the once dear and prized hunters of Olfadr the Everking, in faraway Isgurd. Now, thanks to her, they were creatures of fear. Living tokens of the invisible. Reminders that Watchers were more than legend. It helped foster suspicion in the people, to see packs of ravens flying together.

She would feed the raven soon enough, another pitiful rodent from the cage. It was important to feed his lust for juice and bone. Let it bite the head, pluck the fur. Of mice, there was no lack. She had dozens of cages, hundreds of mice, devoted to one simple, unswerving purpose: vision.

Vision required blood.

Well-trained by fear, the raven did not move, only croaked its hunger. This routine had happened many times before. Without the least bit of pity, the sorceress dropped the mouse into the bubbling liquid. Instantly, the creature's life mingled with the water. The steam changed from white to sickly red. Nemesia murmured strange words. Rather than dispersing, the red steam coalesced into a small cloud, suspended in midair. It swirled, gaining layers, density.

The price of power. This was how it happened. Once more, the visions gushed forth.

"Yes, foolish Gray. Wordlocked," she chortled, crossing her arms. "My word is my gift to you, though you shall never know it. Oh, yes. I know what you are thinking. How could you fall for such a simple trick? How could you not have known? You wonder how *nasmith* could fail."

Nemesia reached for another mouse, tossed it into the pot. It wasn't needed, but she didn't care. When she spoke again, to no one, the chill in her voice caused the torchlight to flicker. "Such a stupid, simple plan. Does Archibald really think children from another world could become heroes in the Hidden Lands? A fool's hope. They are nothing but boys—frightened boys."

Suddenly, with rage, she moved. Grabbed the wire cage, turned it upside down, shook it. Every last mouse dropped into the water. Their brief screams were instantly silenced. The boiling water bloomed bright red, making the vision shockingly clear. Nemesia smiled, babbling strange words that formed like spittle on her lips. Soon, from within the vision, orange light glowed on her face. The beginning of a fire.

More importantly, smoke.

"Sorge, old friend. Now I will watch you die. You *and* the precious outlanders. And with you, with them, the last hope of Aion in this world dies too."

CHAPTER 14

Fey Haven

The trees of Elkwood are tall and old and wild. Forest animals scamper and play. All manner of wildlife live and die in the normal rhythms of forest life.

But Elkwood was not a normal forest.

It was full of *other* things. Invisible creatures with shimmering wings. Slender beings, sprites and pixies, nymphs and brownies, human in appearance, yet entirely otherwise, in ways that drove men mad with desire to possess them, if ever they were seen. Of course, sightings were highly rare, by design. Only in the most unusual of circumstances would a spirit willingly reveal themselves. Random glimpses were equally arcane: in the light of a full moon or reflected in fresh pools of rainwater or pieces of new-polished silver. Still, some few had seen, had lost themselves and been carried away over the years. It *could* happen. These were the Fey Folk.

Creatures of legend on all of the Nine fabled worlds. Luminous beings, mischief makers.

On Karac Tor, they had been progressively herded over the centuries, by the will of the Midland Earls—who had long ago learned the need for such herding—into sun-dappled Elkwood. But Fey Folk didn't follow rules very well. They kept leaking out. Stealing butter and cream, which they craved. Hexing cows and chickens in spite, so that their milk came out green, or their egg yolks black, leaving the common folk in various tizzies of fear. It had led to all sorts of superstitious practices. Copper nails over doors to snag their wings before they could enter a home. Salt thrown in wells, because salt, supposedly, would burn them. Offerings of rice and cheese.

The Fey Folk Queen was a regal presence. Always, the Fey Folk had a Queen, never a King. Such was the way it had always been . . . and always would be.

In a hollowing of the woods near the center of Elkwood, birds and butterflies gathered to drink from bubbling fountains, and colors smeared atop one another until nothing but a fluttering, ethereal sense of wonder was left. Slanting shafts of light reached the mossy forest floor, while blossoms and feathery tufts of seedlings floated in the air, never seeming to land. The center of Elkwood was nearly always in spring. This was the realm of the Queen.

Today, the Queen was in a foul, wintry mood.

"He saw you?" she demanded of the breathless, wide-eyed spirit before her, a five-hundred-year-old pixie named Elysabel. "In plain light of sun?"

Elysabel nodded fearfully. She had known, of course, that the news would anger the Queen. However, not informing her would be even more dangerous.

Queen Marielle was severely beautiful, a melting icicle in winter, filled with sunlight. Her eyes were hard and cold as diamonds. Her skin was perpetually frosted with glitter. Fairy dust, mortals called it. Her hair was sage green and twirled in swirling, unseen winds.

This was Fey Haven—*Aelfheim* they called it—the court of the Queen, a place of constant activity, music, and mirth. Other Fey twittered and darted about the open space, whispering to one another, chittering. Many danced and swayed, oblivious to all but the melodies of flute and drum, lingering just below what a human could ever hear. Nothing truly bothered the Fey. They were their own reality and cared for little more than song and flight and the curve of the moon in the summer sky. The ways of men were endlessly fascinating to them, precisely because they were utterly incomprehensible. A mother's love. A warrior's sacrifice on the battlefield. The pain of death. Tears. Laughter. These were not the way of the Fey.

More to the point, the way of Fey was *secret*. The world of men and the kingdom of Fey were firmly divided, visible and invisible. Material and spirit—one of those immutable certainties upon which all reality hung. Boundaries were for a reason, and not meant to be breached casually—in daylight. Through their own portals, no less!

No, this was not good.

Elysabel tried to soften the news.

"Your mother, a long time ago. Remember? She fell in love with one of them. The black robe. The mirling."

Marielle did not blink, showed nothing resembling emotion. "Tal Yssen."

"He could see, too."

The Queen's wings, blurred beyond sight, made a whisper. She bobbed in the air.

"And so?"

"So it happens. She showed him our secrets. He built portals. She crossed over with him, jealous and devoted. They loved and hated. But she granted him one last wish, and so the fallen king, the great one, was brought back with her. Across the water, with his sword. He came, good as dead. But she sustained him, even then."

"He is here still. Hidden. With his sword."

"And the new Champion. It is not so different. Only that one, *you* allowed."

The Queen's eyes grew distant. "He was so beautiful. But I could not keep him."

Elysabel shrugged. She was not afraid anymore. The Queen was lost in her own enchantment.

"It happens," she repeated. "As with the boy. He may be something special. But he may be nothing."

Other Fey listened, not caring what they heard. Big news and small news were all the same to them. A human captive was certainly special, and rare, but a boy who saw? That was the Queen's problem. Not theirs. This was the way of the Fey.

"Stay near to him," Marielle commanded, refocusing. "I will reward you well or punish you greatly for this task."

No threat, no promise. Just facts.

Elysabel, surprised and pleased, bowed and spun away.

CHAPTER 15

Wordlocked

Wordlocked?! What in Sam Hill does that mean, wordlocked?"

Ewan, acting indignant. Hadyn smirked.

Sam Hill? Really? Ewan was in rare form, but also running a bit ragged. Any other day, Hadyn wouldn't have let that one slip, but at the moment he was too busy trying to recall old reruns of *MacGyver*, hoping to concoct a miraculous escape plan. It was stupid, he knew, but it was all he had. Flogg by now had moved from fist to cudgel for his door poundings. Sorge, studying the results, only half heard Ewan's question, and halfheartedly answered.

"Word. Locked. They bound the metal latch to a secret word, and then walked away with that word."

"Don't we have a key?"

"It doesn't need a key. It needs a word." Sorge seemed not so much puzzled as amazed. "Do they not have such simple magic in your world?"

"No!" Hadyn cried, dragging his brain out of cheesy TV adventures, *circa* 1980s. "We open doors with keys, we don't lock them with words. And we don't peel stone apart with our fingers!"

Sorge thoughtfully considered this new information. "Then who is Sam Hill?"

Ewan's head sunk to his chest. "He's the king of confusion. We're his loyal subjects. Can you get us out of here or not?"

Sorge shook his head. "Not without the word."

"Just do your thing with the wall again!" Hadyn said, more loudly than he meant. "Stick your hand in and shape another hole, big enough for us to crawl through."

"Ah, no, you overestimate me. My thing, as you say, is quite undeveloped. I came late to my vows—as a man, not a young boy. Countless Grays are far more gifted than I."

"*Slobahg*," Flogg retorted.

"Yes, I can waterbless," Sorge admitted. "But I cannot yet draw fire from wood, and I am just learning to stonemold. Such a large area of rock would be impossible for me."

"What about her?" Hadyn said, pointing to Asandra.

"Blacks are skilled in spirit and wind. Mystery," Asandra said. "We are Landhealers. Such powers are not our way."

Hadyn kicked the wall for bravado's sake, maybe for Asandra's, too. He had no idea what her answer even meant, but he managed to hold his poise for about three seconds. Oh, how he *wished* Dad let him curse!

"So the rock is harder than your foot," Ewan observed. "That's a keeper."

Hadyn balled his fist and lunged. "You little turd, I'll show you rock hard."

Sorge caught Hadyn before the two came to blows. "Easy, little brother, easy. Anger is the easiest emotion, and the least helpful. We must think. We must trust Aion."

He knelt on the ground, covering his head, and softly began to pray.

Hadyn sniffed the air. "What is that smell? Is something burning?"

Asandra was the first to look up. "The roof's on fire!"

"What new devilry is this?" Sorge said, rising.

Smoke had already begun clotting the air below the rafters of the thatched roof. Orange flame was blossoming through the fumes, licking at the dry sheets of grass. Everyone began to cough.

"Flogg!" Sorge shouted. "The door!"

"Aye!" Flogg cried. But what could he do? The latch was a large, heavy iron assembly with no locking mechanism other than a simple sliding bolt. Hadyn draped his sleeve over his mouth and nose. The smoke was beginning to press lower into the room.

"Back! Stand!" Flogg commanded, shoving Hadyn away. He struck the latch twice with a shattering force. The bolt scarred but didn't budge. Didn't even rattle.

"Let me try," Hadyn said. He remembered burning leaves at the farm in Newland earlier in the year—how much smoke it made, how noxious it smelled. Smoke killed more people than fire, he knew. One of those useless, fire-safety factoids. It would kill them, too, if they didn't get out soon. The Stone House would become the Stone Grave. He raised the cudgel high above his head, brought it crashing down. The moment the forged iron head made contact, something like a shout blasted across the room—a single metallic word, like the declaration a hammer makes on an anvil. Hadyn dropped the cudgel, grabbed his ears.

"What was that?" he said, panicking. "Who said that?"

"Said what?"

"Someone shouted! Right when I hit the latch. Have they come back?"

Outside, a stiff gust of wind must have whistled through the valley, for half the roof suddenly blazed. The heat became scorching; the noise overhead, a low roar. Charred pieces of wood and glowing stalks of grass began raining down, burning their skin. Ewan yelped as a piece landed on his head.

"Crouch in the corners!" Sorge shouted. "Below the smoke. Cover your face. Breathe through your clothes. Hadyn, give Flogg his hammer. This is no time for games."

"I'm not *playing* games!" Hadyn said. He looked at the war club in his hands, then at the latch. Something was strange. He struck the iron bolt again—this time more lightly. The metal-on-metal sound, he expected. But there was more. A sharp, iron voice underneath the clang, fused into the vibration of it. He touched his ear. It was hard to concentrate. His eyes stung and watered so freely he could barely see. Too much was happening.

"You didn't hear that?" he shouted over the roar of the fire, turning to the others. "It's so clear, but it's a sound I don't understand." He swung again. "The noise is the same every time."

Sorge crawled toward him. "Hit it again, Hadyn. Pay close attention to the sound."

Hadyn swung once, twice. He couldn't believe they didn't hear. Swung three more times, straining to form the sound in his mind.

"It sounds . . . twangy," he said, faltering.

"Tell me exactly what you hear. The roof won't hold much longer."

The hem of Asandra's robe caught fire. Flogg pounced upon her, patting the flames out with his bare hands. Hadyn heard Ewan choking. His little brother. He pounded furiously, over and over.

"What . . . are . . . you . . . saying to me?" he bellowed.

"Collect yourself," Sorge urged, surprisingly calm. "Ignore the fire. Pronounce the sound. It doesn't matter if the word makes sense."

Hadyn cleared his throat. "Nan? Nang . . . No . . ."

A gust of smoke left him hacking. "Ninjang? That's it, but I'm not saying it right. Nuan? Rrgh! It's a nonsense word!"

He dropped the cudgel, feeling consciousness fade. They would all pass out soon from the lack of oxygen. Every breath was now a gulp of poison and seering heat. In that moment, the only thing Hadyn cared about was being with his brother one last time. He heard Ewan calling for him.

"Hadyn . . ."

He fell toward the sound of the voice, eyes pinched tight, groping. Found a hand. He hauled with all his might, pulling Ewan's limp body toward himself. Faintly, he heard Sorge caught in a half-thought, a revelation. Heard Flogg and Asandra somewhere on the floor, gasping like him. He had a vague sense of motion, of the ghostly image of the gray monk, surging with strength in the midst of the smoke, flinging the cloth away from his face. Proclaiming one word, a command. One nonsense word.

"*Njuang!*"

The latch rattled loosely. The bolt rotated under the pull of gravity. Sorge slid it open, pushed hard against the wood. Swung wide, flooding the room with light.

Clean air.

Flogg and Asandra crawled out first, gasping. Sorge pulled on Hadyn next, who clung to Ewan's hand, dragging him along, just as a large section collapsed in a glowing heap where he had lain. All five buckled to the ground outside the open door, hacking, squeezing dry grass and rock between their fingers as though they couldn't get enough good air fast enough to make a difference. They clawed their way on elbows and knees just a few steps farther, black and soot-stained, hair singed, skin red with heat. A few seconds later, the whole roof tumbled inward, sending a blast of smoke and cinders high into the air. Nobody moved. Hadyn lay still, near Ewan, feeling every painful, glorious expansion and contraction of his lungs. He wanted to laugh or cry. Something. He managed neither, just gulped the air as if he were a starving man set to feast.

The door, having finally burned free of its hinges, toppled outward, charred and smoking. Hadyn sat up, gazing from door to grass to sky as if seeing all of it for the first time. He saw the bolt, still clinging to the door. No one spoke. No one needed to.

Ewan lay curled up in a ball, crying softly. He didn't even try to hide it. Hadyn didn't expect him to. Both their faces were dirty webs of tears. They crawled to the edge of the pond together, splashing their faces. Water never felt so good. The other three followed their lead.

They washed every part of their body they could, to scrub away the smell of smoke, to cool their skin. They were alive. But they took no more time than necessary.

Cleaned, grim, made both defiant and wary in their survival, they journeyed on.

Unfoldings

After about an hour of marching, washing their wounds in silence among the barren hills, not daring to stop, Hadyn was ready for answers.

"Sorge, how did you do that?" he asked as they trudged along. His hair was still matted with blood. He was bruised, limped a little, but felt very alive. "With the door?"

"I think the more appropriate question would be, how did *you* do that?" Sorge countered. "The word you heard, *njuang*, is of the language of the S'Qoth, the people of Quil. Idol-worshiping pagans."

"The witch," Flogg growled.

"Nemesia is also S'Qoth. Which would, of course, make the most sense."

"I am part S'Qoth," Asandra said softly from behind in mild challenge. "Am I part witch?"

Sorge didn't take the bait. "So you heard the word, little brother? With your ears?"

Hadyn nodded. "It was so clear. I can't believe you didn't."

Sorge shook his head. "This is a powerful magic, to unbind what is bound."

Hadyn fought to suppress a grin. The fear had settled by now, leaving many questions and a slow, unfolding awe. He stank of smoke, had almost died. He also felt pretty stinking cool. To top it all off, out of the corner of his eye, he knew Asandra gazed upon him with new appreciation.

How did *I do that?* he mused.

"I didn't hear jack," said Ewan with a playful jealousy. He, too, was notably recovered. He never said thank you, and Hadyn didn't expect him to. "Not twang, nang, ninjang. Nothing." Ewan broke into a huge grin. "Dude, that was awesome. Teach me how."

"I don't know how. I just heard it."

Ewan asked Sorge, "What does *njuang* mean, anyway?"

"You will not like the answer," Sorge warned.

"I hardly understand the question. Try me."

"Basically, it means despair, but more as a command. Like telling someone to give up."

"Ahh . . . nope. Don't like it."

Hadyn dreaded to think what might come next. They had been magically bound to a word as a death sentence. Despair. He made a fist, feeling something stir deep within.

"Trackerlings again be followin'," Flogg said at their next resting stop, fingering the earth, lost in a trance. "But gone the croakers."

"A Flight of Crows is a burst. It cannot be maintained."

"I'm not sure why, but the Watcher feels distant. Beyond my reach," Asandra said. "They will have a harder time finding us now."

They traveled light and fast, pausing only to catch their breath, or drink, though barely either. Aiming due east, bobbing over the hills like waves on the ocean, the five drew ever closer to the Argosee. The central Shimlings were tall, just shy of mountain height, but the southern Shimlings were little more than hills. Many were rough with crumbly shale and giant slabs of rock, rather than green with grass and heather, as had been the hills behind. In fact, the farther from the Abbey they traveled, the more hardened and bleak the land became. Past these hills, all the land began to brown. The grass was dead. For many miles it seemed like they made little to no progress. Thanks to Sorge's unrelenting pace, they also saw no sign of their pursuers. Two more days passed in the grinding, dry heat. The trails became easier, the hills shorter.

Along the way, Hadyn found himself relaxing more around Asandra, though with little to no encouragement from her. Gliding along in detached silence, she asked nothing and offered nothing. Hadyn could not help but wonder. She was beautiful but did not seem happy. He tried to strike up a conversation, but quietly this time, so as not to embarrass himself.

"*Umm* . . . my lady."

He already felt like a fool.

"My name is Asandra."

"Okay, good. I was just wondering. Is it rude to ask how old are you?"

A slight breeze billowed her robe. "One less than nineteen summers."

Hadyn played it cool. Only eighteen? Not a big enough difference to count. Not really.

"How long have you been a mirling?"

"Ten years of blue, as a Seer. Training. Only five years robed in purple."

"And your family? Aren't they worried?"

"My only family is the Black Abbey. I have no parents."

So they had both lost parents. A bit of common ground. But Hadyn wasn't sure he wanted to share on that level. He was not one to casually disclose himself. It meant a loss of control. The knowledge of his pain was his own, earned with the hard stripes of life. It was part of how he remembered, how he honored his mother, by hurting for her. By carrying all that hurt, deep inside, crammed and packed like a piece of paper folded over and over again, so tightly you could not make another fold, tucked away and spring-loaded into the lonely core of his being. He did not give away his secrets to strangers. Not easily.

So it was to his great surprise that he found himself saying, "My mother died, too."

"Did I say my mother died? Or my father?"

No, she had not. Hadyn's cheeks burned. Her response proved the foolishness of opening himself up like that. Some Bible verse about pearls and swine rang in his ears. Asandra was colorless, compassionless. He regreted making the effort.

He had decided to give up when Asandra continued, "I only *wish* she had died."

Instant anger. The words were like a slap in the face. Hadyn would have given anything—everything—for his mom to have lived. Asandra kept her gaze on the hard earth beneath her feet. "My mom didn't want me. She left me in the cold at the door of the Black Abbey. I was a little baby."

Ahh . . . so everyone has a story. Hadyn felt foolish all over again. He didn't know what to say. "I'm so sorry. So that's how you came to be a mirling?"

He caught a brief glimpse of one half-lidded eye draped behind her cowl. A mirror full of secrets, full of pain. No, he decided. She was not happy at all.

He tried to fumble forward. "Is it a gift? You said you were trained—"

"Too many questions. I wish to be alone now."

She fell back, leaving Hadyn alone with his thoughts and the befuddlement every teenage boy feels over the perplexities of a woman. It truth, her silence was something of a relief. After that sweet little ice-breaker, Hadyn felt fairly cured of his brief infatuation.

Focus on more than the face next time, he reminded himself.

And yet.

It seemed Asandra was like a child who wanted more than anything to be thought an adult. Impetulant. Stubborn. Trying to prove something. Or like a little girl, acting out to gain her father's attention. More simply, she just seemed bitter, but with good cause. Heaven knew, Hadyn felt justified in his own stewpot of emotion. Life could really suck sometimes.

With shock, he realized their deeper commonality. Asandra had her own little piece of pain folded up tight inside. It wasn't pretty how it came out, but she had taken the same risk he had. She had opened up. Obviously, by her demeanor, the experience was both rare and painful. After all the years, the fact of her abandonment still hurt, quite deeply. So she pushed against him, against all of them, expecting more abandonment. She was a social porcupine, further confirming the story of her life. Maybe hoping, just once, that someone might push in, rather than away.

Hadyn doubted he was that guy. But he felt pity just the same.

CHAPTER 17

Acceptance

A t dusk, exhausted, they set up camp in a grove of oak trees, feasting on a meager meal of salted pork, raisin bread, and badly bruised carrots from the Abbey.

"No smoke," Sorge said apologetically, explaining the lack of fire. "No signals."

"No problem," Hadyn muttered. "If I never smelled smoke again, it would be too soon."

The cobalt sky was a sheet of velvet sprinkled with diamonds. Ewan passed out almost immediately after eating, soon began snoring. Flogg and Asandra each removed themselves a little way from the group for more privacy. Sorge, though, remained wearily awake, his quarterstaff propped against his shoulder, ready. Hadyn lay back, staring into the night. He felt restless. Time passed, during which his thoughts rolled across the dreamland of Karac Tor, wondering exactly how all this had come to be. He saw Sorge glance around the circle of sleepers, his face illumined by the fire. When it seemed the monk thought everyone was asleep, he tilted his gaze toward the quiet stars, as if in supplication. Soundless as the night, his lips began to move. The words softly turned to song, which Hadyn strained to hear. Yielding at last to the night's tender light, the monk's full, husky baritone emerged, night winds and shattered dreams, bare like a tree stripped clean, and all the more beautiful for it.

> *"Across the sea, lo! the stars*
> *Where white gulls cry for shame,*
> *We journey as a thousand souls*
> *In search of our true name.*
> *The way so far, the sea so wide,*
> *Our longing hearts to roam,*
> *As waves rise high, as seagulls cry,*
> *My heart drowns in the foam.*
> *Lo! Isgurd! Silver bright!*
> *Where brave men ne'er grow old,*
> *My soul doth long thee in the night,*
> *But shrinks in daylight's gold!*
> *I ache that your wind holds no sway,*
> *I yearn thy silver shores.*
> *Across the sea, and far away*
> *I fly, I fight to sail unmoored*
> *Across the sea, in light of day,*
> *Across the sea, and far away."*

The sadness of the tune trailed away to silence, gradually displaced by the alternating rhythms of Ewan and Flogg's steady breathing.

Hadyn spoke aloud. "Such a lonely song . . . in search of our true name."

Surprised to hear another voice, Sorge turned, gathered his cloak more tightly around himself. He seemed to be chewing his own words. "The Book of Law teaches that everything, living and dead, has a name. We use the names to help us make sense of the world, to separate one thing from another. Rocks, birds, you, me. Common names are easy. And kind. A form of grace. I know you as Hadyn, and you know me as Sorge. Outlander, Elder. Boy, Man. All these words start the process of knowing. They are useful. But deeper still lies our true name."

"Like a secret?"

"In a way. We all yearn to know and be known. It goes to our core. To know a name is to know a thing for what it truly is, not what it appears to be. It is essence, connection, vitality, but also the difference between surrender and mastery. Or so I am told. Most true names have been forgotten. Only the wise remember. You tasted some part of this mystery back at the Stone House, I think. It wasn't a true name you spoke, yet you named the binding truly. That is a rare gift."

Hadyn, intrigued, had grown sleepy. "Right now, I just need some true sleep. How can you even stay awake? Aren't you exhausted?"

The moon rode high. Sorge studied the stars, deep and layered, glittering like ice. "Our stories tell of a field of memory where an ancient battle was fought, so terrible and so full of blood the land could no longer absorb life or rain. Within a year, the ground was barren. One night, all the trees pulled up their own roots and moved away, lest they die."

Hadyn saw the strange picture of it in his mind, trees hiking their skirts and heaving up their roots from the deep earth. "I have a feeling you have a lot of these stories."

"I do. You may be tired, but what does it say to you?"

In the darkness of another world, a fifteen-year-old boy groped for words.

"I have no idea."

"No, no. You asked me a question. How can I stay awake? I answered it. Try."

"Dunno . . . trees need water, I guess."

"You can do better," Sorge chided. "It means that *we do what we must*. To live and live well, all of us do what we must, when we must, even if it is hard. You have known this battle."

"I have?"

His face was unreadable in the darkness, but Sorge's tone was gentle. "I knew nothing of your mother until just today. I heard you speaking to Asandra. I'm very sorry, little brother. It is not right."

Hadyn lay still, feeling put on display. His heart pounded harder. But there was a strange comfort in the monk knowing. Not a bad trade. Sorge wasn't offering pity but kindness.

"Go to sleep, Lord Hadyn. Today, you have done what you must, and I shall do what I must. I have spent many, many hours late into the night practicing prayer to sustain me. We journey hard again tomorrow and the next. On the sixth day, we make Threefork."

So they did. They woke in the morning and traveled hard, passing each day without further event. No creepy people or spooky birds. Asandra gave no Watcher warnings. Just a long web of trails winding south and east.

Day five, near the little village of Gilford, they began passing simple stone fences and herds of grazing sheep, if they could be called that. The animals were bony and thin, the fields nothing but brown stubble. Overhead, the sky was a globulous mass of unbearable heat. Creeks and streams were bone-dry. They wandered past an old shepherd with long hair and a mustache who was panting in the sun. He did not bother to look at them, just seemed to wither in the parched air right before their eyes.

Sorge sighed. "The land struggles. When blessings run thin, curses prevail."

"Murder, too." Asandra's dark eyes roamed freely. "Look, there."

At the top of the hill to their left, far away, stood a grove of trees. A stone pillar.

"A place for the Wild Dance. For a Summoning. They probably sacrifice to bring rain, only to deepen the curse."

She made the sign of the circle. Both boys limped and complained of blisters. Thankfully, the hills began to thin and flatten. Eastward, Avl-Argosee became plainly visible. Huge and blue. Not like Hawaii's turquoise waters. One doesn't easily forget a color like that, or the vacation the Barlows took together before Mom died. No, the Argosee was more opaque—blue and purple, foggy with minerals and mud. Sorge, angling more south than east now, told them they were headed for the Chin, a part of the western profile of the lake that formed her last major contour before funneling into the three rivers—Luth, Hart, and Argo—and finally, Champion Bay, which, upon crossing, would bring them to Stratamore.

Their food was nearly gone, leaving enough for just one more good meal. Flogg set out to find fruits and nuts for the morning. Ewan protested that Flogg shouldn't be allowed to leave the group. He manufactured some concern about the larger question of safety, for Flogg's own good, blah, blah. Hadyn saw through it.

"Ewan, knock it off," he said. "You're being an idiot."

"That *thing* stuck a knife in my back and never said it was sorry," Ewan huffed. "Besides, he creeps me out. I don't trust him."

Flogg, having zero interest in Ewan's protestations, departed. As they packed their gear, Sorge said, "You are a stranger here, Lord Ewan, while Flogg is a trusted friend. Your accusations mean nothing to me. Tomorrow he will go ahead of us to help make arrangements in Threefork. Settle it and move on, little brother. On this matter, I will pay you no mind."

That was the end of it for everyone except Ewan. The monk went on to explain how they would find the captain, restock supplies, and sail south. Foothills and spotty trees currently hid the city from view, but Sorge assured them it was no more than a half-day's journey by foot. Tomorrow, by midday, they would be at her gates.

As they drew closer to the lake, they began to see the outer tokens of a nearby city: people and homes, simple dwellings with mud walls and thatched roofs, mothers in long dresses with babies on their hip, fathers working the land. Or far in the distance, men on the water flinging huge nets in the air, praying to whatever gods they chose—sea gods, fish gods, gods of net or luck (or Aion if all else failed)—for a mighty catch of bluegill and bass to bring to market.

Sorge guided his charges through the land of these hamlets quietly. Everywhere, the people looked sour, tired. No one hailed them or offered them supper or inquired as to the ease of their road. They were strangers and treated as such. A handful of folks inclined their heads to Sorge out of respect for the robe he wore or offered him the sign of the circle. But the very same folk squinted their eyes at Asandra, or averted them and cursed, or rubbed fresh mud on their doorposts and spat. Mirlings were generally feared for their strange ways, trafficking with spirits. Others thought it bad luck to rile the Darkwings, as Watchers were commonly known. Seeing their soured, resentful expressions, Hadyn felt grateful for the new clothes he had been given. He and Ewan blended well. Without them, they would have no doubt been objects of much scrutiny and suspicion.

Yes, it was a strange world in which he found himself enmeshed. He was now a part, unwilling or no. Had heard a name, had unbound what was bound. He had heard what not even Sorge the Gray could hear. What Flogg, whose fingers drew whispers from the land, could not hear. It was . . . rare. Or was it? Almost challenging his thoughts, he remembered the lifeless tone of the speaker at the Stone House.

You have come for no great purpose . . . nothing matters.

The words brought a sudden rush of claustrophobia, left him feeling trapped at the Stone House, surrounded by smoke and fire. Trapped, really, in the struggle of Karac Tor. *Enmeshed.* Beyond his will and his control. Hardly the adventure he had expected. Plus, he really missed his dad and might have broken down at the thought, except for the embarrassment it would have caused. The lost boy's words swarmed his brain. *Nothing . . .*

The feel of the cudgel in his grip wasn't nothing, nor the curi-ous whisper of the metal latch in his mind. Nor the word known only to him. The battleground formed, between the suffocating foolishness of it all and something else. Something raw and fragile rose to oppose the fear. It snuck upon him like a secret invitation, and in that invitation a burst of intuition pounced, as a lion stalking its prey. The minefield of his mind grew calm.

In the span of a single breath, where before, so many things had been important, now only one thing mattered. It was as if he had only ever known this *one thing*. He recognized the thing as a mirror image of himself. It defied the lost boy (or anyone else for that matter) to define him or his purpose. *Who am I? What is my purpose?*

He was Hadyn Barlow. That was his name. And in that moment, he knew with clarity, the answer. *To fight.*

"Hadyn, are you well? You look disturbed."

The voice was Sorge's. Hadyn was clenching his jaw. He didn't want to speak. Much as the revelation might ring true, he didn't care for the implications.

"I'm fine," he said. "Never mind."

CHAPTER 18

Tower of Ravens

F ind them!" Nemesia roared, green eyes flashing. "Find them. Capture them. Bring them here. I want to know how he knew the word I commanded you. I want to know what they know. I want to know what commission they bring to this world, before I destroy them."

Floating in the vapor, five youths stood among dead, dry hills. They were all roughly the same age, but the central figure appeared to be the oldest, perhaps seventeen or nineteen. His face was slack, but a puzzle lingered in his hollow eyes. A dangerous question.

"I don't understand. How could they know?"

"They didn't. *He* did."

The accursed, oldest one named Hadyn.

Hearing her own words, Nemesia's voice slipped like oil to become softer, more calculating. More maternal. "He's about your age, darling. How does that make you feel?"

"I feel . . ." The boy in the phantom image struggled for words. He grew annoyed at himself. "You know I never know these things. Just tell me the answer."

"Shameface, my precious bomb," Nemesia answered, sticky sweet. "I don't have any answers. No one does. There are no answers to anything. But if"—and here she greatly emphasized "if" as though she were giving them a choice, when really she was further stripping them of thought and will—"*if* I were you, I think I would feel empty."

Shameface accepted her verdict immediately, with relief. "Yes, empty. That's how I feel."

"Horribly empty, I should think! Even more than you already do. And confused, maybe? Angry? After all, why should he get to do special things that you can't? Doesn't anybody else care that you are nothing special?" She raised the volume of her voice to include the four who stood behind the leader, listening, staring with blank, fleshy eyes. The effects of vague emotion passed over their faces.

"We are the Nameless," declared one with monotone matter-of-factness.

"Yes, nameless. All of you, my bombs, so lonely. Such a cruel task, to live this dreary life."

"I don't want to live anymore," said another. "I want to die."

"No, not die, Hurter, Hider. If you are dead, they can mourn you and pretend to feel bad, as if you actually mattered, even though they never really loved you. If they are allowed to mourn, they can bury you and forget you, with their guilt appeased."

They stared at her: five gazes of slavish simplicity. Nemesia spun words like sticky webs.

"Death is a gift to *them* not yourselves," she explained. Her words carried both enchantment and perverse logic. "You must do something more. Something worse. You must shame them."

"How?"

"Hold *nothing* to yourself! No hope, no joy. Become dangerous, by becoming even more worthless than you already are. Feel the anger of your misery. You don't need a reason to rage, my bombs! You are almost completely worthless, but not yet! Not yet enough to truly be free. You still cling to trivial hopes and dreams. Abandon these. However small, they will *never* come to pass. Forget your name, your ambitions. They are paths of iniquity, the tired remnants of love's empty promise."

"What does love feel like? I have never known it."

"Nor do you want to, my bombs! Not anymore. Your fathers did not love you and your mothers did not want you. You were not their choice. They wanted other things, better things. They gave you barely what you needed and nothing you wanted. Why? Because they did not care to be bothered. You carry this poison inside."

"It hurts. So bad."

"Only because you still fight it! You wish to be somebody, to prove them wrong. But this can never happen. And so you hurt."

The girl nearest Shameface raised her timid voice. "But you said we had been cheated. Didn't you? You said that one boy is better than us, just now. No, wait. I can't remember what you said. I'm sorry, tell me again, why shouldn't we fight back?"

"With what, sweet Grayday? Fool!" Nemesia mocked, clicking her nails together. "Simple, foolish girl, it's a wonder I care for you at all! None of you are good enough, smart enough, or brave enough to ever amount to anything. I am so kind to even bother with you. Listen, let me help you. I will speak slowly. If you try to rise above your station and prove your worth, what have you caused yourself? You know the answer."

"Pain, because we will always fail."

"As will love. Love *always* fails. Love of anything, anyone. Tell me why, quickly!"

"Because love gives us a name," Shameface said bitterly. He knew the coming exchange by heart. Nemesia had drilled it into them countless times. It made so much sense.

"Names give identity, which leads to—?" the witch's voice trailed away.

"Hope. Foolish hope."

"And why is hope foolish?"

"Because it is the birthplace of dreams."

"And what do dreams bring?"

"Shame, because the weight of dreams always collapses. Love is faithless when tested. It cannot be fulfilled. It promises what it will not surrender. It gives with one hand that it might gain with another. It demands what cannot be achieved. It remembers wrongs. Love must be earned. It is never given."

"Have you worked hard for love, my dear?"

"All our lives."

"And do you have anything—any love or name or dreams—to show for all your efforts?"

Shameface's eyes were the last embers of a dying fire.

"I am empty," he whispered.

"Empty and nameless. A lonely bomb, ready to explode. Like that silly gnome carries in his satchel. And so you came to me, each of you. And I am kindly trying to guide you through your pain.

There is comfort in numbness and rage if you will be so brave as to find it. Be slave to no man, no woman. Only yourself. Serve no one but your own desires. When you do this, when nobody matters to you, you will matter to nobody. Your nothingness will then be complete. And since they cannot own what doesn't exist, you will finally, truly, be free. This is the gift I offer."

A low murmur rippled through the ranks of the five shadowed figures.

"The girl keeps the Darkwings away. It makes it hard for us to find them."

The image of the five wavered. Nemesia dangled a mouse, dropped it in the water. "I did not expect her on this journey. But she is a broken vessel. A mistake. She means nothing."

"The monk is strong."

"No, he is a little mouse, playing with his cheese. He is afraid to use his strength. His guilt runs too deep."

"Even so, the boy knew your secret word. All on his own. Your spells are not enough."

Grayday broke in with a dangerous thought, her voice tinged with hope. "Do you think we could be like *him* one day?"

Nemesia's eyes narrowed to thin slits. The flames in the black chamber followed, narrowing to thin points of white-hot light. Her fingernails, filed to razor points, dug grooves into the surface of the wood table. As the vaporous image above the boiling pot began to fail, a new thought entered her mind.

"I have a surprise for you. A gift. Something very special for each of you."

"A gift?" said Grayday with surprise.

"But you must do something for me first. Bring the brothers here, to me. Be as devious as needed, but bring them healthy and well."

"We are afraid. They are strong."

"We are not like them. It is torment. Let us kill them quickly and return to you."

Nemesia licked her lips like a hungry cat. "No, my dear Hider! That would ruin my gift. I want to show you your power, the power of despair. Don't you see? Since you cannot be like them, I will make *them* like you. Nameless, just like you."

Slowly, devilishly, the five teenagers smiled.

CHAPTER 19

Threefork

T he city of Threefork was a tightly bundled knot of commerce at the southern split of the Mighty Argosee, where the one great river became three. The city, which the river cut in half, was stitched back together by four great bridges. Homes were packed along tight, winding lanes around the sprawling heart of the city where the wealthy lived and worked, the eastern shore, while countless docks and the cluttered shops and peasant homes of fishermen and craftsmen formed a perimeter north, west, and south.

Here, seamen from Yrgavien brought fat-bellied ships laden with ore, rubies, coal, and pelts, and barges came lumbering down River Conach to the Argosee bearing cedar, pine, and fir. Salty, gray-bearded captains cursed their crews with one breath, then prayed for good tailwinds the next, offering tokens at the

Shrine of the Green Deep to buy favor from the sea gods for their next trek across the Bay to Vineland and back, with holds full of legendary sweet Faielyn wine. Honey mead came from Befjorg to Threefork, and from Threefork to all points of the compass; so too, grain and produce brought by ship, cart, and donkey from traders all around the Midlands and Greenland—Slegling, Lismoych, Brimshane—and countless lesser villages besides. Even the Gray Abbey regularly sent monks pulling donkeys with carts of braghe and ghouda to Threefork. All these converged in a breathless mess of race, language, coin, bartering, trading, cursing, profit, and loss. Threefork was commerce to its bones: down every canal, inn, and shop, down every alley.

"Here," Sorge explained. "The Duke of Düshnoc came with three hundred soldiers to reclaim a large sum of money he had lost in a wager with the Earl of Seabraith. It was a fool's errand, so he was well qualified for the task. Vastly outnumbered, even more vastly outwitted, his lone success appeared to be in greatly offending the Earl, the king's most loyal ally. The Earl captured the Duke and had him taken to the gibbet to hang. But the Duke was fortunate that day. He had come bearing the prized metal *algathon* on the spears and shields of his soldiers. He bargained with the Earl: pardon in exchange for algathon. Instead of bloodshed, the two forged an alliance that lasted for two hundred years. The Duke climbed down from the gibbet and left Threefork that very day with twelve champion steeds from the personal stables of the royal family as token of their covenant." Sorge squinted against the light of the sun. "In other words, in this city, the best deal is always the next deal, and the only reputation you carry is that of your last bad trade. Money talks loudly everywhere . . . but here, *everyone* is listening." He glanced behind him. "Asandra, this is where we take leave of you. Will you continue by land or sea?"

For the last couple of days, Asandra had seemed more compliant, even friendly, at least toward Hadyn. It was admittedly subtle, perhaps existing only as a wish in his head. But as she studied the whole group now, none more than he, her almond-shaped eyes, like Sorge's, were so intense that he feared he might have food stuck in his teeth. She was dark and lovely.

"There's no hurry on my errand to Seabraith," she said slowly. "Perhaps I should continue with you a bit longer."

Sorge was adamant. "I do not agree. You should press on."

"The errand is from the Bishop to me," Asandra replied, "not you."

"And these boys are my charges, not the Bishop's. You are on the path to pride, young Asandra."

The mirling flushed. "I can only assume you speak from experience," she shot back. "Consult at the Chantry if you like. We need not decide this very moment."

Rather than argue, Sorge stomped ahead, picking his way from the outer docks down several streets and narrow lanes, finally bringing his party to the door of an attractive looking inn in a well-appointed section of the west quarter.

"Hoods off," he advised. "No need to look like we're carrying secrets."

From the shadows of the adjacent alley, a voice called to him with surprise. "Sorge! Sorge, is that you? How goes your road, old friend?"

Everyone spun. It took a moment for Hadyn's eyes to adjust to the alley's dim light, but Sorge's face split into a wide, troubled grin. "Cruedwyn? What are you doing here?"

The man motioned him closer. He wore a sword at his side and bright colors. He had a toothy, nervous smile. He did not step out of the shadows.

"Wait here," Sorge commanded. Gripping his staff, he and the man named Cruedwyn began conversing out of earshot. Hadyn saw Sorge shake his head. Cruedwyn grasped at his sleeve, pleading. His worried eyes glanced over to where they stood in the middle of the busy street, studying each in turn. His lips moved faster, more urgently. Again, Sorge shook his head no, then again, emphatically, *no*. The other man dropped to his knees. Sorge hesitated, touched his friend's shoulder. Turned and walked toward the inn.

"Who was that?" Ewan asked.

"An old acquaintance. A swordsman and singer. He wishes to join us. I refused him."

They entered the inn, with a faded sign hanging above the door that read, Possum and Peacock. The innkeeper, a busy man, greeted Sorge by name, knowingly motioning toward the back room with a flick of his head. Hadyn and Ewan kept their mouths shut and their eyes straight ahead, but Asandra seemed quite at ease. The inn, though noisy, was not raucous; dim, yes, but neither cheerless nor deviant. Actually, it felt rather friendly. And by the rich aroma, Hadyn decided whatever beef stew was simmering in the kitchen, he wanted a bowl. Or two.

"Brother Sorge!" declared a lilting, cadenced voice, coming from a lean man with a shock of white hair and sagging jowls meant for a heavier man.

"You've lost weight, Gregor," Sorge said, eyeing his friend with a wry smile. "Running from pirates, still?"

"Ha, t'would be an easy task. Running from me wife, more like it! Me lady wants me up on the roof, thatching for autumn rains.

'Course I come here only to think about how best to serve her every whim." He reached out to clasp Sorge's extended hand, fingering the cloth of his cuff.

"Brother no more, from the look of it. The gray of an Elder? How long?"

"Nearly two years."

"Well then, I'm too late to throw a party and not enough to claim senility, eh? Sit, sit, my friend! 'Tis been a long time."

Sorge glanced around the room. "Where's Flogg?"

"Auginn's eyes, man! Would ya sit first and chat awhile? Let me buy you and yer young friends here a pot of stew. Flogg'll be back soon enough. Had matters to attend to, he said, after finding me. Hello, boys."

He smiled pleasantly, took note of Asandra, but studied the brothers like an auctioneer assessing value. The boys nodded politely. Sorge pulled up chairs for all three. Together, they sat. The back room was small, just six tables. Only one other was occupied.

"I need a favor," the monk said quietly.

"I know, lad. Flogg made it clear. And yes, I'll help, o course. How soon?"

"Actually, we are in haste. Now would be best."

He almost started to rise again. Hadyn's cough drew his eye. The boys eagerly clutched their wooden spoons. Hadyn did his best to look famished.

"Alright then. *After* that pot of soup."

CHAPTER 20

The Oracle

By the time the meal was over, Flogg had rejoined their party. Ewan treated him with open contempt, but in quiet, sullen fashion. Captain Gregor parted company to begin preparing his ship, and the four travelers followed Sorge to the House of the Noble Way, a Gray Chantry.

For the spiritual health of the people and the land, each abbey had outposts like this—the Grays with their spare, humble Chantries; the Whites with glorious, light-filled Kirks; and exotic Sanctums of candles and incense for the Blacks—scattered throughout Karac Tor, typically in major cities and larger towns. The Way of Aion centered upon these three primary branches of devotees. Of course, there were plenty of pagan temples, too, boasting strange ways and stranger gods. Plenty of peasant witches and fortune-tellers in their street booths, offering to spill the bones and read your future, or sellers of charms and talismans, promising everything from love and fortune to blights upon your enemies. Plenty of normal folk, devout folk, heathens, superstitious fools, poor, rich, proud. A smorgasbord.

Yet, suffusing all, to the deep bones of the earth, in rock and cloud, in the hidden soul of man, was Aion's circle of three strands: the Book of Law, the Book of Names, and the mystical Gifts of Nine. The Gifts—like lore, oracles, wind, healing, might, and others—were transcendental endowments given by Aion for the good of the land. In typical fashion, the Whites viewed the Nine with contempt. More solid stuff, stone and ink, was all that was needed for a holy life.

Today, Sorge needed more. He did not share much, only that he felt troubled in his spirit, needed wisdom beyond his own. The voice of Aion, he said. At the Chantry, a gray robed monk greeted him with the sign of the circle. They were in a quieter section of town. Wind chimes above the door tinkled lightly in tones of seashell and crystal. A gilded sign read: "For Patrons and Seekers." Sorge turned to the Barlows before entering.

"Would either of you like to come with me?"

"Depends on what's in there," Ewan said cautiously.

It was a muggy day. The monk's eyes glimmered. "Surprises. Truth. Revelation. Warnings. One never knows. Discover for yourself. Cats need no eyes for milk."

Ewan cocked his head. "Cats what?"

"Sometimes you just know when something is right and good. Like a cat with milk."

"Okay, never look a gift horse in the mouth. I get it. But what are you doing in there? Seems kind of weird."

From the corner of his eye, Hadyn noticed his brother's furtive glance, appealing for guidance. "If we trust him to get us home . . ."

Of course, *he* wouldn't have gone in the Chantry, but what did that matter? He wouldn't have crawled into the briar patch after the birds first flew in, either. Ewan was often bold and unpredictable. He loved roller coasters. Hadyn did not. Tomato, tomahto.

"Does it cost anything?" his brother asked warily.

Sorge reached into his coin purse, placing a copper *shil* in Ewan's open palm. "No, but it is good to give."

Hadyn saw the decision in his brother's eyes. Ewan closed his fingers on the round coin, a shape without beginning or end. A circle. He stepped up to the door, made the sign. Together, he and Sorge entered.

"What will they tell him?" Hadyn asked Asandra.

The mirling's brown skin glistened with perspiration. "Aion's breath blows where it will."

Hadyn groaned. Could someone please talk normal? The pithy little proverbs were a bit much. He sat on the steps in a small corner of shade, waiting. After nearly an hour, Sorge emerged without Ewan. He stared into the faceless crowd. "At the Fourth Coming, Olfadr commanded his son, Aion, to bring gifts to men. *Lira, orn* and *nasmith* are three of Nine."

Hadyn was exasperated. "Lira and . . . *what?*"

From where she sat on a ledge of sun-baked brick, Asandra said, "Lore, Oracles, and Mysteries. Strength of Heaven. Light of Sun. Radiance of Moon."

"Oh, right," Hadyn said. "Why didn't you just say so?"

"Was any insight granted?" Asandra probed, rising.

The monk's eyebrows gathered above his face like storm clouds. "None I comprehend. One of the brothers spoke an *orn* upon me:

In division, completion
In darkness, door shone
Of water, wood dreaming
To sunlight, from stone"

Flogg patted Sorge's arm, "Timing times. Elder will see. *Nasmith,* maybe yet."

Hadyn blinked. He was lost. Where was Ewan?

As if summoned by his silent question, the younger Barlow exited the Chantry, equally thoughtful as Sorge. His face was peaceful. "Two of the monks prayed with me. They listened. For Aion, they said, for the feel of his breath. They said I was Called." He smiled. "Isn't that strange? No riddles. Just that I am Called. They said my magic is meant to be heard." He looked at Sorge. "What does that mean?"

"Ahh, you must puzzle it out. A gift is one thing. Discovery is another." The monk turned to Asandra. "We all need wisdom, and Aion knows I have stumbled often in pride. Though I do not see this road with clarity, I see that it *may* be best if you come. If you still wish."

Staff in hand, he strode away, passing from smaller lanes to wider, more bustling avenues. The noise and color and movement turned the teeming central thoroughfare into a restless river of humanity. Merchants standing behind carts and under awnings loudly hawked their wares, while young children dodged in and out of traffic, playing games and screaming. Odors from bodies and countless shops assaulted them, both pleasant and foul—donkey manure and sweat on one hand, mingled with the warm, yeasty smell of freshly baked bread, flowers and apples, and a host of other aromas besides.

"Have you noticed," Hadyn whispered to Ewan, glancing around the streets. "There's old people here, and there's lots of children. But there's almost no one our age. No teenagers. They're all gone."

Ewan looked around. "Creepy."

Near the end of the central boulevard of the city, they passed a great stone fountain at the intersection of two streets. In the center of the fountain, a statue of a bearded man, royally dressed, was slumped over as if he carried a great weight. In his hands he held a golden crown.

"Eskobar the Weak," Sorge explained. "The last King of Karac Tor."

By the smell of the air, Hadyn knew they were nearing the docks. He matched his stride to the monk's. After chewing on the riddle for a bit, he was more irritated than ever. "Is that all there is to the *orn*? It's nonsense. Just words."

"*The stumbling dancer says the ground is uneven.*"

"Fine, but if we don't understand it, how can it help us?"

"Because at some point, we *will* understand. Remember . . . *the difference between vine and wine isn't taste, but time.*"

Hadyn rolled his eyes. "No, serious. Please tell me you're running out of those."

Sorge chuckled. Hadyn pressed on. "Is it for when we see Archibald? When we get on the boat and sail down the river? I mean, the *orn* could be nothing, right? Just a riddle."

"Nothing is *just* from Aion. All his gifts have meaning. Otherwise he wouldn't have given them."

And that was that. They entered the fish markets. Vendors gutting fish and rowdy pubs selling cheap beer. They passed warehouses and docks and sailors lying drunk on rotting wooden slats. They passed alleys and guild halls, and the tall-masted warships of Duke Pol Shyne of Greenland, passed under a rotting sun, to Gregor's small vessel. Unbeknownst to them, they also passed a man who had trailed them since the Chantry. Even now, from the shadows, he watched which vessel they boarded. They did not see him. But he saw them.

CHAPTER 21

The Wildstar

They arrived to find Gregor already ready to sail. His vessel was not large, with a tall, single mast and clean, beautiful lines. Near the bow, in gilded silver, Hadyn read the name: *Wildstar*. The name and the vessel struck him as utterly seaworthy, though in truth, he hadn't a clue what that meant.

"I've trimmed me back to a keelboat," Gregor offered apologetically. "Don't need nothing that requires a crew n'more—just have to get on the water every now and then, y' know? Anyways, there's no room in the hold for sleeping, only stores and a bit of cargo I'm haulin'."

"I didn't think you were hauling anymore," Sorge commented.

"Oh, not really. But got me an offer too good to refuse on this here load, and just a short run. Down toward the cursed Argo"—he made a sign, as if warding off evil—"but only near, not on. Then we be on our way. I figure we take the Hart to the Bay if'n it suits ya. It's clean 'n swift. Shouldn't take too long. I've got a couple more barrels coming, and some food stuff, besides. Crossing the Bay will be a few days."

"So now we wait for the evening winds?" Sorge asked.

"Aye, we wait."

Sorge saw Asandra, standing alone on the starboard rail. "You are welcome on this vessel, as I have said, but I wish to be clear. You are welcome only if you do *exactly* as I say. Agreed?"

One eyebrow raised. It was a gesture of one part acquiescense, one part defiance.

"Agreed."

"I see your disrespect in your eyes. Take care, mirling."

Hadyn, nearby, heard Asandra's bitter whisper as Sorge strode away.

"Sorge the Gray, friend of Corus. For whom do *you* care?"

Though he considered inquiring as to what she meant, he quickly decided it was wiser and safer to simply enjoy the turn of events which now allowed her to continue through the next leg of the journey. Though his feelings were decidedly mixed, he had to admit a certain tinge of sadness had accompanied the thought of parting her company. Yes, she was too old for him. And if someone had accused him of being a glutton for punishment, he couldn't have argued. Only days ago, he was done with her. At her worst, Asandra was icy, rude, antagonistic. At her best, beautiful and compelling. And he was a red-blooded male.

But for now, he was also a tired teenager with nothing to do but wait. Asandra had already retreated back into her shell. Both Barlows seized the opportunity for some rest. They lay on the warm, oiled wooden planks of the ship's deck, watching the slow current drift ponderously south. Ewan nodded off first. Soon, Hadyn followed.

When the ship finally unmoored from the docks, drifting into the open harbor, they stirred. The sun had long ago peaked and begun arcing lower in the sky. They stood on the edge of the deck, leaning over the railing—two Missouri boys who had never been sailing. Foreign land or not, this was fun: gulls lofting on unseen pillows of air, dangling just out of arms' reach; salty air in their noses; the clean cut of the ship through the water, awaiting her sails. They watched the old captain run his hands along the rail, surveying other boats, closing his eyes to better feel the wind on his face. It was almost something mystical, the way he seemed to feel the water, the wind. When he opened his eyes, it was to measure the harbor, waiting for the right moment to unfurl.

"C'mon boys," he said. "You're my crew, see? Grab there. Now untie that knot. And there, too. Now pull! That's right."

Soon it was done and the boys felt almost like real sailors. The mainsail hung limp for several moments before gently rippling a bit, then suddenly snapping full as a good stiff breeze blew in from the east. The boat lurched forward. Hadyn grabbed at a rope to steady himself, was startled at the touch, what he heard. The rough woven fibers whispered in his mind, a particular bending together of sounds. Like a word.

He smiled, gratified, but couldn't form the sound and frankly, was too lost in the moment to care. The pleasure on Gregor's face was like a sort of rapture, and Hadyn felt it too.

"There it is!" Gregor cried, heaving at the ropes, "By the gods, I love it when the wind finally grabs her!"

It was, indeed, an awesome feeling. Gregor took the helm with an easy, steady hand. The current was swift, the waters deep. The

distance from the city to the branching, triplet rivers which gave it
its name was short indeed. Sorge told the boys that the Hart had
waters that were swift, but tame, and offered the shortest, most
direct path to the bay.

"Aye," was all Gregor would say.

It only took fifteen minutes, maybe less, before the juncture of
each waterway became visible ahead. To port, the Luth and Hart
were still a good ways away. But just off the bow, south and west,
Hadyn saw dark, murky waters. Beyond it were the shadows of
many trees.

"Redthorn," Sorge said warily. "A cursed forest. Home to
jackals."

"Quick landing, 'tis all I need," Gregor said, wagging his finger.
He secured the rigging, began steering hard to port, angling for the
Argo. "This be where I drop me cargo. Then we be done with it.
No worries, mates. Hardly worth the trouble for such a short trip."

Sorge eyed the countryside nervously. They were only a
couple miles south of the city. The shipping lanes were clear.
No other vessels could be seen up or down the channels. A few
small huts dotted the land heading west, but that was about it.
Gregor aimed the vessel for a small, dilapidated dock on the
western shore, no doubt used by local fishermen. He put down
the gangplank, handed each of the boys a thick rope, and began
barking orders.

"Take these down to the dock'n lash 'em to the piers, lads. I'll
follow in a moment. Go! Missy, you can go with 'em, but let them
do the work, see? Sorge, my friend, you and the gnome, come and
grab some of these barrels and heave 'em up the ladder to me. I'm
too old for this anymore. Down there in the hold, against the far

wall. Careful now, she's got a low ceiling. *Rat Trap* I should call her, not *Windstar*. That's right . . ."

Hadyn and Ewan didn't know any good knots, but they worked their way to the dock and began tying the ropes as best they could. In the dark belly of the ship, Sorge and Flogg waited for their eyes to adjust.

"I don't see barrels anywhere—"

A creaky sound. An unoiled hinge, loud above them. The monk glanced up in time to see the hold's door slam shut. Smooth and practiced, Gregor slid a thick iron bar through heavy metal hoops on either side of the door frame, sealing the door fast. "You're the cargo now, mates," he smirked.

Sorge and Flogg began yelling, pounding. The sound of the staff banging against the underside of the deck drew both boys' attention.

"What's going on?" said Hadyn.

"Betrayal," Asandra said ominously.

Gregor straightened his back, took time to cooly adjust his tunic.

He laughed. "That's a smart lass ya' are, missy. As for me, I can't figure why they don't want you instead."

He unsheathed a thin rapier from his side and began slowly advancing down the gangplank, the tip pointed straight out, swishing back and forth, boy to boy. He glanced dismissively, though not without fear, at the mirling. "None to hear you scream lads, so go ahead. And I know for a fact a mirling's powers got nothing to do with sword fightin'. So it's just me and you here. The four of us. And some buyers with deep, deep pockets. No need for this to get ugly."

"You can't do this, Gregor!"

"Oh, but I can. It's like I told Sorge. Sometimes an offer comes along that's simply too good to refuse." He put fingers to his lips and whistled loudly. Following his line of sight, Hadyn saw five figures emerge from behind scattered trees near the shore, fanning out, converging in a half circle around the dock where the boys stood. Their march was methodical, maddeningly slow. One of them carried a small bag in his hands that jingled. The other four held long knives. They were trapped—by water, Gregor's blade, five hunters. Hadyn scanned the dock, the boat and shore, trying to formulate a plan.

"Why are you doing this?" he whispered.

"Why does anyone do anything? Cause I wanted to. Cause I can."

Dimly, another voice could be heard coming from the belly of the ship. "Lord Hadyn! Lord Ewan!" It was Sorge. "How many?"

"Five on shore!" Hadyn shouted back. "The ones from the Stone House I think. They have knives."

"Hold your ground!"

Gregor glanced back nervously as the hold's door rattled and buckled with every blow; yet it held.

Again, Sorge called out. "Gregor! Repent of this. You are a better man!"

"Gave up on being a better man," Gregor shot back angrily. "Gave up on you. Gave up on Aion, most of all. I've lived long enough to see no punishment for evil, no reward for good. Besides . . . never much liked being told what to do." He paused, allowing his words to sink in, showing stained, crooked teeth. "How do you like that, Gray? Huh? Do you still believe in your invisible, legendary prince? If he be so all-powerful, why did he not warn ye you were walking into a trap? Eh? One of his own holy servants?"

He waited for a reply. None came. Only a single, solitary, defeated thump against the hold's door.

"Aye, he didn't protect you!" Gregor shouted, his voice echoing on the water.

Off in the distance, a gull cried. Then there was silence. A slight breeze rustled the green leaves of the few trees on shore. Otherwise, the only sound was the soft whisper of the feet of five people folding the grass with each measured step, drawing closer, closer—three boys, two girls, all robed in drab brown. With hoods drawn and hands outstretched as if they meant to consume their prey all at once, the five advanced. Standing on the gangplank, Gregor swished his rapier in the air. The raucous thumping coming from the ship was done.

"Sorge is stuck," Ewan whispered. "What do we do?"

Gregor heard him and mocked, "Methinks what you're gonna to do is win me a prize, and then go far away. On a lovely holiday I'd wager." He called out louder to one of the five, "That better be a money bag I see in your hand there, lad. Otherwise, I'll just have to haul me cargo back on board."

Nearly to the dock, the leader of the five gazed upon Gregor dispassionately. He tossed the bag to the older man, who caught it in midair, opened it, pulled out a gold coin, and promptly bit the metal. The sailor smiled greedily, began jingling the bag, counting the number of coins.

"Outlanders," the leader of the five said calmly, eyes fixed on Hadyn, "do not struggle, and you will not be harmed. You must come with us."

He had to act, no time, but felt a wave of indecision. Thoughts piled up in Hadyn's mind, one on top of another, like a traffic jam at noon. All the adrenaline in the world was pointless if he couldn't *think*. Every muscle felt poised for action, cued and ready. Every muscle but his brain, which felt dipped in neural molasses. The mental fog was a projection of the lost ones, he knew. The nearer they drew, the more powerfully their torpor became his own, exactly as he had felt it at the Stone House.

Ewan made a slurred, shushing sound.

"Get *away* from us!"

He was bent over, holding his head, his ears, wobbling on his knees. He seemed pained, though his eyes were steel.

"Get out of my head!" he shouted.

As long as he lived, Hadyn would never forget that moment, standing on the dock. As mild waters lapped the shore, something about Ewan's defiance, the desperate posture of his hands clutching his face, cut through his own dullness. He knew, at the very least, one thing. They must *not* be taken. He had to do something, for himself.

For Ewan.

His plan was not a plan. It was motion. Roaring wildly, he charged. He had no weapon, not even a stick. One against five. But standing still would solve nothing. If he distracted them, perhaps Ewan and Asandra might escape.

His movement was so jarringly unexpected, the five wavered. They had formed a wall on the edge of the dock, but now the wall shook. Plus, Hadyn was a sprinter. He might have made it, except for the explosive force that knocked him forward, slamming him against the dock.

From deep in the hold of the ship came a blast that shattered planks and splintered the cargo door. The sound was deafening. A piece of flying debris cracked Gregor's head, splattering blood. He tumbled facedown into the water. Ewan and Asandra were blown to their knees. Crawling from the smoke and tumult, Sorge heaved himself over the side into the water between the ship and the dock, howling in pain. Behind him, Flogg seemed to have fared little better. Then came the monk's hands, grasping at the pier, pulling himself to the platform. Of the five, three lumbered toward the dock, slashing randomly with their blades. Hadyn tried to clear his head. Rattled or not, he had to fight.

He heard something, saw something. For the second time, was saved.

A flash of color, a musical, laughing cry, and the whisper of a blade scraping free of its scabbard. Hadyn whipped his head around. There, swirling about with a naked blade, was the man from Threefork, Cruedwyn. He looked like a hawk diving from the sky, leaping into the path of the three assailants before they could reach the dock, before they could adapt. One of them cried out and lunged, but he was awkward and slow. Cruedwyn parried, spun, thrust his weapon deep into the boy's flesh. The second swung hard, hissing like a rabid animal. Creudwyn sliced, spun again, cutting across his robe, leaving a gash of bright blood.

The first one folded toward the earth, never to rise again. Two more stumbled away, crying in pain. The remaining two held their ground for a brief moment. Then they, too, fled.

Cruedwyn lowered his sword, but Flogg wasn't finished. Hobbling past, he heaved a bulging, leather-strapped ball in their direction. It exploded loudly above the heads of the fleeing four, knocking two more to the ground. They wailed aloud, collected themselves again, then disappeared into the trees heading north toward the city.

Sorge knelt beside the boys.

"Are you well?" he asked. Both, obviously shaken, nodded.

Satisfied, the monk wheeled round, leaned out over the dock, ready to aid Gregor with his staff. The seaman's body, facedown, floated slowly away.

"Mercy, Aion," the monk whispered, touching his closed fist to his chest. "Once, he was my friend."

The boat bubbled and frothed as it took on water from the hole blown in its hull. It slowly began to sink into the river. Sorge leaped aboard, gathering a few quick supplies, any food he could find and the personal belongings all five had left on the deck. He threw them over to Flogg, one by one, then jumped back to the dock, landing hard. The vessel creaked, lurched, rolled onto its side. Within minutes, it had slipped below the surface and disappeared.

Sorge's soot-stained face was bruised and bleeding. Flogg looked even worse, though he had a wild, gleeful look in his eye. The monk said grimly, "There were five last time and five this. By Auginn's eyes, we have survived their treachery each time. Cruedwyn, my thanks. Flogg sensed someone trailing us, but we assumed the worst."

Cruedwyn, panting for breath, flashed a playful smile. "You know the saying. *A lame donkey blessed is better than oxen cursed.*"

"Blessed with a sword and you are better than ten oxen. We are in your debt and surely won't refuse your company this time, though now perhaps you see why at first I did. Join us at your own peril."

"Fair enough. I have my own reasons to travel, if you'll accept that for now."

Sorge nodded. "A return to Threefork is probably unwise, but we mustn't wait for Nemesia's brood to regroup. We will not face them in such low numbers again, I think." He looked at Flogg, limping, felt the sticky blood on his own fingers when he wiped his face. "Our first task is to bind our wounds and carefully plot our next move. For now, the best thing we can do is hide. And to hide safely, we must hide dangerously, where no one would search for us."

Hadyn felt a pit in his stomach. He looked south, down the river. The sun was setting. Not far away loomed a wall of dark trees. Sorge confirmed their destination, speaking it like a curse.

"Redthorn."

CHAPTER 22

Archibald

Vast swaths of evening light streamed through the great windows in the Hall of the King. Luminous, rose-hued beams diffused into the air, reflecting off the large, square tiles, catching fire on the gold filigree of the Hall's six massive columns, the silver etchings trimmed into the ivory throne, and the line of polished metal shields and crests hung so precisely upon the walls.

In this Hall, a man shuffled aimlessly up and down the heavy blue carpet runner leading from the great double doors at one end to the ivory throne at the other, muttering, "Where are the Champions?" Though he was neither very young nor very old, he stooped as if great with age.

"*Where* are my Champions!" he bellowed again, his ragged voice echoing off the marbled walls. Turning circles, as if searching, he murmured, "*Why* are there no Champions? Why am I alone left to rule with no aid among men?"

A dozen elite palace guards stood stone-faced at attention, spears held tightly upright. They did not move or reply or even blink. Four other men in richly embroidered robes stood at a distance with mixed expressions, either fretting or scoffing, looking bored or scheming. Another man, also richly arrayed, walked beside the troubled ruler. He was a slight man, full of poise and syrup, skilled in the meaningful pause, the clever phrase, the subtle gesture or expression capable of bending another mind to his point of view, however slightly. He could cloud an issue enough to seem wise, then later clarify the distortion with a simpler, more comprehensible half-truth. His name was Jonas, the Minister of Justice—a title of extravagant irony, to be sure.

"My Lord Archibald," Jonas whispered, folding his hands behind his back. On the underside of his left wrist, he bore a strange mark, like a tattoo or birthmark, shaped like a wild beast. No matter. It was always buried beneath his sleeve. "You are Governor of this great dominion. Why trouble yourself with negligent heroes and other petty matters? We have no need of relics of days gone by. This is *your* domain!"

Archibald was unimpressed. "My domain is crumbling to ruin."

"My liege . . . I must beg to differ. Consider, are the coffers empty or full?"

"Full," grumbled Archibald.

"Are barbarians from Quil threatening our borders?"

"Not *yet.*"

"And haven't, not for many generations. Our spies tell us all is quiet in that land. Now, is your own person healthy or ill?"

"I am well enough."

"Have peasants gathered in an uprising or refused to pay the tax?"

Archibald shook his head irritably. "No, no, no."

"What then? Are Dukes and Earls plotting against you? Is Har Halas? Or Pol Shyne?"

"They are loyal to a man. Lazy, but loyal."

"Then why do you wring your hands, exaggerating woes that do not exist and may *never* exist? Why agonize and compromise your health and sanity—in the prime years of your life, when you should be enjoying song and hunt and fame—grinding your teeth on unfounded fears of doom?"

Archibald grumbled low in his throat. Beneath the pasty skin of his lips, his thick teeth formed a wary, cunning smile. "Do you think I do not see through you, Jonas? With one hand, you seek to flatter me, and with the other, play me as a fool—"

"Lord Governor, no!" Jonas pled, lowering his head.

"Yet you laud the stability of my kingdom while insulting my concerns as its ruler!"

Jonas withdrew two steps in humiliation, but continued pace with the Governor. Archibald nervously fingered his thin gray beard in a manner bordering on obsessive. He was a solid figure, or at least once had been. Short, beefy, and broad shouldered, with blue eyes still capable of piercing through layers of worry, Archibald carried a scepter but wore no crown. He was not a king and he knew it. His hands often trembled with this knowledge, and he ever felt that someone, somewhere, was measuring his royal deficit. Even now, the Governor studied the chamber walls, the polished floor, with distracted, weary effort.

"The land is sickening, Jonas. Crops are yielding barely half of what they did a generation ago. Rains are flooding Vineland

and forsaking the Midlands. The mountains quake in the north. My armies are thin, my Champions are in decay. The League of Assassins grows in power. And those are but trivial concerns. Across the bay but a few miles, the witch in her tower watches me. I feel it. Her shadow grows and I am powerless to stop it. Children are crossing over to join her dark ways. Hundreds, perhaps thousands. Every day, we see them. My spies cannot penetrate her sorcery, but they give reports of phantoms wandering every village, of dark ships at night, full of these youths, slipping secretly toward the Isle of Apaté. They roam as gangs, plundering through the night, stealing other children away. I have stacks of letters from priests, parents, dukes, and duchesses, describing them, dreading them. Blaming me. I saw one once, when I rode the hunt. A young lass, maybe fifteen years old. Her eyes were empty, like a wraith. She had lost her soul, her very memory."

He paused, ashamed. "I fear them."

"Troublesome, to be sure," Jonas said sympathetically, stepping closer once more. "But if I may be so bold, haven't children always been difficult? I was, I regret to say. Perhaps even you were a handful, great lord. In fact, tell me a time when parents haven't worried and prayed over their children. Yes? But what happens, every time? They grow up. They learn and change, and eventually tomorrow resolves the troubles of today. Always, tomorrow."

Though he was not of royal blood, Archibald could summon a commanding presence when needed. Now, his blue eyes turned a pale shade of winter. "Your tongue is made of witchcraft, minister. These children aren't merely stubborn or troubled. Or even rebellious. They are *lost*. They have no connection to the land of their birth, their families, or the goodwill of the people. Good and evil are alike in their eyes, and the gods are mocked.

They are our hope for tomorrow. If we lose them, we lose our future."

Jonas replied with a thin, tight smile, "Heavy matters indeed. I stand entirely corrected and will act with force. Tomorrow, I shall appoint a delegation to study these criminal activities at once."

"You appointed a delegation," Archibald said wearily, "six months ago."

"Then with your lord's leave, I shall have their report, or create a new commission!" Jonas smacked his fist in his palm. Then, smooth in its suddenness, he angled the conversation away. "But if I may be so bold, my lord, I daresay you *were* a spot of trouble as a child, weren't you? Great leaders are like that, I have found. Always a bit rowdy and raucous? Always charging ahead, eh?"

Archibald continued to pace, determined to maintain his fretting. But Jonas had found the mark. A gentle twinge of memory wet the governor's lips, tasting sweet. Pride swelled in his voice. "Well, I don't want to boast or anything . . ."

"For shame! Truth is never a boast, my lord."

"True, true enough. The fact is, I was the finest swordsman among all my brothers."

"Among all six? And you, the youngest?"

"Indeed! Have I ever told you of the time I found my father's sword in the livery . . ."

On and on. On and on. Jonas smiled.

CHAPTER 23

Eldoran

On the morning of the fifth day since his guests' departure, Eldoran rose early, as was his way, and laid a new sheet of fresh parchment on a small table in his private study. He lit two candles. The twin flames burnished the wood with a haze of waxy light. Taking feather in hand, he dipped the quill in a small copper inkwell, began scratching the paper with his thoughts.

> *To Alethes, High Priest of the White Abbey, and*
> *Cassock, Bishop of the Black,*
> *From Your Humble Servant, Eldoran the Gray,*

> *Troubling news continues to increase across our fair land. For more than a decade now, we have beheld, first, warning signs, then strange*

happenings. Most recently, truly dark events have begun to unfold. We have varied and wavered and argued as to their cause. But I trust your heart (as I hope you trust mine), that within our respective duties, our mission is to safeguard the ways of Aion for the health of this land. As sobering tales continue to reach our gates from every province, I have profound news to convey. Though it may be difficult to conceive, two young brothers from another world beyond the reach of ours entered the Gray Abbey some five days ago. They came in response to Call Birds which passed into their world, dropping royal invitations signed with a golden A. I saw these tokens myself, and am compelled by numerous particulars to believe the veracity of their tale without question. In such troubled times, I need not tell you the importance of their coming. But I share my thoughts, knowing you will have wisdom and insights by which we can each glean a larger share of truth, to whit:

First, I am surprised that Archibald summoned the courage to send Call Birds. Such an audacious move! I know not how he came by these legendary creatures. I thought them extinct. But I fear treachery within his ranks will undo his will and betray his plans. How can we undergird him and prevent Jonas and his ilk from bringing all to ruin?

Second, my brother Alethes, I know the White Abbey is in the midst of the Days of Awe. As you review the Book of Names, I think we should look for these two young men. They are brothers named Hadyn and Ewan, surname Barlow. Since Yhü Hoder, the first man, was commissioned with divine wisdom to compose the Book as part of his doom, might not he have recorded their names and deeds and place in our history? Such travels between worlds are not entirely unknown to us, are they? Tal Yssen and the great king Artorius? I know the boys' deeds will be invisible to us, but we might still gain reassurance of their purpose if their names are recorded. Please send word immediately regarding this with the trusted Brother who bears this message.

Third, my friend Cassock, I implore you to stir the seers and mirlings to greater dreams. We are blind, sickly, and wingless without them. Speaking of wings, you are so good to keep the pigeons in flight, bearing record of their dreams, but we have seen fewer and fewer for many months. Hold fast in your dark sanctuary, friend! The Black Abbey has chosen a severe solitude far in the north, but do not forget why. It is for the good of the land.

Know also that Asandra was invaluable in her time with us. By now she is well on her way to Seabraith. However, her presence raised another issue: the number of Watchers roaming the land is becoming intolerable and will soon outstrip the capacity of your few pupils. One recently banished at our Abbey had stirred a nearby village to madness and the slashing of their flesh. This abomination must be addressed! But how? The land is poisoned, and the great rituals of fire, land, and water have been obstructed for generations. Since the Severing Blade is lost, is there no other provision in the Book of Law that the Taines may be restored? Pressed by the urgency of the hour, I feel compelled to make every inquiry.

As always, the Grays stand with you, ready for the good of the land. If we lack in anything you require, do not hesitate to lay such burdens upon us, as part of our service to the Way. Even now, my most trusted Elder escorts the two brothers to Stratamore. Brothers, let us pray our fortunes are revived!

In devotion of Olfadr, Everking, and the Imperial Prince, Aion, I sign with my own hand,

Eldoran

The Father signed with a flourish, then made a second copy exactly like the first. Upon finishing the latter, he rolled both parchments into tight scrolls. He took one of the candles, tipped its flame so that hot wax dripped on the folded edge of each, waited a moment, and then pressed his ring deeply into the warm pool of wax. Rising stiffly, he opened the door, where two light gray Brothers waited patiently. He caught them both in mid-yawn and gently roused them. Led them to the courtyard, where horses were saddled and ready, handing each a scroll.

"Brothers, your task is great. Sleep no more! Melanor, south. Velusi, north, with haste! The three Abbeys must be of one mind if we are to survive the days ahead. Go!"

He slapped the rumps of both horses, sent them jumping. Iron-shod hooves clattered on the cobblestones as the men thundered away. Eldoran turned back to the Abbey, heavy in his heart. Before he could even reach the doors, another set of hooves came clicking on the cobblestones. He turned, expecting that one of the Brothers had forgotten his water bag.

"What is it, my brother?" he said kindly. "What do you need?"

A yellow robed emissary of the White Abbey reined into the courtyard, slumped against his beast's neck, obviously exhausted. The horse was lathered with sweat and heaved so hard into the chill morning air Eldoran feared it might collapse.

"The Holy Hills, brother! What—"

"I am an Interpreter of the White Abbey," the man declared, pushing himself to an upright position. His hair was short and blond, his face was dirty. "I bear urgent news from Alethes."

"Yes, yes. I know your color. What news, man? Speak."

"Alethes bids me give you grave tidings: On the first morn of the Days of Awe, according to our tradition, we entered the Hall of

Ages to find our people in the Book of Names, to read the names born on that day. Such has been our custom for many thousand years."

"Yes, yes, and . . . ?"

The Interpreter shifted his weight uncomfortably. He seemed near tears.

"Speak, brother!"

"The Book of Names, Father. The pages. They're *blank*!"

"What do you mean, blank?"

"They're simply gone. Years of names, gone. The future is gone. Even the scrolls of previous days and years, names we have already seen, are now empty. The record of two decades of children and life is stricken. Alethes has torn his robe and cancelled the Days of Awe. Even as I bear this news, the White Abbey is in fasting and mourning."

He panted for breath. The Brother in charge of the stables crossed the courtyard to offer him a flagon of water. The Interpreter gulped thirstily, wiping his face. Water ran down his chin, neck, and robe.

Eldoran's mind reeled. "The pages of the Book are . . . are. . . ." The Interpreter filled the void with a dull voice of doom. "Nameless, Father. The pages of the Book are nameless. Karac Tor is undone."

Cruedwyn

is full name and title, it turned out, was Cruedwyn Creed the Silver Tongue, Bard of Clan Fergisfencreed. The Fourth. Of Slegling-by-the-Sea. Wooer of Women. Master Verseman. Tormenter of Evil. Bastion of Justice.

He had a lot of names. Hadyn grinned.

Ewan wanted to talk swords. "Where did you learn to fight like that?! Like Jackie Chan or something. Can you teach me?"

Cruedwyn basked in the praise like a flower reaching toward the warm sun. "Teach!" he cried. "Why, young lord, I could make a master of you in a fortnight—perhaps even a week. Days, really, that's all I need, skilled as I am. Why if I put my mind to it, I daresay I could have you fencing like Corus himself by morning!"

A low, warbling sound rose in response to his boasting. It was a slight, irritating noise. No one could tell exactly what it was or where it came from, but Creed immediately became apologetic.

"Ahh, never mind that. Not sure what's afoot there."

Ewan tilted his head at the sound. Everyone tilted their heads, including Cruedwyn.

"Could you really teach me that fast?" Ewan continued doubtfully, straining his face.

It was a comical sight, six people in unison trying to drain the vibration out of their skull. Cruedwyn began hopping about as if his boots were on fire.

"Well, ha ha, of course it might take longer," he stammered, "you being a beginner and all. A fortnight is awfully fast. Could take years, really. Waste your whole youth. Besides, you look like a poor study if I may be so bold."

The warbling sound began to fade. Cruedwyn wiggled his pinkie finger in his ear. "Right! Done, and gladly! Now, as I was saying, before I'm done with you, you'll parry like any Champion in the realm or my name's not Cruedwyn Creed!"

They all knew his name quite well by now, because he said it often. In fact, he had hardly stopped talking or singing since they left the river for the safety of the trees, which, Sorge made clear, was a foolhardy notion. Redthorn could hardly be called safe. It was simply all they had.

Cruedwyn continued his curious pantomime. "I'll have you know, when the Duke of Greenland, who's practically family, being my father's brother's cousin's uncle by marriage—when he needed a guard for his lovely daughter Sáranyása, who did he call?"

"You?" Hadyn asked with mock surprise. He found it odd that Ewan was so taken with Cruedwyn, yet so spiteful to Flogg.

Cruedwyn made a grand, sweeping gesture, as if to wild applause. Right in the middle of the rolling grass, he bowed low.

"Me, none other, 'tis true. Thirteen swordsmen of unusual distinction are known throughout the land. Since Duke Shyne insisted on the absolute best for his daughter, he sent couriers on steed, until one found me lying naked in a bed of lilies, offering prayers for the flowers of the field, that they might be blessed with even sweeter fragrance—"

The warbling sound began again, in earnest this time. Cruedwyn made no attempt to hide his irritation. He glanced impatiently at his hip, surprisingly unembarrassed.

"Oh, shut up. You know it's the truth! Okay, maybe not naked—"

A little cry escaped his lips then. A nervous sound, like laughter, like one might make if sentenced to be tied up, tickled, and pinched to death.

"I *could* teach him! That's all I said!" Cruedwyn shouted angrily. Shouted to nothing, except perhaps his . . . pants? "And I was with a Lilly. That was her name! A brief, chaste kiss, nothing more."

His eyes watered. He was in obvious pain. But he never let go of his thin, strained smile. Still, the sound grew. Growling, he yanked at his scabbard, talking to it as if it were a person. "Don't you dare! You besotted wedge of cursed metal! You fiend! Traitor!"

The high wail grew into a knife of pain boring into everyone's skull, but only Cruedwyn spun and writhed. When he could bear it no longer, he jerked on the haft of his blade with a gloved hand, whisked the sword free, and flung it to the ground. It landed in a patch of dark, mossy earth, glowing as if heated in a smithy's fire. The air smelled burnt.

Sorge leaned closer, impressed. "I've never seen the like."

Indeed, the long blade was polished and razor sharp, with a handle of silver dragon teeth wrapped around the grip. High on the haft were two seething, amber eyes. It was a work of remarkable craftsmanship.

"All in fun!" the bard cried. "I've shown you nothing but kindness! Why am I cursed with your wretched ways?"

As if in answer, a dry leaf touching the blade caught fire. Then, silence.

All this took place like a one-act play before the eyes of a rather stunned group of curious onlookers. As one, they all burst into laughter, even Flogg. Everyone except Cruedwyn, whose feelings appeared more than a little hurt.

"Easy, friend," Sorge said at length, patting him on the back. "Maybe you should get another one. That one seems pretty testy." But he studied the blade, even as he smiled.

"Oh, it'll cool down," the bard said irritably. "Maybe minutes. Maybe tonight. The hothead! I can't get rid of it—traded my own, beloved harp for this sword, and what's a bard without a harp? Cursed by Loki himself, I think. Can you believe it?"

Flogg made a warding sign against that name. Loki, Prince of Mischief. A Fey Folk.

They changed the subject, still bearing south, shadowing the Argo, drawing ever nearer to the northern rim of Redthorn. The woods loomed larger and larger on the edge of the land. Hadyn's knees felt weak to look at them, though he couldn't fathom why. From here at least, dark or no, they just looked like trees. Asandra didn't help.

"It is said even Watchers avoid these woods," the mirling said softly.

"True," Sorge observed. "I would expect evil to be drawn to evil. But not here."

"Tell me about Watchers," Hadyn said, trying to divert himself. With each step, a foul and sullen mood had increasingly fallen on the whole group. Watchers hardly seemed the right topic to lighten it, but hey, it was a start. Even Cruedwyn had grown glum. The heat of his sword, safely returned to its scabbard, still caused a slight limp as he walked. "What are they?"

"Fallen spirits," Sorge answered. "Slaves of the Devourer. When evil reigns, they fly with the Horned Lord, Haurgne, on his wild hunts. They are dreadful."

"Long ago," Asandra said softly, "before memory, they were the eyes of Olfadr, at the making of the world. But Haurgne, the Devourer, ensnared them. Now they are his. Dark, birdlike spirits."

Sorge continued. "When a mirling captures them, as Asandra did in a mirror of blessed water, they are bound by the code which binds all the earth together. And in this Law, all waters lead to Hel, which is their prison. That day, Asandra took the frame of water to the river near the Abbey, with the Watcher still trapped inside. She laid it in the flowing waters and cracked the glass. This released the Watcher into the river, from which it traveled, bound in liquid, down to the rushing current of the Goldfoam. From Goldfoam to the bay, and eventually—as all waters must—it passes deep into the sea, into Undrwol. There the water is purged of its evil. In this way, Watchers are removed from the earth."

"I thought you said they were banished to Hel?"

"Helheim, the kingdom of ice and terror in the northern mountains of Bitterland. It guards the entrance to Undrwol, where the living do not enter."

"Nor should they enter *there*." Cruedwyn pointed straight ahead. They had arrived. Redthorn sprawled before them, dark and somber. Sorge scouted the area before the last light of day faded. There was a good campsite outside the forest amongst a few straggling trees, where the land gradually sloped down the embankment toward the Argo. Pleasantly, on the way down, a large bit of soft, flat earth was hemmed in by enormous boulders. There was a makeshift fire pit and old ashes. The place had been used before.

"Good lines of sight," Sorge said, peering below to the water's edge. East was the river. "To the west and north we are hidden by the rocks. We can defend this place if needed."

"Pray not, brother monk. Remember, I am regrettably swordless." Creed slapped his sheath, not so much to emphasize the point, it seemed, as to insult his weapon. "Even when the blade cools, and wearing gloves, the haft can be unbearable. Sometimes it gets so hot the blade actually deforms. It melts. Or something. But then it always comes back, curse it." He shook his head ruefully. "Strange magic, the Fey."

"Why were you following us?" Ewan asked. "I mean, don't get me wrong, I'm glad *you* were." He glanced toward Flogg with baleful eyes. No one noticed but Hadyn, who smacked him lightly on the head as a warning.

Cruedwyn was unfazed. "Take no thought of it, my young friend! A Creed seeks adventure wherever it may be found. Luck and happenstance led me to you, simple as that." The warm sword began moaning again in protest. "All right, fine! I'm being hunted. Sort of. It's nobody, really. Just a man named Quillian. I needed help getting out of the Midlands and quickly. So I thought I might wave you down from the shore for another try. Like a poor, pitiful beggar. There, are you happy?"

For a moment Hadyn couldn't tell if Cruedwyn was lashing out at Ewan or his sword. The bard's blond, moppy hair, receding chin, and fast, toothy grin already reminded the oldest Barlow of a puppy, which Hadyn wisely decided was not a good comparison to make at the moment. Nor was it an easy thought to avoid, for whenever Cruedwyn moved, his mail undershirt, tucked safely under a blue vest, tinkled. Like a dog collar. Hadyn had to bite his lip.

Sorge swooped into the conversation. "Did you say Quillian? Of the League?"

Creed feigned surprise. "So you've heard of him?"

The monk's eyes narrowed. "You should have told me, Creed. You know it."

"Pish-posh! Let's not dwell on the past, shall we? He thinks he won my sword in a game of Bones, which he plainly didn't. 'Tis a simple misunderstanding. I might have been happy to be rid of the blade if I had thought it through. Hear that, old girl? I'm not afraid of you." He brightened, clapping his hands together. "Now let's do something useful and plan for tomorrow, eh? We know we can't enter the woods—that's a fool's errand—and we can't camp here indefinitely because I'm not the only one with enemies." He eyed the brothers, mostly with respect. "Boys, let me give you some advice. An enemy is nothing to be ashamed of. Fact is, if you don't have at least one enemy in your life, you're probably doing something wrong."

Deep within Redthorn rose a lone, wolfish howl. Its barren cry, ragged with hunger, triggered a chorus of other howls all over the forest. The voices emanated outward, surrounding the band of six as they made camp, clinging like fog to their tingling skin. Ewan unconsciously edged closer to Hadyn.

Flogg tromped off, "Going to trees for listening. Come to tell again."

"It's a bit dangerous, but I'm going to risk a fire," Sorge said. "Hot food might lift our spirits, and the fire will keep the jackals at bay. We will all need our strength tomorrow."

Cruedwyn gasped. "You're going to do it then? No, Sorge, not with an army! Before it's over we'll all be mad. Or dead."

Ewan leaned closer. "I don't care for either of those options."

Hadyn didn't either, but what he noticed, strangely, was Asandra. She was studying Sorge's face. Waiting. Almost imperceptibly, one eyebrow arched.

"I'll take your counsel over rabbits and onions, happily, Creed. But not one more word on an empty stomach. Build me a fire. Asandra, tend to wounds. I'll be back soon."

He stalked into the night, following Flogg. Asandra's gaze lingered on him as if searching for an answer, or waiting for a visit from an old friend that will never be seen again. When she felt Hadyn's eyes resting upon her, her countenance fell.

"Leave me alone," she said.

CHAPTER 25

Night at Redthorn

Later, with a mercifully cool breeze from the north bringing relief, the fire crackling warmly, and three rabbits hung on a spit, Sorge called for attention.

"A night fire is the time for stories. Hadyn, Ewan, listen to me now. You have learned much in a short period, but mostly of the Grays. It is time now to learn of the Blacks, they who listen to soil and water, trees and rocks, who purge the land wherever evil takes root. Their construct is spirit. Grays are material. Whites are mental. Among the Blacks, mirlings are second in rank." He turned to Asandra. "I know these woods weigh heavily on you, but please do not withhold your grief. Tell us the tale of the darkening of Redthorn."

Asandra removed her cowl so that Hadyn could see her eyes again, brown and warm. He was surprised that she did not resent the request. As the embers swirled, dancing in the updraft like fireflies, her face shone, and she began to speak.

"Redthorn was once the most beautiful of forests. It is also called *Salieré*, which means Red Rock, though no one can remember why. Here, Aion and Yhü would go hunting together. Aion would ride his great steed and laugh and tell tales of Isgurd. But sometime long ago, lost in mist and sorrow—some say even before the Age of Crowns—a great evil occurred in these woods. An evil so great even the trees themselves were forever defiled. The Argo was darkened, as were oak, ash, and elm. One of the Five Great Trees, the Ash of Uisnwch, once put down roots here. It would have died had not Soriah the Gray carried from it a seed, long ago, replanted now in the court of the White Abbey. He saw in a dream and obeyed."

Her voice took on a certain cadence, broken only a little by Flogg's return from surveying the forest perimeter.

"Quiet bugger," Hadyn said admiringly to Ewan. "I didn't even hear him coming."

Ewan curled his lips, whispered back. "More like sneaky. Why'd he have to go to the woods, huh? And why does it seem like we're always attacked after he leaves for a while?"

Hadyn rolled his eyes. "Would you get over it?"

"No, I won't, and neither should you. It happened in Threefork, right? He went ahead of us, then the whole Gregor thing happened. If he can listen through the land with his fingers, all weird and stuff, who's to say he can't *send signals* through the land? Same thing, but reversed, telling them where we are? Maybe that's what happened at the Stone House, with the ravens."

Hadyn poked at the scabs on his head from the bird peckings. "He almost died protecting us. Both those times."

The camp had strangely quieted. Night birds, crickets, the hissing fire. Asandra had either paused, or finished, he wasn't sure. Sorge and Flogg were whispering. Creed was staring at the flames. He coughed lightly, in apology. But as the mirling brushed a strand of hair from her eyes, in that gesture, Hadyn realized she had fallen silent on her own. He had returned to a heavy moment. For the first time since meeting her, in the smallness of that gesture, Asandra seemed like a human being. A frail, little girl, not just an angry mirling.

"Have you ever had a feeling that something was wrong?" she said, her voice fragile. She was looking toward Sorge, deep in conversation with Flogg, or past him into the dark night. "You can't prove it. You can't measure it. But you can't shake the feeling."

The question was like peeling a crusty scab back to fresh, pink skin. Hadyn felt a rush of unwilled memory rise to the surface like droplets of blood when the scab is pulled too soon. He couldn't help but think of Mom—how the cancer had claimed her one inch at a time. Slowly at first, so much as to not be noticed. She had always been so *alive*! And then, merely sick. She and Dad said they were fighting it, that they had hope. They believed. They had caught it early, traveled across the country to the best doctors. But every night, as he drifted to sleep, the black hole in Hadyn's stomach would remain. Over a period of weeks and months, what wasn't so apparent in a single day slowly became obvious. Something was wrong. Very wrong.

And then, one day, a day like any other, Dad woke him and Ewan before school and took them downstairs. He would never forget his dad that day, pale and trembling. He said he needed to tell them something. Things weren't so good. Mom had been taken to the hospital during the night, while they slept.

The very next day, she died. The single worst day of his life.

He tried to swallow the knot in his throat. Shape thought into words. He sighed, a long slow release, as if shedding his skin, purging sorrow. "Yes, I've had that feeling."

"Well, the people of Aion feel it *every* day. At least those of us who care to notice. Something is not right, and it haunts us. Right now, it bears a name: Nemesia. But there is something greater, great enough to consume us all. Greater than Redthorn. Something terrible is coming. We know it, but we don't know why. Or what to do."

She paused, gesturing toward the murky, hidden woods as if apologizing. "Redthorn is not truly evil. It is defiled, and that is a very different thing. Thorns cover the trees like a disease. The forest aches. It has been filled with poison for a long time."

Sorge chose that moment to rejoin the conversation. "The thorns are real, not poetic. You cannot walk without being pricked and you cannot be pricked without going mad. Jackals now call these woods their home. Worse, when the world grows dark . . ." His voice trailed away.

"What?" Ewan whispered.

"In every age, when the world grows dark, and the tides turn toward evil, Haurgne is seen riding these woods on his wild hunt. He is torn by a thousand thorns, but he is already mad with evil and power. And Hel goes with him."

Asandra hurriedly made the sign of the circle.

"Please, my friends!" Cruedwyn exclaimed, emerging from his own private reverie. "If the boys had wanted a show, you should have taken them to the amphitheater in Portaferry, or let them watch the Revlons dance and sing at the Cirque. Haurgne, really?

He hasn't been seen for, what, ever? When was the last time? In the reign of Gwylfal? The time of Prophet Iff?" He turned to the boys apologetically. "Midlanders call him Herne, and say that he has antlers like a great, wild stag, cavorting with the Fey Queen on her bed. The Bittermen say he is Kurg, an evil changeling who steals children and drinks blood. For the Highland folk, he is Kr'Nunos. A man . . . no, a beast. No, a spirit! And the Abbeys," he glanced at Sorge, "they will tell you he was once the great Champion of Aion himself." He pulled a knife from his bootstrap and began sharpening it on a piece of soapstone from his satchel. "I say we've got enough problems that *can* be seen without making up those we can't."

"Only a fool would make such claims," Asandra murmured.

"Fools and fanatics," the bard answered equably.

Sorge picked up one of the spits, cut a wedge of sizzling flesh, and tasted it. Licked his lips, pleased. He knew better than to argue theology and philosophy on an empty stomach.

"Enough talk. Nemesia is quite real and evil enough for all of us. Let's eat."

A fourth rabbit would have been nice. And more onions. Fried chicken would have been even better. Or a hamburger. *Oh!* The thought of a double Whopper made Hadyn's mouth water. He wondered how long it had been. It seemed like months.

Still, something about food around a campfire always tasted good. Cold water on a hot summer evening was even better, but the water in his flask was warm. Regardless, it was nice to feel full and slaked. Since they were all fairly sore and tired, and mostly talked dry, the meal passed swiftly. Afterward, Sorge put out the fire, and each member of the party picked a spot to spread their blanket on the soft earth. Asandra and Sorge, each to themselves, bent low for silent, evening prayers. The mirling prayed a warning hedge around them. It would not keep jackals away, but would, at the very least, startle them awake. Sorge again offered to keep the first watch. Flogg and Cruedwyn agreed to later shifts. Pillowy clouds grazed the sky, swallowing stars whole then spitting them out again. One by one, each fell asleep.

Ewan lay awake, quietly playing his tin whistle. For once, Hadyn didn't mind. The sound was comforting, the song strangely stirring.

"That's really good, Ewan," he murmured sleepily. "You're getting better."

Ewan paused. "Really? 'Cause I haven't practiced much. It just seems easier now, since coming here."

"Well, it sounds good."

Ewan thoughtfully played a few more notes, breathy and soft. The song ended. He lay with his arms folded behind his head, staring at the stars as if they could lead him back in time. "Sometimes I still hear her voice," he whispered. "Like when people would tell her she should have a girl. Don't stop with four boys. Don't get stuck. Remember? She would just smile and walk away, holding our hands. 'I'm not stuck with boys,' she would tell us. 'I'm blessed!'"

Hadyn scrunched his eyes, wanting sleep. Asandra had pressed enough of his buttons for the evening. Frankly, he didn't want to think about Mom right now. But Ewan pressed on.

"She'd be worried sick if she were still alive, you know? I mean, this isn't like losing us on aisle nine at Wal-Mart. This is another world. She'd freak." Sympathy flooded his voice. "Poor Dad."

He had a knack for thinking and saying stuff like that. Hadyn sighed. "One step at a time Ewan. Before long, we'll be home."

Dreamless, they slept.

CHAPTER 26

Divided

G one! He's gone!"

Full of soft urgency, the phrase soaked slowly into Ewan's thoughts like rain dripping through the branches of a tree.

"Auginn's eyes! How could we have lost him?"

As the red morning slowly crept up his face, peeling back sleep, Ewan caught little pieces of conversation volleyed back and forth. Sorge, Asandra, Flogg.

Must just be wandering . . . no, too long . . . by the river? . . . where?

Then lots of shouting. They were calling Hadyn's name. Everyone, including Asandra, scurried up and down the embankment, roaming near the black woods.

"What's going on?" Ewan mumbled, blinking. Sorge knelt beside him to study the soil around the campsite.

"There are many footprints here. Three. Four. Ewan, awake!"

"Okay, okay. Fine."

Then he saw the blank earth where Hadyn should be, but wasn't. He bolted upright.

"Where's Hadyn?"

Sorge put his hands on both Ewan's shoulders. "Don't worry. We'll find him."

"How was he *lost*?"

"No one knows. I counted, Cruedwyn counted, before we slept. Flogg was at watch. Now he's gone."

That was it. Throttling a cry of rage, Ewan dove headlong into Flogg's chest, knocking him to the ground. They tumbled. Ewan flailed his arms and fists.

"You overgrown rat! You Judas! What did you do? Sell him out? Like Gregor? Did they pay you, too?"

Sorge and Cruedwyn heaved him off, kicking and thrashing.

"Ewan, cease!" Sorge ordered. "You're acting like a fool."

"No, you are! Why can't you see it? Flogg set us up. Ask *him* where Hadyn is!"

"Nonsense," Sorge said. "You are afraid and angry, but Flogg is no more a traitor than you. Will you keep your peace if I let you go?"

Ewan fumed. Flogg adjusted his green vest, rubbed his wrinkled snout. In morning's light, his hair and beard looked like fire. Ewan spasmed a lunge once more, then quieted. When Sorge released him, the tears came. He quickly moved away so that no one could see.

Only one thought mattered. Hadyn better not be dead. He repeated that again and again. *Better not, better not.* A sense of foreboding settled on him like a trail of bread crumbs for his thoughts to follow. He tried to leave it nameless, illusory, but it kept sneaking up on him, breathing threats. *Five attacked us. Four remain. They want us dead.*

He knew what that meant for Hadyn.

"Hold fast," Sorge interrupted, "we have a plan. Listen well. I know you fear, but this tale is not yet told. We have clear tracks: three figures, no struggle. Hadyn was dragged to the river, where the tracks end. There are gouge marks in the soft earth, where they must have pulled a boat or raft ashore. Here are the facts. If they wanted him dead, we would not be having this conversation, because you would likely be dead too."

"Why three tracks? There were four that survived?"

"Only three entered camp, it appears. During Flogg's watch last night, he heard noises coming from the woods. He left camp to investigate. He saw nothing. When he returned, with the fire out and the moon covered, he failed to notice Hadyn was already gone. My guess is that the fourth made noises in the woods to distract him while the other three snuck in and carried Hadyn away." He lifted his nose, scenting the air. "Hadyn was probably drugged. The air reeks of sorcery."

Ewan peered over the gray's shoulder at the gnome, standing like a tree stump, inspecting his satchel. "Sorcery? Or deceit?"

"Ewan, you are most likely alive *because* of Flogg."

Asandra agreed. "They would have stolen you, too, if they could have. Flogg's return probably scared them away." She set about restoring the earth around their camp.

"With five, they might have tried to take you both. With only four, they could not risk it. Cruedwyn and his sword gave us the edge."

"Cursed blade," Cruedwyn mumbled. But he held the weapon lovingly.

"How are we going to track them?" Ewan asked, sinking to the ground.

"You and I are not tracking them. We're heading for Stratamore."

Ewan grit his teeth. His eyes were the gray color of steel. "I'm going for my brother."

"Lord Ewan, my job is to get you safely to the Governor. Though Helheim be emptied against me, that is what I shall do . . . deliver you safely. With my last breath, if needed. Do you understand? I am responsible for your life."

Ewan did not understand. Did not care. His legs felt rooted to the ground.

Sorge gently encouraged, "The plan is good. Flogg and Asandra will track the raiders. They listen to the land better than I. It will speak to them, lead them to Hadyn. Cruedwyn will be with them for strength of arms."

"I want a better plan."

"The raiders barely have the lead. Ewan, speed is our *best* plan. We mustn't waste time."

On cue, swordsman, gnome, and mirling passed by, hurrying toward the river. Their gear hung from their shoulders. Flogg did not look at Ewan but held his head high.

Asandra spoke as she passed by. "Solstice is in three days. I do not know what the winds say to me, but I feel a warning. Be careful, Elder."

Sorge offered his own warning. "Likewise, don't fight the jackals unless you must. The blood will only draw others. When you are trailed, don't meet their eyes and don't appear to run. Flogg, fire will help if you are outnumbered. You know this."

Flogg patted his bag, but under his crusty grimace was a look of worry. Cruedwyn, for his part, carried no such doom. His eyes sparkled, "Fear not, lad! The sword of Creed is cool and sharp again. We *will* find your brother."

He proudly brandished the metal of his blade, glinting in the sun, then tromped along. Within moments, all three had disappeared down the slope of the land toward the river's edge.

The search for Hadyn had begun.

CHAPTER 27

Crossing Argo

Ewan was growing more irritable by the minute. They needed to *go*. If he could just get in motion, he might feel part of the search for Hadyn. He needed to feel busy.

Sorge packed their few belongings and laid out the plan. They would cross the Argo, then head east, he said. Over the river, they would have open fields that bordered the woods. After a short distance, they would be on the shores of the river Hart, near to a couple of small villages, a couple of decent docks. From there, they could secure passage on a ship—very likely one heading to Stratamore.

"Sailors give wandering monks free passage," he explained. "It is considered good luck."

Even with so little gear, packing still took nearly half an hour. Then morning prayers. Then a quick scramble down to the river. By then, Ewan could only recognize the barest hint of the three figures receding in the distance, picking their way south over muck and rock. He longed to be *there,* not here.

"Blood River," Sorge said, wrinkling his nose. A well-earned name. The river was wide, deep, and foul, stinking of dead fish and bugs. Shriveled, sickly grasses clung to the rocky edge. In the early sun, the waters shone with a crimson hue.

Ewan gagged. "I can't swim that. It looks ill."

"It *is* ill. No one swims the Argo, or even sails the Argo. But there is a bridge. Just inside the forest—an old rope bridge. We must be quick."

The bank was mostly wide enough for speed, but it required intense concentration and footwork to avoid the low, stray branches, all of them covered with thorns. What Ewan had not comprehended from Asandra's story was how violent and unnatural the woods would seem. Like thousands of porcupines fanning their quills, the trees of Redthorn exploded with thorns. They were abominations of nature: tall, bulging, angry, reeking of loamy, molded earth. Their gnarled bark oozed sap like sticky gray pus. Roots curled atop the soil, feeding and drinking from an earth perversely alive: bugs and worms and mice—all deformed, elongated, blind. Even the leaves were somber toned, olive and black. Ewan felt like the forest had swallowed him alive.

"Don't look. Keep your eyes level, but speed up," Sorge urged. "Jackals watch us."

Ewan focused straight ahead, tromping over pebbles and sand and the cracked husks of freshwater mussels, measuring his stride to that of a brisk walk. Behind, Sorge shoved him even faster. Out of the corner of his vision he saw red, gleaming eyes in the underbrush and heard soft, hungry snarls.

"Don't look. Don't appear to run. The bridge is just ahead."

A blood-curdling howl ripped the air. Dozens more echoed—a chilling cacophony of bloodlust. Slashes of black and gray began darting more quickly between the trees, barely hidden in shadow. Bristling fur, wet teeth. Another howl rent the air, much closer. Ewan nearly bolted.

"Steady . . . almost there."

A sound of snapping twigs could be heard nearby, mirroring their path. They were definitely being tracked. Maybe herded. When the rope bridge finally came into view, Ewan almost laughed out loud and totally without humor. Sorge's description had failed to mention that by *old* he meant falling apart; just like by *forest*, he had actually meant Satan's obstacle course. The ropes looked ratty and old enough to have been built by Adam and Eve. *Not* confidence inspiring. But this was not the world of Adam and Eve, Ewan sorely reminded himself, breaking into a trot. The narrow footpath followed the water's edge, ending at the base of the tree.

"Climb."

Ewan stared upward. "No way."

It looked even worse up close. On the near side, several ropes were attached to a massive oak. Far across, they were lashed to another sprawling giant. In the middle, high above the river, the bridge sagged like a fat man's belly, swaying in the wind. Wooden slats that once formed the floor of the crosswalk had long ago rotted away. Only the main framework of ropes seemed secure, with a few tangled crossbracings.

No way. Not. A. Chance.

Over his shoulder, no more than forty feet away, a half dozen pairs of eyes appraised him through the thickets with cold, predatory malice. He only caught a hint of their beastly form, but they appeared much larger and more primitive than any wolves he had ever seen on the Discovery Channel. The stuff of nightmares.

Sorge spoke in steady tones, "Don't think. Just climb. When the jackals gather great enough numbers, they will attack."

Ewan panicked. He didn't like heights. "Wait, what about Cruedwyn and Asandra? How can they possibly make it all the way down the river with those things following?"

"The same way we will make it across this bridge. With courage. But be careful! If you are pricked, stand still. I will come to you."

A crude, winding staircase, carved into the trunk of the tree, wrapped steadily higher three times before reaching the bridge above. The steps were gnarled and split, barely wide enough for feet. Sorge began whacking at the thorns around the steps.

The jackals began inching toward them. Suddenly, they lunged.

"Ewan, climb—or become their next meal!"

Sweat dripping down his face, Ewan leaped up the stairs. His eyes stung, no time to wipe. Sorge was pushing from behind. He heard Sorge's staff crack against bone. A yelp. Below, the jackals snapped their frothy jaws, pawing at the base of the tree. He could barely breathe on the narrow steps, but somehow eventually reached the top platform.

"I can't do this," he quavered, looking out across the huge span, the rotting rope, the sickly waters below. "We need to do something else. Drive them away with fire. Build a raft. Anything but this. I don't do heights."

"Too late," Sorge said.

He was right. Gray everywhere. Gray streamers in the sky, lacing the sun. Raspy growls beneath, gathered in a thick knot of gray fur among the rough, gray-skinned trees. Ahead of him, a monk in gray placing sandaled feet on a very old, weathered rope. Sorge leaned out to test its weight and strength. The full braid was about half as thick as a man's clenched fist. It creaked, but held.

There were two ropes for hand grips (one notably more decayed than the other). And two for their feet, both of which seemed passable. To Ewan, it didn't matter. The rest of the bridge was a yawning chasm of water and air below. It might as well have been a hundred miles to the other side; might as well be a high-wire act over the Grand Canyon.

Sorge drew inward for a moment of silent prayer, then shuffled carefully forward. His black, bald head caught the speckled reflection of light filtering through the trees. Though the ropes wobbled, his feet gripped. Halfway across, he turned.

"Now, Ewan. Come."

He couldn't. Physically *couldn't* move except to twitch his head.

"I'm stuck."

The water passing below sounded velvety and warm. Strange as it was, he almost felt tempted to jump. The fear, boiling inside. It was absurd.

"Your world does not lie on that side of the river, Ewan. Your father, your brothers, your home all await you on *this* side."

Ewan shook his head more emphatically. No.

Sorge edged his way back. When he got close enough, he extended his staff.

"Reach for it, little brother. I can bear your weight."

No . . .

"Just stretch out your hand."

Ewan extended a trembling hand. The staff was too far. "Please come closer."

"No, you come to me. I'm here for you."

Ewan inched forward, looked down; shouldn't have looked down. Thought he might throw up. Glinting light and water, stalking, gray fur lay below. Ready with snapping teeth, deadly jaws. Ready for blood.

Blood River.

He closed his eyes.

"Easy, easy. Keep your head up. Eyes open. Head *up*! Now grab the rope with your left hand, take my staff with your right. That's it. Good."

The feel of the wood on his fingers felt like hope. He nudged along the bottom cord with his foot, put weight on it . . . slipped. Foot plunged downward. Balance off.

Pitching forward, he clawed for the staff.

"Sorge!"

"Hold!" Sorge shouted back, bracing himself, as Ewan free-fell between the ropes.

Finding, grasping the staff, Ewan held.

It was a desperate one-handed grip, swinging like a vine, until it occurred to him to reach for the staff with both hands. All kinds of thoughts flashed through his mind. Dangling above the water, Ewan thought of what his dad might be doing that very moment, sitting at his computer, unable to type, pacing, praying, on the phone with the police. Filing a Missing Person's Report. Two of them. Not having any idea that his son hung from a rope bridge above a poisonous river, lost in another world. All because he had crawled through that stupid rock!

Anger surged, but it was the sadness that focused his thoughts.

He said, "I'm not a great swimmer, Sorge."

"Get ready. One, two—"

He closed his eyes, felt a mighty heave.

"Put your feet out," Sorge said. "Now, feel the ropes. That's it, catch your wind. Slowly. Now grab here. Ewan, you need to open your eyes . . ."

His whole body felt rubbery, like boiled meat. He wrapped his arms around the ropes, catching himself like a fly in a spider's web. When he finally peeked, the view had changed. Sorge now stood behind him, *between* him and the first tree. He was on the other side of the bridge.

"You did that on purpose," he said indignantly.

"A happy coincidence, I assure you."

"Sorge, I can't do this. I feel like I'm going to throw up."

"Just take a step, Ewan. Just one. Your foot won't slip again, I promise."

"You don't understand. I *can't* do it!"

"Then we have nothing but time," Sorge said, exasperated. "So answer me a riddle."

"I don't want another stupid riddle."

"Of course not. You just want to play games. An easy life—"

"I want to be a million miles away! I want to be home with my Dad. I want Hadyn back!"

"But you can't do that!" Sorge thundered. "Just like I can't save my friend, Corus, no matter how much I wish I could. You aren't a million miles away, Ewan. You are *here*. And I am done coddling a spoiled young man who won't make up his mind." Sorge collected himself, though his expression remained stern. "I'll tell you my riddle and you'll answer it. It's a simple riddle, really. If a person pretends to sleep, *can he be awakened?*"

"That's it, that's the riddle?"

Sorge repeated it again for clarity.

Ewan snarled, refused to budge or give in. Stupid riddle games.

"Make a choice, little brother. You make much noise about how deeply you care for your brother. You rant and spew at Flogg. You want to go home. It's all very impressive sounding. And maybe I believe you. But none of that matters right now. This moment is far simpler, much weightier: What do *you* want? What do you really want?"

Ewan narrowed his eyes, didn't know how to answer.

Sorge sighed. "Just as I thought. If a man pretends to sleep, he *cannot* be wakened."

The rope bridge swayed in an unseen breeze. The dark leaves fluttered. Ewan wanted to strangle the monk.

"What in the world—?"

"Think, Ewan! It's really very simple. A sleeping man can in fact be wakened, since he is truly asleep. But a man who only *pretends* at sleep—what can you do? Ewan, we all pretend to sleep in some way or another. Likewise, we all must choose the moment of our waking. Face a thing, or do not face a thing, whatever it is. Wake or sleep. Or just sit there and talk. But I'll believe you want to go home—that you really want to see Hadyn—*when I see you standing on the ground on the other side of this river.*"

Ewan felt color rising in his cheeks, felt Sorge's eyes searching his face.

"So do you want to find your brother or not?"

Ewan bit his lip until it bled. Tears stung his eyes.

Then, lifting one foot, he stepped.

Forward.

CHAPTER 28

Death on the River

Hadyn, in a fog of pain, slowly came to realize two things: first, he had been kidnapped by zombies, and second, he was likely going to die on a foul-smelling river in whatever world lay between earth and Planet Oz. He felt like he had taken the Matrixian red pill, but instead of waking free, was now imprisoned even deeper in the nightmare.

On a raft.

It was a crude raft, barely seaworthy by the feel of the rough splinters pricking his skin and the sloshy feel of water underneath him. Almost certainly the Argo, he guessed. It had the same, unmistakable smell.

At first, still groggy from the drink they forced down his throat—a nasty, smoky liquid—he had slept. Upon waking, slack-mouthed and numb, he lay still, attentive to the sounds around him. As the concoction finally wore off enough for him to collect his wits, he realized it wasn't dark, he was blindfolded. And he wasn't paralyzed, his hands were simply bound behind his back.

A delicate lacework of light falling through the trees moved across his face. He felt the web of warmth and brightness. In the stillness of water, wind, and leaves, he sensed the nearness of others on the raft. Intuitively, he knew what had happened.

Stay calm. Breathe.

He thought of Ewan first, followed by a rash of wild fancies. Jump and swim for shore? Wouldn't do any good, not with his hands tied. Nor would it matter to shout, or they would have gagged him. And, since he was alive, they must not want him dead. Yet.

The others were probably searching for him even now. Maybe they were close?

Ewan. Are you here? Are you alright?

He cleared his throat, feeling timid. These were brutes. Would he be struck for breaking the silence?

"H . . . hello?" He craned his neck like a blind man. The raft bobbed. Water splashed his cheek. "Can someone talk to me? Will someone tell me what is going on?"

Whispers. Silence. Whispers. He felt the weight of eyes staring at him. Then a shadow blotted out the gossamer sun. Something hard, metallic, cuffed him across the forehead. No time for pain. Only swooning darkness.

Yes, he would be struck.

He awoke later—how long?—in a crumpled pile on the same raft, hearing the same watery sounds. His elbow, bent under his body, tingled as the nerves awakened. Everything was as before, except for deeper shadows and cooler air, smelling of evening. That, and a splitting headache. He was getting tired of being pecked, chased, knifed, and whacked. Blood stuck to his cheek, in his hair. He stomach-crunched himself into an upright position. A blinding light shot through his head. He nearly wretched.

That one's gonna leave a mark.

"My eyes hurt," he said softly. "My head hurts. I can't run. Will someone please . . . will you please take off this blindfold?"

More whispering. His captors seemed conflicted by his request. He recognized the first speaker's numb, ashen tone as the voice from the Stone House.

". . . no, Grayday. She would be angry."

"Nemesia said 'healthy and well.' Does that gash on his forehead look healthy? Hider remembers what she said. Don't you Hider? Maybe it needs tending."

Hider answered with a grunt. A sort-of argument followed, grousing and mostly incoherent. In the end, hands clumsily pulled the blindfold from his eyes to hang in a loop around his neck. Hadyn stared into the face of a young man, perhaps seventeen, with deep, storm-colored eyes and a face of pale, sculpted ivory, or at least it seemed like it might be, under all the grime. The boy had no instinct for space, staying within inches of Hadyn's face. Curiously, though he had just argued with the girl, he carried no trace of a grudge in his eyes. He was entirely unbothered in his yielding.

Perched on his haunches, he fixed his eyes on Hadyn. Behind him, sitting cross-legged, was a girl and another boy. They also stared.

Grayday. Hider, he guessed.

The girl looked as if she might be pretty underneath the dirt and unkept hair. She was thin, waifish, ruined, like a puppy who is never fed. Maybe sixteen. Maybe thirteen. Hard to say. There was little shape to her. Her expression was a watery mixture of wide-eyed curiosity and wide-eyed dread, as if she were constantly holding her breath and constantly wondering why. Hider was overweight, with sweaty cheeks and a double chin. His shoulder and side were wounded, his cloak torn and streaked with dried blood. Leaning to one side, favoring the wound, he winced on occasion, but little more. Based on the gashes Hadyn saw, he should have been wailing. His eyes conveyed minimal recognition of pain.

And then there was another, a young lady roughly Hadyn's age. She was clothed in layers of scarlet and white, embroidered at the neck, clasped with silver. She wore fine sandals. Her hair was long and brown. Hadyn only caught a glimpse of her, knew she was afraid. She lay crumpled like a pile of rags, bound and blindfolded.

Hadyn gathered all this in a few brief moments: the vessel of rough cut logs, lashed with vines, barely afloat; the bare movement of thick brown water grown fetid with moss and slime and small, decaying animals—frogs, rats, and such—lining the rocky shore; the ghostly, contorted trees all around, carpeted with red thorns. There was little sky to see above the clutching branches. Little warmth to feel from the hidden, setting sun. The trees looked like some force had exploded from within, spined and angry, vomiting blood.

A rush of adrenaline demanded he flee, cry out, leap. Madness leaned toward him with leafy arms. He felt like joining the other prisoner, the silent girl, crumpled beyond hope. The nearness of the three who watched him, who had stalked and now captured him, caused the air to shrink around him, siphon away his lucidity. Almost.

Hadyn licked his lips. "There were five of you."

The leader shrugged. "Your swordsman felled Hurter at the river. The other was too wounded and weak. Poverty, my sister. We left her to the beasts of the forest."

Hadyn struggled to maintain a flat expression. Though horrified at the leader's matter-of-factness in disposing of his own sister, he could not afford to appear weak.

"Do you have names?" he said quickly, to cover himself. "Real names?"

Grayday offered a wan smile, as if at a memory. Hadyn took it as a good sign.

"Come on," he said carefully, prodding for more. "Everyone has a name. You know . . . what your parents named you when you were bor—"

"Names mean nothing. Names are illusions," said the leader. "I am called Shameface. But in truth, I am nameless."

"Alright," Hadyn said slowly. "But I don't really feel right calling you that, if that's okay."

"I am nameless, also," Grayday joined in. Her eyes were a cradle of wounds, her lips a plastic grin. "My parents named me something else, once. Then they sold me in the village to a fisherman who had lost his wife. He wanted a cook, a maid. He had . . . needs. My parents couldn't feed me, didn't care to try.

They already had five mouths besides theirs and mine. I was one too many, they said. A mistake. Said I should go be somebody else's mistake, not theirs."

Solemn, matter-of-fact, she did not lower her eyes or look away. Hadyn did. But Grayday was not finished. "Hider will not tell you, but he was the son of a wealthy merchant. His father called him pig. Said he was slow, stupid. Fat. Worthless. Shameface was the son of a blacksmith in Bitterland. Trained to make pickaxes and hammers for the miners. He was a poor apprentice, made soft hammers that broke on the rock. He brought shame on his father. His father cast shame upon him, as did all the village. The Bittermen take pride in their metal."

"Our old names were lies," Shameface explained in monotone. "Nemesia has given us newer names. Truer names. We borrow them only to speak to one another. The new names tell a story, stripped of lying words. And we are glad."

"Birth names lie. Names of pain do not," Hider mumbled.

Grayday brushed a hair from her face. "You see, life is pain. So . . ."

She waited for Hadyn to catch on. When he didn't reply, she finished for him.

". . . only the nameless escape."

Water lapped at the raft, squirting through the gaps between logs. It was a miracle they stayed afloat. Hadyn felt a battle beginning. He felt a funnel spinning inside, sucking conscious thought toward a dark edge. Grayday's twisted logic had left him open-mouthed, speechless.

"You have had pain," Grayday said, cocking her head to one side. It was a statement, more than a question. "Everyone has."

Hadyn managed a thought in the swirling tide. Grayday's eyes climbed into his own, bored through his skull, demanding response. Three words slipped out, knifelike.

"My mother died."

"And the name she gave you?"

"Hadyn."

Shameface picked at the words as if they were pieces of food stuck in his teeth. "There you go. Hadyn is a name of memory and memory is linked to hope. To hold on to your name is to always remember the falseness of that hope. You, that boy, the one named Hadyn—*you* are the one who has felt the sorrow of a mother dying. Hope and life and promise. Lies, all of it, for they died with her. Another boy with a different name has not felt these things, because he has not borne your name. But you have, and so you are bound, name and being, to a lie."

Hadyn reeled. "No."

"Yes, you cannot avoid it. Because hope and memory are also bound to that name."

Hider spoke softly, "Those hopes will never come true."

Grayday still wore her eerie smile. Almost singsong, she said, "The nameless are free. Free to be. Free to see. Only the nameless are free."

As if on cue, Shameface pointed to the other prisoner. "This girl. She is rich and unwise. She thinks she is loved. She has no future. But she *believes* she does. What good is such a worthless one, clinging to lies? Clinging to old words and names. We have offered her truth. We offered to let her soul become lost, as ours. She refused."

Shameface scooted near to the girl, who shivered at the

awareness of his unfelt hand. The boy looked at Hadyn, then rolled the girl, hands bound, off the raft, into the water.

His face was blank as stone. He didn't even turn to watch her, as she writhed and kicked for help.

"No!" Hadyn cried. He tried to leap to his feet, to wrench his hands free. But like the girl in the water, he was bound. As he clumsily gained his legs, Hider slammed a knee into his stomach, doubling him over. He was clubbed, again, on the back of the head. Collapsing to the raft, darkness closed upon him swiftly. The last sounds he heard were that of the girl, thrashing in the water.

Thrashing. Screaming. Then burbling silence.

And Grayday, almost sounding pleased, singing again, "Now she is nameless. Now she is free."

CHAPTER 29

The Devourer

They will enter the bay soon," Nemesia informed the shadowed man before her. He was a towering figure, horned and helmeted with iron, caped in purple the color of spilled wine. He wore shimmering chain mail. A huge sword was slung at his back. In the low light, all else was hidden. If someone from the mainland were to see him, they would fearfully salute and call him Baron—Baron von Gulag. (They might wonder, for rumor was that the Baron had died many years ago.) His name was true enough and came with all the right trappings, but his appearance was more like a suit of armor, a change of clothes—the latest fashion, for convenience among the world of men. The being inside was far more ancient than the once-powerful Baron. His potency stretched back to the beginning, from whence he earned his true name.

Devourer.

Devourer of life, of peace. Deceiver of old. He was there at the Pillar of Reckoning, when the world was young. There, convincing Yhü Hoder, full of bitterness and shame for the doom laid upon him, to pull the string and release the arrow. Ripe with malice, the Devourer had watched as Hoder's poisoned dart struck true, killing the great Aion where he dangled in the air. The Devourer had laughed then, with a voice that tore mountains apart. Laughed and known terror when Aion returned to life nine days later. Aion had passed judgment. Kr'Nunos was the cunning voice, the witness of death, the spark in the thought of evil. He was not allowed to remain, banished by the reborn Aion. So came the Horned Lord to the Wild South, long ages past. So began the ruin of the world. Kr'Nunos, Lord of the Wild Hunt. Eventually, Keeper of Hel. Knowing his true identity, Nemesia addressed him with something near reverence.

"I have sent a swift vessel to retrieve them and bring them here. It won't be long now, Great One."

"Them, you say?" the warlord rumbled. His deep voice rippled as thunder rolling over hills, shifting in and out of phase. It sizzled with dark energy. "Both brothers?"

"No. Only one. The other remains under the monk's protection."

The Devourer slowly clenched his gloved left fist. The sound of the black leather stretching was a warning.

"I am not pleased, witch."

Nemesia was no coward. She held her head high. The emerald in the circlet of silver on her brow gleamed like stars dancing in the sky, falling to earth. Her dark eyes flickered. She stood alone with the huge figure in a room of twilight and rock deep inside the Isle of Apaté. From above, javelins of light rained down through a series of slits in the central chamber of the Tower of Ravens. The air smelled of sandalwood and cloves, of ancient, dusty scrolls and leather-bound books, scattered about, marked with ominous, unreadable characters. The room was suffocating with malice.

"I have foreseen," she said quickly, softly, "That the oldest is the key to finalizing my . . . *our* plans. He has caused my leaders to question, which has not happened in many moons. When he falls, their spirits shall fail. Never to rise again. The work will be at long last complete."

"You underestimate the younger. He, too, has power. I have felt it. My Watcher sensed it, before he was overcome by the mirling. *Your* mirling."

Nemesia flicked her eyes nervously, ignoring the implication.

"Perhaps. But the boy is unaware."

"He stands on a threshold, passing from boy to man."

Nemesia dared to challenge. She raised her voice, slightly. "*I* have also watched, Great One. I have spilled blood that I might look into his soul. I have seen fear."

Baron von Gulag laughed. The sound was uproarious and mocking. It shook the Tower. "Such a mighty S'Qoth witch, yet such a great fool! Never, *never* doubt the raw power of a young human heart, especially one trained upon destiny. Wherever they wait, fate finds them, and one day, wakes them. It is the way of Aion, whom I hate."

"No, Great One. Surely . . . he is caged. He thinks his brother is more special than he."

"Silence, woman! He carries a name, unstripped, with fierceness and pride. He is not like your others. A name, like oil to fire! Provoke such flames in the boy and they will rage in the man. You are surely a woman, or you would know this."

Nemesia's face flushed. In her shame, she was made brave. "Are you so strong already?" she cooed. "Is your shape true? Or will you bellow at the moon tonight, dripping dew from your antlers, forgetting who you are? Are you seated in the north, ready for battle? Are the ships yet built, the Goths yet ready? The Cleavers awakened? The jackals amassed? The Watchers released? You have spent centuries roaming. You have claimed the shape of Baron von Gulag. Clever! But are you ready to face the mustered will of this land?"

The Devourer smiled dangerously. "My time is near."

"Well my time is now," Nemesia hissed. "I prepare the way before you. I weaken the will of both land and people. I prepare the shadows that sap the soul. Ten thousand Watchers will soon pour through the door I shall open for them. Why? Because I have the strength *now*. And I have brought the oldest outlander here by my power! Not yours, Baron von Gulag! You forget the ally I am. You forget the power I offer. I am stealing a generation—an entire generation—all for you. Even now, my fleet of ships is bringing thousands to my shores." She approached the heavy drapes of the massive northern window, flinging them open with a thought and a twitch of her hand. Outside, sweeping down the expanse of misty, dark grass, down a long, shallow hill flowing toward the sea, she pointed. There, streaming up the hill toward the tower, line upon line of hundreds of lost plodded along, shoulders hunched, eyes adrift, faces void of passion or thought or meaning. Like shifting fog, clinging and curling up the grass and rocks, the Nameless came, beckoned to the numbing lure of forgetfulness. And beyond, in the midst of the sea, more ships coming.

"I have amassed an army of the living dead, walking bombs, waiting to explode. They are my own, empty shells waiting to be filled with whatever I tell them to believe. They have no conscience. No power of thought. They are entirely mine. Has such a thing ever been done? Has it, O, Great One?"

As she spoke, the air around Nemesia became gray and blurry. She seemed to grow in both stature and terror. The Devourer, cloaked as a man, watched from the shadows, arms folded, unmoved. When he stepped into the beams of light, his dark eyes narrowed threateningly. He had a scarred face that was fierce and seductively handsome. Almost imperceptibly, he stretched two fingers toward her. The air in the room became a marinade of power.

Nemesia convulsed. Her body shook. Her exalted stature shrunk as if melting. Within moments she was on her knees, limp, bowed over, gasping for air.

From someplace deep under his armor, deep within his barreled chest, he spoke, his voice pushing outward against the stones of the tower until they strained against their mortar. In truth, he never spoke above a whisper. "You are useful to me, witch. Never forget that. It is all you have."

He lowered his hand. She thirstily gulped for air.

"I have been planning for a thousand years," the Devourer said, "and a thousand more before that. And a thousand more before that. Unfathomable plans. Unstoppable plans. The power is mine. The plans are mine. The kingdom is mine, and all it contains."

Nemesia rubbed her throat. Her face was white. "Yes . . . Great One."

"This is what you will do," he said. "Find out how the outlanders have come to be here . . . come to my world. Who called them? Archibald the fool? The coward? Why did they answer the call? Discover this. Then either convert them or destroy them. Do this, and perhaps I will allow you to continue to serve me."

He spun round, plum cloth rippling behind him. Then stopped, glancing once more out the window. He did not turn, did not need to see Nemesia glowering, spittle gathered at the corners of her ruby lips. Her smooth skin had turned pale with rage.

"One more thing," he said. "Your army is nearly gathered. It pleases me. It is greater than I thought you capable of. At Solstice tomorrow, release the darkness. It is time."

Staff of Shades

The rest of the day, Nemesia fumed and fought and cursed the Baron. She focused all her strength to spite his last instruction: *release the darkness.* She found no peace.

But powerful or no, she was, in the end, a witch. Which meant her soul was broken, a city without walls, constantly emptying itself, able to hold nothing in reserve. Hers was a brutal burden, a playland of iron and thorns. Ever, she was in torment. Ever, she was spent.

Sorcery was a grand illusion, lawlessness masquerading as power. Acolytes of the dark arts usually discovered too late the lie: they do not truly *gain* power. They surrender it. Slowly, in hidden ways, they are reduced to mere slaves, servants of darker, more clever spirits, who exert their cunning and will, leaving shells behind unwitting channels, transmission points, that evil might gain a foothold in the world of men.

So it was that the will of the Devourer now pressed hard on Nemesia's soul. As the day wore on, she tried in vain to compose a moment of unconflicted silence. But vengeance and blood beckoned and she could not resist. Thinking she mocked the warlord, in rage and defiance, she slaughtered a cage full of mice, drank their blood until it ran down her neck and belly. She cut herself and called upon gods of fire and darkness. She screamed until foam formed on her lips. She pulled her hair out in chunks. Nothing she did was absent of emotion. Having long ago surrendered the sovereignty of reason to blood and fervor and vile compulsions, she had grown strong in the dark arts, for this was the terrible secret at the heart of witchcraft.

Long ago, light and joy had passed from her world. Ever, she *thirsted*.

As the tormented day turned to a sleepless, tormented night, and then dawn turned to noon, she was, at last, compelled to obey. She had no choice. She was a city without walls.

So she took the Staff of Shades and climbed the steps of her high tower to the crow's nest atop, fluttering with wings. The flagstone floor was warm in the sun. A dozen birds ringed the tower ridge. Their beaded eyes watched her, ruthless and focused.

The weakened blood of Auginn. Watching. It was a delicious irony.

The Staff of Shades was a prized possession. Long thought lost, she had paid a dear price to find and reclaim it from the Abbey, before they cast her out. For what? For pursuing deeper things, deeper truths? Truths beyond mystery, yes. Beyond the covering of light. It was, in fact, the beginning of her great plan. The Staff was a relic of a different kind of menace, the age of old Hhyss One-Eye and the traitorous Raquel, wife of the great Duke Tiernon. It was Raquel's ancient ring, and a long-buried manuscript of her sorcery, that first began twisting Nemesia's mind in her private studies at the Black Abbey—the brightest of Bishop Cassock's young pupils—two decades hence.

The Staff was carved of willow wood, trimmed in silver, marked with evil runes that seemed to shift shape with the light. It was a weapon of great power. Though it was heavy in her hands, once she took it up, she could not be free of it. It spoke to her in the voice of the Baron.

Release me . . .

The stone atop the tower was carved with odd geometries: concentric circles, star shapes, other markings. Around the edges of the platform, Nemesia kept a garden of snapdragons and flycatchers, and in the center was a socket. Here, she mounted the Staff. Today was High Solstice, the peak of summer's light. A holy day, by design perfect, therefore, to challenge the sun's supremacy. More than that, to challenge the hidden despotic rule of Aion in faraway Isgurd.

"Thus I pervert thee, O brightest of days," she whispered. It was called *Alban Heruin*. The irony might have been even more delicious if her plan could have fallen on one of the great Taines. But High Solstice wasn't a festival of ritual cleansing, as were the Holy Festivals of Tyr Taine, Gwyl Taine, and Ayl Taine, when land, fire, and water were renewed and defilements broken. Part of the glory of the Blacks was to execute the Taines, but it had been a long time. The books that spoke of them had long ago crumbled to dust. Gray-haired nannies had no memory, nor their grandparents, nor their grandparent's grandparents, of ever seeing one performed.

Only the Abbeys remembered, and they were now powerless. With the Severing Blade lost, what could be done?

For Nemesia, these were rich, but distant considerations. With High Solstice, her aims were far simpler. Alban Heruin was a bright day of merriment and feasting, joy and wine. She intended to make it a day of darkness and dread. Light offered color and hope, but darkness was an oily beast, a thief of virtue. All the vices of man were committed mostly in darkness: murder; theft; the secret, unrestrained sins of the flesh. So, too, the Nameless were held in the spell of her power most easily when night fell or a storm came and the sky turned foul. Darkness invited evil. Thus the brilliance. To plunge the entire realm into shadow, colorless as winter, empty as a starless sky, would serve a threefold purpose: First, to sap the will of already weakened men; second, to lay out honey for the Watchers, to summon what few were scattered across the land and, in succoring them, gain strength for the release of many more; third and most important, Nemesia foresaw that it would at last complete her grand design. The Nameless would be plunged beyond mere lethargy into the final throes of irreversible despair. The collapse of the outlander would seal her plans.

Release the darkness . . .

At long last, their faltering souls would yield name and nature—no more resistance. As the hues of a living world fell into gloom, gladly would they surrender the emotional burden of hope (and with hope, responsibility) to the numbing comfort of insignificance. To gaze at a sky burdened with shadows would seem a fitting conclusion to the pain of their lives. Meaninglessness would offer them a way out. No need to struggle anymore, to believe it could be better, much less that the task might fall to them to make it better. In a colored world, they might have been known or loved.

They might be tempted to care. In a gray world, there was nothing to care for. Give in. Expect nothing. Feel nothing, except rage. And blame. Blame others and give rage to all. Pour out rage, like water from the fountains of the deep.

A world without hope is not worth keeping. Best to just destroy it and end the pain.

So might the kingdom pass into oblivion.

Though she hated the blind obedience forced upon her by Kr'Nunos, High Solstice had been her plan all along. Indeed, the day of Tyr Taine was the perfect day, the perfect symbol; for all the world to know that she, Nemesia the S'Qoth, had brought them to despair. The very thought unleashed insatiable hunger within.

As the sun crept to its apex, she raised her arms, began chanting, calling for the winds of the east to mingle with the winds of the south, to rise in fury, to become unnatural. She spoke the name of each rune on the staff, along with its matching word in the old languages of Hel and suffering. She called for Watchers to gather to her, unseen, to add their will and lust and energy to her purpose. It might have been hours or days she stood in that moment, transcending time, but slowly, she sensed the gathering of invisible malevolence around her. The presence of many minds began rattling in her own, growing with intensity, gnawing at her awareness. The air grew thick with gnashing and claws, swirled with the windless flapping of many dark wings. A crescendo of voices threatened to tear Nemesia's thoughts from her conscious control, to shred her personality. She began to tremble and shake violently. As the Watchers slipped through, taking possession of her body, her eyes rolled into the back of her head. She screamed. The sound became a stream of strange words. It sounded like a nest of iron hornets scraping wings, like tearing metal, over and over.

When the last word left her lips, she collapsed. The voices stopped. The air around the Staff seemed to draw inward, bending light and time. It compressed a moment, held, then in a rush of air, dilated outward. Darkness spewed from the crown of the Staff like a sick man's vomit. Incomprehensible quantities of thick, oily smoke—unlike any fire ever created—spat skyward. The substance was drawn from unseen realms, from the soul of murder, from the world of Watchers and the deep reaches of Undrwol. Passing through the rune-carved wood the way blood leaks from a wound, it stained the sky. It did not block the sun; it ate the sun. It did not dissipate, as might steam or smoke. It thickened. It was Unlight.

Then came the winds. Stirring at first from the south, then the east, crosswinds sucked the shadows high into the sky, began blowing them north and west across the island. Heading for the Wyld Sea and the mainland. Over the immediate vicinity of the Tower of Ravens, the sun was already being blotted out.

Nemesia lay unconscious on the ground for many hours as the Staff of Shades worked its ill design. When at last she awoke, a great shadow covered half the Isle.

It had only just begun.

"Now . . . ," she whispered, rising. The darkness fanned into the air like ink spilled in clear water. In her inner ear, she still heard the shrieking of many Watchers, urging the darkness on, feeding it with their malice, feeding *on* it. Watchers tore at her thoughts, consuming her mind. They would devour her entirely if they could. The Staff was the beginning of their long-awaited doorway back into the world of men. They could sense it. They had been imprisoned for so long. They, too, were rabid with thirst. She knew this, knew the danger.

She also knew they could not devour. Not yet. They were trapped still behind the thin veil of spirit. Bound to the coldest depths of Helheim if they did not pass through soon to the other side, to the living world of men. Only temporarily, and only if summoned by power, and the will of another, could they breach the Law and roam the world of men. Even then, only as disembodied spirits. How they longed for flesh! To have it, to eat it. To wear it, as did their master, the Horned Lord. At present, they could only torment. Nemesia heard their laughter, like a knife in her mind. She squeezed her eyes against the pain.

"Now . . . ," she whispered again, tensely. Her pale skin had turned blue, and there was no sun to warm it. Fed by Hel, the Staff would not stop spewing poison until the farthest reaches of Bitterland were cast into shadow. For days and weeks and months—as long as needed.

She raised her head, heavy and haughty.

"*Now* the world will know. Now the Abbey will know, and Cassock, who cast me out. Now the Nameless will know. Now even the great Horned Lord of old will know. I am *Nemesia*. I bring all the world to ruin."

CHAPTER 31

Tales of Old

Ewan stood placidly beside Sorge aboard a broad-bellied frigate named *Python's Eye*, loaded with casks of Befjorg mead and crates of prized whitefish, fresh from the cold waters of the north, packed in salt. The vessel slid, windborne, down the river Hart, a mercifully clean and mild waterway compared to the wretched Argo. The liquid sun sank low as sweeping columns of clouds boiled upward in the western sky. Mild breezes from the south had been with them all day on their trek across the stretch of grassland separating the two rivers. With each step away from the woods, Ewan's heart had lightened. But it wasn't until they had hailed a boat and boarded that he felt he could truly relax. Still, he wasn't entirely free. To the west, fanged with red, like jackals grinning after a kill, Redthorn grasped leaf and tooth toward them. But its reach fell short. Soon, they passed safely by.

"I think I was even more terrified of the thorns than the jackals. We barely made it."

"Two great evils, and the wisest of the wise do not understand why. It has simply always been so."

"Let me try that again," Ewan said in a chiding tone. "What I was trying to say is thank you. In case you didn't notice."

Sorge rumbled uncomfortably. "Say it then. Don't dance. A man should not pretend with words."

Ewan rolled his eyes, as water foamed beneath the keel. "Are you *always* this way?"

"Yes. No," the monk faltered. He coughed. "What I'm trying to say is you're welcome."

They both grinned, fell silent. Ewan's thoughts, drifting from Hadyn to his father, felt like bruises. They were tender, but he pressed against them anyway, needing to feel the sting. Before long, his dad would have no choice but to assume they were kidnapped or dead. Two more lives to grieve. It seemed awful to think about. And for what? Reggie would have no answers. Only one more mystery to drive him further into silence and despair.

Staring across the gently folding current, Sorge apparently noticed his need for distraction. Under normal circumstances, what he offered would have been better than money and iPods. "Let us pass the time usefully, yes? Ask me anything, Lord Ewan—three questions, if you will. Then you must rest."

It was a good offer because Ewan, if nothing else, was a very curious young man. He was a compendium of trivia. He liked to know stuff. This time, his heart simply wasn't in it. Running his forefinger along the deck railing, feeling the waxy grain of the wood, he said, "I just want to go home, Sorge." He sighed. "Tell me about the Watchers, I guess."

In response, Sorge slumped against the rail, lowered his hood over his face. He paused, as if carefully selecting his words, then began to sing a melancholy song. It rolled out from his chest, mixing with the frothy music of the river, mixing like wine and sorrow and sunsets.

"Auginn fierce and Runinn wise
Talons, feather, endless cries,
Great black wings, taking flight
No more, no more, to soar the skies
Brother-blood, Olfadr's friends,
No more, no more, be seen again"

He took a deep breath. Ewan was surprised at the depth of sadness in his eyes. "So begins the tale of faraway Isgurd, and its ruler Olfadr, great and ageless. And of the two giant ravens, the brothers Auginn and Runinn, Olfadr's most beloved animals, whose names meant 'War' and 'Glory.'"

As the frigate *Python's Eye* cut south through better waters, Sorge explained, "A long time ago, Olfadr banished Kr'Nunos to the Wild South. To secure his exile, guards were placed upon the borders, that he might never return. Auginn, the larger of the two brothers—the most loyal and warlike and given to anger— was chosen for this task. Before he departed, Olfadr bestowed upon Auginn and his descendants many, many eyes to enable their constant vigil. To see in all directions, see and never sleep. In truth, Auginn probably did not need them. He knew the Devourer well, having traveled hill and dale on countless hunts with Aion."

"Aion. Olfadr's son. The High Prince."

Sorge nodded. "This was in the time before the days of evil, when Aion and Kr'Nunos (whose true name is now forgotten) had been the best of friends. Then came the betrayal at the Pillar, and the exile, and Auginn's vigil to *watch*. To protect Karac Tor from Kr'Nunos's evil.

"Meanwhile, in the Wild South, Kr'Nunos turned his vigor and craft toward shape shifting. Eventually, he became so skilled he lost his original shape and could not get it back. Yet with Auginn and his children ever watchful at the borders, the land remained safe."

Sorge sighed, feeling the wind on his face, like memory. "Kr'Nunos was tireless in his attempts to return. He hated the Watchers and their ruthless, righteous patrol against him. Eventually learning of the wild magic of water, he devised a plan. He would hide himself in the belly of the great sea monster, Lavtalion. Promised rulership of the seas, Lavtalion agreed and swallowed him whole. Thus, Kr'Nunos passed under the Watchers' eyes, deep underwater. But it was a long journey. In his hunger, the Devourer began to consume the great beast from within. Lavtalion went as far north as the Hödurspikes, searching for the coldest water possible to ease his pain. He found the hidden passage to Undrwol in the underground river Gjoll, at the deep roots of Helheim where all the world's waters eventually flow. There, Lavtalion was betrayed, and gutted from the inside out, for Kr'Nunos would not share dominion of the seas."

Ewan shriveled his face. "Gross."

"Brutal, cunning, and powerful in shape shifting, Kr'Nunos emerged from Hel disguised as a prince of men. The northern Watchers did not recognize him, having never seen the Devourer, nor having any knowledge of his shape. On the high peak of Mount

Agasag, Kr'Nunos coaxed and seduced them, bemoaning their unfair restraint at Aion's command, lauding the freedom to fly as they wished, as they *deserved*, if only they could abandon their sentry. He promised them great fame if they ever flew among men, rather than being confined to the extreme borders where no eye could behold their beauty and strength. At Agasag, he told them, he would summon power to liberate them forever. Sufficiently overcome by his smooth words, the northern Watchers tricked all their brethren into attending a great council on the mountaintop. Even Auginn himself attended. None knew the trap that was laid. With the body and blood of the great beast, Lavtalion, Kr'Nunos had already laid a thick web of sorcery on the whole mountain. In the presence of his many sons, Auginn was slain. Thus passed the great lord of birds.

"The Watchers found themselves trapped now in both witchcraft and bloodguilt, able neither to fly nor fight, for the power of Auginn's murder and Lavtalion's blood had dedicated the mountain for evil. Weighed down by the magic of Kr'Nunos, he disembodied all ten thousand strong, ripping their spirits from their flesh. So it is, they remain evil spirits to this day."

Sorge shook his head, as if still hearing their cries. "It is said their screams were heard for weeks thereafter, all the way to Röckval."

Salty breezes caught in Ewan's hair. A sailor timidly approached the two of them, grinning doltishly. The man was ridiculously skinny, even more ridiculously tall.

"Don't mean to interrupt or nothing, but may I fetch ya anything, Elder? Water or wine or apples?"

"We are quite fine, thanks. Grateful for passage to Stratamore. We require nothing."

"I'd like an apple," Ewan said. His stomach was growling.

"An apple then for the Elder's charge. Coming right up!" The man shuffled away quickly and hurried back, eagerly shining the red fruit on his dirty shirt. He handed it to Ewan. Ewan bit into the pale flesh hungrily, wiping the juice from his lips.

"Delicious. Thank you."

The praise emboldened the man. He turned to Sorge confidentially. "The captain's seeing a storm on the morrow's winds. Changin' south to east, which aren't normal. Never a good wind come from the Jawbone, so they say." He coughed, not bothering to cover his mouth. His breath stank of rotten gums. "Pray yer blessing on the ship, Elder—if'n we find favor with ye. And I'll be sure to pitch a coin at the Chantry in Stratamore when we land." He ducked low, shuffled off, putting his hands on the first mop he could find and swabbing with the hard dedication of nervous superstition. His shipmates, busily at work lashing lines and hoisting cargo, drew near to him to whisper and, perchance, console their fears with news of a sacred blessing.

Sorge, scanning the near horizon, said, "The Bay of Champions is usually mild this time of year. But a summer squall is to be feared for sure." He whiffed the air, glancing at the swirls of color in the clouds gathering to the east, then at the crewmen stealing furtive glances his way. Ewan thought he looked perturbed. "They are slaves, full of fear. But something has shifted. A storm *is* coming. At High Solstice, no less."

Ewan, whose imagination was still trapped on the peak of Mount Agasag, said, "But how can the Watchers escape Hel? Like that one Asandra caught? If they're trapped there, how do they get free?"

Sorge put his back to the railing, propping both elbows behind him. "Worship. Flesh. Since they were seduced by the promise of human praise, they gain power from devotion. Holy places cause them pain, while darkness gives them sanctuary. Drawn to the dark mysteries of unseen realms, men often *feel* them and wrongly perceive their presence as divine. They build sacred groves and shrines, as we saw in the Shimlings. It is a dark circle. If enough devotion is given, the veil of their curse lifts and a door opens between worlds." He paused, noting Ewan's wrinkled brow. "It is not so hard to understand. Since they were given to protect men, the will of men directs them, attracts them. Passage from Undrwol in spirit form is the beginning, but when blood is added to the worship, the evil is multiplied. The Watchers consume the flesh of the sacrifice. Whatever flesh they consume is the flesh they gain—never again lovely bodies, but maggoted corpses of claw and wing. Once more embodied, they kill without mercy. Nights turn red with slaughter. And generation after generation, the people never learn."

Ewan shuddered. A memory crested like a wave in his thoughts, of a Watcher, covered with eyes and hatred, raging. Watching *him.*

The story was finished. Night had fallen, time for stars and moon, masked in the east by a heavy drape of clouds, just as the sailor had said. Sorge spread his fingers on Ewan's head as if bestowing a blessing. He smiled playfully, even winked. "Now I will show you how wise I am, by guessing your next question: If Auginn's line are the Watchers, what are the Call Birds that brought you here? Eh? But you are a smart boy. You already know the answer to that, don't you?"

Ewan thought for a moment. "I'm guessing the other bird, Runinn."

"Indeed. Runinn and his four sons became the legendary Call Birds. They summoned many great souls." He frowned, puzzled.

"But here, my knowledge fails. All five were slain calling the Champions of the greatest age of peace Karac Tor has ever known. Yet . . . *four* birds came to your world?"

Ewan nodded.

"*Hmm.* I can only guess what is at play here, based on old legends. Archibald alone will know the answer. I must say, with this one, he has greatly surprised me."

He folded his arms. "Time for sleep. Last question."

"Okay, where'd you get that armband? The one you try to hide."

Sorge held his gaze, then slowly drew it away toward the moon, still visible on the dark rim of the eastern clouds.

"I had a friend once. His name was Corus, the second son of a second son of a second son, stretching back many generations—a special thing for the Lotsley clan. He was an extraordinary man, the last, great Champion of our world. He gave it to me."

His face closed tight as a lock without a key. He shuffled over to the captain.

"Swing round the horn due west before morning," he said. "You'll miss the storm, I sense. I have friends we need to pick up on our way to the city."

Night came. Sleep came. Before drifting off, Ewan played a few simple songs on his flute. Laying on his back, staring at the stars, hearing his own music, it felt like maybe if he closed his eyes, he could wish himself back home. Then came sleep and many dreams. In one, he heard again the melody that had opened the runestone. Only this time the tune was sung by a bright, haunting female voice—too high to be human. In the dream, he was blindfolded, groping for the voice, spellbound by the quiet power of the song. A song of doors opening, closing. Suddenly, the woman appeared before him. She had silver skin. He asked her name. *Nine,* she answered. In another dream, he was given a treasure chest. When he reached inside, his hands found a long, thin object. It was his tin whistle. When he pulled it out, it became a sword.

The visions came fast and hard, fading just as swiftly, replaced with a deep, dreamless slumber. Later, Ewan would struggle to recall them at all, though they seemed so vivid at the time. He woke, briefly, sweating, then laid back down. A breeze blew. Crickets chirped. The steady, rolling waters of the Hart carried him and Sorge under a starless sky toward Champion's Bay.

CHAPTER 32

The Book of Names

Nestled in the lush valley at the base of The Great Rim, the White Abbey was a towering monument to the brilliance, strength, and long life of the first man, Yhü Hoder. Not so much the Abbey, per se, as the enormous edifice of white marble at its heart. The structure was a huge, perfect cube, one hundred paces square, polished white, blinding as the noon sun. It had no adornments, no spectacular, gilded columns or ornate craftsmanship, yet its simplicity and sheer size commanded awe from everyone who beheld it, with mortarless seams that were finer than human hairs and nearly invisible to the naked eye. This was the Hall of Ages, built single-handedly by Yhü to house hundreds of thousands of vellum sheets which comprised the venerated Book of Names.

". . . and here, planted in front of the Hall nine hundred years ago, is the great tree, the Ash of Uisnwch. Brought by Soriah, may he be blessed in Isgurd forever." Alethes, High Priest of the White Abbey, waved his hand absently ahead of their path to a great and beautiful tree, but his voice was flat, his eyes sunken. Having fasted for days without food or water, his features were more severe than normal (which was saying something) and his white hair smelled of smoke from the ashes placed upon his head as a daily symbol of shame and repentance.

Melanor knew to be appropriately sober in the presence of the Abbey's stern leader. After all, it was the most famous Abbey of all, a place of legend—from its location along the Kinsman River (whose headwaters at Avl-on-Bourne were formed of Aion's sacred snow), to Uisnwch, to the great Hall and the long traditions of the Book of Names. Everything about the Abbey commanded both reverence and reflection. For his part, Melanor had to squelch a kind of giddy awe. Having come of age in Tinuviel, he was well versed in the legends of the great Soriah, and old Aventhorn Keep, from which the city of Tinuviel sprang. But, being initiated into the Order of the Grays at a young age, he had never traveled much. This was his first visit to another Abbey, first time to lay eyes upon one of the five Great Trees, and the dwarfing splendor of the Hall of Ages. He was nearly overcome.

It had been a hard five days' journey. With the frosty white crown of Mt. Bourne looming ever larger to the east, he had arrived exhausted, his lathered horse near to collapse. The mood of the Abbey did little to restore him. It felt like a tomb, a commune of solemnity. Much more than normal, he felt sure.

The only color in sight was that of garb and rank: green, yellow, tan. Scribes, Interpreters, Master Wordsmen. Only one wore pure white, and he walked a pace or two ahead, speaking in monotone. Everywhere around Melanor, learned men and scholars bowed in alleys and lanes and courtyards, in private rooms, alone, together, whimpering, anguished, afraid. Contrite.

Indeed, such a thing had never happened.

"Such a thing!" Alethes moaned, as if reading his thoughts. His voice cracked with emotion. "Has *never* happened. Yet I wear the white. I am the High Priest. I am responsible." His face hardened. "May Aion forgive me. I have horribly failed him. My sins stretch to the sky."

Melanor wished to comfort, but could find no words. Wisely, he kept silent.

They passed under the cool shade of Uisnwch, sprawling and green, lined with white stones and yellow lilies. The tree was the only decoration marking the entry to the Hall of Ages, whose south-facing door was positioned due north of it. There was some symbolism to this, but Melanor could not recall it.

The door to the Hall was enormous, a solid slab the height of three men and at least four hands thick. A massive iron band formed a locking mechanism, yet when Alethes gave the door the slightest push, it swung easily open, eerily silent.

"You shall have much to report to Father Eldoran," Alethes said. He still held the letter in his hand, which Melanor had faithfully delivered. "I must confess, I am quite curious at the tidings of these youths who have come to our world. You say you saw them yourself? It hardly seems possible." His voice held more than a hint of doubt.

"Indeed, High Priest. I saw both. They came separately and seemed quite disoriented. They wore strange clothes."

"S'Qoth perhaps? Or children of the south?"

"No. Of that I am certain. It was unlike anything we have ever seen, but not barbarian. They used strange words and phrases."

"Are you sure they were not playing an elaborate game with you?"

"I can only tell you that Father Eldoran is convinced. Even now, they journey to Stratamore. They asked nothing of us and offered no aid. Although they were impertinent at times, they struck me as quite sincere. They only wanted to return to their father and their homeland."

"And where is that, I wonder?" Alethes mused thoughtfully. "Eldoran mentioned Tal Yssen in his letter. And Artorius, the fabled King. Tell me, does he have reason to believe these boys come from the same world? I must confess, that would seem a good omen, indeed. But we cannot afford to traffic in unknown realms, Brother Melanor. The Book of Law does not allow us to experiment with these things. It could be very dangerous."

They passed together down an arched hallway full of pictures chiseled into square frames of stone. The pictures were simple, looping up and over the arch, then back again—row upon row, layer upon layer. Hundreds, perhaps thousands of carvings.

"The Mosaic," explained Alethes. "A history of the world, from the First Wind to the Final Fire and the War of Swords. After centuries of study, we don't comprehend even a quarter of it. Yet as you know, all of this, what you see here, the building itself, and every scroll inside, was written, built, and carved by one man." The High Priest held his hands behind his back. He was tall and lean, with a prominent hook nose. His voice was stern with the strictures of faith. "You stand in a living prophecy made of rock, Brother

Melanor. One which has never failed to guide and confirm the Way of Aion to man."

As a White to a Gray, his comment implied more. It was both diplomatic and mild spiritual rebuke. Melanor hardly noticed and frankly, didn't care. He was too busy marveling at the Mosaic. Some carvings he recognized, or at least could surmise. But there were far too many to see at once. "It seems impossible one man could do all this."

"And yet, it is. And was. And will be. And so we believe."

Then, without warning, the Mosaic ended and the Hall of Ages flung wide before them. The sheer expanse of the space was staggeringly unexpected. The high, impenetrable ceiling was lost in shadows, save for many wide circles cut into the marble, each domed with one of three shades of crystal: clear, topaz, and amethyst. Through these, light drenched the floor like effulgent waterfalls. The gold and purple effect was so startling amongst the white, so ethereal, that at first Melanor did not notice the true wonder of the Hall. Lining the high walls to half their span, forming row upon row upon row within the cavernous middle, were wooden shelves bored with holes. And tucked into each one of these holes, a scroll.

Scrolls beyond number. Scrolls beyond imagination.

"Every soul who has ever lived, or will live, in Karac Tor," Alethes breathed. "Every scroll you see is a page in the Book of Names."

To gaze into the room, drenched in soft color, was like looking into the heart of a night sky full of stars. A kiss of light from above caught on the lip of each coiled sheaf, as it barely protruded past its shelf. Millions of twinkles. The ordering of history. Blue. Yellow. White. Each light a life. Alethes allowed Melanor space to linger for several moments before aiming toward the far corner of the Hall.

"These rows are decades, centuries, millennia. Advancing through time."

And so they, too, advanced past row after row lined with tall ladders on wheels, and green-robed Scribes milling about, carefully tending to the parchments, the oil on the wood, the shine on the floors. He had expected the air to smell musty and old. It did not. Even at a brisk pace, it took a while to get wherever Alethes was going. Melanor felt himself getting sticky with time—the strange nearness of forgotten epochs, the sprawl of history. Having dared to enter such holy space, he had become a mere gnat before a great fire, transfixed in wonder, worthy only of being consumed. Even the sound of his feet on the floor seemed noisily rude to his ears.

"Here," Alethes said at last. "This is where *we* are in time. Way over there is where Time began. And here," he moved back two steps, "is where we were two weeks ago, at the beginning of the Days of Awe. All of these," he swept his hand forward, "are blank."

Melanor studied. His eyes moved forward across time and could not help but notice that only a few rows of scrolls were left before the wall terminated at the near corner. Bare marble lay between the shelves and the corner—the only spot he had seen in the entire Hall not entirely covered with scrolls. Instead, it was overlaid with a flat sheet of pure gold, floor to ceiling.

"What's that?" he said.

"Who can know until it comes?" Alethes said enigmatically. "The end of the world? Of time? A new and glorious age? Or does the gold represent an age of fire? Karac Tor rising or falling? We don't know. But if it is the War of Swords, as many of our wisest scholars suspect, then you can see with your own eyes, we are near to the Ninth Coming. Aion, soon, shall return for the final time."

Melanor swallowed. "And the outlanders? Where might they be, if they were recorded here?"

"Eldoran mentioned that—a puzzling thought. Obviously, having just read your letter, I have not had much time to consider the likelihood. The fact is, we would have no way of knowing how to align their birth seasons with our way of keeping time. If we knew the year and moon of their births, it is *possible* they are in our records, but that would require much more research from our Scribes than you will have time for during your stay."

"What if we were to use the date of their arrival into this world. A few days ago."

"Perhaps you haven't heard," Alethes said rather testily. "The pages of the Book are *blank*."

Immediately, Melanor recognized his mistake. Of course. He felt foolish. The boys' arrival would fall into that period of time.

Standing in a pool of amethyst light, the High Priest nearly glowed. His cheekbones, made sharp and black, gave his face the look of a skull. His voice droned, echoing in the Hall. "As I see it there are three possibilities. First and most likely, the letters of the pages are not blank, merely hidden, probably the result of some sort of witchery coming from the Isle of Apaté. May that sorceress be cursed to Hel! If this is so, however, we should truly be afraid, for then her power is far greater than we ever thought. Nothing has ever breached these walls—neither man nor magic. Second, as stewards of the Book of Names, the White Abbey has in some way failed to maintain the standard of the Book of Law and fallen short of the worthiness required to behold this gift any longer. If so, perhaps through our fasting vigil and repentance we might once again be found worthy. Third, some other mystery is at work, which we have never encountered, because we have never reached this point in time. This is, of course, entirely possible. But it does not ring true in my mind."

He waited, letting the silence bear down upon his guest. Melanor, instead of feeling doomed, felt a surge of inspiration. He pointed to the sheet of gold laid on white marble. "Or fourth, the end of time *is* coming. A dark age of mounting chaos, according to the prophets. So the Book, rather than steering the way and predicting our future, now holds the names of this generation in safety. It preserves them in hiddenness, until they are strong enough to throw off their shackles and take their place in the battle at the end of the age."

Alethes's eyes slowly narrowed to hard, iron points. His was the soul of a holy warrior, rabidly persuaded of the unique virtues of his Order. A devotee of objective truth. Melanor's tone, smacking of too much fluidity and the subjective pitfalls of personal revelation, did not enjoy his approval. He stepped forward, out of the wash of light.

"Do you enter this hallowed space trailing strange ways behind you, speaking *orn* and *lira*? In my presence, no less? If the Blacks and Grays wish to pursue the dangers of the Nine, it is their business. We have prophecy in rock, we need no more. Only the way of the Law. Tell Eldoran what I said to you. All of it."

Feeling scolded like a puppy, Melanor shrunk back. He had never experienced any of the Gifts of Nine before, nor had he presumed to do so now.

"I'm sorry, High Priest. Forgive me."

Alethes sniffed. "There is nothing more for you to see here."

They both turned to leave. Yet while Brother Melanor the Gray might have thought himself done with bursts of holy inspiration, the inspiration of *lira* was not yet done with him. As they passed through the Mosaic again, another epiphany seized him.

"My lord, will you show me where in Time we are in the Mosaic?"

Alethes, irritated by now, was disinclined to further conversation. He pointed.

"Somewhere in this range, in these carvings. So we think."

Melanor studied them carefully for several moments. Each picture was a simple scene or symbol. Sun on rock. A burning forest. A frightening mountaintop. Many, fierce boats on water. A dragon with a sword. Alethes tapped his sandaled foot impatiently, but Melanor ignored him. After some time, when he was near to giving up, one caught his eye. Yes, there. There! He tried not to register surprise, did not move closer and stare, nor reach out his hand. Yet for a moment, the Gray monk felt as if, within the Hall of Ages, a new line might have just been added to the scroll of his own life. A line of simple discovery. The hairs on the back of his neck stood tingling to attention.

The carving was simple: Four boys. Four birds. And a curve of stone in a field.

Carved at the creation of the world by Yhü Hoder. In a realm called Karac Tor.

He smiled, said nothing, exited. Low-hanging clouds had begun knotting together like fists in the sky, casting gray upon the valley. More rain. All of Vineland had been inundated for weeks. Villages had flooded. The Abbey, positioned on higher ground, felt no less bleak. All the world felt bleak.

Yet Melanor held his head high. He had seen with his own eyes, a carving.

Inexplicably, there was hope.

CHAPTER 33

The Nameless

He had seen the other girl rolled into the water, had shouted in horror. He vaguely remembered the blow to his head, had the bloody scab to prove it, along with a trail of dried blood down his cheek. At last, he slept, waking once more to the darkness of the blindfold. It was maddening. Worse still was the memory of the girl's body sinking slowly beneath the surface, her voiceless thrashing. The watery silence. He remembered wishing for release, to vomit, but couldn't. Instead, he cried softly. He didn't care what the other three thought. The sickness in his stomach grew worse. He had never before witnessed something so brutal, so cold-blooded.

He was going to die; he knew it.

Not too long after, as he passed in and out of consciousness, he felt the current of the river briefly speed up, become more choppy.

The flimsy raft threatened to capsize. In the near distance, he heard other, urgent voices. Many voices. Then the raft bumped into something, bobbing in the water on large waves. The air smelled briny and open. Over the sounds of gulls, Grayday and Shameface discussed matters with other voices positioned higher above. It seemed obvious they had been approached by a larger vessel. From the tone of conversation, it was equally obvious that this was one of Nemesia's vessels.

Hadyn was hauled to his feet. A thick rope was tied around his waist. Blindfolded, bound, he whispered, "What are you doing to me?"

"Teaching you despair."

He was hoisted onto the larger ship. Shoved here, there, down a ladder, tripping over ropes and rigging. He heard the rusty hinges of a door creak open. He was roughly shoved . . . down. No ladder. No steps. Free fall. He landed with a crunch on his shoulder and side. Air exploded from his lungs. He groaned. He thought of his mom, thought of slipping into darkness. Thought of the beauty of light and the green of trees.

I'm never going to college. Never driving or getting married.

Pain greater than his need for air seized him. A memory danced at the edge of his awareness, a story he knew well, told many times around the dinner table. This time, it was just the two of them, in his father's office.

When I first saw your mother, his dad said. *She was standing in the green grass. Green like a dream, like only Ireland can ever be. She was surrounded by a bunch of us from the dig. Your mother was always in the middle of things, always the center of attention. It suited her. I'll never forget it. Her hair was so blonde I thought she was an angel. Too beautiful for this world.*

The yearning of the memory made Haydn flinch. He squeezed his eyes shut, trying to block it out. Laying on the planked floor of the ship, he focused on the unpleasantness of human sweat, combined with fish odors, lamp oil, grime, salt, yeast. The stew of smells was overpowering. It was stiflingly hot. He sat up, gingerly feeling for a spot of wall to lean against. He felt old and dead inside, hollowed out like a tree near to falling. And puzzled. Puzzled as to why *that* memory should float to the top.

Maddeningly, it continued. It had been shortly after the move to Newland. Mr. Barlow had been working on his computer, staring out the window. One of many lonely reveries. Hadyn had walked in, and, feeling the rudeness of his presence, almost walked right back out. This time, for some reason, perhaps having no other friend to confide in, Dad had chosen his oldest son to share his burden.

It's like my heart is still searching, Hadyn. For another world, for heaven, I don't know. I lay awake at night and wish I could just fly away. Never come back. Hadyn remembered well the rambling, delicate anguish. His dad pointed to his head. *I know what's true here. I know what the Bible says. I guess when it comes down to it, I just want to know that I'll see her again. That I could someday sail that dark ocean and find her, waiting for me on the other side.*

Dark ocean, that was it. That must have triggered the memory. Hadyn shivered in the belly of his own dark ocean. He remembered Mr. Barlow's bloodshot eyes flicking around the room, searching desk and sky, moon and stars, new computer, old books, for any way to find *that* world. Any door. Any bridge to leap from . . . to wherever Anna might be. He was lost without her, had lost himself in her. He sat across from his son, sunken, sleepless, eyes rimmed with tears. The light of one lamp offered soft illumination, little comfort. Perhaps for the first time, Hadyn comprehended the naked pain of his father. Such wounds might never heal.

But it was the haunting recall of his next few words that chilled him to the bone.

We have to make it, Mr. Barlow had said with gritty determination. *Do you hear me? All of us, together. We're five now, not six. I can't ever lose any of you, ever again. You are the only world I've got.*

In the belly of a ship, Hadyn could do nothing but cry.

When he woke, Hadyn decided it was time to sort things out. He knew he was trapped in the hold of a boat. He knew that others were watching. He heard their whispers, curious and surprised.

"Hello?" he said. His tears were dry. "Am I alone?"

More whispering. He struggled against the ropes on his hands, but they were too tight. The effort burned his skin. He tried pressing his cheek flat against the wood to snag his blindfold. It did little but scrape the wound on his forehead, freshly split from the fall. Blood leaked down his temple, his neck.

"Is anyone else here with me? I can hear you talking."

"We can hear you," a young woman answered blandly. In the warm darkness, Hadyn could not judge whether she was annoyed or merely weary. Or just another one of *them.*

Added another: "Seventy-two . . . now seventy-three."

"Is that how many of us there are?" Hadyn asked. "Someone tell me your name. I'm Hadyn. Where are we going?"

"The Isle of Apaté. To Nemesia, who calls us."

Hadyn scoffed. "Do I look like Nemesia called for me and I willingly came? I am bound and blindfolded. Are you?"

A long silence followed. Presently, gentle hands began unknotting his blindfold. The fabric fell to the floor. Except for a few thin bands of dusty light leaking down through loose slats and high portholes on either side, the hold of the ship was quite dark. The tattered, downcast faces of many Nameless took form—the brush of light on eyes and cheekbones, huddled bodies. Most were curled up on the floor, not bothering to move or peek at him. A few stood. No one else was bound.

"What are you doing here, so special?" demanded one young man whose head was shaved. "You aren't fooling anyone. We know you aren't one of us."

Another Hadyn could not see added, "We go to a place for losers and lost. Are you one of us?"

Bodies closed in threateningly. From within the crowd, a girl intervened—the one that had first spoken.

"Let him be, look at him. He's lost as any of us."

Pushing against the others, she stepped forward into a meager swath of light. She had a normal girl shape, a little full, not at all heavy, blonde hair, with timid doe eyes, and a sweet half smile. She still had spirit.

"Back!" she demanded with vigor. "Let him breathe."

Feet scuffled. Voices grumbled. Most returned to uncaring slumber. To them, Hadyn was simply one more body in an already crowded space.

"To be true, you *don't* look as lost as the rest of us," she whispered, kneeling beside him. She began daubing at his wound with a wet rag. "I am Kyra, from Portaferry."

"Is that your real name?"

"As real as any name can be. It is the name of my birth."

It was a glimmer of hope. Hadyn seized it and told his own

story. "My mother dreamed my name when she was pregnant with me. My dad wanted to call me Ransom. I don't know why. But one night, Mom dreamed Hadyn. They both knew it was right. It was like a gift. She always said I was a gift." He looked away. "That's what my name means."

"I don't know what Kyra means. I just know I don't like it. I never have."

"You should. It's very pretty."

"And *that* is why," she said bitterly. "My name outshines me."

Hadyn was taken aback, quickly realized he needed to be careful. He did not want to risk offending whatever new friend or ally he had just gained. Kyra had smooth skin and bright eyes flecked with mischief not yet lost to Nemesia. Like the others, she was dirty and worn, but most anyone seeing her would have thought her attractive. Not beautiful, but cute. And feminine, with a girlish, fluttering voice.

"I don't much like being a girl," she said, as if reading his thoughts. "Always guessing what other people think about me. I grew up watching the Revlon Cirque in Portaferry. Now those are beautiful women! So graceful, with those huge feathers in their long, twirling hair."

"I'm sorry. I don't know what that is."

"The Cirque? Are you even from here? You talk funny."

"To be honest, I don't know how to tell you where I'm from."

"Well, *everyone* here loves the Revlon Cirque," Kyra smirked. "They are the most marvelous carnival in all the world. Men desire them. Women envy them. Paintings of them hang in the streets. They are rich and famous." She lowered her eyes. "I do not have their shape, their face, or their fame. And I never will. When I told a friend once how I wished I could be a Revlon, she laughed at me."

Hadyn spoke gently. "Not much of a friend, I'd say."

Kyra snorted, unmoved. She pulled out a small round mirror from the folds of her gown. It fit in the palm of her hand. She gazed into it sadly. "That is only because you do not see what I see every day in the looking glass."

"What do you see?" Hadyn asked. His eyes fell on the rag she had used, clotted with his own blood. He began to feel lightheaded at the sight of it.

"Nemesia says there should be no boys or girls. Not male or female. We should all simply be."

"Be what?"

"Human. Free."

The hold began to spin. Kyra's voice had begun to sound as if she were underwater. Hadyn shook his head to clear it. He couldn't tell whether he was woozy from blood loss, or if that freaky mind thing was happening again. He struggled to speak.

"I'm sorry, but that's the . . . dumbest thing . . . I've ever heard. Humans come in two flavors: boy and girl. If you don't start there, nothing else makes sense."

Kyra put her mirror away, pressed the rag against his wound, a little harshly. Hadyn winced. "Are you so sure?" she said. "Hatefully sure? Unbendingly sure? Arrogantly sure? Are you like all the other boys who can only think like boys? You think your strength gives you the right to hurt others. A man thing, right? Well, that is why a woman's thing is to control men. So they don't get hurt in turn." She sighed, softened. "It doesn't matter, really. In the big frame, girls hardly matter at all."

Hadyn was incredulous. "What?!"

"Well, girls like me. Pretty girls matter, of course. They matter a lot."

"Who *told* you these things? Nemesia? She's a liar. Any girl—"

"Ahh, you haven't been listening." Kyra smiled without joy. "Another poor trait of men. Did I say I wanted to be just *any* girl?" She laid her hand hesitantly on his chest, searching him in the dark, for common ground. "Is it so hard to imagine? To want to be a Revlon?"

Hadyn swallowed. "I wanted to stay in Independence. I wanted my mom to live."

"And did she? For all your wishing, did it matter?"

Hadyn swallowed hard. "Things change. Life goes on. We have to be strong."

"Yes, well . . . I guess we all want to be something we are not. That's why we are all lost. That's why we go to Nemesia. To forget what we will never be. I know I don't have to go. I *want* to go. I want to drown on her shores."

Hadyn remembered another drowning girl. Grayday's haunting, almost envious, declaration. *Now she is nameless. Now she is free.*

"If you go, you mustn't forget your name," he whispered, pleading. Somehow, that single thought still made sense to him. "What about the Book? The one everyone is written in. Doesn't that mean something to you? Doesn't that matter?"

"The Book of Names?" Kyra giggled. "Scribblings from thousands of years ago? I've never even seen it. What does it have to do with me?"

"Maybe everything. Right?"

"Or maybe nothing at all."

Hadyn moaned. The sickening murk was growing worse, coagulating in his thoughts. His tongue felt thick. "I wish you could see."

Kyra faded back into the shadows.

"I see things you don't want to see. Perhaps you are the one who is bound."

No sooner had she gone, no sooner had the darkness loomed, than Hadyn forgot what was so important about their conversation in the first place. All around him, bodies swayed gently to the rocking motion of the boat. He felt queasy in both his stomach and his head. Like newspaper ink imprinted on a ball of silly putty, then pulled, he felt the shape of his thoughts slowly stretching beyond recognition. Words—those simple containers of thought and meaning—grew mushy right at his point of actually thinking them. Feeling became an indistinguishable gallimaufry. The more he tried to concentrate, to follow a single line of thought through to clarity or resolution, the more his brain hurt.

Focus. Breathe. Think . . .

But focus hurt. He needed an outlet.

Perhaps . . . you are the one . . . bound.

And he was. He could feel his binding: the ropes, the knot around his wrists. Desperate for focus, he directed his thoughts to them. He remembered standing on Gregor's ship, when the sails first lurched and he grabbed for the rope. Something had spoken to him. Another peculiar word. Now, he stroked the fibers with his finger, honed in on the tone and feel, the warp and weft of the rope at his wrists. He recognized the same, strange sense of something unfolding within. The sound of a name, whispering itself, unwrapping in his mind like a soft piece of candy, teasing him with secrets. It was so hard to focus, hard to hear.

He struggled to form the word. The word of rope. Of knotted rope. He was a namer. An opener. Somehow, this was his gift. He tried to sound it out, as he had in the Stone House. He practiced, trying to pronounce it. It was a foreign word. They probably all were.

Under his whispered command, the fibers relaxed. The knot suddenly loosened. He felt the slack. He stopped short. For appearance's sake, he needed to leave the rope intact.

Focus. Breathe. Think . . .

Even as he struggled, he felt himself slipping deeper and deeper into stupor. It pressed upon him like a weight.

Hadyn, wake up! Focus. So sleepy . . .

So hard. In forgetfulness he found a semblance of peace. When he mentally relaxed, didn't fight it, relief flooded in. Each time, it became harder and harder to gather the resources to think again. The sensation was unsettling. The farther they traveled, the greater the feeling that he was being transformed. Like the putty, too elastic to recognize, too squished together to distinguish. An obvious contradiction: stretched and squished.

He slumped over, closed his eyes, biting his lip. Tried to use the pain to help him concentrate. He became porous. Language drained away. *Contradiction. Contradiction. Contradiction!* What did that word even mean? *Contra. Diction. Dictionary. No, constitutionary. Con . . . tra . . . fiction. Consternation. What was it again?*

"Are Shameface and Grayday your leaders?" he called out suddenly, sounding drunk. "Why do you follow them?"

No one answered. No one cared.

As he struggled to stay upright, his thoughts drifted to Shameface on the river. A seventeen-year-old boy. Shameface had argued with Grayday. Then, uncaring, he had simply yielded the point. No more challenge. No flare of temper. It had seemed so puzzling to Hadyn at the time how Shameface could acquiesce so easily. Now, in his slurry mess of thoughts, he finally understood why. It wasn't innate agreeableness, or maturity, or some sort of inner peace Shameface possessed. Quite the opposite. Shameface was simply well acquainted with defeat—of losing everything, every pleasantry, every argument, every challenge. He no longer pretended to expect otherwise.

In this, all the Lost had one thing in common. They had never felt important. To anyone.

No one cared about Hadyn either. No one was here to rescue him from becoming one of them. He was unimportant. Like Kyra. Like Shameface. He had been forced to move against his wishes. Forced to watch as his world fell apart. Forced to clear that cursed spot of land on a farm he hated. He wouldn't even be here at all if it hadn't been for how uncaring and selfish his father had been. And his brother! Getting up in the middle of the night. Chasing dreams. How foolish. How selfish. How typical. No one ever thought of what Hadyn wanted or needed.

The thought of his brother—what was his name?—made Hadyn realize he had no brother. Soon wouldn't, at least. He had no hope, no future. He was trapped in a surreal world, a dream. Nothing made sense. The fog in his mind—a dark, angry beast— demanded he yield, be silent. Find peace. Surrender.

Your name is Hadyn Barlow. Your name is Hadyn Barlow . . .

He clenched his teeth as he tried to remember. It seemed impossible.

CHAPTER 34

To Stratamore

I f spoken at all by sailors, the word *Argo* was usually flung like
an angry fist by greasy, unshaven men after a bad roll of the
bones, in dimly lit taverns, around tables covered with candle
wax and spilled beer, part of a larger effluence of highly colorful
verbiage, and never polite.

In short, the Argo was to be avoided at all cost, even in speech.
So when the sailors let up a shout that they were "Argo borne!" it
made Sorge laugh. But in truth, the crew was mightily cheered.
Next to the crosswinds of a summer squall pinned against the
Jawbone, or the mountainous waves and fierce gales famous for
battering ships headed north to Yrgavien, nothing could make a
crusty old seaman spit and holler worse than the mention of the
cursed, red river.

Yet Sorge had spoken truly, and the *Python's Eye* hadn't felt nary a drop of rain. When the captain followed his advice, heading due west upon reaching the bay, rather than cutting a more southerly course to Stratamore to attempt a quick landfall on the southern shore—as a bold captain might have preferred—the rising storm split around them, leaving them in safe waters. To aft, strings of lightning lit the tall, black thunderheads, booming with thunder, but the waves ahead remained ever steady and smooth, with a good west wind to boot. So when Sorge informed the captain that his friends were at the mouth of the Argo, no one even blinked. You don't want to risk offending the gods, or their servant, when they've brought good fortune to your ship.

As they rounded the last jut of land to the river's mouth, Ewan could hardly sit still. He nearly made his hands bleed, digging his fingers into his palm. Would Hadyn be there, smiling, waving? He opened one eye, held his breath. Three figures on shore, not four. Flogg, Cruedwyn, and Asandra hunched over their fading campfire. Ewan's heart sank.

Drifting as near as they could, the *Python's Eye* dropped anchor, and the captain sent a dinghy of six men to row ashore and collect the friends of his honored guest.

Ewan was crestfallen. "They didn't get him. Why didn't—"

"Take courage, Lord Ewan. Our plan was to search to this point, and then rejoin. I see the Chantry riddle at work. *In division, completion* . . ." He scanned the shoreline again, shading his eyes with his hand. "It looks like they failed. But the oracle still holds, and they no doubt tracked him a good way. We'll soon know more."

"This is not how it was supposed to go. What if there is no completion? What if he's dead?"

"What if he's not? What other choice do you have, but to believe?"

"I want to know that *you* believe it, too," Ewan said stubbornly.

"I do."

Still, Ewan was unsatisfied. He fidgeted. "Okay, but what if you're wrong?"

"What if we're right?" Sorge laid a hand on his shoulder. "Either way, providence is at work."

Out of the corner of his eye, Ewan saw a flash of silver.

"What's that?" he said.

Sorge, who saw nothing, deeply inhaled the southern wind. Thinking Ewan spoke of providence, the monk turned toward the far eastern horizon, toward Isgurd. "It means the Everking still dwells on the Shining Hill. And so there is hope."

Ewan wasn't listening anymore. He had seen the shimmering of air, the flit of motion. It only took a moment to remember the dance of liquid hair, the glittering dragonfly wings. He nearly jumped, feeling eager. He had thought of the Fey creature numerous times, wondering if he would ever see her again. To port side, near the rear—aft, the sailors would say. There she was, flitting away. He wandered past men, heaving on ropes, toward the back of the ship.

Elysabel was there, in a corner, empty except for crates of cargo. As the morning sun rose, she was nearly transparent. Her wings blurred the air around her. She stared at him impassively.

"Are you following me?" he murmured. She was numinous and beautiful. He wanted to touch her wings, wanted to fly away with her.

"The Queen. She bid me watch over you. But you are *never* supposed to see me." She raised her chin slightly. "I do not like it that you see me."

Her eyes were hard, her tone firm. But not entirely. Ewan thought that maybe, just maybe, she was not telling the whole truth. After all, if she did not want to be seen, just fly away . . .

Please, please don't fly away.

He heard Sorge behind him, calling his name. The monk's voice was urgent. Ewan didn't care. He saw Fey.

"Will you stay with me?"

"I will not."

"Can I touch your wings?"

Elysabel fluttered back. Ewan cried out, as if stricken, afraid she would disappear.

"I'm sorry! I'm sorry!"

The pixie was not afraid. But she watched him curiously. "You are full of sadness. Why?"

Ewan shook his head. "There's nothing you can do."

"How do you know what I can do?" Elysabel said with a hint of petulance. "I can tell you a secret. Your brother lives. That is why you are sad, yes? Even now, he sails to the witch's isle, beneath the great cloud."

It took time for her words to sink in. "Cloud?"

She pointed. He followed the line of her delicate fingers. Morning continued to brighten, but far to the south, a knot of darkness was growing. It didn't look like a cloud.

When he turned back, she was gone. Dazed, he heard Sorge again, calling him.

"Ewan!"

A sailor bumped him, jolting him out of his reverie. "The monk be callin' ya, lad."

Ewan wandered, found Sorge. He, too, was staring at the southern horizon. Anxious lines creased his face.

"Where have you been?" he snapped, probably more irritably than he meant.

Ewan spoke as if still waking. "I saw her again. The Fey. She said Hadyn is alive. He is being taken to Apaté."

"That *is* Apaté," Sorge replied tersely. A half moment later, his head whipped toward the younger Barlow. Ewan didn't move, didn't blink. Slowly, Sorge turned back to the sea. In the distance, darkness rose like a pillar into a brooding, foul sky. Beneath it lay a smallish, nondescript mass of land, floating free, shrouded in mist. He raised his voice impatiently. "Swords and blood, captain! Get my friends aboard. Make haste, man! And then, full sail to Stratamore!"

The crew scurried. The captain fumbled an apologetic reply. The monk had brought them luck. Best not to anger the monk. At the moment, Sorge did not seem to mind taking advantage of their superstition. Ewan heard him whisper.

"What are you doing, Nemesia? What evil have you begun?"

CHAPTER 35

High Council

They were all gathered: that crusty old warhorse, Earl
Har Hallas of Brimshane; Sáranyása, whose veil of
gossamer blue accentuated more of her porcelain
beauty than it hid, daughter of the Duke of Seabraith, surprising
all by standing in her father's stead; pale Thorlson Hammerföe,
Captain of the Guard of the Lady Odessa in faraway Bitterland;
cunning Diamedici, from the fallen house of Faielyn, visiting in
secret; and Lor'vrkeln, son of the Highland Jute, ever impatient,
with blind Mac'Kalok at his side. These, the regents of government
from the Five Dominions, both pretenders and those of noble birth,
sat at a long, massive stone table alongside the embroidered, robed
figures of the Governor's many advisors and ministers. Lastly, but
not least, three clerical emissaries, too. A Wordsman, an Elder, and

a Seer, in the respective colors of their rank, representing the holy interests of the Abbeys.

This was the High Council of Karac Tor, a throwback to the days when Kings ruled, and the table was surrounded by noisy Barons, Earls, and Dukes of every province of the land. Now the table was half empty, seating barely twenty, though built for forty. At the far end, Archibald slumped in a chair carved as one piece from the massive trunk of an ancient, felled oak. His scepter lay on the table, untouched. His swollen cheeks were sallow. Beside him, Jonas watched over the proceedings with a calculating eye.

"—and still my crops are dying!" Har Hallas of the Midlands was roaring from the far end, pounding the table. The implacable stone surface (wisely foreseen by a King long ago) disallowed the drama of a wooden table, as Har was used to in his own hall in Brimshane. In Stratamore, the impact of an angry fist was nothing but a dull thump. Still, Har bellowed well enough to make his point. Everything about him was big: voice, face, arms, hair. "I've had no rain since three springs ago. And not much before. It's summer! My corn should be gold and ripening. Instead, my farmers bring baskets of shriveled, black husks to my table. Not to mention thieves and jackals raiding the villages around Redthorn. And Fey Folk! *Aargh!* Prowling and stealing like I haven't seen in fifty years, witching the cows, frightening the townspeople. You may think it small, but they require all my will to confine to Elkwood."

"We have no crops or Fey Folk," Thorlson of Bitterland said in his heavy, gravelly voice. While most Bitterland *viks* were fair-skinned and blond, Thorlson was a true albino: shockingly white skin, hair like morning frost, a blush of color in his eyes. The effect on people was usually profound, which made him an unnerving adversary in the political arena. "But our herds are sickly. Our spring foals have barely gained weight, and many are lame in the leg. This is the ninth season of puny foals. Dozens of gorse were stillborn. Our best sires no longer stud, and the mares give no milk."

Lor'vrkeln rose. He was dark like all Highlanders, with high, narrow cheekbones and black hair. He wore several necklaces of colored stones and had feathers in his hair. "*Water is life*—so the Highlander has ever said since being led to this realm by the will of Aion through our forefather Gil. We scratch our existence out of rock and wilderness and desert. For decades now, we have warned that our deep wells are turning to sand, yet our petitions to this court for aid have gone repeatedly unanswered. Now even young children suffer with thirst as our wells run dry. We cannot grow food. Our prey die before we can hunt, before our hawks can kill." He sat down, defeated, making no attempt to mask his fear and contempt. "Man cannot live without water."

"What about the Vinelanders?" someone asked. "They are being flooded with water. Can they not help, or share?"

"Vinelanders have no compassion for my people," Lor'vrkeln sneered. He refused to acknowledge Diamedici's presence in the room. The young prince responded only with his own brand of cool detachment. "Anyone who thinks they will offer succor or aid should drink less wine."

"Speaking of children," Har cut in, droll. "Has anyone noticed? We're running out."

A low murmur circled the stone table. A few pounded their fists in approval. He roused them further, saying, "Even if my farmers did have corn, they would have no sons of age to harvest it!"

The representative of the White Abbey stood. He wore tan and spoke with practiced solemnity. "It is time we acknowledge the truth. Our children have turned to rebellion and witchcraft. Sons and daughters are ensnared in the spell of the sorceress across the water." His eyes roamed slowly over the assembled guests. "Everyone at this table knows this. We have all heard the excuses, the superstitious nagging of hags and old women: Ghosts wander the land! Wraiths have stolen their souls!" His voice grew icy. "I tell you, the answer is far more simple: our sons have forgotten family, duty, and obligation. They must be brought back hard to the Way."

"Brother, the *only* Way you know *is* hard," replied the Gray across the table. A few snickered. While the Gray's tone was light, even playful, his expression wasn't altogether charitable.

"Only because *truth* is hard, Brother," countered the White. "It pierces. Not everyone likes to hear the truth. That doesn't make it any less true. This is the Way of the Whites."

"And what of the Way of Aion?" the Gray answered deftly, quickly adding, "Yet I yield the point, and quite concur the seriousness of the issue. It should be obvious and terrifying to all of us, that the unprecedented recent events of the Book of Names have come as a judgment on all the land. They tell the story of our sins, passed down to each generation." He bowed his head politely. "I know the Whites have doubled their devotions in fasting and prayer. Yet . . . something is still missing."

"It is because Aion is *not* the way of all," whispered Sáranyása. Through her veil, she seemed to be staring at Diamedici. "Across Greenland, the Old Groves are being restored. The pagan ways are practiced again. The people dance to dark rhythms when the moon is full. They cut themselves and call down fire. My half-brother has even tracked the shape of Haurgne north past Befjorg and across into Bitterland."

A low rumble of voices, sounding both concerned and disbelieving, rolled up and down the table. Some simpered, some sighed.

"I have not seen Kurg, but his old mountains stir," agreed Thorlson. "The land shakes. Though they have been quiet a thousand years, they shake again. Many have seen shapes of the Stag Lord in our dreams."

"As have the Blacks," added the emissary of that Abbey, a tall woman with a humorless face. "Our Seers dream of nothing else. Nemesia is a face we see and know all too well. We see also young men with hollow eye sockets, like skulls, becoming snared in a great spider's web and devoured. We see young women tear off their clothes, stand naked in the sun, full of bruises, and shake their fists at the sky. We see mysterious images of the Hall of Ages cast down in ruins. But ever, of late, a great shadow, shaped like a stag, lingers in the background of every picture of our dreams."

As she spoke, shadows and dread lay upon the great hall. The doubting voices seemed to fade. Jonas watched in careful silence while Archibald, slumped in his chair, scowled.

"Kr'Nunos, Lord of the Hunt, Lord of the Flies, is to be feared," said Mac'Kalok. He had a scarf tied over his sightless eyes and faced forward, back straight. His scarred hands were laid flat on the table before him. "But that is not our struggle. Not yet. Not today."

"You speak wisdom, great Champion," Diamedici said kindly. Or was it sarcasm? Turning his attention to the Master Wordsman, he stroked his neatly trimmed beard. The room hushed to hear him. "Master Veritazian, perhaps you do speak the truth. Yet if I may be so bold, the whole truth may require a larger telling. Perhaps our youth have not forgotten their families so much as their families have forgotten *them*."

It was a political calculation draped in moral outrage. Everyone who knew Diamedici's exile status—which was everyone—understood the double meaning. But many agreed.

"Hear, hear!" boomed Har, loud and full of bitterness. "I lost three sons. Three in five years! But not to some witch. Disease and hardship took them. Now I have no more heirs. You all know this. You know I would have given my soul for any one of them. I raised my boys with a firm hand, and full of love. But now what do we have? What has happened to the fathers of this day?" His eyes circled the room slowly. He jabbed his finger at the table. "If we wish to speak a hard truth, let us begin here. If the Devourer returns, then we shall be forced in that day to face the dread of our forefathers. But . . . but! *If our children are taken from us, we are already doomed, and tomorrow will not matter one whit.* Nothing will be left to devour! If dames and sires value their own flesh and blood and soul so lightly, is it any wonder the children of this land eventually drift away and leave our fair shores?"

"Perhaps it is for this the herds and crops grow weak?" the Black suggested thoughtfully. "Perhaps the whole land is cursed?"

"Then do something!" Har roared at him. "Get Cassock out of his tower and do something!"

"Gentleman! Ladies!" Jonas stood at last, carefully tucking each hand into the length of his sleeves. He smiled broadly. "Esteemed guests of Lord Archibald, all. Youth have always pushed against their elders, until such time as they become elders themselves. Then, as we are doing now, they complain about the next genera-tion, just as our parents worried and complained about us. This is the way of the world. It has ever been thus and always shall. Let us deal with crops and gorse herds and necessary things. Water wells and life. Let us not grow frightened with trivial fears of wayward children."

"You are a snake, Jonas," Thorlson said simply, loudly. "My Lady made clear our Dominion shall not deal with you, only the good Governor Archibald, whom we wish would be free of your voice."

Jonas's lips thinned. "If you wish to have dealings with this court, then your Lady will recognize that I support Archibald in the many, heavy burdens he bears. I offer wise counsel. He decides on all things. And in this, he has decided that you shall speak to me."

"And what of the cloud?" asked Diamedici. "What of the darkness in the sky over the Tower of Ravens? What do you say about that, Jonas? Is it simply a wayward cloud?"

Many chuckled openly.

Jonas clicked his tongue. "Does a Vinelander ask these things? Lord Diamedici, firstly, let me sadly remind you that you are present in this court only by the good favor of our Lord Archibald, cousin to your uncle, whom you have greatly grieved. Second, Aion's mercy, young prince! Vineland is a muddy, flooding mess! Have you not seen countless dark clouds and storms? Where, pray tell, do those storm winds begin? To the east, in Isgurd, yes? Then, passing over the Isle of Apaté, to the mainland. Are dark clouds so rare? Truly, tell me?"

Diamedici set his jaw. "This one is different and you know it. Just look at it."

"Different? What does that mean? Are there different kinds of dark clouds?"

"Clouds in the sky. And clouds that shoot from towers."

"Bah! A trick of the light. The Governor needs wise counsel, not poor eyesight."

Flushing red, the prince fell silent. No one but Sáranyása caught his secret glance. Lor'vrkeln, ignoring the Minister of Justice, stood to his feet. "Lord Governor, I do not know what the point of this meeting is. We have done this before, and it has only grown worse since the last time, and the time before that. I call upon you to lead us. The land will not bear compromise any longer, while you languish in your den of comfort."

One of the court's gray-haired advisors hobbled to his feet, shaking his finger indignantly. "Mind your place, Bird Man. I will not tolerate such a tone in this court."

Lor'vrkeln did not retreat, motioning toward Diamedici. "You willingly harbor a scoundrel. Yet you take offense at *my* tone?"

Har rose. "If the son of the Jute will not be heard, then what of true and noble blood? My lineage goes back twenty generations. Will you hear me, Lyson? Or what of the son of the Duke of Greenland. Why is he not present to speak?"

"Illegitimate son," Jonas countered warily. "You know the delicate diplomacy of this issue, Lord Hallas."

Lor'vrkeln shook with anger. "At least he is a fighter! Do we have so many willing souls that we can throw them away if their blood is mixed? Through no fault of his own?"

"I agree with you, son of the Jute," Har said. "But for once, Jonas is right. This is not the time or place for that dispute."

"When will it be the right time? Many issues are brought before this court time and time again. They all fall on deaf ears. We talk till we have no more breath. I am ready to be done with talking. I say we act. And were he *allowed* to be here, Win Shyne would say the same. Meanwhile, his father only builds more boats to tax the shipping lanes. Others with a clearer eye call it what it is: piracy."

The air grew still. Lor'vrkeln glanced to Har for support. Har lowered his eyes.

The Highlander clenched his jaw. "None of you may have the courage to say it now. But in the privacy of your own halls, you already have."

"You are as unwise as you are stupid," Sáranyása said tensely. "Little Bird Man, with your clipped wings. With your silly little hawks. How is it that the Jute sends a brute like you as diplomat to a court of your betters?"

"I fall over my tongue at your beauty," Lor'vrkeln said, bowing. "Perhaps you should stay home next time, if the speech of men offends you."

"Challenge my father all you want. The Duke of Seabraith has kept the warships of Karac Tor at ready with a *reasonable* tax. For the safety of *all* the land, even your accursed wilderness. And for what? Is he thanked?"

"He doesn't have to be. He is paid."

"My father is twice the man you shall ever be!"

"Twice the coward, more like, sending a woman to tend to the difficult work of governing. But that is probably unfair! In truth, does he even know you are gone? Did you come of his schemes, or your own, for love? Little girl, you and the exile are fooling no one."

Sáranyása's eyes turned ice blue. "You are fool enough for us all, Bird Man."

"I agree! Guilty! Or at least I would be if I kept silent one day more, turning a blind eye like the Governor, while your father rapes the seas for profit."

Sáranyása jerked to her feet. Suddenly, everyone was standing, shouting. Swords slipped free, pointing from half a dozen men toward half a dozen throats. Har bellowed, Lor'vrkeln raged, Diamedeci drew his knife, white Thorlson coiled like a snow leopard, ready to pounce.

Archibald gripped the armrests of his great oaken seat, staring at each face around the table with open malice. He ground his teeth together, a stew of anger. Jonas lowered himself to the King's ear, began furtively whispering secrets. He looked nervous.

"Lord Governor, what have you to say to these things?" Thorlson cried out amidst the clamor. Archibald shoved Jonas away. Guards rushed to the table, silently lowered their spears. The shouting stilled. No one moved, or sat, or relented. Again, Thorlson said, "Lord Governor. Look at us. The land, your people. We have need of you."

Shifting his weight, knees creaking, Archibald hauled his beefy frame upright. He took his scepter and flung it across the length of the table.

"You do not need me. You need a King!" he shouted, red-faced, before collapsing back into his chair. "And *I need a Champion*. One with eyes that work. One with a sword that cuts! Not another fool to join those already present round my table. Olfadr's beard, rot you all! Where is the Champion who will fight for me? Who will vanquish my foes?"

A deep, unexpected thud answered him, followed by the slight whisper of heavy hinges needing oil. The doors to the great hall swung open. As one, all heads turned. Silhouetted in the doorway stood a haggard group: a monk robed in gray, a swordsman, a mirling, a young boy, and a gnome. With Sorge flanking him, Ewan stepped forward into the columned hall.

"I've come to see the good Lord Governor, Archibald," Ewan declared, his voice shaking, trying his best to speak as Sorge had instructed him. He held up the silver tube and scroll, his invitation. "He Called for me. I have come at his request."

CHAPTER 36

A Is for Aion

L ater, the four of them sat in private chambers: Ewan, Sorge, Jonas, Archibald. After a brief explanation and a moment of shocked surprise, the High Council had been summarily dismissed, still hot and bickering, to meet again come morning after everyone's temper had cooled. Jonas had seemed quite flustered but welcomed the visitors with a tight smile. Having sent a chamberlain scurrying to the kitchen, a platter of freshly cut fruit was soon laid before them. Ewan was famished.

Archibald seemed thankful for the break. With his forefinger, he traced the jewel-crusted rim of his goblet of wine, sounding irritated and weary to the bone. "They want me to raise an army. They want to send spies north into the caverns under the Hödurspikes to see why the mountains shake. They want me to command Pol Shyne to launch his ships against the Tower of Ravens. They want me to give more money to the Abbeys. They want me to take less advice from the Abbeys. They want me to make their corn grow tall, their gorse strong, their water clean and abundant." He sighed. "Am I a wizard or a man?" He allowed everyone to consider the question as if it were more than rhetorical, then answered with disappointed pragmatism. "I am a man. But the world is failing. So they ask me to save it . . . as long as I save *their* part first."

Ewan fidgeted, feeling too nervous and urgent to worry about breaking protocol, or keeping it. Though the outer court had been lavish and huge, and would have been intimidating to a thirteen-year-old American kid, the plainness of the present chamber temporarily allowed him to forget his fear. He did, at least, remember Sorge's main instruction.

"*My lord*," he said carefully. "You must have something planned. Why else would you send the Call Birds?" He spread his invitation on the table before the Governor. The thick vellum glimmered with golden ink. Jonas, doing his best to appear uninterested, leaned closer. He was a creepy old man, with rich robes and a little cap on his balding head. He had a strange birthmark on the back side of his wrist. Or was it a tattoo? His sleeve almost always covered it.

Jonas read aloud, sounding weaker than normal. "*You have been chosen for a life of great purpose. Adventure awaits you in the Hidden Lands.*"

And then the signature flourish, shaped like the letter *A*.

Sorge preemptively took the blame. "Lord Governor, blame me for our tardiness. I do not know when you released this Call, so please forgive me if we have taken longer than expected. We were unusually resisted."

He explained the events leading up to this point, beginning with the four Call Birds, the stone arch, the Abbey, Hadyn's coming, the five who hunted them, and everything leading up to the capture at Redthorn. Both Archibald and Jonas listened without comment, sipping at their drinks with the practiced nonchalance of men who were always being told something important. Sorge further explained, as he himself had only recently learned, how Flogg, Asandra, and Cruedwyn had tracked Hadyn's raft downriver, but being greatly slowed by the difficulties of the path and numerous encounters with jackals, were prevented from ever coming near enough to attempt a rescue. They had tried to signal him through the trees, had heard his voice, saw him clubbed on the head and pass out. When they finally reached the bay, they saw him transported to one of Nemesia's larger vessels, bound for Apaté. That was it.

"Four invitations, you say?" Jonas clucked his tongue. He fixed his filmy gaze on Ewan. "An unlucky number, to be sure. Pray tell, where are the other two boys? Did you lose them, also?"

Sorge directed his response to Archibald. "The youngest two, though Called, did not come. At least not yet, not that we know. How can a Called one not answer? It is but one of many riddles I do not understand. Yet in truth, forgive me, but even the two that have come do not truly wish to answer your Call, Lord Governor. Could it be for this reason that the younger ones were not allowed to cross over? I only know that the Grays have sworn to help these boys. Once the older brother is retrieved, it is their wish to return to their home and father. And so, after a long and perilous journey, we humbly request your aid and seek your counsel."

Archibald stared blankly at the burnished rim of his cup. Flame and light played in the jewels. "You humbly request *what*, exactly, good Elder?"

"Call Birds, my lord. We did not even know they flew anymore. This is far beyond our knowledge. But the Grays wish to aid you in whatever manner you require. So how will you send the boys home?"

Archibald snorted. "Send them home? What have I to do with sending them anywhere? Yours is the province of the divine and supernatural."

"Or at the very least, of cheese," Jonas buzzed, dragging out the last word. Archibald chuckled. Jonas showed a toothy smile.

Sorge smiled politely, but he pulled back, confused. "But . . . you Called them."

Clearly annoyed, the governor snapped, "Elder Sorge, I have warm regards for Father Eldoran and your fine work together. But I haven't the foggiest notion of what you are talking about."

"The letter is marked with your own hand, my lord. There, see? The letter *A*, for Archibald. Has it been so long since you sent them? Have you forgotten?"

Jonas hissed lightly at the monk's tone. On cue, the Governor leaned forward, his jowls quivering with rage. "I am not the doddering old fool you and half the kingdom suppose, Gray. Do you think I don't know what I have or have not written? As if all the other demands placed upon me were not enough, now this! I've got to somehow get this boy to another world? Is that what you are telling me? Elder, I have neither seen a Call Bird nor directed one, ever, in my life. Nor have I ever seen this letter you show me now. By Aion's sword, that is not even my hand—"

A strange, distant expression passed over his face, like a cloud passing over a green field. In much the same fashion, Sorge looked down, began studying his hands very hard. The air grew vivid, even perilous. Ewan didn't know why, but his pulse quickened. Jonas's eyes were wide and white. Archibald stared at the scroll.

"Could it be?" Sorge whispered, finally daring to speak what all were thinking.

"No," Jonas said dismissively. But his lips were pale and trembling.

"*A* is for Aion? Could this be the seal of the High Prince himself?"

Governor and monk slowly turned to Ewan. While Archibald seemed mostly baffled, Sorge's eyes were lit with new admiration and more than a little surprise. Ewan, dressed in every manner like a boy of Karac Tor, felt their scrutiny. All he wanted to do was shrivel away. Yet even he could not deny the numinous turn of events.

Clearing his throat, he said, "So this is like . . . a big deal."

Sorge spoke, drawing words as from a deep well. "To be sure, little brother. To be sure."

Jonas hurriedly whispered in the Governor's ear. As they spoke, Archibald measured his young guest in age, feet and inches, with his eyes. He put up a hand, a warning. Jonas dutifully retreated. Heavy-lidded and superior, the old man nodded once more in decisive fashion.

"He is too small, too young. It is impossible."

"What?"

"Aion's chosen? You can't seriously expect me to accept this," Archibald said.

"I assure you the letter is real," Sorge said, challenging carefully.

"You can assure us of nothing except that this young boy brought a letter, which you *believe* to be real."

"What about my brother?" Ewan said. "What about rescuing him?"

"Oh, don't play on so," Jonas smirked. "This has been a grand charade, really, but you go too far. You both should join the Cirque, I think. The bait is too large for the fish to swallow!"

Archibald twirled the rings on his fingers. He seemed to have passed a door in his mind, a point of no return. Before, he was cautiously intrigued. Now he was dismissive. "Your brother is no concern of mine. I have much more important matters of state to attend to. You may have fooled the Grays, but you will not have me chasing my own tail with your fancy schemes. I do not have time for such things. Tell me, did Lady Odessa put you up to this? I dare say you have a bit of a Bitterman's accent, eh?" He turned to Jonas, who nodded in agreement. "Now she's one that would be this clever, don't you think?"

"Oh, absolutely, Lord Governor. Definitely the Lady could scheme such chicanery, to goad you into attacking the island. It's appalling, really."

Ewan saw Sorge's fist clench and unclench in his lap. "Are the attacks and the kidnapping part of the charade? Or do you call me a liar, too?"

"Careful, Elder. Do not puff your chest at me. I do not deny the threat of the witch, or her possible interest in these children," Archibald grumbled. For a brief moment, he sounded apologetic. "It seems she is interested in many children. And so she may be a threat, or she may be nothing. But *if* a threat, she is one too great to face. We must wait, be wise. Look for weakness. In either case, there is nothing I can do about it right now. Perhaps you should take comfort in the fact that she has attacked nothing thus far. It has been all tricks and theater." He turned away. "I've made up my mind. I will not risk inciting her to rage simply because some young people are drawn to her in curiosity, drawn by this and that. It is the way of things."

"Lord Governor," Sorge pleaded. "You know the connection of leader to land, the sacred bond—"

"I do not need your lectures, monk. Good day to you both. I am not a king. I am a steward."

He rose, twirled round. His robes flowed behind him. At the door, he paused. "Even if your story were true, even if I *wanted* to help—I have no knowledge of portals and no knowledge of how to return you. That is all there is to it."

Meeting adjourned. Ewan fumed. With Sorge beside him, they wandered out of the city to rejoin the other three, climbing the low hills to the west. Sorge needed space to think, Ewan to vent.

Cruedwyn was unusually thoughtful. "So Archibald laid no claim on the letter. And you still hold to your story, Ewan?"

"Of course. What's that supposed to mean?"

"Well, to be honest, I thought perhaps there was some other motive at work here. I've never met a world-traveler. Good day to you."

He made a motion, like tipping his hat. Sorge was lost in thought. "Jonas had a mark. Did you see it, Ewan? On the underside of his wrist. I've never noticed it before. The antlers of a stag."

Ewan nodded. "I figured it was a tattoo. An ink mark."

Sorge chewed on his own words to get the taste of them. They followed a footpath that wound up rock and scrub brush, eventually finding a small pinnacle of green surrounded by trees. There was something strange and familiar about the place. Ewan decided it reminded him of the woods outside the Gray Abbey, when he first arrived.

Cruedwyn, serious, but cheerful again, said, "None of this matters, friends. Who needs Archibald? We go to Apaté! A Creed never turns his back on a challenge, never breaks a vow. A Creed never . . ."

From his side came a low, insistent throbbing. But he was on a roll. Open-mouthed, mid-sentence, the sound grew louder. Cruedwyn clamped his mouth shut.

"I am willing to help," he said tersely.

The humming stopped. Feeling safe, he jerked the haft.

"I'm about this close to tossing you in the ocean, do you hear me?"

No hum.

"That's right, you *know* it's the truth."

"Perhaps you consider flowers and wine for your lovers' quarrel?" Asandra teased. Ewan laughed. Cruedwyn gave them both a fake, honeyed smile.

"Even a blade of your skill is not enough for this challenge, Creed," Sorge said gravely. "First, we have to get there, and we can't just walk. There's not a captain at the docks that will take us." In answer to Ewan's silent question, he shook his head. "Yes, I already asked. Our captain made a warding sign at me like I had just cursed his ship. If we combined *all* our funds and Creed sold his sword, we would still not have half the fare for any captain to ferry us. Not a chance."

Flogg, meanwhile, had begun pacing, muttering, hands clasped behind his back. His words were mostly incomprehensible.

"Black. Croaker," he seemed to be saying. "Only way."

Sorge noticed, chided him. "Don't, my friend. You would be banished from your kin. I will not allow it. We'll think of something else. Not the Raven Trail."

Flogg stomped a foot. "Will monk be telling Flogg what Gnome-kin thinks and does?"

"What's the Raven Trail?" Ewan asked.

"A famous rollwol. One of the secret gnome tunnels that run under Karac Tor. The Row of the Black Croaker, gnomes would say. We say Raven Trail. Supposedly, the Raven Trail goes under Champion Bay, connecting the mainland to Apaté. But there's no guarantee we could even find it. It could be a huge waste of time."

Flogg offered a rascally grin. "Seekings and peekings. Find Croaker Way, feets to witch."

Ewan was tired of puzzles and figuring things out. He just wanted to be done. He wanted a good video game, a soft couch, some hot chocolate by the fire. As his gaze drifted to the south, he saw a stream of blue along the base of a green valley. Faraway, which was where he wanted to be. Even from his vantage point on the hill, the river looked swollen from rain. The river ran parallel to the sheer face of a high cliff, stretching west as far as the eye could see. An enormous cliff. Ewan had never seen anything so huge. Grand Canyon huge. Below it, the river streamed roughly east, toward three towers. Three white towers, rising over the ridge, in the City of Kings. A black bird flew high in the sky.

Suddenly and vividly, the scene surged within him, like a waking memory. Watching the bird soar overhead, he felt a rush of recognition. He *knew*.

". . . they are prized secrets," Sorge was saying. "It would be unprecedented for Flogg to break faith with his kin in this way."

Flogg grumbled, "Kin forget Uplanders, be forsaking Aion. Forgot not and forsooken."

"What kind of bird is that in the distance," Ewan whispered to Cruedwyn, pointing.

The bard squinted into the sun. "I dunno. Looks like some sort of raven. They fly over to the mainland from Apaté all the time and feed in this valley. The island is covered with them."

That was enough. Ewan found his faith, took the leap. Providence had come rushing in.

"We take the Raven Trail," he declared with finality. The strength of his voice surprised everyone, including him. "I've dreamed this. In my world. *Before* coming here, when I dreamt the song, I saw those towers, that river, that bird, high in the sky. Cruedwyn says the ravens come from Apaté. We take their trail. If Flogg will let . . ."

He turned to face the gnome, his words trailing away almost before he spoke them.

"I'm not sure what to say. I'm sorry. But if you will do this for me, for my brother. . . ."

Flogg grew still. His worn face betrayed no emotion—not sadness, nor anger, just stillness. Like a stone planted deep in the earth. He was proudly unbeautiful.

"Not for manling, Flogg does. See? For Aion, alone, who Called."

Pulling his satchel strap tighter to his chest, he stomped away.

CHAPTER 37

Raven Trail

They stood on the rocky shoals of the coast just south of Stratamore. The sun, bleached and globulous in the sky, grew ever darker under the weight of shadows billowing toward the mainland from Apaté. The capital city had prospered around one of the most pleasant coves in the kingdom. As it wrapped north and east toward Faielyn, the beaches turned to fine white powder, with water the color of *quoi* stones, like the Highlanders gave as gifts to their wives. Blue and green, like a peacock's feathers.

This was not one of those shores.

Flogg had led them instead to a long promontory of limestone and chalk rising perhaps thirty, maybe fifty feet above sea level. The jutting crescent-shaped wall bordered the sea a few miles before diminishing to the north, nearer Stratamore. The beach below was nothing but flat sheets of rock and rough mixtures of sand and broken seashells caked with dried salts. Roots from a handful of small, particularly tenacious old trees leaned out over the water from pockets of soil collected from the sea, eroded into the stone, leaving a dramatic patchwork of nooks, scoops, and crannies, and green-leafed trees on the white shoreline fence. Long ago, some had suggested building the King's City on top of the bald earth here as it was a more defensible position against seaborne raids. But old King Radygaar, who first chose the site, preferred other locations for bloody war campaigns. Stratamore was meant for peace and commerce, fine art and illustrious diplomacy. For that, the quiet cove to the north was far more suitable.

"Findings and bindings!"

Flogg was clearly agitated. They had been searching up and down the most obvious and likely stretch of land for nearly three hours. The footing was treacherous, with countless potholes and gullies of worn stone. Some were quite deep. The limestone wall was honeycombed with possible caves, though most terminated after only a few feet. "Wonderings, blunderings in Flogg's head. Black Croaker long traveled ago. Ten tens of years."

He wiped sweat from his bulging brow, panting.

"Tell manling riddle," he barked.

Sorge winked at his young charge. "You might have noticed, we have many riddles."

"No, really?" Ewan said, feigning surprise.

"How do you comprehend life without riddles? Anyway, gnome children sing this song. My translation isn't exact, but it's close:

"Trail of Birds, heed the words,
High tide no. Low tide go."

He poked the ground with his staff. "It's here somewhere."

"I've *never* heard that riddle," said Creed thoughtfully, as if he were disappointed in himself. "In any event, we've looked and looked. The shoreline has probably been reshaped a dozen times or more in the last hundred years. Eh, Flogg? Sorge, my friend, it's time to rethink. *Every windcraft needs an oar.*"

"You think we need a backup? Just what do you suggest? This *is* our backup plan."

"I dunno. Creeds are excellent swimmers."

The monk ignored him. "Even if the shoreline has changed, it is doubtful the caves have. The entrance must be somewhere near."

Asandra was in water up to her knees, furiously splashing about. "When the tide is high, the riddle must mean the entrance is hidden, right? We are now at low tide. We've searched up and down this shore. Flogg, are you sure the Raven Trail begins here?"

Flogg bent down, put his fingers to the ground as if sucking the earth into his arms, his brain. "Kneeling, feeling rulvôl deep below rock. Water like blood through veins. But cannot find door. Big gnome magic."

"Use some of your own magic then, dwarf!" Cruedwyn exclaimed. He laughed. Everything was a joke to Cruedwyn.

"It's not that kind of magic," Asandra said nearby, pulling strands of wet, clinging hair from her face. Though she worked near Sorge, she never spoke to him, never looked at him. Ewan couldn't help but wonder why was she even here. "Flogg refers to the way they build, which keeps things hidden. Gnomes are highly secretive. The skill to build something so well, to hide it in plain sight so craftily that even one of their own cannot find it, is highly prized. It is part of how they rank themselves. Who built what? How known, or *unknown*, is it?"

They kept searching. Ewan grew more impatient with each passing moment. Gazing across the narrow channel of water between
the mainland and Apaté—some ten miles perhaps?—the island
rose gray and stained from the sea. Steep shores and sharp rocks
faced toward Stratamore. Greener fields and shallower hills curved
north around the island. On the edge of that transition, between
cliffs and fields, stood a tall, black tower. Just a speck from here, but
Sorge had pointed it out: The Tower of Ravens. A ribbon of black
vapor funneled up from the tower, like ash and soot billowing from
a volcano. Unlike smoke, it did not dissipate in the wind.

If Hadyn was alive, he was *there*. So near, yet unreachable. To
think his brother was being held prisoner, possibly in pain, in danger, so near, made him sick.

The plan was perhaps too simple: find the Raven Trail, sneak
across, underground, onto the island, then Ewan would pretend to
be one of the Lost and hopefully locate Hadyn. After that . . . well,
they would just have to wing it. If they ever got there. Ewan's eyes
wandered back to the island. This time he noted what looked like
distant ships streaming toward the small harbor on the northern
side, and thin ant trails of people climbing the hill toward the
tower.

The Nameless.

Hadyn, possibly, with them.

"C'mon, guys, we can do this!" he blurted with sudden conviction. He started a cadence, like a drill sergeant on a twenty-mile
run. "High . . . Tide . . . No . . . Low . . . Tide . . . Go! High . . .
Tide . . . No . . ."

Waves crashed on the rocks, whispered on the sand, slurping
back to the sea. Wind scuttled amongst brittle stalks of dune grass

high above them. These were the only sounds. Water, sand, and Ewan's chant. Sorge started laughing.

"I don't believe it. Do you hear it? Listen to what he's saying. It's in the song!" he exclaimed. "Ewan just revealed the magic."

Everyone froze. Blank-faced, Ewan said, "I did?"

"Same words, different emphasis: 'High tide—no low tide—Go!'" He paused, thinking. "By the Nines, could it really be that simple? Is it a translation error, Flogg?"

Flogg scowled at the ground, irritated to have missed something so obvious, to have forgotten. As a gnome, he could not help but take it personally. Ewan was pleased to have figured it out, although he still wasn't sure exactly *what* he had figured out. Cruedwyn remained dubious.

"So it's exactly the opposite of how it sounds at first, right? Is that the best we've got?"

"I guess we'll find out when the tide comes in. Maybe the water drains into one of these holes or caverns." Sorge's eyes lit up. "That's got to be it."

Glad to be done with critical thinking, Cruedwyn slapped his palms together and rubbed.

"By my sword," he exclaimed, "I'll grow gills if I have to! We Creeds tire of too much talk. Tonight, we swim!"

ΠΟιε SECΙΕΤS

Πemesia's dark hair was a starless night, a raven on her shoulder. Eyes gleaming, she strolled leisurely around her prized captive.

"My honored guest," she cooed. "I've *so* looked forward to this."

Hadyn slumped in a rickety wooden chair, shirt torn, still ragged from the long hike up the slopes of Apaté and the many winding stairs to Nemesia's tower. His cheek and forearms were bruised. Though bound, he was no longer blindfolded. One eye was nearly swollen shut.

"What do you want?" he asked. The words scraped in his dry throat like sand. His eyes rolled here and there. Six torches burned in brackets on the walls, causing the circular chamber to nervously leap with bat-like shadows. Outside, all was darkness.

"I want everything you have to give," Nemesia said sweetly, trailing one finger across his face, "which is to say, nothing, since you have nothing. You *are* nothing."

"Release me then," Hadyn said. Pain and exhaustion made him reckless. "If I'm of no use, release me."

"Oh, my dear," purred the witch. "It's not what you can give me, it's what I can give you that matters. You will be part of my grand ceremony. As I said, my honored guest."

Hadyn flopped back, laughing hoarsely. His head felt like lead. Nemesia swept her hand toward the far wall, on which hung a huge map of all Karac Tor. She grinned, wild and beautiful.

"Behold, the banishment of hope, the darkening of the land, and the collapse of Aion's pitiful kingdom. A fitting retribution for the false promises of a faraway King, don't you think? On the morrow, we shall journey to the Sacred Grove—you and I and all my bombs—and there I shall begin returning the land to the ways of the Old Gods. The stone I throw from Apaté shall ripple out to the farthest corners of the kingdom. And my army of children shall lead them."

Head slumped to his chest, it was hard to tell if Hadyn had heard or not. In the witch's tower, clarity was constant warfare. But something was funny. He didn't know what, but *something* was funny. He snorted. Nemesia smiled uncertainly with him, at him. Hadyn began to roar hysterically.

"Sacred Grove, is that what you called it?" he laughed until tears rolled down his cheeks. "Sacred like my butt, maybe! Your butt!"—that really set him laughing—"I mean, I may just be a teen and all. But I'm not an idiot. You can't just rename evil, call it good, and have that mean anything." He stared at her cross-eyed, struggling to focus, "I dub thee Scary Bird Lady. Snake Charmer. Katie

Couric. They're all just words. Just because you use a word doesn't make it true. You're Nemesia, the witch. The deceiver. You've stolen these kids' minds and promised them a lie. Old Gods is just another way of saying false gods."

Nemesia showed her teeth, a terrible smile frozen to her face. Seductively, her gown flowing in the light breeze, she strolled behind Hadyn, placing her hands on his head, holding it forward. Her fingernails scraped against his skin.

"You want truth so much, let me give it to you now. You will *never* return. You know that, right? That map is the only world you'll ever have again. Bye-bye, Daddy."

Hadyn slurred his words. "You're bluffing."

"Am I? A person only bluffs if they have something to gain."

"Or lose." He felt daring. Probably going to die anyway, right? "I've learned a bit since coming here. I know the Book of Names is older than you, older than all your magic. I know Aion is more powerful than *anyone*."

Nemesia hissed. "You know nothing! You probably cannot even spell *Aion*. A few stories told by a failed monk—a failed warrior, a traitor—and you think you know all about my world? Tell me, Hadyn Barlow. Did Sorge tell you his story. *Our* story?"

Hadyn hesitated.

"No, of course not. It might cause you to lose faith, to know the failings of the one trusted to get you home. But since you are *so* interested in truth, allow me. It's a simple tale. Twenty years ago, I believed like you. You see, I come from another place, too. Another country, far to the west. I am of mixed blood, the illegitimate daughter of a S'Qoth cult priestess and a wandering Bitterman warrior, a father I've never known. At thirteen, my gift was revealed—a foreign gift in the eyes of my mother's people, terrifying even to me at the time. When she saw my mirling power, my mother beat me, calling me heretic. I fled Quil in search of my father's land, but never made it there, eventually stumbling half-dead across the threshold of the Black Abbey. There, I was trained and nurtured. I was powerful. They found a use for me."

"Sorge traveled all the land in those days, with Corus, the great Champion, as Initiate to Master. They were both skilled with bow and sword and deep friends. They took the oath of Bloodkin together, and each bore the Mark of Twine on his arm for the other. When Sorge and I met by chance, our hearts briefly entwined. But Corus also loved me. Sorge was young and temperamental. When he discovered my attraction to Corus, he became wild with jealousy. He feared that Corus, with all his fame, would win my heart. And it was true. In spite of Sorge's many charms and skills, Corus became my lover. Seeing us together one night, Sorge went mad and attacked Corus. They had a mighty duel of blades. In the end, Corus would have killed him, but withheld. Sorge fled, humiliated. In revenge, he struck a rash bargain with the Fey Queen to betray his master. Pretending repentance and submission, he led Corus into an ambush—one mere mortals could not thwart. Corus, my love, passed into shadow and bondage and was gone. No one knows where. He is captive still."

Nemesia stared out the window with vacant, hard eyes.

"Do you know what I did, Hadyn Barlow? I cried out to Olfadr, cried out to Aion his son. Do you hear me, outlander? I cried out! Like you might, even now. I called upon my mirling skills to undo Sorge's plans, to find my love. When this failed, I dared Aion to stop me as I turned to darker arts, older ways. I embraced the paths of my mother's people. Yes, I dared the Great Prince to intervene in judgment, and feared him, until one day I realized I no longer cared . . . and no longer feared. By then it was *I* who was feared. So the Black Abbey cast me out. I drifted away, to this island. I was drawn to the ravens, and they to me. And with every step I took I cursed Olfadr's name."

She grew quiet. Crooked shadows crawled like vines across the paved slabs underfoot and the mortared walls. Dark, breathless firelight caught in her eyes.

"Now," she said, and the resolve in her voice made courage drain from Hadyn like blood from a wound. The sorceress's voice had become a silken, husky whisper. "Now, I have drawn you and thousands more like you. All to me. To the darkening which *Aion* has brought upon this land by his neglect, his lies. When you understand this, you will see I do not truly cause the darkness. The darkness I create merely clarifies and reveals his abstention and neglect. Hah! Let him hide in faraway Isgurd forever. Let him rot in all our minds as myth and legend. The fact is, if ever Aion lived, he abandoned us long ago. Good riddance! Thus I bring liberation. Let the world fall from him forever, that it might finally stand on its own."

The more Nemesia spoke, the more her words smudged together in his head. Hadyn tried to form an answer. "He . . . will come again." He heard his own voice as if from the bottom of a hole. For some reason, he believed. He truly believed.

"The famous Ninth Coming? Oh my dear, if you are really hanging your hope on such folly, then you are more lost than all my precious little bombs put together."

But Hadyn was thinking of something else. "My brother."

"You think he will come, too? Foolish boy, he's probably dead. Don't worry, you will join him soon enough if you like." She laughed. "See, outlander? It's like I tell all my bombs. Nothing matters."

She strolled away, a flurry of wind and drama, her words echoing over and over.

Nothing matters, nothing matters.

A raven croaked. Hadyn heard his own ragged breath reflect off the stone walls.

Really, what did it matter? Evil was so strong and he was so weak. Bad things happened. Terrible things. Mom was gone. He had lost his friends. He was stuck, here. *Nothing . . . matters.* The repetition grew stronger, beating down on his mind, further wearing his defenses. Sitting alone, trapped in her tower, for the first time, Hadyn couldn't remember why he ever believed otherwise.

CHAPTER 39

Under the Bay

F inally, night had fallen. The outline of the moon, lost in a haze of low, black vapor, was quite full. High tide had filled the beach with froth and foam and lapping waves noisily crashing against the limestone, gleaming like milk in the moonlight. The five sojourners slopped through water up to their knees, fighting the undertow, searching in the dark for what could not be seen. They were systematically sweeping north, wet, tired and frustrated. Ewan felt like giving up. But they couldn't. Another hour passed. Then another. Then Sorge called out, "Listen! Do you hear that? It sounds like a roaring."

"I hear it!" Asandra shouted. "There, right where Ewan is about to—"

Ewan put a hand out to steady himself, leaning against the wet ridge of stone. He was in water up to his waist. Instead of the expected wall, he heard a roar, then a rush of water underneath him. In a blink, his silhouetted form disappeared into the salty depths. Sorge dove toward him, was sucked down. Flogg was next.

The short ride tumbled and twisted down a tube of rock mercifully smoothed by the long ago gnomish builder of the Raven Trail, whoever he was. They spilled in sequence, all five, from the slick channel into thirty feet of open air, plummeting into a deep reservoir fed every night by the tide.

Darkness engulfed them. Ewan could hear the steady roar of the falling water, but saw nothing, not even a shimmer of movement when he waved his hands. It was blacker than any blackness he had ever known. Treading water, he heard Cruedwyn's voice, spluttering.

"To what shall I compare thee? To a sow giving birth? Ahh! . . . grunt, squirt, snort, *splash*!" He paused for effect. "At the moment, I think I know how they feel. The piglets, not the sow."

"Flogg," Sorge said, spitting. "Can you see?"

"Aye," the gnome answered. "But flint no good."

"Asandra?"

"Yes."

"Good. Ewan?"

"Here."

Someone was swimming tentatively away. Flogg called them.

"This way. Come shoreling."

Bumped and bruised, but no worse for wear, all five pulled themselves sopping wet onto an embankment of solid rock.

Cruedwyn declared, "I just *love* wet chain mail! Is anyone else wet but me?"

Ewan heard what sounded like hands fumbling through loose rocks, followed by Sorge whispering a command. Soon, a soft blue glow appeared, blossoming from a roundish stone in the monk's palm. He whispered to it, coaxing soft light. The darkness receded.

"Some stones are better than others," he apologized. "A greater skill could draw out more. But this helps." He looked around. "The water must somehow drain during the day, and fill again at night."

Ewan stared at the rock, pulsing like a winter star in Sorge's hand. Though it brightened the cave, it had the opposite effect on his mood. He tried not to whine, had tried ever since the Stone House, ever since Hadyn's little trick with the latch. No one liked to admit to jealousy. But Sorge's rock tipped him over the edge. "I don't get it," he complained. "Hadyn has a power. You can do cool stuff with rocks. Asandra catches Watchers . . ." He let his words trail away, hoping Sorge would catch his unspoken question. When you compete against your brother for everything, you don't like to have to spell it out.

Sorge studied his face in the dimness, taking careful measure of the moment. Surely, Ewan thought . . . surely the monk could remember what it was like to be younger, dreaming of greatness? "Secrets unfold over time, Ewan. But I daresay you are missing the obvious. How did you come to this world? Who dreamed the way?"

Ewan reached for the inner folds of his loose-fitting shirt, relieved to feel the Irish whistle's thin metal shaft, intact. It had survived the waterfall.

"It's not the same. You know it."

"So you are telling me your *flute* is magical. Is that it?"

"Look, Hadyn can't open locks on my world, not with words at least. And I'm wondering why not me?"

"Ahh. Well, you should know, I asked the opposite question when you first came. Why you, I thought? When Father Eldoran said you were marked with power, I wasn't sure I believed. Nemesia fears you, and I am glad for that. But Ewan, power alone is an empty road. If you wish to envy something, envy strength of heart. The choices you make, the one you serve—these are more powerful than all the world's magic."

"Maybe, but on my world, magic is bad. Here . . . I want it. I don't want to be the only one without."

He glanced around self-consciously, not wanting to broadcast his little moment of confession more than necessary. Cruedwyn was busy with a cave crab dangling from his britches, hopping about and cursing. Flogg and Asandra were still wringing water out of their clothes.

"I do not know your world," Sorge said, bending low, placing the blue stone between their faces. "But Magic is a word, like *Pleasure* or *Fun*. Or *Pain* or *Knowledge*. There can be pleasure in evil, pleasure in selfishness and lust, but surely not all pleasure is evil? And discipline can be painful, but also healing to the soul. Does that make me enjoy the pain of it? No, it just makes me understand the word better, with fuller meaning. The source from which a thing comes, and the end to which it is put, reveals the worth and goodness of the thing. Magic is no different. On the one hand, it is just a word. On the other . . ."

His voice trailed away. Ewan shrunk into himself. "Nevermind. You don't understand."

"Don't give up on me yet, my young friend! You're talking about magic and power, not just common stuff—grace and kindness and the power of decency—although those are quite magical, too, when they touch you. No, you wonder about the strange realms of shadow and light, Fey Folk and Watchers, the nether regions."

Sorge smiled. "Even the mysterious possibility of twinkling worlds in the far-flung night sky high above our heads."

Ewan lifted his face toward the cavern ceiling. His heart fluttered. "Do you think that's where I came from?"

Sorge followed his gaze into the darkness. "You mean, up, up, up? Or perhaps from some other place entirely? Like where we are now, below Karac Tor, yet still *within* Karac Tor. Worlds within worlds. But don't you see, it's all part of the same magic? You are interested in power. I ask you, how did you come to the bottom of a tree outside the Gray Abbey?"

"Exactly. That's what I'm asking you."

"I don't know!" Sorge said with relish. "That's my answer. Magic is everywhere, but it must be perceived. Aion speaks in the Nine, the Book of Law, the Hall of Ages. But who listens? Who notices? Why you and not another? Or not you? And so it is that realms of wonder inhabit the invisible places all around us. This is the true magic. Pick another word if that one doesn't suit you. But now you're merely choosing the best way to describe something, not whether the thing is right or wrong."

"*Better to live with no eyes,*" said Asandra, who, apparently, had been listening all along, "*than with eyes closed. So say the Highlanders.*"

Ewan sagged, feeling defeated. "I just want to know what *my* magic is!"

"Halt magicals! Time for budging and trudging."

Sorge breathed onto his stone again, putting more strength into the light. The illumination expanded, revealing an enormous cave with a vaulted ceiling beyond the glow's reach. The walls curved upward, rough and glittering. Cones of rock jutted upward and downward gave the cavern the look of a giant mouth lined top and bottom with ragged teeth. Intermittently, tidal water fell from above into the dark pool behind them. The only visible tunnel headed . . .

"East, I think," Sorge guessed, pointing. "Easy enough."

"Definitely east," Cruedwyn added. "Creeds are born with a keen sense of direction. Like bloodhounds. Never been lost. Follow me!"

He stumbled forward, tripped on a low shelf of rock. His sword whined and warbled.

"Probably best if I guard the rear," he said quickly and hopped to his feet, brushing himself off. "You lead, Sorge. I insist."

They gathered their belongings and set off. The Row of the Black Croaker was a mess of twists and turns, but fortunately, remained a single shaft for many miles, with room enough to walk two beside. They wound up and down narrow stairs of slippery rock, climbed steep walls, where they had to boost one up and then reach down for the next. More than once, they were forced to hug the rough stone with their back and inch along while huge, open pits of darkness yawned before them. Ewan just stared straight ahead, thankful now for his practice on the rope bridge in Redthorn. He never would have made it, otherwise.

They pressed on, as Flogg said, trudging and budging, passing veins of yellow crystal and blue gemstones that glittered like light on water. They entered cavern after cavern of sweeping scale, with stone formations that soared beyond the reach of Sorge's light, only to pass next into narrow, claustrophobic tunnels where they had to crawl single file, on all fours, or scrape along on their bellies and elbows. Everywhere, the air was cool, mossy, damp. Once, a blast of heat hit them, but no once could tell from where.

Asandra asked, "How many miles under the bay to the island?"

Ewan hadn't even considered the fact that somewhere far above his head a boat might be gliding past. The thought made his throat constrict, made it feel as if the caves were closing in around him. His skin felt clammy.

"Five miles. Maybe ten. I'm not sure. Flogg, how do we get out of the Raven Trail? Is the exit a trick, like the entrance?"

Flogg had no answer. They stopped twice to rest, munching on dried apricots and pork (which was slimy from the water dowsing), then huddled together for warmth in their damp clothes. Then, more trudging. They walked until their legs ached, until they were sick of blue light and dark caves and glittering rock. When they reached a fork in the tunnel, faced with three possible branches, Flogg knelt and placed his fingers on the rough stone. His eyes became vacant and his ears no longer mattered, only the connection of flesh to stone, the voice of the deep earth, the hearing of touch.

"Trees, grass," he pointed to the center shaft. "Cry of blackwings."

No one spoke as they moved deeper into the center passage, but Ewan felt fear rising like the tide. Fear turning to desperation, boring inside, subsuming his thoughts. Perhaps they *had* been hasty?

Sorge held the cool, radiant stone aloft. The path became tighter, steeper. They moved slower, breathing hard, dragging their feet. All save Flogg, who seemed downright cheerful. Ewan noticed even Cruedwyn starting to grow haggard. There simply wasn't enough light. The weight of the earth pressed upon them like a tomb. The air felt close, suffocating. They kept crawling along, every step more tedious than the last. Ewan felt near to collapse. The surface of the land, the promise of grass and light and stars just above, felt so utterly far away it caused jolts of anxiety to consider if he might ever get out. Plus, they had been walking for hours and he hadn't slept at all. He trailed a finger along the wall to his right, wanting to feel connected to something, earth and stone, more than the swallowing darkness. He felt the surface of the rock gradually become more porous, sulfurous—less the rock of common caves and mines, and more like the remnants of ancient molten flows.

"The stone is changing," he said.

"Fire mountain," Flogg replied. "Burnings and churnings, Apaté. Ages gone."

"We need rest," Asandra declared. Her tone was not belligerent, just fatigued. When Hadyn had been kidnapped, she seemed to soften. Strange timing. "We've traveled all night, with no idea where we are or how far we've come. Clearer heads will serve our purpose better."

"Speak for yourself," Cruedwyn boasted, sounding half drunk. "A Creed never tires."

But his hair was disheveled and his eyelids sagged. When his sword wobbled in protest, he slapped tiredly at his thigh. "Oh grow up! It was just a joke."

Ewan, too, was exhausted. Sorge relented.

"There is a large chamber ahead. We'll eat there and rest for a few hours. No more."

CHAPTER 40

Tree Dreams

They found a river in the next chamber, flowing opposite the direction they were moving. It ended in a swirling pool, presumably disappearing next into the water table deep underground. Sorge scooped his hand in the flow.

"Fresh," he said, surprised. But then his face wrinkled. "Fresh, but strange."

They all drank, and all felt the same. The taste was nearly clean, but felt unwell in their stomachs. Several planks of old, rotten driftwood were scattered around the chamber. They found pulleys and moldering rope dangling from somewhere up high, the ruins of what looked like carts and crates, and a platform of some sort, decades old, with rusted gears and a metal tube that reached down into the water. Like an old pump.

"*Rulvôl* diggings. Gnome camp," Flogg explained.

He and Cruedwyn set about gathering any scraps that looked like they might still have fire in them. The gnome pulled a bulging pouch from his satchel and sprinkled a little black powder on the wood.

"Back," he warned. Then lit it.

With a whoosh and pop, the wood caught fire. They fed it and leaned close, grateful for dry heat. They ate and slept and warmed their bones. Ewan had not realized how chattering cold he had been, for so long.

When they broke camp several hours later, they followed the river. The deeper they went, the more Sorge's stone dimmed. More than once, Ewan stumbled, even though his feet had not slipped. After resting, though more alert, he found it harder and harder to concentrate. The others staggered as well.

They passed through chamber after chamber connected by long, snaking tunnels. None of the passages were sculpted or refined—no arched doorways or carved columns of stone. There was evidence of workmanship in pulleys and carts, but even these were fairly primitive.

Then things changed. Ewan began noticing faint marks, black birds painted on the rock. Ravens. For so long, their path had drilled deeper into the earth. Now they seemed to be moving *up*, steeply at times. The only constant was the water, flowing down channels of rock on either side of their path. They crossed single file over natural, curved bridges of rock, while underneath the current bubbled swiftly by; again, at a dead end, they had to leap across. Ever it flowed beside them. Like salmon swimming upstream, they climbed higher and higher, creatures of darkness, wishing for light.

"I can't think straight anymore," Ewan said hopelessly. "It's like my brain's in a vice. Everything is closing in."

"The confusion of Nemesia seeps into the earth itself here," Sorge replied. "You are not tired, so much as bedeviled."

They were almost climbing vertically now, up long, steep flights of cut-stone stairs—more evidence of basic craftsmanship. Small hope, but it meant someone had created the path and therefore eventually it must lead somewhere. Such was the logic, Sorge reassured. But the strange thickening of air continued. Ewan felt near to fainting. He just wanted to sleep.

So tired . . .

At the top of what seemed like an endless ladder of crumbling steps, splashed by water from above, Asandra's foot slipped. She cried out. Cruedwyn barely caught her wrist. Flogg barely caught Cruedwyn. They pulled one another onto the next ledge.

"Blarmy that," Creed breathed. "I think we're buggered."

And so they were. At the top of the last flight of stairs, they had come upon what none were expecting: a broad, flat pool of water in a large, circular chamber. No other tunnels or paths. Dead end. The narrow ledge was the only patch of rock not submerged. It overlooked the vast, still water.

"No way out. No other paths."

Sorge said, "Something doesn't feel right. Asandra, what do you sense?"

"The water is foul. Or the air. Or the trees. I'm not sure."

"Black witch," Flogg grunted. "Close. Poisons all."

Sorge hiked up his robe and stepped into the water, tracing the perimeter with his light. The lake stretched a couple hundred feet from front to back. Water poured over the sides in a shower of noisy rain.

"There must be a spring in the middle," he called back to the others. "Or a collection point for runoff water from the surface. Either way, this is the beginning of our river."

"Any tunnels back there?" Ewan called. His voice echoed over the water.

Sorge shook his head. The water seemed an even depth, above the knee. After his circuit around the outer edge, the monk sloshed toward the middle. His light brought a strange revelation. The low ceiling was stone, as expected, but also thickly matted with earth and roots. Gnarled, twisting fingers of wood hung down from perhaps thirty feet above, smelling like moss. Here and there, wherever they broke through the bed of stone, they groped toward the mostly pellucid pool like jealous, clutching hands, plunging deep. Ewan figured this was a good sign. They must be close to the surface. It made him want to scream.

So close! And so strange. The roots seemed to hang from nothing. As his eyes adjusted more, Ewan noticed the tangled masses formed a pattern of two circles, one inside another. The outer circle of roots was nearly the size of the entire area of the pool. But there in the center, another enormous clump snaked downward, drinking lustily. Ewan could almost hear the roots gulping. The tree above must be enormous.

"Of water, wood dreaming," Asandra said thoughtfully.

Sorge started. "What did you say?"

The mirling raised her eyes. "Where did I hear that?"

"From me," Sorge said. "The riddle."

"In division, completion
In darkness, door shone
Of water, wood dreaming
To sunlight, from stone"

He turned a mad circle, tensing.

"We were divided when they stole Hadyn. Now we want to be complete again. Do you see? The promise is that in the darkness, we will find a door. What does wood dream of? If you were a tree, Cruedwyn, a mighty oak, what would you dream of?"

"Oh, I think a pretty little maple, don't you? Maybe a willow, they're so graceful and—"

"Water!" the monk reached down, splashing in the pool, pointing to the hanging roots. "We will find our way to sunlight, out of the stone, through the dreaming woods." He barked a command. "Flogg!"

Already, the gnome was splashing his way toward the center tree, grasping the low roots, scuttling up with ease. Moments later, he called down: "Flogg cannot join tree."

"He means connect with it, like he does the earth," Sorge whispered to Ewan. "This has to be it. Keep looking!" he cried.

"Maybe you should turn off your light," Ewan observed. "The riddle says, *in darkness*."

"Of course!"

Sorge snuffed the rock like a candle. Slowly, everyone's eyes adjusted to the total darkness. Very nearly total.

"There!" Asandra whispered.

On the far wall, a thin beam of light poured down from the ceiling. Hanging beside it, like an invitation, was a long, coiled tree root.

". . . or maybe a birch," Cruedwyn continued, finger to chin, grinning. "They have that nice, white bark. So lovely."

Sorge grabbed the swordsman by the sleeve of his shirt, hauling him toward the light. It was time to rejoin the land of the sun.

CHAPTER 41

Sacred Grove

Really, it had been so simple, so obvious, they might have never found it. One of the largest roots had been carved of stone, weathered and shaped to perfectly mimic the gangly mass of other roots around it. On the back side, the rock was knotted into primitive, climbable steps, which wound upward into a hollowing of the trunk above, from which the faint traces of light could be seen.

They emerged carefully, one leg, one arm at a time, from the rotund belly of the great tree. Remarkably, it was still alive. Cruedwyn went first, in case there was resistance. Then Sorge, Flogg, Asandra. Lastly, Ewan.

Hunched low to the ground, all five took time to squeeze clumps of grass in their fists, reveling in the feel, the smells, of earth and open air. Though the sun was mostly choked by the violence of

the black cloud, there was still *light*, and it felt sweet to the soul. In
the twilight gray, Sorge guessed it to be late morning, nearing noon.

"See," he said, pointing. They scooted close enough to peer
over a rim of rock. From here they could see their position, on a
flat-topped bulge of land, part of a series of low hills overlooking
a broad sweep of valley. Not too far away, and very nearly level to
their height, across a shallow ravine where a series of smaller creeks
gathered water for the river in the valley below, the Tower of Ravens
was sculpted from the black stone of the hillside. The structure was
dominated by a tall central tower, mostly windowless, with few
additional fortifications around the base. Not a true fortress, but the
steep hillside offered a natural defensive position, and the walls of
the tower looked imposingly solid. To the west, they saw the three
white towers of glittering Stratamore and tall-masted ships gliding
tranquilly in and out the King's Port. Spanning their field of view,
the blue waters of the bay crawled wave upon wave toward land.
Ribbons of golden beach traced the face of the island's shores.

It was a lovely sight, even draped in shadow, but it was the
procession below that immediately grabbed everyone's attention.
Streaming down the hillside from Nemesia's tower, a huge swath
of people teemed across the shallow ravine, slowly marching up
the hill toward . . . them. To the very circle of trees where they
lay. The crowd was still hundreds of yards away, but the distance
would close fast. A thousand glum youths, maybe two, trod along
in silence, their faces nothing but unrecognizable globs. Their
clothing was drab and common, their line impossibly long and slow
and noiseless, except for the low stampede of feet.

"I think that's Hadyn," Ewan said, his voice catching. "In the
front. I'm not sure."

A hard, lovely woman with black hair led them. Nemesia, holding the Staff of Shades aloft. She wore a seductive gown, shimmering in dark hues, with a high collar, a tiara of silver, and a billowing cape. Viscous streamers of unlight trailed from the tip of her staff, chewing at the air, as if eating it.

"Unexpected," Cruedwyn murmured, watching the crowd.

"They don't see us, do they? Is that why they're coming?"

"No, no." Sorge scanned the high grassy bluff. Their location was a natural outlook; yet unnatural, also. The trees were arranged with perfect symmetry, forming an outer circle of beech at the perimeter, many feet apart, with an inner circle of some sort of cedar. At the very center was a massive, ancient willow. Its great, feathered branches hung low.

"*Um*, Sorge. Are you seeing what I'm seeing?" Ewan said carefully.

Sorge grunted disconsolately. Everyone saw. Trees and trunks laced with intricate carvings. Each and every one. With strange symbols that made Ewan feel as if he were crossing his eyes to look upon them. The sight made him wobbly and nauseous. In the center, the large willow trunk was the worst, carved not with symbols, but the grotesque masks of beastly creatures, of fangs and claws and horns. Furthermore, all the branches dangled with an assortment of chimes and bells, glass beads, amulets, daggers, and talismans made of brass. Ewan hadn't even noticed the multifaceted sounds, so sudden and grateful was their arrival to light and land. But he heard them now. The whole grove tinkled in the gentlest of breezes, a cacophony of eerie noises.

"Now tell me, I dare you, tell me that's not a pretty tree," said Cruedwyn admiringly. "Just like I said. So graceful, folding over—"

"Creed!"

"Right. We'll need to spread ourselves. I'm thinking Flogg can lay some powder for distraction. Ewan is best positioned higher up the hill, out of harm's way." He pointed. "Behind that outcropping of rock should be perfect. The mirling should be with him. She is of no use in this battle."

"Wrong, swordsman," Asandra said cooly. "Nemesia is coming to this grove to summon Watchers. I hear them already. But I will stay with Ewan, and that outcropping is as good as anywhere. You will see the strength of the Blacks is not forgotten."

"Everyone's a hero," Cruedwyn said dismissively. He turned his attention to Sorge's rosewood staff. "You remember metal, don't you? Or do you still want to play with sticks?"

Sorge tightened his grip. "This will do."

"Hey, what are those for?" Ewan cut in nervously, his throat catching. Sorge followed his pointing finger to the outer ring of trees where stacks of crude bows and bulging quivers were laid against the trunks. Likewise, propped against the inner cedars were dozens of small, freshly carved wooden wands. All bore similar mystic runes.

The implications were clear. Nemesia was building an arsenal. Sorge crawled a few paces and touched one of the wands, jerking his hand back as if burned. He spat on his fingers and wiped them on the grass. Something deeply unsettling was at work.

Ewan whispered, "Will somebody please tell me what's going on?"

"This is a Sacred Grove—a mockery of the term. Old magic dwells here."

Sorge struck the earth with his fist. "I knew I felt something in the water below. It all makes sense now. The roots are not only drinking, but depositing blasphemy into the earth. The water we drank was defiled. It is spreading underground. How could I be so dense?"

"*I*, even more," Asandra said ruefully. "I'm ashamed. We are in a place of great evil. My skin is crawling."

"Mine, too," Ewan whispered.

"All very spooky, I'm sure," Cruedwyn said. "As for me . . ." He quietly pulled out his sword. Ewan was struck again by the beauty of the blade. The metal was more than merely long and sharp, it was sober and clean, like a holy relic of old, or a song that stirs the hearts of men. On the haft, two amber eyes gleamed above the dragon jaws. Creed glanced down into the ravine, grinning wolfishly. "Never taken on a thousand before. Not sober, anyway. What was my previous high? Thirteen?" Sweat trickled down his cheeks. "Looks like today's my lucky day."

Sorge tapped him on the shoulder. "If you're finished . . . ?"

"Yes, yes, fine. Next, Flogg makes some noise and smoke, while you and I hit the front line and scatter their ranks. They aren't fighters. Blarmy, it looks like they're doing good to all be facing the same direction. But there are so many."

Sorge warned, "Do what you must, Creed, but only wound them, if possible. They are just children. Spellbound, not evil."

"Right," Cruedwyn said with obvious irony. "No killing. Seems fair. One, two thousand, against five." He assessed his team. "Strike that, against two. Are you seeing the same thing I'm seeing, Sorge?"

"I mean it. None. If possible."

"Shall I just beat them across the shoulders with the flat of my blade?" Cruedwyn teased. "Or wave and make threatening hand gestures? Hurl clever insults? I know, I'll charm them with the mirling's tender personality!"

He winked at Asandra, who rolled her eyes.

"Perhaps if the bard would just wave his sword and talk," she said, "the heat might scare them all away."

Ewan snickered. Cruedwyn said, "Lovely girl, Sorge. Does she have a sister?"

"Stop it, both of you. I said none *if possible*. Do what you must. We have your sword and my staff. It will have to be enough."

Ewan gently intervened. "Sorge, look at how many of them there are. Your staff is not enough. Take one of the bows."

"Second," said Cruedwyn.

"Aye," said Flogg.

Before the monk could protest, Ewan pressed further, "Eldoran gave you permission, Sorge. You're a Master Bowman."

"Was," Sorge corrected.

"So what? What about all that big Champion speech you gave me? Or was that only for me, the *thirteen*-year-old? Sorge, we've come all this way—"

"No more!" the monk muttered dangerously, his eyes twitching. "You know nothing, little brother. I was skilled and strong once. Even more proud. And stupid and brittle. I betrayed my own Bloodkin. I lost my way."

Flogg, having left the conversation, was furiously at work with his bags of black powder.

"All lose way. Fallings, crawlings."

Sorge faced the gnome, lines of anguish traced in his dark skin. "For what, my friend? For fame? Swordplay? The last Champion of Karac Tor is lost because of me."

Cruedwyn groaned. "Allow me to pause and invite us all back to the *real* world, where a *whole lot of weird people* are coming this way and, forgive me, I don't think it's to invite us to tea. We have a narrow moment, a decent element of surprise. Time to buck up and fight."

Sorge took a deep breath, found Ewan's face. "I'm sorry, little brother. I will fight for your brother on my terms. I will not risk losing my honor again."

"Honor?" Ewan spat, his eyes turning gray like iron. "*To you falls the privilege of righting the wrongs.* What is honorable about hiding in the past when my brother needs you now?"

For the first time since the two had met, it was Sorge who looked away.

Cruedwyn picked up where he left off. "So we hit the front line. If Sorge is right, we will have profoundly confused them by then with our daring originality and wit. Grab Hadyn. Pray the gods the short one gives us some explosions right about that time. After that, we aim for the secret tree, drop into the water, and . . ."

"And?"

"Fly. Like the bats of Hel."

Sorge didn't answer. He and Ewan were locked in a stern, complicated silence.

"They're getting closer," Asandra warned, peering down the ravine. "Our height will not hide us much longer. Minutes at most."

Cruedwyn ran his finger along the razored edge of his sword, caressing the cool steel almost lovingly. He looked to Sorge, waiting. They all did.

Sorge ran a slow hand across his bald head. He seemed pained. "A good plan. A good plan," he mumbled to himself pensively, touching his forehead, tracing the circular scar in a slow pattern. He refused to look at anyone, only the grass right beneath his face, the crowd drawing ponderously near. He squeezed the wood of his staff, moved his mouth, as if confessing secrets to the earth. A slow, bitter grin split his face. He looked up, found each set of waiting eyes. "I'm a decent monk, but truth be told, I've never been very good at making cheese."

"Then it is on!" Cruedwyn said, eyes shining.

"Yes, but listen. I have a deep rumbling in my spirit. This has become more than a rescue, I think. Aion's own sacred purpose in the land is at stake. If we fight—if *I* fight—it must not be merely to snatch Hadyn and flee, but to bring deliverance. We must somehow thwart Nemesia on a larger scale."

His tone had changed. His face had changed. Everyone leaned toward him as a slight breeze blew. Overhead, sun and sky were unrecognizable, void of both comfort and guidance.

The mettle in Sorge's voice was guidance enough. "We must buy as much time as possible. Master Flogg . . . how much black powder *do* you have?"

For the first time Ewan could ever recall, the gnome grinned.

CHAPTER 42

Witching Hour

S ilence. A gathering of energy.

Ravens darted and swooped above, offering faraway, throaty cries. A slight breeze swirled seaward, pleating the grass and heather. Land and water washed together at the shore. The illusion of calm left Ewan anxious that the cannonade of his heart was as loud as it sounded in his ears and might ruin everything. He crouched with Asandra behind the rocks and scrub and tall, knotted grass lining a shelf of rock higher up the hill. He didn't know what else to do but pray. Same for Asandra. Each had barely found their place to hide in time.

The tip of the staff crested first, curling thick undulations of oily vapor into the air, like emptiness or midnight. The corruption of it first repulsed, then inexorably drew Ewan. He could not stop watching. Nemesia appeared next, bearing the staff, marching the

last few steps up the ravine into the grove. Ewan sucked in air at
the sight of the stunning woman. She embodied the fascination of
darkness. Hadyn stood beside her, heading a throng of Nameless.
Ewan choked with emotion to see his brother up close. Hadyn
looked drab, colorless, hollow, like all the rest. He stooped as he
walked, shuffling his feet. His eyes drifted, focused on nothing. He
was badly bruised, and his face and eye were swollen.

Nemesia stood outside the grove but did not enter. She turned
to address the shiftless crowd behind her.

"My precious bombs," she purred. "There is a time of power
called the Witching Hour—a time when darkness spreads forth.
This is our Witching Hour."

The Nameless murmured, like the soft moan of the wind.
Hadyn was a blank stone, with no hope in his eyes. Ewan had never
seen his brother like this before. He found himself turning away,
willing his brain to reject the imprint of the memory, but he could
not. As he watched, he saw Hadyn straining the muscles in his face,
as if battling for five seconds of concentrated thought. Then, like
a balloon deflating, the defeated expression returned. Strain again,
defeat again, many times.

Ewan could read the story in his eyes. He had been kidnapped,
beaten. He was trapped, alone. No one was coming. For all he
knew, Ewan might be dead. His face told a story of numbness and
resignation. Really, what was there to live for?

He feels completely abandoned, Ewan thought.

It was nearly too much for him. He wanted to shout some word
of hope. *Hang on!* Subconsciously, he even tried to inch a little
closer. How could he sit idly by? He couldn't, not for one second
more.

"Easy," Asandra whispered, calming him. "Hold tight. Be wise."

"It's no good," Ewan moaned. The reality of the situation was beginning to sink in. "He's as good as dead. And us, with him. There's too many."

"They are empty shells. Watch and wait."

Nemesia still held the Staff of Shades aloft as she addressed the crowd of youth. "We must build a new world. A world done with pretending. In a world where light and grace and love have no meaning, our first step must be to summon the courage to admit the awful truth. In their place, we embrace what we do know: darkness, sorrow, despair. These are the only things that are true, for they are the only things that are honest. Everything despair promises, it gives."

A sickly chant rose from the crowd.

"Nothing matters. Hope promises, but fails," they answered as one.

"Come, my children. Today, the future of Karac Tor will be boldly decided. By you." She swept her arms toward the grove. "Take your places, my captains. The Witching Hour is here."

Twenty or so young men and women began filing into the grove, forming a circle around the base of the central willow, but Hadyn stayed by Nemesia's side. The remaining mass pressed farther up and around the eastern perimeter to observe but did not enter the grove at the crown of the bluff. Many hundreds trailed down the hill, unable to come closer.

Ewan strained for a glimpse of Sorge, Flogg, Creed. Couldn't. They were well hidden. But it was such a hasty plan. Ludicrous, really. What were any of them thinking? Why bother?

Doesn't matter . . .

His own words bounced off the inside of his skull. He jerked, as if struck.

You are not tired, so much as bedeviled.

Ewan blindly felt the ground for a sharp stone, squeezing it in the palm of his hand until the pain made him gasp.

It matters.

As the leaders of the Nameless took their places, so did Nemesia. Her stride was slow and imperious. She moved past the outer circle of beech trees into the inner ring of cedars. Her gown, cut to be sensual, caught the breeze, weaving its own black spell. Hadyn shuffled slavishly beside her in baby steps, as if compelled. The sorceress approached the willow with her back to the east, to Isgurd. A symbolic gesture. Some inner fire caught in the thin, silver circlet in her hair, dazzling. There was no sound of crickets. No birdsong. The silence was unearthly.

Nemesia mounted the Staff of Shades into a square socket set in a paving of stones before the base of the willow, a votive offering to the animal gods carved into the wood. Like a snake licking the air with its tongue, the staff flicked and spit venom into the sky. Nemesia began to chant. Her tone grew louder, more cruel. Her captains joined hands, began to mirror her chant. As their noise swelled, outside the grove, hundreds more began droning a single note, more on the level of vibration than music. The hairs on Ewan's arms and neck rose. The sound was hypnotic, drawing him in. Asandra's tense voice jolted him back to awareness.

"*Mismyri!* They call for Watchers."

Ewan couldn't see what she saw, but he felt the stirring in the air, the movement of unseen wings. The leaves of the trees began to rustle in the still, heavy air.

"How many?"

She didn't answer. Which was answer enough.

The unlight of the Staff of Shades began to coagulate like an angry, living thing. Streams no longer slithered skyward. Instead the energy became tar-like, sticking to itself. The cleft of land on which they stood, high and green, as well as the grove and wider isle, all paled of color. A rift opened in the air, then widened. Light passed from memory. Darkness writhed like a pit of cobras around the staff. Nemesia's eyes rolled back in her head as ecstasy overtook her. Her fingers flexed, became splayed, bony claws, shaping and molding the dark vapors like clay, gathering the power for release. But there was no release.

The air pressurized. The ground began to shake. The willow at the center trembled. Otherworldly sounds, cries of ancient betrayal and murder, the traitors of Olfadr, leaked into the realm of hearing. The droning of the Nameless reached a fever pitch, demanding release.

But there was no release.

Ewan thought the staff might explode, if not the whole world. He covered his ears, unable to drown the awful sounds. The trees began to thrash in a storm of invisible wings. The noise escalated.

"Merciful Aion," Asandra said beside him. "There are thousands. We are undone."

Below, Nemesia made a dying sound, as air and light sucked inward. Worms of darkness shivered from the staff toward the same rune carved into every tree in the circle, like a sponge absorbing water. Coagulating, then dripping with unlight. Nemesia waved her hand. The chanting stopped. Only the low hum continued. And the rift. She smiled.

"Now," she said. Just one word.

Those in the inner circle obeyed. Ewan watched, not knowing their names. He did not know Shameface or Grayday, or the others gathered around the great, bowing branches of the willow. But as they fanned out, they carried the wands to the many trees, began dipping each in the pools of inky blackness. The darkness, like a leprous wound, transferred the infection from one shaft to another. Each wand began producing a small stream of unlight. A smaller version of the Staff of Shades.

"Merciful Aion," Ewan heard himself say, noting the stacks of dozens of wands, maybe hundreds. The process was repeated with the flinty tips of the arrows.

It seemed clear now. Nemesia intended to transport the darkness all over the land. The Staff of Shades would darken the heavens, and the mass of Nameless would darken the earth. Having stripped them of name and will, they would carry her malice with them—wands for where feet could tread and arrows for where feet could not.

It was diabolical. They needed more time, Ewan knew. More time for Flogg, wherever he was. He had been wrong about the gnome. He knew it. Too late, he knew it. He hoped to be able to tell him one day, if they made it. A sense of finality was creeping upon the ritual. The window of opportunity to save Hadyn and stop this evil, however paltry it seemed, was closing.

"We can't wait much longer," he whispered.

Asandra hushed him. Nearly fifty dark wands had been created. Now eighty, now two hundred. It was a fast process. Wands and arrowheads both. Each, touched to the dark rune in the center of the trees, came away with self-sustaining darkness.

Hadyn, slack-jawed and bound, seemed to comprehend none of it.

One of the young leaders turned to Nemesia with a curious expression on his face. "My lady, this tree has no bow. No arrows!"

The witch arched a wary brow. "Don't be a fool. I placed them myself."

Then there was Sorge. Ewan's heart leapt. There, from behind the largest birch, Sorge.

"Not a very good bow," the monk said distastefully, taking his stand to the north. His feet were dangerously close to the cliff edge, where the knuckle of the grove dropped suddenly to the valley below. The bow was stretched full, arrow notched to string, aimed straight at Nemesia's heart. Ewan and Asandra faced him from above the grove, on the opposite side.

Nemesia inclined her head to the sound of his voice.

"So, the little mouse has decided to come out of hiding after all?" she teased, as if this had been her plan all along. Her lips played with a smile. "I'm flattered. But really, shouldn't you be among the other little Gray mice? Pretending to be one of them, as you have for so long now? Eating your cheese. Saying your prayers. Have you come to pray for my soul, Sorge, is that it? Surely you haven't come to fight."

A strange tingling brushed Ewan's skin. Like someone watching.

"She's searching for us," Asandra said. "Feeling outward. Get down."

Ewan froze. Beside him, the mirling began to pray. The tingling on his skin became slippery, wouldn't stick. She was shielding him. Nemesia made a full survey of the grove, turning back to the man in the charcoal robe with the scar on his forehead. "Rather short-sighted to come alone, wouldn't you say, Sorge?"

"I never travel alone. I come and go in the name of Aion, with his authority." Nemesia curled her lips in reply, but Sorge wasn't finished. "And my daughter. I've come with her, too, Nemesia. *Our* daughter."

Ewan frowned. Did he just say—? He glanced sharply at Asandra, whose mouth was gaping. *Daughter?* The monk's voice sounded heavy, but full of pride.

"Release the boy," Sorge commanded. "I will let you live. It's not too late for mercy."

The sorceress clicked her long nails together, laughing; a mocking, seductive gesture. "So far, just to be refused? That's our story, isn't it Sorge? Did you think bringing the little mirling with you would play on my heart? Of course, I should have known you would figure it out eventually. You've had twenty years to put the clues together."

Asandra's chest heaved. Not once during the whole journey had she exhibited fear, until now. She squeezed Ewan's arm so tightly it hurt. Her eyes welled with tears.

"Why didn't he tell me?" she whispered. "I've hated him all my life. But he knew."

"Where is she?" Nemesia said coolly. "I sense her."

"Hidden. Safe, as she has been all her life, though she did not know it. She looks like you. She has your spirit, your gift. Your anger. But there is one difference," his voice surged with obvious pride now. "Unlike you, she is utterly loyal to Aion."

"How dare you lecture me on loyalty!" Nemesia snarled. Everything in the grove, light and leaf and limb, tensed together. Nobody moved. For a moment it seemed that only Sorge and Nemesia were real. "Would you be so righteous before Corus, under Aion's sky, if he stood in my stead? Would you tell *him* of your great fidelity? Do you bear his gift of friendship on your arm still?" She chewed each word like a poisoned piece of fruit. "Come now, Elder Sorge. Are you sure you're ready for this? Does a coward suddenly turn so brave?"

"I have repented, made my peace with Aion," Sorge said. He never relaxed his hold on the bow. The thin shaft of the three-fletch arrow was pressed against his cheek. "My knees have bled with prayer. I am sorry for many things. About Corus. About you." He bent the bow tighter in warning. "Do not give me cause to repent for more."

The throbbing of magic in the grove did not subside. Hundreds of eyes were fixed on the monk, the witch. Still, the Staff gushed its darkness. Still, the trees sucked it in. But the Nameless were frozen in place and Nemesia's captains had paused. They no longer dipped the wands. When Ewan glimpsed Flogg—that small, hardly visible streak of green blending with the grass outside the field of view, moving from tree to tree on the outer rim, dropping pouches at the base of each tree—he understood.

Sorge is buying time. He's stalling.

The others did not see. Nemesia did not see. Again, Ewan understood, noting the sweat and strain on Asandra's face. The mirling labored hard. She shielded them all with prayer.

"You will not release Watchers today, old friend," the monk said solemnly.

"Oh, but I will, *old friend*. And so much more. The Darkwings are only the beginning. Soon, they shall have blood. *Blood bound, blood released.* Isn't that how it goes, Sorge the Gray? From Nemesia the Black?" She touched Hadyn on the shoulder, smiling wickedly. "I shall give the *mismyri* his blood and call them forth, while Aion slumbers on the green hills of Isgurd, far away. Of course I'm willing to change my mind. If he wishes me to stop, let him stop me." She blinked coyly. "Do you think he will?"

Hadyn lifted his face to Sorge, desperate and blank. Even at a distance, Ewan could see the lack of recognition.

"But I am not entirely unfair. I shall let the outlander choose." She took Hadyn's face in her hands. "Join me, fool. If you willingly do so, I shall spare your life and another shall take your place. Their blood shall open the door, rather than your own. Regardless, know this: *the monk cannot save you.* Nor the four with him, scattered around this grove. He does not know my power. He does not know he has brought them all to ruin, including my wretched daughter. A thousand Watchers have been summoned. They are waiting. They press hard against my mind, but without blood, they cannot cross over. Magic and darkness have drawn them, but I cannot keep them here. They will return to Helheim unless there is a sacrifice." She shuddered in a spasm of pain. "I offer you this. Join me, and all my precious bombs shall be made complete in despair, to see you fall. Or resist and die. Only do not ask for compassion. I will not give it, even to my own."

Sorge tried to break the hold on Hadyn's mind. "Hadyn! Don't give up! For Aion, for all that you love . . . *fight* her."

Ewan's stomach sank at their bitter plight. This was the part where they had to wing it. Sorge with an arrow, yelling at Hadyn. Hardly a plan. Hadyn gave no indication he heard his own name, much less anything else. Not Nemesia. Not Sorge.

Yet on some level, he understood. Perhaps it was nothing but the primitive, sheer will to live, but drooping forward, he pushed one foot away from Nemesia. A silent cry for freedom.

That's when Ewan noticed the chain. Nemesia kicked her foot and the iron between her ankle and Hadyn's snapped tight, bringing the boy to his knees. Hadyn had stayed close for a reason. He had no choice.

Sorge released his arrow toward the woman he once loved. One moment it was in his hands, pulled tight against the bow. The next it was plunging toward Nemesia. No time, no space in between.

Yet somehow, the witch had time to laugh. To take the staff in hand, to raise it. Time for the darkness to blossom and consume the arrow, turning it to ash, blown away on the wind. Three more arrows loosed by the former Master Bowman—faster than Ewan could truly see—were notched, released, all turning to dust mid-flight.

Nemesia pointed the Staff at Sorge.

"Fool," she said. "I don't know why I ever loved you."

She flung unlight toward the monk like water from a bucket. The web of darkness connecting the trees turned gray and weak, then failed altogether, as the full force of immaterial evil struck Sorge like a physical blow. Ewan almost cried out to see how it slammed into his body. Sorge had to lean into the darkness to remain upright, as into a gale force wind. The strain on his face was terrible. Black slivers of oily residue slithered into his mouth, his nostrils, like mercury. The boundary of his flesh had been breached.

"Ewan," Asandra said. "I have no magic for this."

It was obvious what she meant. "And you think I do?" he whispered.

"You have come with power. Find it now or it will be too late."

The younger Barlow panicked. You don't just find power! He started to grow angry, desperate. Dreamlike, he heard his own voice, after visiting the Chantry in Threefork. *No riddles. They said my magic . . . is meant to be heard.* A string of revelations occurred in a blink. He remembered three dreams on the boat. Remembered the number nine, over and over. He saw Sorge, saw Hadyn, as if in slow motion. He didn't know what to do, what else to do, except stand. So he did. It was a wild impulse, and immediately he felt foolish and exposed, but the time had come. He feared, but no longer feared, for the fear was too large a thing to truly be felt. It was, and he was, and yet this moment required something more.

His brother needed him.

Below, Hadyn raised his eyes. Saw him. Ewan wanted to weep at the shocking bareness of recognition, like a tree stripped clean by a tornado, or a field of charred grass after a fire. Deep within Ewan, a point of brightness flared. Yes, they were ridiculously outnumbered. There was no chance. But that hardly mattered anymore. What mattered was Hadyn, his brother. All his life, he had looked up to him, pranked him, argued and screamed at him, laughed and fought with him. Now it was very simple, he would fight *for him*. Come what may. He wiggled his foot nervously, summoning courage. Even took the time, for some reason, to pull his baseball cap from his pocket and place it snugly on his head. It felt good, felt right. If he was going to fight, it could only be as himself.

He had wondered, laying low behind the rock, what this moment would require. Now he knew. He did the only thing that made any sense to him.

Any sense at all.

Song of Aion

I n the roaring chaos of his mind, Hadyn saw a strange figure rise, standing on a ledge of rock above him and to the left. The boy was close to his own age. He wore a cap, with letters on it. He held a sword in his hands. He looked familiar. With tremulous fingers, the boy lifted the sword to his mouth, filled his lungs, pursed his lips. Strange sword. It made a song.

And oh, such a song! It was a song of memory, of beginnings and endings. A piercingly bright sound, clear as morning. Instantly, it cut through the murk of darkness, like a candle set in a window to bring travelers home. A murmur went up among the Lost. The boy began, but could not finish. Nemesia, chattering words from her mouth like a nest of rattlesnakes, knocked him backward with a thought. The weapon of his music clattered to the ground.

But it was enough for the fog to lift, even just a little. Hadyn finally saw, knew. Ewan, his little brother, struggling to rise again, groping for the thin, metal whistle. It was a gift from their mother, from Ireland. Pain stabbed his heart.

The music had not been anything Hadyn recognized, but, dreamlike, it carried him. A long time ago, to another life. With a father and mother he loved. Even the sorrow of that life now seemed sweet to remember. Remembrance of anything seemed sweet. His mother, Anna, had held him, had known him. She was gone from his life, but not from his soul.

He saw her in his mind's eye, laughing, her blonde hair catching the light of a new day like silk and pearls. There had never been any woman like Anna Barlow. The memory came with pain. He could not stop it, could not pick and choose. It was all or nothing, good and bad. He grit his teeth to feel her again, slipping away, beyond the touch of his fingers. Fighting to live. Then gone. Hadyn might as well have been alone on that hill, as tears streamed down his face. His whole world, in that moment, was held together by the brother in his eyes, and the blonde-haired woman in his memory. In a flash, behind the pain, came a tender, aching sweetness. He remembered dancing with her, after school, acting like fools. He remembered her making up silly songs, just for him, then singing them at bedtime. Even when he was older, Hadyn would sing along, even when he should have felt silly. Something clean and free of regret stabbed him like a knife. He was *so glad* he sang with her! The pain was a searing heat. A healing heat. He remembered her teaching him how to listen to the quiet voice of God, to find him in the darkness, right before bed. He trembled.

Too much. The darkness is too much. Mom!

She could laugh and the rain would stop just to listen to the sound. Not true, of course, but that's how it had *felt* growing up with her.

She made living fun and bright. She told stories, and the retelling was always better than the actual event. He remembered the story of her dreaming his name, giving it to him like a gift. She gave it to him now, once more, in his memory. A final gift. A command, to live again.

Hadyn!

He heard it with his ears. His brother was shouting the same word. Standing on the high outcropping, shaking his fist in the air, shouting his name.

"You are Hadyn Barlow! Son of Reggie and Anna Barlow! You are *my* brother. I am *your* brother. I am Ewan Barlow! We are lost in this world, but we are never lost, because we know who we are!"

Nemesia's face became a dark mask of rage. She screamed at her captains, "Get him!"

Ewan did not back down, still shouted, waving his whistle like a banner on the field of battle. "Do you hear me, Hadyn?! Do you remember who you are? You have to *want* it."

The pain. The loss. The memories that burned like hot metal, that could make a day a hated thing. The move to a new place, the loss of friends. Dreadful days. Better days, yet unlived. Somehow worth living. All of it, wrapped up in human flesh, shaped of a life, given a name.

His name.

He wanted it.

Some things come hard and take a long time. Others turn course in a moment. Another day, maybe, would tell the difference. For now, he only knew that he *wanted*, he chose—and in the choosing, the haze lifted, like a harbor fog pushed by the wind. His eyes cleared. For the first time in many months, Hadyn knew himself and was glad for the knowing. He felt his bound hands, his tender, swollen cheek. Felt a tidal wave of anger rise from his core.

Nemesia flailed one arm wildly toward Ewan, demanding action from the Nameless. The staff bucked wildly in her hands. She dared not lift it from the monk, who shuddered in a bubble of darkness, eyes bulging. His skin had turned from a deep, natural color to a pale, sickly brown. He was dying. Hadyn absorbed all this in an instant. Saw a man—what was his name? . . . Creed?—sprinting from somewhere, sword drawn—why was he laughing?—crashing against the tide of Lost youth who pressed toward Ewan, brandishing their dark wands and sharp-toothed arrows. He saw Creed move like a man consumed, his blade an extension of his being, like a brush for a painter, an artist, flashing with silver and fire and death.

Hadyn knew his task. He spoke a word, the word he had learned while bound on the raft. Hushed thoughts, of ropes and knots. The fibers quietly, quickly unraveled; the knot grew slack. It could not do otherwise. Its name had been spoken, unbound, by one who knew the power of names.

Nemesia's captains surged toward Ewan, while the mass on the hill watched, stunned, incapable of thought. No different than any other day.

Except for one difference. This time, their eyes were on Ewan, not Nemesia.

Hadyn tried to wriggle his foot lose from the iron band. The metal bit into his ankle.

"I can't get free!" he shouted above the din. "Somebody help! Creed!"

Then there was music again. The same haunting, familiar melody, played to fullness now, unbroken. Nine notes, played once through, then twice. Ewan had reclaimed his flute, his footing. From the ground where he lay, Hadyn was awed. Seeing some twenty people climbing toward him, carrying rocks and wands and magic, blind with rage, Ewan did not flee. Thankfully, the scree-covered hill slowed his pursuers. But they were getting close. Three times Ewan played. One of the Lost threw a large stone.

"Watch out!" Hadyn cried.

Ewan ducked, immediately putting the flute to his mouth again, losing nothing. Somehow, he had become even more deeply rooted to that place on the rock. A part of the land itself. A conduit of the truer power of light.

Nine notes, again. Only nine, but the melody was beyond compare. Five times, six, the melody played. Doorways to other worlds.

"The Song of Aion!" Nemesia howled. "Who taught him *that* song?"

In his mind, Hadyn answered her fiercely. *Aion did.*

Ewan repeated the melody again, for the eighth time. A pulse. The witch felt it first.

Then, nine.

"No!" she screamed.

Power quivered in the ground, down the rock to Haydn's body, to his feet. Something sharp and metallic pinged loudly, multiple times, like firecrackers in succession. Every link in the chain which bound him snapped, and the shackle tore. He fell backward and scrambled away.

"The Song of Aion!" he shouted. He was free.

Nemesia turned her staff upon Ewan, away from Sorge, but the darkness never reached him. Waves of energy rippled outward from the song like the crest of a wave, colliding in the center of the grove. A battle ensued between the song of light and the staff of dark. Ewan continued to play. The darkness wavered. Gasping, Sorge stumbled through the breach, finding air. When Ewan paused for breath, the darkness waxed strong again.

Hadyn heard the monk grunt, making a circle motion with his hands. More, more.

"Keep playing!" he shouted up the hill.

A girl passed by Nemesia. Grayday, marching toward Ewan, to stop him. The sorceress grabbed Grayday by a handful of her hair and threw her to the ground. A fount of strange words bubbled from the witch's mouth, foaming. For a moment, she released the staff. It fell to the earth, sizzling and sputtering. A second reprieve. Growling, the witch seized a blade of black onyx from the folds of her gown and lunged for Grayday's throat.

Hadyn lunged, too. He caught Nemesia broadside, knocking her to the ground.

"Grayday," he groaned, his face on the ground near the girl's. Grayday's eyes were white. "Don't die, not for her. Wake up. Run."

Nemesia kicked at Hadyn. Her foot landed in his gut. She slashed at him. He rolled away. Coiled from the force of her swing, she uncoiled even faster in a backward slash that caught Hadyn off guard and bit deeply into his arm. He fell back, squeezing the wound to stanch the blood.

Meanwhile, a half-dozen young men—those that had escaped Cruedwyn's sword—were nearly upon Ewan. Though their footholds were weak, they were close enough it hardly mattered. Ewan's song began to falter. He was not trained to play for so long, and his lungs burned. He stopped, took a large stone in hand and lobbed it toward the nearest two. They tumbled into one another, down the hillside. Instantly, Creed was upon those two. They did not rise again.

"I will climb!" Creed called. "You play! Keep your song!"

Ewan stumbled, light-headed. But he played. At the bottom, Grayday cowered underneath Hadyn, sobbing. Nemesia screamed in rage, pointing to a different girl amongst the stupified throng on the edge of the grove. "You! Come!"

The summoned girl did not flinch. With wide, vacant eyes— same as the rest—she came.

"No!" Hadyn wailed.

"I am Shy Eyes," the girl said demurely.

"How many times have I told you?" scoffed the witch. "It doesn't matter!"

Like the strike of a scorpion's tail, Nemesia drew a quick, sharp line with her knife. The girl's throat ribboned with red. She fell to the ground, bubbling. Nemesia chanted strange words. Shy Eyes's body shook. Nemesia lifted her face to the sky. It was now or never. The darkness had prepared the way. They were gathered.

"Watchers, traitors to Aion! Mismyri, come! I shed blood for thee. Enter through my gate."

Through the rift, Watchers poured forth—a thousand in a moment. Immediately, they began tearing at the flesh of the dead girl. Hadyn didn't even have time to look away. Since they could only consume dead flesh in their disembodied state, living spirits were beyond their reach, save for terror and dread. But when the grisly meal was done, they swerved lustily toward the assembly on the hillside as if a banquet had been laid. Their shrieks were the sound of tearing metal, or a rabid sow giving birth. A basilisk

sound, cold and bone-chilling. It was madness in the brain. Some
Nameless were overtaken with awe, their eyes rolling back in their
heads. Hundreds more scattered in terror. Hadyn felt himself
slipping again into despair, to hear that sound, to see the earth
beneath where Shy Eyes had fallen smeared with red.

Still Ewan played. Like a Champion of old, he stood his ground,
as dark wings raked around him. Hadyn clung to the lifeline of his
brother's flute. Aion's song. Of the thousand Watchers that had split
through, nearly every single one had already taken wing to the high
skies, bent on seeking vengeance and worship elsewhere. But with
words of power, Nemesia seized the will of the last three, ordering
them to strike at Ewan. At first they fought, squealing. Their long,
toothy beaks and many eyes—their black, foul feathers—stank
of maggots and decay. But then, shuddering with delight, they
understood. More blood. They reared in the air and swooped. If
the Lost could kill him, they could drink their fill. They had not
the flesh yet to kill him themselves, but they could drive him to
madness and distraction.

"No!" Hadyn whimpered. Out of the corner of his eye, he
saw Sorge struggling to his feet, pale as death. Living tendrils of
the darkness clung to his body like seaweed. The monk steadied
himself, gathering energy for prayer, from prayer. One by one, the
last tendrils fell away, but he was too weak to do more. Hadyn saw
a dash of movement among the base of the far beech trees. He saw
Cruedwyn roll and flow like a river among stones, his sword pale
and efficient, bringing the last three of those he could reach to
the ground, one after another. Scattered, bleeding bodies writhed
around him.

Lastly, in the anguished slowness of a single moment, he saw
three Watchers, wretched and vile, streak toward his brother with

death and lust in their eyes. Their claws were outstretched, like razors, ready for blood.

But Ewan was not alone. Rising from behind the rocks with her hands lifted high, the daughter of Nemesia met the Watchers in flight. Her eyes were closed, serene. A translucent sheet of energy sprang from her gathered fists, catching like a sail in an unseen breeze to form a canopy above her. Above Ewan. The Watchers reared back.

"*Mismyri yl maal eStyblerian! Aione portismaal sanos!*" she declared.

Watchers, you cannot come near. Aion forbids it.

The Watchers beat their wings furiously, scouring the humans with their many eyes full of loathing. They snapped hungrily, chomping their beaks, bone on bone. Asandra had no mirror of blessed water, had no ring of men trained in the Wall of Binding. She was a strong mirling, but it was still just one against three. Her barrier would not hold long.

Growling like an animal, Nemesia took the staff from where it lay on the ground.

"*Mismyri, om!*"

The Watchers immediately responded, swooping toward the staff like moths to a flame. They drank its viscous fumes, gathering their strength.

"Kill them," she said in a fell voice. "Drink their blood. Gain flesh."

"Look around you, Nemesia!" Sorge rasped from a distance. "Your plans are undone. You will not have this generation. Relent!"

Hadyn, nearby, continued to shelter Grayday, if only because he could think of nothing else to do. The arm of his shirt was torn and soaked red. Then a daring thought entered his mind. He edged nearer to the witch with a single goal: steal the staff.

As if reading his thoughts, Nemesia spun to face him. "You could have been among my best and most wretched."

She jabbed at him and he ducked, choking on the vapors of the staff. In a limber twirl, she spun to face Ewan, releasing a burst of darkness. Asandra's covering wavered. The Watchers pounded against it. Then back to Hadyn, she swung again. It was a desperate dance, between the two brothers, but she was strong and fast, and fueled with sorcery. Nudging his thoughts toward the chain where it lay shattered by Aion's Song, Hadyn stretched his awareness, feeling for the secrets and substance of iron. He saw it in the half-light, cold, dark, and gray, untouched by the sun, moldable with heat and light. Hard as night. He asked it questions. It did not answer. It was iron. Unfeeling.

Too hard. Not enough time or skill yet. He needed something else.

She swung again. He rolled, nearer to Sorge this time, who still heaved for air and had no strength. Unlight was like drinking poison from a cup.

"Hold on, Sorge. Just . . . hold on."

The monk groaned. Watchers pounded against Asandra's canopy. She bent low under the weight of their wings. Their cries were torment to the mind of a mirling. They were three, she one. She began to crumble.

Creed, having scrambled up the hill, clutched for the heels of the ones above him, who had also made the climb. The highest of these had his fingers on the ledge of rock at Ewan's feet.

"Shameface!" Nemesia screamed to the boy. "Kill him!"

Ewan tried to step on his fingers, but Shameface grabbed his foot. Twisting, he dropped Ewan to his knees. Ewan cried out in pain, shouting a name like a plea or a command.

"Fllohhhhgg!"

But Flogg did not respond, and Ewan and Shameface, who was older and stronger by several years, tumbled together down the slope, tearing at each other's face and throat. Seeing their prey emerge from under the cursed Black's protection, the Watchers screeched, dove.

Hadyn hadn't even realized he was on his feet, running toward Ewan. Then he had no feet as the ground rose to meet him, lifting, throwing him like a ragdoll. As if waking from a long sleep, the earth shuddered. A massive explosion rocked the grove, followed by a quick series of lesser explosions. *Flogg!* Earth and grass shot into the air. A cloud of thick, gray smoke followed. Tree trunks along the outer rim splintered, sending chunks of wood flying. The last Lost boy still on his feet howled as a large, sharp piece struck his leg, shattering the bone. Cruedwyn, who had slipped down the hill near to one of the trees, was thrown twenty feet. Trees began falling toward the center and outward down the steep cliff face. Roots groaned, snapped. Nemesia fought for balance. The Watchers drew back in fear.

For a split second, the force of the explosion left everyone rattled, including the witch. In that brief silence, the only sound was the gruff voice of a gnome, fuming somewhere amid the smoke. Only a moment, that's all any of them had.

It was enough.

"Smashings and flashings!" Flogg bellowed. "Want *crashings!*"

There, lofting above the smoke in a near perfect arc, was Flogg's leather satchel. When it landed, the explosion was deafening.

Instantly a stress line formed in the stone, cracking loudly, creeping first left and right and forward, then spidering out, following thin places in the rock down to the dome underneath their feet where the pool of water lay unseen, roots plunging for drink. Hadyn no longer saw Ewan fighting for his life, nor Sorge staggering forward. Dazed from the explosion, he could focus on nothing but Nemesia's staff. He chided himself. Iron had been unwise. Too difficult, wasted time. Besides, he didn't need it. There was something else he already knew. He bent down, carefully, took it in his hands. On the one hand, it made no sense to try this. He knew the folly of it. It was too soon, he was too unwieldy in his skill. Still, he *knew*. In his heart. The fibers, the weft, the shape of the knot, the strength of the thing. He knew the binding, for it had bound him.

The timing was right. Nemesia was distracted by Flogg, by Sorge stumbling toward her. She, too, was dazed. He would have no better chance. Ridiculous thoughts scurried through his head, like how it would have helped if he had ever been a cowboy, ever been in a rodeo. At the moment, he wouldn't mind getting that chance someday. He made several large loops with one end of the rope, gathering them quickly into his fist. Sent them spiraling toward the Staff while he held the other end.

The rope sailed wide. Nemesia didn't even notice.

City boy, they called him at school. Newland was sounding better all the time.

"Nemesia, have done!" Sorge said.

She paused, staring at the monk with a strange look on her face. Visible fissures laced through the earth around her, tearing apart the grass. Rock and stone grated together. Loud, random reports, like cannon blasts, as the stone skeleton of the grove fractured. It happened in mere seconds. Hadyn threw the rope one more time.

His aim was better this time. Midair, he said the word for knotted rope. The appellation was as foreign to his ears as a clanging lock in the Stone House, yet as true as his own name. He spoke, and as the rope looped around the staff, it found itself again and wove together. He didn't hesitate. With all his might, he jerked, tearing the staff loose from Nemesia's grip. It arced up and over and landed in his hands. And then he ran. Didn't even think about it, just ran.

"I will bring all of Hel to your door!" Nemesia screamed, wheeling round.

"Back!" Hadyn shouted, scooping under Sorge's arm, helping him hobble away. "Everyone, back!"

Nemesia's eyes flashed. She opened her mouth, had barely begun her final incantation when the earth split. The belly of the grove collapsed. Willow tree and all, earth and rock, folded upon themselves, dragging Nemesia down. She clawed at the ground briefly. Sorge tore free of Hadyn, stumbling back toward her, grasping for her hands. He could not get close enough. The ground was too fragile. Nemesia looked up at him with one last terrified look.

"Find Corus, Sorge. Find him. Tell him Nemesia stayed true."

She plummeted below.

CHAPTER 44

Completion

As the dust settled, streams of pebbles rattled and clattered into the pit where the grove had once been. A giant, open bowl of earth had been formed. For a long time, nobody moved or spoke. Overhead, the heights of the sky remained clogged with darkness, but around the island, the lower shadows began to dissipate a little. Some few, stray sunbeams made their way through, as the winds drove the darkness over the bay to the mainland.

The Watchers fled, ready for power and spoil purchased elsewhere at lesser cost. They had no desire to remain so near to a mirling, risking recapture, if they did not have to. With Nemesia gone, they did *not* have to. Sorge lay near the edge of the cavity, clenching and unclenching his fist, shaking. Asandra lay beside him, weeping.

"You knew?" she said at last, bending over the monk. Hidden in her words was something fragile, a question of worth. Of years and tears and anger. Sorge was unwilling to look at her, but he nodded.

"I was a different man, then."

"Why didn't you come to me? I suffered so much, piecing stories together. I came to hate you."

"Every day, Asandra," he heaved with sadness. "Every day I carried you in my thoughts. I have failed at so many things in my life, but you were never one of them. But I could not risk it. I needed you to be free of my sins. So I hoped you would never have to know. It was a risk, but I thought you might have a better chance, a fresher start, without me. Without the burden of knowing who your mother was."

"I was born to a woman, not a mother," Asandra said bitterly. "At least I could have had a father."

Sorge stared at his hands, the ground. He had no words.

Ewan hobbled toward his brother. Hadyn watched him approach with a curious expression, probing the air between them with hesitant fingers, as if reaching toward a dream. He was in his right mind, but couldn't shake the sudden, irrational fear that Ewan might be an illusion, and that a single touch might shatter it all.

"It was so dark," he whispered. "I thought I was forgotten."

Gingerly, he touched Ewan's cheek. Something broke inside him. He grabbed fistfuls of Ewan, his clothes, his hair. He couldn't get enough, would not let go. Ewan held tight.

"Never," said the younger brother, his voice muffled from where he was pressed against Hadyn's chest. When he finally pulled away to study Hadyn's battered face up close, his conclusion was blunt. "You look pretty awful."

Hadyn smiled weakly. They both did. A relief valve had opened.

All six took turns gazing down upon Nemesia. Her body was broken, her legs and arms bent at odd angles, splayed across the belly of a cedar tree in the water below. Sorge extended a hand, palm out.

"Aion be merciful. To us all."

He took Asandra's hand, and she allowed it. Realizing many eyes still watched them, the monk addressed the stragglers that had not already fled, that waited for some direction. Their confusion was almost painful to witness. They truly were *Lost*.

"Nemesia was a cruel master to you," he said, raising his voice. He had regained a measure of strength, but shook as if he was cold. "She stole your name. Your future. She was going to use you for great evil, whether you lived or died." He pointed to the bloody streak of grass where Shy Eyes had lain. "If you do not believe me, ask this one."

Gradually, as he spoke, the darkness broke, and with it, the stupor over their minds. Faces stared at the green grass, the blue water far below, each other, as if for the first time. They murmured amongst themselves. One voice grew loud. Though Hadyn could not see her, to his ears, it sounded like Kyra. The girl from the boat.

"What do we do now?"

"Go home to your families," Sorge said. "Most have not been as wrong toward you as you think. You have been bedeviled. In fact, they likely grieve, thinking you are dead. If they have wronged you, forgive them. If they do not want you, go to an Abbey for sanctuary, or find work in a village. Most of you are of age. Claim your name again. Make a life."

He had no strength to say more, and there was nothing more to say. The Nameless crowd slowly dispersed, shushed away by a hobbled Creed. To where they might go, Hadyn had no idea. How do you strip a soul, and then put it back together again? He had felt that ravaging, if only for a few days. Healing would take time.

Asandra began tending to the wounded, and there were many. As it happened, Cruedwyn had not dealt a single fatal blow fending off Nemesia's captains. Such was his skill, striking only non-vital areas, maiming without killing. Some few had plummeted to their deaths in the explosion, but most were scattered around, moaning.

"Impressive," Ewan said. "It looked like you were on a rampage."

Creed put his arm around Ewan's shoulder. "Ah, my boy. A skill as precise as mine is closer akin to a surgeon's blade than a brutish club. I do what I intend, strike where I aim. Never more. Never less."

Ewan flinched, but the sword was quiet. His eyes widened.

Together, the six picked their way around the areas of tangled carnage which had survived the blast. The trees that were not exploded or toppled, they defaced. Sorge, though weak, displayed an angry passion in cleansing the bark of all wicked markings. Asandra gathered elements of wood, stone, water, held them in her hands and raised them to the sky, offering prayers to heal the land. It would take more than she could give, but it was a start.

Since the ritual was never completed, the strange darkness did not seal itself to the wands and arrows, eventually fading to nothing. Sorge ordered all the implements collected, thrown in a pile, and burned. He remained until he personally witnessed each consumed to the very last puff of ash—except the Staff of Shades. Its power, fire could not destroy. Sorge wrapped the profane thing in his cloak.

"Such great evil," he said thoughtfully, glancing at the clearing sky. For days, the Staff of Shades had burned, stolen light, sending shadows across the bay. It would affect the people it touched. Perhaps not as far and wide as Nemesia's full intent. But darkness was a sticky thing. It fascinated, preparing souls for evil. It would require attention, care, prayer. The land was already so weak.

Steadfast spirit. Mercy of Aion.

This, too, would take time.

Hours had passed. The cleanup took time. Hadyn felt an urge to look upon Nemesia once more, for closure. She had nearly destroyed him. Standing near the edge, he peered into the gaping hole. A cry escaped his lips.

Sorge and the others dashed over. Nemesia was gone. Where she had lain, she lay no more.

"Should've killed her when we had the chance," Creed said. "Made sure."

"Fallings not can live," Flogg said. "Not human."

Sorge was quiet. He lifted his hood so that none could see.

They made their way, limping, torn, down the ravine, into the valley, to the shore below. They found empty, waiting boats— skiffs, schooners, keels, flat-bottomed barges—and selected one they thought they could manage. None of them were sailors. Some of the Lost milled about the shore. Several young men and women asked to go with them. One of them was Grayday.

"What is your real name," Hadyn asked her. "You can tell me now."

"I don't remember."

They took her on board, with a few others who seemed most ready to leave. They did not have room for very many. They did their best to mount a single sail and caught a northerly wind, for Stratamore.

Elysabel had seen many things in her five hundred years. But nothing quite like this. Power and courage. Pain and betrayal. Tears and blood and hope. Maybe it had always been so. Maybe she had simply never taken the time to watch so closely. But the Queen had commanded: *watch.*

So she had. For days. After seeing the older brother hauled to the island, she had stayed with the younger. She had been with him in the chamber with the one they called Governor. Such fancy, important men. So much talking! She had followed them under the waters, through the caves. The younger brother was fiercely devoted. The older was strong. He had held firm. She saw all this, but did not understand.

It was not for her to understand, only to convey. The Queen would expect a report soon. She had much to tell. But for the first time she could ever remember, it seemed strange to leave, to go from here to there. She had grown attached. She wanted the boy to see her again. To talk to him.

It was forbidden. Dangerous. Didn't change the wanting.

Away she flew, leaving them on the blue water, in their old boat. As she lifted into the sky, the younger one turned unexpectedly, as if he had heard a noise. His gaze followed the slant of light she disappeared into. Just in time, she hoped.

Still, she wondered.

CHAPTER 45

A Hero's Welcome

ll the next day, prior to their audience with Archibald, they rested in private rooms beneath the castle's three white towers. They didn't know it, but stable boys, chamberlains, scullery maids, and cooks were abuzz with tales of their deeds. Court officials whispered nervously, being highly attuned to any shift in the balance of power. Some called them heroes; others, troublemakers.

Asandra slept all night and half the next day, rose, ate some bread, then slept again. Sorge recovered more quickly, though either the darkness, or Nemesia's loss, or both, had clearly taken its toll. He was quieter, his gaze less intense. He spent most of his time alone. Flogg wandered in the small woods within the palace grounds, looking for mushrooms, grumbling over the loss of his satchel, though of course he would soon fashion another one.

Cruedwyn, whose back was miraculously unbroken by the force of the blast, suffered with a smile while two flouncy, pretty-faced maidens nursed his bruised bones and muscles.

Hadyn and Ewan were mostly a mess. They felt elation, relief, dejection, triumph, and were still no closer to home. Upon waking, they sat in their room, eating grapes, honeybread, and dried meat, contemplating the last month. So much had happened. So much gained and lost.

"The scrolls talked about adventure," Ewan said, mostly to himself. "I didn't expect this."

Hadyn touched the long scab near his shoulder where Nemesia had cut him.

"Nope."

His face was a blank slate. He wanted to say more, but the words that came to mind all seemed too flimsy. He felt as if he had aged ten years in the last ten days. While this was definitely not what he had bargained for, it also seemed more than he could've dreamed.

Light slanted into their room. Motes of dust danced in the luminous beams like tiny fireflies. The silent, awkward proximity of the brothers was like magnetic poles repelling one another. Neither seemed sure what to say or how to say it. How do you shape pain and magic into words? How was it possible to feel both foreign and strangely alive in the *same place*? In the same breath, homesick, yet glad? Discomforted, yet delighted and determined? The tumult of holding antithetical, irreconcilable emotions together in the same heart, with equal vigor, felt exhausting. He was already exhausted.

Bugger! Hadyn thought. He could not help but smile, hearing Creed in his mind.

There, finally. There was the rub. For Hadyn—likely Ewan, too—the only thing worse than the thought of staying one more day was the thought of going home. The contradiction was delicious, fearful, riddled with guilt. What about Dad? The twins? What about Karac Tor?

"What now?" Ewan said with appropriate vagueness.

Hadyn nibbled at a grape, held up empty hands. He determined not to be the first to speak it. "Honest to God, I don't know." He studied the floor, the crumbling mortar of the ancient walls, as if they might hold hidden clues. "But I get this weird feeling Dad might have known about a world like this, don't you? Or at least suspected. They bought the old farm for it."

"For the runestone. The ACP."

"Just what did he expect to find, besides the rock? Or *behind* the rock, in our case."

"Heck if I know. And what's that even mean? Ancient Civilization Portal?"

They both fell silent again. Finally, Hadyn said, "Dad's got some weird history stuff. He's always been knee-deep in old Celtic stories. Wales. Ireland." He paused, strumming his chin. "It kind of feels like that here. Like an alternate universe. Know what I mean?"

Ewan nodded, smiling. "Like . . . Camelot."

He said it fighting tears. Hadyn dropped his head. "Something like that."

Ewan's voice began to crack. "Hadyn, I won't lie. I kind of like it here. I kind of want to stay longer. But what if we're stuck here forever? I can't do that. I don't like it that much."

"I know, I know. But a part of me feels like I have two homes now. Here *and* there."

Hearing his own words, Hadyn was taken aback by their gentle truth. Newland had felt like a friendless prison sentence and Karac Tor had only brought great pain into his life. But deeper still was the revelation that home was more than a place, more than a spot on a map. Home was an idea, a strange convolution of emotion, identity, and experience. He took note of Ewan's gray-green eyes, the shining rim of hope he saw there, colored with tears. It was the belief that one day, somehow, they *would* make it back. But not yet. Ewan groped for words.

"I see Fey in this world. My music means something. We've made friends . . ."

It was a surprising admission for both of them, that Hadyn might want to go home to Newland, and that Ewan might want to stay in Karac Tor. Bouncing between the extremes, from the quiet urgency of returning to Dad and all the desperation and anxiety that caused, to never leaving and embracing the wild adventure of Karac Tor, both groped toward the center again, toward one another. The space between their words became an apology of sorts, for questions without answers and feelings beyond explanation. A muddled blessing emerged: at least they had each other.

"We were Called," Hadyn softly confessed. "You know that, don't you?

"And we did answer," Ewan agreed.

Trapped as they were on this side of the equation, that part felt certain and settled. Returning home did not. Though Ewan did not complain, Hadyn understood the toll it would take on his loyal soul. He was a tough kid—had proved it in the face-off with Nemesia—but Hadyn knew his brother's soft side. Setting aside his own questions, his own need for answers, he marshaled his strength to reassure Ewan, and in that moment, became more of a man.

"One way or another," he said firmly, "we'll make it home, Ewan. I promise."

By mid-afternoon all six of them were rested, collected, washed, fed, and ready. Sorge had already privately briefed Archibald earlier in the day, worriedly informing the others that he had gained no sense of the governor's pleasure or displeasure in reply. Now Archibald received the ragtag troupe into his courtroom, surrounded by a full fleet of advisors, minus one. The Minister of Justice was notably absent.

"You've stirred up a real hornet's nest, monk," Archibald groused, lifting his sagging chin in contempt. "Nemesia was not a friend. Any fool could see that. But at least she was docile. Now you have made issues for us all."

Hadyn and Ewan turned to one another in shock. *Issues?* Had he not listened to Sorge's tale earlier that day in the Governor's private study? Did he not understand that an onslaught of darkness had narrowly been averted, that a thousand Watchers now streaked across the Hidden Lands *unbound.* Their presence would be manifest very soon, since little was required to enflesh the cursed creatures. And what of the darkness of the Staff of Shades? Such arcana was difficult to calculate, but light had literally been consumed by unlight. It could never be restored. What opportunities for evil might now be possible that had not been before? How could the unimaginable be properly anticipated? Darkness, fundamentally, was blindness.

"Nemesia was destroyed," Asandra offered, but Sorge subtly motioned her. *Shh . . .*

"Is she?" Archibald scoffed. "Then show me. Show me the body!"

"Clearly, she was moved."

"By whom? Fool of a mirling. A renegade may act as he, or she, likes, but a *ruler* must consider all factors. I said she was docile. Do you think she will stay tame if she lives?"

"Unlikely," Sorge said calmly. "But it is even more unlikely that she lives."

"Hah! Are you so knowledgeable of these things? Is it so easy to kill a witch?"

Sorge shrugged. "Is it not?"

"Jonas believes she survived. We consulted, before he left on matters of state."

"Be that as it may, with respect, the pot you say we stirred was boiling before, and most certainly would have soon spilled over. The only difference would be a dead outlander—a guest in your land—and even greater evil unleashed. Far greater."

"So you say," Archibald sniffed, unimpressed.

"My lord, you saw the shadow. You heard the explosions. She sat at your doorstep and mocked you with her schemes. It is she who stole the names from the Book. Her power could not be ignored."

"Quite right, power *should* not be ignored! So why do you feel comfortable ignoring me? My will?" Archibald shouted so loud spittle shot from his mouth. "You know nothing of diplomacy, Gray. Or affairs of state. Do you think me a mongrel by the trash heap, to speak to me so, telling me what to do, who to fear? I will decide what is right!"

He stood quivering for several moments, red with rage. Then collected himself. Looping his thumbs in the hem of his robe, he turned his attention to the Barlow brothers.

"And here we have the young heroes, eh? Boys, beware that you take up with the wrong sort. You should learn to keep better counsel."

"Kindly sir," Hadyn said tersely. He felt no loyalty to a fool. "The only counsel we really need is how to get home."

Archibald narrowed his eyelids at Hadyn's impertinence. "As I have already informed your brother, I cannot help you. I have enough problems, and now a dead witch come back to life. Thanks to you."

The Governor fell heavily into his seat, smacked his lips dismissively, and waved them away. Most of his advisors behaved in similar fashion, though a few seemed troubled, even embarrassed. Sorge did not dawdle. He rose, bowed curtly, and left.

Their sandaled feet padded softly across the polished slab, past the great doors guarded by the Governor's Elite, with their spears and helmets plumed in blue. From behind in the council hall, Hadyn heard Archibald call out, "Elder! I think I should see this staff you spoke about. The shadow-maker. It may have usefulness!"

His request rang out, sharp as the spears in the hands of the silent guard. Sorge left it hanging in the air, just as silent. He did not break stride.

CHAPTER 46

On the Road

Outside the castle, Sorge vented his rage.

"Give him the staff?" he spat. His braided pony tail snapped on his head. "Does he really think?"

They stood now in the bustling lanes of the city outside the outer wall and ramparts. Street performers danced. Merchants hawked beads, silver, wine, rope, food. Metalsmiths clanged upon horseshoes and shovels and links of chain in a cascade of sparks. The air smelled of smoke, meat, and unwashed bodies. Though Archibald had called for them once more, no guard rose to prevent them. No escort had been detached.

Sorge tilted his face toward the sky as if wringing answers from the clouds. "We should go to the White Abbey," he said slowly. "The Book of Law will tell us how to deal with the Staff. It absolutely cannot be left with Archibald, but I will have no power to

withhold it if we are challenged. And the open road is too long to
the Bishop of the Blacks."

"Maybe the Whites can help *us,* too," Hadyn gently reminded.

"Perhaps. I am not a scholar of the Law, but it seems wise as
any other course."

"Speaking of course, it is time to adjust mine," Asandra smiled
wanly. Her eyes were on her father. "My task in Seabraith cannot
wait any longer. I'll have a good scolding from Cassock as it is."

"And I, too. Must go," Cruedwyn declared with false bravado,
squinting into the sun. "Somewhere."

"Really?" Ewan said. "Like where?" He let the question trail
away. He had grown quite fond of the bard, but hardly believed a
word he spoke. Cruedwyn took the bait. He always did.

"Oh, the Highlands, perhaps. Or maybe Aventhorn Keep. A
charming place, the old city. And Tinuviel, the new. Perhaps I'll get
inspired to write a song."

"Truly, music?" Asandra teased. "Because I might have thought it
was the fact that Pol Shyne has driven the League out of Tinuviel."

"Has he? I had no idea!" Creed exclaimed, putting his hand on
his heart as if wounded. "Elder, will you allow this from your own
daughter? What does she take me for? I'll have you know I come
from a long line of courageous minstrels. An even longer line of
Creeds. 'Never walk away from an honest fight,' my pappy always
says. Never—"

"Cruedwyn," Hadyn warned, giving a knowing look.

The bard flicked his finger in the air. "She's packed in my bag!
Allow me my moment!"

Sorge grinned. "Come with us as far as Faielyn. Then sail
to Tinuviel if you need. Truth be told, we may need your sword
again."

He extended his hand, awaiting a clasp. Cruedwyn shadowed his eyes. "Still the lame donkey, huh?"

"Not at all," Sorge said with mock gravity. "I would never speak so poorly of donkeys."

"Marvelous. A witty monk."

Ewan laughed out loud, but Cruedwyn's smile was tighter than usual. "Truth be told, I could probably use a friend even more than you could use a sword."

He took Sorge's offered grip, winking at the boys. "Somebody has to keep you two alive. Otherwise, all you've got is Sorge. And his Mighty Stick of Peace."

Sorge thumped Creed in the stomach. Both chuckled.

They bade farewell to Asandra. The parting was especially bittersweet for her father. With no easy means of closure, Sorge had avoided the moment as long as he could. Their road from this point was unknown, but a common future was no longer impossible to imagine. Not that it would be easy. They didn't know how to talk to each other about the guilt, the hurt. They simply pulled aside, exchanging whispered words, meant only for each other, where both expressed a willingness to start. The fact was (and all could see it), Asandra had noticeably lightened in the last two days. There was a new grace. As she offered the sign of the circle to her five friends, she lingered most in her farewell to Hadyn. Even Ewan felt the intensity of her eyes on Hadyn. He was mildly surprised to see how Hadyn returned it in measure. He was a typical boy, nearly sixteen and clueless. Unsure what her gaze might mean, he simply held it, unwilling to let the moment slip away.

"Good-bye, Asandra," he said. "Maybe another time."

She smiled. "Another place."

Then turned and walked away.

The journey to the White Abbey took every bit of two weeks. Nearly three. The road, a well-used merchant's path, many centuries old, was usually hard packed and rutted, but not in the fickle weather of late. Amazingly, it still bristled with traffic, even in the mud; carts pulled by oxen or donkeys, laden with produce, rugs, or barrels of wine, headed to market in the King's City or one of many lesser villages along the way. The road stayed a stone's throw from the broad curves of the Kinsman River, which bulged and frothed as it spilled its banks, leaving broad swaths of fields under water, including, at times, the road. It was slow, messy going.

Likewise, Sorge happily overflowed with stories of the land. He seemed eager to share them, perhaps buoyed by the relative blessing of a second chance with his daughter. In a short span, the Barlows learned more about the Hidden Lands of Karac Tor than they could ever remember, probably more than they even knew about their own world. Creed joked, but seemed mostly content to simply listen, which offered the added blessing of never having to peel off his sword. Perhaps he was learning.

It rained frequently. They traveled soaked as often as dry, tramping and stamping, as Flogg might say, through mile after mile of soft mud. Quite wearisome. Even Cruedwyn's normally high spirits were hard pressed at times. Their campfires would not burn. Their skin seemed permanently pruned and chilled. But at least there were no jackals, no Watchers. No Nemesia, no Lost. And maybe, just maybe, the rain was washing them clean.

About midway, the road forked. One leg headed north to Faielyn, becoming paved with brick. The other continued toward the Abbey. Everyone watched the swordsman.

Cruedwyn shrugged. "A bit farther, I suppose."

The dramatic beauty of Vineland was undeniable, a long valley of lush grass and wide open skies that one day might turn blue again. When at last the sun burst through and the rain dried, colors shimmered with a vibrancy that caused even the memory of Nemesia's dark island to fade. Vineyards of fat, sweet grapes filled the air with fragrant aromas. Red stucco homes dotted the hillsides. Young children played and danced and sang, in the mud, of all things. But they looked happy.

On the other hand, the effect of marching in the constant shadow of the Rim was disconcerting. It made one feel very small.

"No avoiding the Rim," Sorge said. "It shrinks you to size."

He was right. The mammoth cliffs broke the land in two for nearly a hundred miles from Stratamore all the way to the White Abbey. Whereas the valley below was soothing to the soul, the Rim was an intimidating spectacle, paralleling the Kinsman's path on a scale that boggled the mind. The plunging scarp face of solid granite had no foothills, no transitional rises. It was as if the earth had merely split into two giant slabs along that line, with one part collapsing into the green swath of Vineland, and the other jutting two thousand feet straight up to form the arid Highland mesas.

"Fierce warriors," Sorge explained, pointing to the top. "Shapeshifters, once. Aion welcomed them to Karac Tor long ago from the Wild South, but banned them from shape shifting, for that was the way of Kr'Nunos. Hawk and kestrel do their bidding. During times of war, they will swoop down from the Rim on great, false wings they wear on their arms. It is a fearsome sight—a sky darkened with Highland warriors. They are called Bird Men, but not kindly."

They kept a leisurely pace, continuing to regain strength, eating often, gathering fresh, wild herbs, vegetables, and wild game. With Flogg's help, they ate like royalty. Ewan had apologized to the gnome and the two were actually beginning to be friends. Every night around the fire, more stories flowed. As the rich history of the land began to seep into the Barlows, Karac Tor slowly began to define their frame of reference as much as their own world.

After roughly a week of travel, Ewan noticed a series of structures high on the ridge, identical in shape and size—giant, flat stone slabs. Perched on the edge of the Rim, they overlooked Vineland and Redthorn like guards at attention. They looked enormous.

"The Sentinels," Sorge said, before Ewan could ask. "No one knows who built them or what purpose they serve. They have marks that no one can read."

Ewan glanced at Hadyn, mouthing, *ACPs?*

Hadyn counted, musing aloud, "What's the deal with nine, Sorge? There's Nine Gifts. Nine notes in Aion's Song. Nine Sentinels if I'm counting right."

Sorge grinned. "Good, little brother! Nine Powers, Worlds, Elements, Nine Sacred Names, Nine Secrets, Nine Sentinels, Nine Sleepers, Stars, Sorrows, and Songs."

"So there must be a pattern," Ewan said wryly, "of *nine*."

"It is our most sacred number, the number of Aion, who has come to us eight times before, and will come again in the Ninth Coming. The War of Swords. Which reminds me!" Sorge tousled Ewan's hair. "Where *did* you learn his song?"

"I thought I told you. It was the song at the portal that opened the door."

Sorge took two more steps, then froze. "What did you say?"

"The song that—"

"Opened the door," he murmured, closing his eyes. Ewan couldn't tell if he was suddenly tired, smelling the air, or praying. "That's what I thought you said."

He spoke to Flogg in low tones, as if quoting.

"Do you remember? Doors shall open, doors shall close . . ."

"Even I know *that* one," Cruedwyn exclaimed. "The Ravna's Riddle. It's been set to at least a dozen different tunes over the years. The old land barons love it cause it's spooky." He began to chant in singsong fashion:

"In final days, come final woes
Doors shall open, doors shall close
Forgotten curse, blight the land
Four names, one blood—fall or stand"

Ewan felt a chill rush up his spine. Sorge began to pace in circles, poking the ground with his staff. "It's an old riddle. But many think it's a prophecy. From one of the Huldáfolk, centuries ago. A crazy old seer." He turned to Flogg. "Forgotten curse. How would you say that?"

The gnome thought a moment. "Curse of forgetting."

"Merciful Aion," Sorge whispered, his face turning pale. "Nemesia. The Book of Names."

After that, he would not speak for many days.

CHAPTER 47

Revenge

H e had lain in the woods all night, his body covered with thick fur, glistening with the milky dew of early morning. Had ridden hard for two weeks, then three, then four, on his great steed named Vyle, a midnight stallion with blood-red eyes. Jackals had run with him through Redthorn, howling. Watchers, fresh from their release at Apaté, swarmed overhead and hailed him with loud and bitter shrieks from the sweltering Midland sky. They hated him, for he had made them what they were. But they were sworn forever to his will.

As he stared at the broken body of the Gray Brother named Melanor, the Devourer relished his plan. He was a thief, a pretender, and Melanor's shape would suit his needs just fine. He discarded the corpse with neck snapped in a crevasse of rock and dirt in the woods near the Gray Abbey. Chortling, it pleased Kr'Nunos

367

to contemplate his deception, that the shape of the man before him, already cold on the earth, would wield the knife. It was a good and wicked plan.

Kr'Nunos had long ago learned the usefulness of false forms, gladly trading his natural essence for the ability to wear another shape, be it bear, wolf, bird or man. His favorite was the great stag. He was a shapeshifter, a lord. A god. He would not be beholden to some faraway princeling in Isgurd, who sought to ban and limit his craven needs. No, he would doff and don the shapes that pleased *him*. From olden times he had loved running with the wild beasts. Loved their power, their wild mating, their killing, and thunder. It was drunken rebellion for his soul. And so it happened, in the ancient, darkly spun past, that he lost himself, became the beast.

He was in his natural form now—the only body that felt natural anymore—with muscled man legs, a pelt of fine hair on his naked chest, a beastly, handsome face and a heavy crown of giant antlers. He was not masked as the Baron. From time to time that form was needed still, as were others. The shape and memory of the Baron in the hearts of the people served him well, mainly because it inspired fear without raising too much suspicion. Having once been a legend himself, the Baron's reputation was cruel enough to fit his schemes. His shape would prove even more valuable in the days to come, he knew. But it wearied him to hold another shape. Ages ago, he could only do it only with great effort, for short periods of time. Yet as time passed, every year, every decade and century, he had waxed stronger. Now he could go for weeks in whatever form he chose. His patience had paid off, with hundreds of generations passing through the glass of time, born, dying, and he, moving among them, known, but unknown. Ageless. Killing in secret, taking their place as needed so no one would know. He could do that, *become.* As long as their body was freed from their soul, liberated in death, he could steal their shape. Thus, all over the kingdom, Kr'Nunos was known by many names, many faces, young and old, male and female. While he relished the mythological dread of the old names, his current identities were more profitable. They were brothers and sons, trusted among men, a tactic far more cunning, in that it merged fear with surprise, and strategy with timing, then laced them all together in the weak interdependencies of men. His plans were many layers deep and bent on total dominion.

A low sound of pleasure bubbled and frothed on his lips. He nursed it as he nursed his anger. For eons, he had drunk deep from the well of hate. At long last, his time had come again. His army of Goths was nearly ready under the deep mountains of the north. An entire generation of youth was now stranded on an island of inward emptiness, incapable of resistance. The Watchers were released. Jackals multiplied. Yes, he was very near.

Rising now from the earth, he bayed at the waning moon, overcome, as a beast will be, by forces deep within the light in the sky, the sway of the night. He expelled hard air from his wet nostrils in great, gushing breaths, saw them feather out and fade in the moonbeams. His hair was matted with maggots and sticks and creeping bugs, and the still-wet blood of Brother Melanor, who had come out to the forest, late at night, to pray.

The smell of the monk's blood drove the Devourer mad. He thirsted for more. For revenge. The old man would become a problem soon. He had already interfered too much. No more. Outside, in the woods, Kr'Nunos had left Vyle where he was tethered and begun walking. His enormous shape shadowed the dark ground. The branched horns of his antlers waved slightly to and fro. As he strode, he shook. Cried a pained, beastly sound. Sounds of squishing and cracking came from his skin, his teeth, his bones.

By the time he reached the Abbey wall, wrapped in the warm blanket of night, his form had changed.

"Brother Melanor," one of the night watchmen greeted him, whispering softly, nodding.

And so he passed easily through the halls. Some few other brothers had also risen by now, so early, but most still slept. Those who were awake were sealed in their rooms, kneeling for prayer. None knew his plan. None could have known.

Melanor reached his destination swiftly. The door was unlocked. Eldoran never locked his door. None of them did. This was a place of peace. They prayed, tilled the earth, tended orphanages, made cheese.

Melanor reached into his gray robe, pulled out a knife. A special knife. It burned his skin. He shivered at the pain, but would not relent. The irony was too rich. A blade meant for cleansing, now used for murder. It was one of his special treasures, locked away in the cold belly of Hel under the mountains of the north. He entered the room where the Gray Father snored rhythmically. His gray beard and hair were mussed. Only the faintest traces of light passed through the small window, enough to see the pale white circle burned onto the skin of his forehead so long ago, some fifty years, when he first took his vows.

The Devourer waited in the room for a long time. He wanted more light. Wanted Eldoran to see the shape of Melanor. To despair of the efforts of his life, thinking betrayal, before he died.

As it slowly brightened, just enough, the lips of Melanor moved.

"Father, awaken."

Eldoran stirred, saw his friend. He sat up in bed, still groggy. His lips were dry and a trail of spittle had collected in his beard.

"What's wrong friend?"

"I came to tell you," Melanor sneered, "that the day of Aion has passed. The time of the Horned Lord has come!"

A swift stab of the blade. Again and again. Eldoran did not even have time to gasp. Crimson life spewed from his belly and chest, trickled from his mouth. He dropped to the ground, gurgling, clutching the hand of his friend, his brother, the one who had taken his life. But the hand he held was not Melanor's. There was a mark that Melanor never had, which the Devourer could never hide. Some things cannot be hidden.

It was a little thing, like a tattoo. A birthmark on the underside of his wrist. The young outlander had noticed it on his arm in another shape, in Stratamore.

The antlered shape of a great stag.

The Ravna's Riddle

The acolytes of the White Abbey greeted the five with a mixture of warmth and reserve, as honored guests—dusty from the road, weary—and potential trouble. Especially the Barlows. Yet hospitality was a holy command, especially travelers, and a Gray with them, no less, so the sign of the circle was offered and they were allowed to enter in peace. An older man dressed in tan with a shock of white hair addressed them in friendly tones.

"How goes your road, friends?"

Sorge leaned on his staff, smiling. "Wet. The Crown Road was worse than I've ever seen."

Their guide chuckled and then led them across a series of paved stone walkways to a large building made of mudbrick, whitewashed with lime. Inside, down a narrow hall, they passed room after room with men in tan robes bent over tall desks, fastidiously studying the Book of Law.

"Master Wordsmen," Cruedwyn whispered. He pursed his lips and wiggled his nose with high, snooty drama. "*Learned* men."

At the end of the hall, the narrow corridor swelled to become a large vaulted space, with more desks and younger looking men dressed in yellow. The faces of the men were taut, anxious. Each had a quill, a pot of ink, and several sheaves of paper. Letter by letter, they transcribed sacred writ. The room was heavy with silence, shuffling paper, scratching quills. A stern, regal man wandered slowly behind each, like a white flame burning over their shoulders. When he noticed the visitors, his eyes immediately drifted to the brothers with cold appraisal. He came forward, raised a steady, hushing hand, then escorted them outside.

Sorge was deferential. "High Priest . . ."

"No need for pleasantries, Elder. Word travels fast. We have heard of your dealings with Nemesia. Though you may be surprised, I agree with Governor Archibald. Your actions were rash and ill considered. You should have consulted us first."

"The boy's life was in danger, your grace. We were *all* in danger."

Alethes let silence tell his doubt. Sorge procured the folded mass of twine and fabric slung over his shoulder, opened it, held up the Staff of Shades for Alethes to see. The High Priest reflexively formed a circle with his hands, warding off evil.

"Aion's mercy. Put it away," he snapped. "This is holy ground."

"All the more reason to entrust it to the Whites. How does the Book of Law say to destroy such things?"

Alethes ignored him, would not even touch the staff. Sorge wrapped it up and continued to carry it. They ambled along a garden path past various smaller, whitewashed abodes. Young green Scribes tended herbs, squash, and lentil patches, diligent in manual labor until their spiritual rigors, come afternoon. They did not look happy. Though the White Abbey had finally set aside fasting and mourning, none of the monks felt any peace.

As they strolled, Alethes did not move his head, but his eyes strayed constantly toward the boys. "So. You are the visitors from another world?" He made no attempt to hide his skepticism.

"Yes, sir," Hadyn answered.

"Of that, I will make my own judgment, with no speculation. We must be sure. We must test. We must *validate.*"

"Okay. How will you do that?"

They approached another building, with two green monks on either side of a door, standing at attention, as if guarding the entrance.

"A test," Alethes said. "The simple test of recognition."

He pushed against the door. As it swung open, almost instantly a cry rang out. A cry of surprise and joy. "Hadyn! Ewan!"

A flurry of arms and legs came tearing toward them, as a warm, familiar body pounced Hadyn first, then Ewan.

Hadyn gasped, "Gabe!"

Gabe grinned fiercely, full of noise and excited hand gesticulations.

"I can talk to birds!" he exclaimed. "Can you believe it? I come here—wherever we are, Kractor or whatever—and I can talk to birds. They know my voice! Is that the coolest thing or what?"

Dumbstruck, Hadyn and Ewan could only stare at their little brother. Alethes carefully observed their interactions, stroking his chin. He had apparently heard this much already. Oblivious to the test, Gabe kept gushing and chattering away. When he finally saw Flogg, he jumped back, clapped his hands over his mouth. Flogg crinkled his snout in retort. Gabe jumped again. Creed burst out laughing at both of them.

"Hold it, hang on!" Hadyn shouted, throwing his hands in the air. "Wait, what . . . how?"

Beaming, the youngest twin unrolled a scroll, gilded in gold, signed at bottom with a large, fancy *A*.

Basically, at ninety miles an hour, it went like this . . .

He and Garret had found the scrolls under Hadyn's bed, right? The morning Hadyn and Ewan went missing. *(Sorry, we know. It's your room, not ours.)* Thought about telling Dad, didn't want to worry him. Figured Hadyn and Ewan had gone to the briar patch early. Risky. Knew they weren't supposed to go. Grabbed a backpack. Flashlights. Other stuff. Took the scrolls. Why? Don't know. Just seemed right. Crawled to the back, through the tunnel. Lights glowed. Then through the rock thingy. *Bam!* (Gabe made a smack with his hands.)

"What was the name of that place again?" he asked Alethes.

"Ga'Haim," the High Priest replied, mostly unamused, but relaxing. The test, it seemed, had largely been passed. "Ga'Haim, capital of the Highlands."

Anyway, right. Gaimm. Or Ga'Haim. Whatever. Landed in a wilderness there. Near the city. Hot! Surrounded by birds. Don't know what kind. Heard them talking. Can you believe it? Birds, talking! Then a Bird Man showed up. Oops, a Wingman. A Highlander. Took me to the city, to their leader. The Jute?

"K'Vrkeln the Jute," Alethes clarified. "Clanlord of the Highlanders."

"And boy, is he one serious dude!" Gabe said. "He didn't know what to do with me, so he sent one of his Wingmen to bring me here. I flew! Off the rim. About peed my pants, but here I am. Can you believe it?"

"Totally," Hadyn said, smiling. "How long have you been here?"

"I dunno. A few weeks."

Sorge clapped his hands, grinning ear to ear. "Bless you, Ravna, and your glorious riddle!" He burst out laughing, shouting. "To live in such a day!"

Everyone turned toward him. Sorge drew out his words. "Hadyn, Ewan, Garret, Gabe. *Four names, one blood.*" He glanced at Alethes. *"Doors shall open, doors shall close."*

Flogg nodded slowly. *"Final days. Final woes."*

Color drained from Alethes's face. He staggered back as if pushed, reaching out to the wall to steady himself.

"Can it be?" he murmured.

"Your grace, look at them! How can it not be?"

"Yes, yes, I see. Obviously, something." He wiped his eyes. His voice was dry and rattly, like a bag full of stones. "But is it true? Because if it is, then it can mean only one thing."

"The War of Swords," Sorge acknowledged. "It is coming. We approach the Golden Plate in the Hall of Ages. The end of time."

Alethes nodded slowly. "Hush, hush. I will not go down that road. Not yet. We must not pretend to understand what is not specifically decreed. And yet, it is clear to me now, I have been stubborn and blind. Aion have mercy, I am twice a fool. Unwilling to admit both the turning of the age and the full scope of evil. The blank pages. I should have known."

"Where's Garret?" Ewan said suddenly. Hadyn spun. They all looked at Gabe.

Gabe shrugged. "For the millionth time, I don't know. He's with some guy. Someplace else. I tried to tell the Jute."

"Start over, Gabe. Tell us exactly. What happened?"

"Doesn't matter, you won't be able to do anything about it. Besides, the guy said he'd be fine."

"Gabe, *what* guy?" Hadyn said carefully, trying to swallow the knot forming in his throat.

Gabe put his hands on his hip, as if put upon, or caught giving away a secret. "Okay, here's the deal. When we both went through that arch thingy, it got all dark and weird and stayed that way for a couple of minutes. I couldn't see anything, couldn't see Garret. But I heard him talking. Like someone else was in there with us. When it got all bright again, I was laying there on the rocks outside—"

"Ga'Haim."

"Right. And Garret was gone."

"The other voice," Hadyn pressed him. "What did it say?"

"It said Garret needed to go with him. He sounded nice. He apologized."

"Him? Who's him? Did he say his name?"

Gabe scrunched his face. His mop of blond hair hung over his eyes.

"I think it was Taliesin."

Sorge drew a sharp breath. Alethes's knees buckled. He plopped heavily onto a nearby chair. Even Hadyn seemed to pale at the sound of the name.

"Gabe, say it again. What was his name?"

Gabe rolled his eyes. "Taliesin. Taliesin. He said he would take Garret to another place, and that it was for the good of all. Garret asked about Dad, then they left. I don't know any more than that, I promise."

Sorge began rubbing his fingers in slow circles. "Gabe, I am a friend of your brothers. We've been through many adventures. Let me say the name I hear you saying. Please listen closely."

Gabe nodded, waited. Sorge fixed his eyes on the boy, and then carefully pronounced the name. "Tal Yssen."

"That's it," Gabe smiled. "You got it."

A cold chill filled the room. Even Cruedwyn seemed dumbstruck. Hadyn had heard that name, had read it many times. From old earth legends. A name of legend on Karac Tor, too.

Alethes slowly lowered his head into his hands, moaning. Sorge seemed caught up in a trance. "Alive? The greatest mirling of the Black Abbey . . . *alive?*"

Hadyn tried to stop shaking, wasn't having much luck. He repeated the word. *Mirling.* A door connected to a series of more doors, revelation upon revelation, all suddenly opened at once. In his imagination, epiphany roared.

"Tal Yssen was a *mirling?*" he said softly, swallowing hard. His heart pounded.

"They said he talked to Fey," Sorge mused distantly, caught in his own stream of thought. "That he built doorways to other worlds."

Dazed, Hadyn could hardly believe his next words. "Sorge, you need to know. This man, Taliesin, is part of our history, too. Sort of. From a long time ago. Most don't even know about him anymore, at least not by that name. Nothing more than legend, now. But he is better known by another name. Now I know why. To us, he's *Merlin.*"

"What!" Ewan gasped.

Alethes pounded his fist on his knee. His white hair was nappy and frayed. "No, no, too much! I need quiet, to think. This is beyond all reckoning. I must consult the Books. How could I have missed so many things? If war is coming, how do we prepare?" He stared at the three brothers forlornly.

Gabe, suddenly alarmed, said, "War? What war?" Then, doe-eyed, "Do we win?"

The innocent question instantly pressurized the air in the room. Not so long ago, on another day of magic, Hadyn had felt a similar pressure. Today was not *that* day, not gray and cold, as it had been in Newland. Still, the same clean smell of ozone tingled in the air, from lightning and rain all across Vineland. Then, the oldest Barlow couldn't see. He didn't have the eyes for it, or the heart. Hadn't known anything about anything, really. He had been consumed with the pain of starting over, missing Mom. Grief. Had been a stranger in a strange land, spending all his time and emotion hating life.

Things were different now.

He glanced at Ewan. His brother's face held a devotion that matched his own. It made him feel proud all over again to be a Barlow. In a moment of such confusion, he felt remarkably clear-headed. How could he deny the amazing turn of events? Gabe looked up at him, depending on him for answers. The oldest brother. Hadyn knew the twins would have to find their own answers along the way. Sorge on the other hand, and Alethes and Flogg, had all grown strangely quiet, as if they, too, were troubled and searching for an answer to Gabe's question. Cruedwyn, alone, licked his lips, smelling battle.

"Whatever you say next," he offered, eyes firm on Hadyn. "You have a Creed with you."

Hadyn had no idea what he was about to say. Not a clue. For some reason, he trusted himself to say it anyway, if he would just open his mouth. So he did, calling the moment what it was. Clearly, a summons to war.

"You all know that a Call came, from your world to ours, and we answered it." He found the eyes of each man in the room, young and old. "Gabe has asked if we will win, but that is not the question. Not for now. I don't know if we will win, but we must each determine how to answer. I give you my answer now. For all of us. With our four names, with our one blood, I tell you the truth . . . *we will fight.*"

TO BE CONTINUED
in Book 2
Corus the Champion

VIEW A PORTION OF CHAPTER 1 OF
Corus the Champion ON PAGE 385 OF THIS BOOK.

About the Author

Dean Barkley Briggs has worked in radio, marketing, and new product development. He also pastoredfor eleven years. After losing his beautiful wife at an early age, Briggs decided an epic fantasy might help his four boys live courageously through their loss. *Corus the Champion* is the second in a series of adventures set in the Hidden Lands of Karac Tor. Briggs has since remarried a beautiful widow named Jeanie, and now has eight amazing kids.

Enter Karac Tor at www.hiddenlands.net.

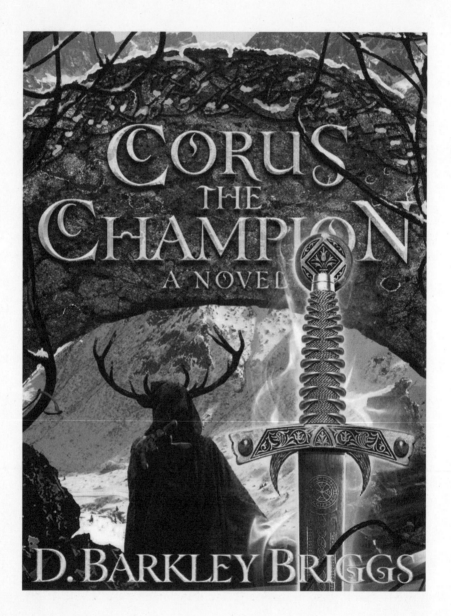

CHAPTER 1

Taliesin

Darkness like a blindfold. Warm air close to his skin. Garret felt panic rising. For some reason, it stayed in his belly. He heard his own voice, as if from a great distance: *"Who are you? And where am I?"*

So much had happened in such a short period of time. Only moments ago, he and Gabe had scampered to the back of the tunnel with scrolls in hand. Winter cold, this morning. Cool light, falling from the sun, rising from the gray earth. Strange marks, glowing. An arch of rock. He hadn't known what to do. Neither had Gabe.

Curiously, Garret went first. Not the usual way of things. But there he was, under the arch. Through the arch. Behind him, Gabe followed. That's when the darkness came, when light was swallowed up. He had heard Gabe, laughing like it was a ride at Six Flags or something. Even felt him nearby in the brush of arms and legs. There was a swirl of air, a sensation of movement, of falling. Something like wetness splashed over him, like plunging into water headfirst. Yet he remained dry. In the confusion that followed, they were separated.

"Gabe!"

Faint and far away, he heard his brother calling his name too. Then another voice, chuckling. A near, touchable voice. Not mocking, not vindictive. Amused. An old man's voice.

"Who are you?" Garret asked nervously. "I don't like this."

The voice that answered from the warm darkness was clear:

Before my release, I was many shapes:
I was a slender, enchanted sword,
Raindrops in the air, a star's white beam,
A word in letters, a book in origin;
I was a lamp of light for a year and half again,
A bridge that stretched an estuary for sixty and six;
I was a path, a kestrel, I was a coracle in blue water.

The voice was pleasant, crackling with humor. "Many words have been written about me. For me. Words like these, wondering how I survive through time, how I move between worlds." A pause. "It makes for nice poetry, at least."

"Where am I?" Garret demanded. He was blind in the darkness.

"In between is the best I can tell you. We're on a journey, you and I. You'll see your brothers again, soon enough. All of them. Don't worry, lad. I've been waiting for this for a long time."

Garret's tone became quite serious. "How do you know about Hadyn and Ewan?"

The old man's voice became even lighter. "Ah, how many times have I been asked that question? Eh? *How do you know? How did you do that?* How, how, how! I know the same way I know about your letter—signed by the High Prince himself, no less. I just *know."*

"So you know about the scroll, too?"

The old man chuckled. "Many things, lad. I know many things. I have lived a very long time."

He spoke another poem:

O'er the nighttime winds that howl,
O'er the darkened roar,
Comes the whisper calling me,
Enticing me to more.

Garret tried to sound calm. "Tell me your name, then. I can't see you."

In the darkness, he felt a firm, gentle hand on his arm.

"Tal Yssen," answered the old man. "My name is Tal Yssen."

The rushing sensation came again. Gabe's voice became distant, then became nothing. The next awareness Garret had was of sudden, pale blue skies and the smell of goats. His feet stood on firm ground, no more floating or plunging. He took a step, moving through something. Turned. Energy vibrated around him. At his back was another arch, similar to the one in the briar patch but much larger, made of fitted, mortared stone. They stood alone, he and the man named Tal Yssen, on a solitary hill of green, surrounded by flatlands.

Other than hedgerows of wild hazel and scattered oak and elm, the hill was the only major feature, like someone had dropped it there by mistake. It rose, tall and sudden, shorn of trees, utterly alone, with vast sweeps of green on every side. A worn footpath wound down the hill, past a stand of trees, toward a clutch of wattle-and-daub buildings. One of them, larger than the rest, was circle shaped, with a cross made of beams rising from the center of the thatched roof. It looked to Garret like an old church. Near to these simple structures, small brown figures worked in rows, tilling the earth. The way they were hunched over made Garret think of giant mushrooms. He stood very still, trembling, not quite willing to believe his eyes.

"What is this place?" he said softly. He looked at Tal Yssen, saw a man perhaps sixty years old, with a short-cropped, silver-white beard and a nose like a hawk's beak. He wore long leather breeches, a blue tunic, and a dark blue cloak, fastened at his neck with a silver brooch. His eyes were the color of new tilled earth and just as warm.

"You have not merely come to a place, but also a time," said Tal Yssen. "You stand in Ynys-Witrin, in the year of our Lord 539. This is your world, my boy. A long time ago."

He spoke calmly, almost calmly enough to soothe Garret's nerves.

"Ynys whatdja say?"

Instinctively, Garret put his watch to his face. The timepiece, shaped with the red arrowhead logo of the Kansas City Chiefs, seemed strangely out of place here. It had been a gift from Dad last year for Christmas—their first Christmas without Mom. The Chiefs were Mom's favorite team, and Garret never took it off. It kept great time. Now, however, the digital display was frozen at 7:13:28.

"Ynys-Witrin," Tal Yssen repeated. "But don't trouble yourself with words. By the time of your day and age, it will be known by other names."